Praise for *All the Winters After*

"[An] absorbing second novel… Their love story is engaging, and the spectacular setting and delightful supporting cast infuse the plot with vitality. A surprise ending is a perfect capper."

—*Publishers Weekly*

"With sweet, heartfelt characters and a richly described setting, Halverson blends mystery and suspense into a love story of many layers, not the least of which is a declaration of love to the Alaskan wilderness and its people."

—*Booklist*

"*All the Winters After* is a beauty of a story that reaffirms what love is and what love does. You'll want to race through it to uncover the mysteries, while simultaneously slowing to savor this enchanting tale in hopes it will not end."

—Julie Kibler, bestselling author of *Calling Me Home*

"Seré Prince Halverson delivers another riveting story about the bonds of family. *All the Winters After* is a beautiful and compelling tale set in the wilds of Alaska. A young woman broken by love sets a collision course with a family torn apart by grief and guilt. The secrets are deep. The winter is long. And the characters are unforgettable. I loved this book."

—Amy Franklin-Willis, author of *The Lost Saints of Tennessee*

"A book that makes you hug the pages and believe in love's transformative power. Against the rugged enchantment of Alaska, Halverson mesmerizes us with the unforgettable story of Kachemak Winkel and generations of hidden secrets. This isn't just a novel; it's a journey to territories of land and heart."

—Sarah McCoy, *New York Times* and international bestselling author of *The Mapmaker's Children*

"Set in the wilds of Alaska, *All the Winters After* is a vivid exploration of landscape and community. Sensual, insightful, and deeply affecting, Seré Prince Halverson's new novel illustrates how reckoning with the past is sometimes the only way to move forward. I read this book quickly, compulsively, and thought about it long after I turned the last page."

—Jillian Medoff, bestselling author of *I Couldn't Love You More*

"This novel is like the Alaskan landscape it so vividly depicts: beautiful yet mysterious, layered and unforgettable, revealing its secrets at the exact right moments. Perfectly paced, deeply felt, and gorgeously written, *All the Winters After* will burn bright in your memory like the midnight sun."

—Melanie Thorne, author of *Hand Me Down*

"It's not often that writers from outside Alaska make the effort to understand and convey the hold our state has on those who live here. Halverson has delivered a recognizable version of ourselves within her larger, very satisfying story about strength of character and the power of love."

—Nancy Lord, *Alaska Dispatch News*

all the winters after

after

Seré Prince Halverson

Published by Sourcebooks Landmark, an imprint of Sourcebooks, Inc.
P.O. Box 4410, Naperville, Illinois 60567-4410
(630) 961-3900
Fax: (630) 961-2168
www.sourcebooks.com

The Library of Congress has cataloged the hardcover edition as follows:

Halverson, Seré Prince.
  All the winters after / Seré Prince Halverson.
    pages ; cm
  (pbk. : alk. paper)
  I. Title.
  PS3608.A54943A79 2015
  813'.6--dc23

                          2015006220

      Printed and bound in the United States of America.
            VP 10 9 8 7 6 5 4 3 2 1

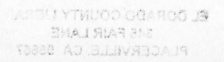

For Daniel, Michael, Karli, and Taylor

COOK INLET

ALASKA, U.S.A.

TO ANCHORAGE

WILBUR

ALASKA

KACHEMAK BAY

FOX CREEK

ALTAI

URAL

THE
HOMESTEAD

CABOOSE

CABOOSE SPIT

KACHEMAK BAY

HALIBUT COVE

KENAI MOUNTAINS

part one

breakup

2005

chapter
one

EVENING CREPT ITS WAY into the cabin, and she went to get the knife. Always this, the need to proclaim: *I was here today, alive on this Earth.*

Here.

Still.

She took the knife from the shelf to carve a single line in the log-planked stairwell that led from the kitchen to the root cellar. She'd carved them in groups of four one-inch vertical lines bisected with a horizontal line. So many of them now, covering most of the wall. They might be seen as clusters of crosses, but to her, they were not reminders of death and sacrifice but evidence of her own existence.

There were left-behind carvings too, in dated columns filling the doorjamb on the landing at the top of the stairs. These notches marked the heights of growing children, two living in the forties and fifties, and two in the seventies and eighties, one of whom had grown quite tall. She saw the mother standing on a footstool, trying to reach the top of her son's head to mark the wood with pencil, while he stood on tiptoes, trying to appear even taller. She almost heard their teasing, their laughing. Almost.

Six stairs down, she dug the tip of the knife into the wall. The nightly ritual was important. While she no longer lived according to endless rules and regulations, with all those objects and gestures and chants, she did not want her days flowing like water with no end or beginning—shapeless, unmarked. So she read every night, book after book, first in the order that they lined the shelves, turning them upside down when she finished reading and then right side up for the second read and so forth, returning to her favorites again and again. And during the day, she did chores—foraging, launching and checking fishing nets, setting and checking traps, gardening, tending house, feeding chickens and goats, canning and brining and smoking—all in a certain order, varying only according to the needs of the season. Her days always began with a cold-nose nudge from the dog, and not one but two enthusiastic licks of her hand, as if to say not just good morning, but *Good Morning! Good Morning!*

Then there were the mornings she ignored the dog and unlatched the kitchen door so he could push it open with his nose to let himself out while she returned to bed to stay, dark mornings that led to dark days and weeks. During those times, only under piles of blankets did she feel substantial enough not to drift away; they kept her weighted down and a part of the world. But her dog's persistence and her own strong will eventually would win over, and she'd drag herself up from the thick bog and go back to her chores and her books, carving the missing days into the wall so they did not escape entirely.

It was surprising, what a human being could become accustomed to—a lone human being, miles and years from any other human being. She balanced two more logs and a chunk of coal in the woodstove and, with the dog following her, crossed the room in the left-behind slippers, which had, over time, taken on the shape of her own feet. She'd been careful to keep things as she'd found them, but those slippers were another way she'd made her mark, left her footprint, insignificant as it might be.

She sat in the worn checkered chair and picked up one of the yellowed magazines from 1985. Across the cover: *Cosmetic Surgery, the Quest for New Faces and Bodies—At a Price.* "A new face, this would help," she once again reminded Leo, who thumped his tail. Unlike the people in the article, she said this not because she was wrinkled (she wasn't) or thought herself homely (she didn't). "It would give us much freedom, yes? A different life."

She opened the big photography book of *The City by the Bay* and took in her favorite image of the red bridge they called golden and the city beyond, as white as the mountains across this bay. So similar and yet so different. That white city held people, people, people. Here, the white mountains held snow. "And their bridge," she told Leo, closing the book. "We could use that bridge." He cocked his head just as she heard something scrape outside.

A branch. In her mind, she kept labeled buckets in which she let sounds drop: Branch, Moose, Wolf, Bear, Chicken, Wind, Falling Ice, and on and on. Leo's ears perked, but he didn't get up. He too was used to the varied scuttlings of the wilderness. She drew the afghan around her shoulders and opened a novel to the page marked with a pressed forget-me-not.

Yes, she knew a certain comfort here—camaraderie, even. How could she be truly alone, when outside her door, nature kept noisy company and at her feet lay a dog such as Leo? Then there were the books. She'd traveled inside the minds of so many men and women from across the ages. And she had such long, uninterrupted passages of time to think, to ponder every turn her mind took. For instance, there was the word *loneliness* and the word *loveliness.* In English, one mere letter apart, and in her handwriting, the words looked almost identical, certainly related. This she found consoling, and sometimes even true.

But now, another sound, and then many unmistakable sounds—determined footsteps coming toward the house. Leo's ears flipped back before he plunged into sharp barking and frantic clawing. She froze. All those years practicing what she would do, but she only sat, with the book open in her trembling hands. Where did she leave the gun? In the barn? How had she grown so careless?

The knife on the shelf in the stairwell. She bolted up to grab it. Flipped off the lights, took hold of Leo's rope collar, tugging him from the door and up the stairs to the second floor. She peered out the window. Though the moon was full, she couldn't see anyone. She pulled the shade, but it snapped up, so she yanked it back down. With all her strength, she dragged Leo, pushing and barely wedging him under the bunk bed with her, and clamped his nose with her hand just as the loose kitchen window creaked open below. A male voice, a yelling, though she didn't hear the words over Leo's whining and the blood pum-pumming in her ears.

It was him, she was sure of it. Shaking, shaking, she squeezed harder on the handle of the knife and wished for the gun. But she was good with a knife; she was sure of that too.

chapter

two

THERE HE WAS, KACHEMAK Winkel, on a plane of all things, finally headed home of all places. Yes, his fingernails dented the vinyl of the armrests, and the knees of his ridiculously long legs pressed into the seat in front of him, causing the seat to vibrate. A little boy turned and peered at Kache through the crack between B3 and B4. Kache motioned to his legs with a sweep of his hand and said, "Sorry, buddy. No room." But he knew that didn't account for the annoying jittering.

"Afraid of flying?" the man next to him asked, peering above his reading glasses and his newspaper. He wore a tweed blazer and a hunting cap that made him look like a studious Elmer Fudd but with hair, which poked out around the earflaps. "Scotch helps."

Kache nodded thanks. He had every reason to be afraid, it being the twentieth anniversary of the plane crash. But oddly, he was not afraid to fly and never had been. If God or the Universe or whoever was in charge wanted to pluck this plane from the sky and fling it into the side of a mountain in some cruel act of irony or symmetry, so be it. All the fear in the world wouldn't make a difference. No, Kache was not afraid of flying. He was afraid of flying *home*. And that fear had kept him away for two decades.

He shifted in his seat, elbow on the armrest next to the window, his finger habitually running up and down over the bump on his nose that he'd had since he was eighteen. The plane window framed the scene below, giving it that familiar, comforting, screened-in quality, and through it he watched Austin, Texas, become somewhere south, just another part of the Lower 48 to most Alaskans.

He had spent the majority of those two decades in front of a computer screen, trying to forget what he'd left behind, scrolling column after column of anesthetizing numbers and getting promotion after promotion. Too many promotions, evidently.

After the company had laid him off six months ago, he replaced the computer screen with a TV screen. Janie encouraged him to keep looking for another job, but he discovered the Discovery Channel, evidence of what he'd suspected all along: even the world beyond the balance sheets was flat. Flat screen, forty-seven inches, plasma. That plasma became his lifeblood. So many channels. A whole network devoted to food alone. He learned how to brine a turkey, bone a turkey, smoke a turkey, high-heat roast a turkey. The same could be said of a pork roast, a leg of lamb, a prime rib of beef.

Branching out, he soon knew how to whisper to a dog, how to declutter his bathroom cabinets, how to flip real estate, and what not to wear.

Then he came across the Do-It-Yourself Network, and there he stayed. "Winkels," his father had liked to say, long before there was a DIY Network, "are do-it-yourselfers exemplified." Thanks to all the TV, Kache finally knew how to do many things himself. That is, he could do them in his head, because, as Janie often reminded him, head knowledge and actual *capability* were two different animals. So with that disclaimer, he might say he knew how to restore an old house from the cracked foundation to the fire-hazard-shingled roof—wiring, plumbing, plastering, you name it. He knew how to build a wooden pergola, how to install a kitchen sink, how to lay a slate pathway in one easy weekend. He even knew how to raise alpacas and spin their wool into the most expensive socks on the planet. Hell, he knew how to build the spinning wheel. His father would be proud.

However.

Kache did not know how to rewind his life, how to undo the one thing that had undone him. His world was indeed flat, and he'd fallen off the edge and landed stretched out on a sofa, on pause, while the television pictures moved and the voices instructed him on everything he needed to know about everything—except how to bring his mom and his dad and Denny back from the dead.

❧

The little boy in front of him grew bored and poked action figures through the seat crack, letting them drop to Kache's feet. Kache retrieved them a dozen times but then let their plastic bodies lie scattered on the floor beneath him. The boy soon laid his head on the armrest and fell asleep.

On Kache's first plane ride, his dad had lifted him onto his lap in the pilot's seat and explained the Cessna 180's instruments and their functions. "Here we have the vertical speed indicator, the altimeter, the turn coordinator. What's this one, Son?" He pointed to the first numbered circle, and Kache didn't remember any of the big words his father had just spoken.

"A clock, Daddy?" His dad laughed. Then he gently offered the correct names again and again until Kache got them right. It was the only memory he had of his father being so patient with him. How securely tethered to the world Kache had felt, sitting in the warm safety of his dad's lap, zooming over land and sea.

Why had it been impossible to hop on a plane and head north, even for a visit? He tried to picture it: Aunt Snag, Grandma Lettie, and him, sitting at one end of the seemingly vast table at the homestead, empty chairs lined up. Listening to one another chew and clear throats, drumming up questions to ask, missing Denny's constant joking and his father's strong opinions on just about everything. Who would have believed he'd miss those? His mother's calm voice, her break-open laughter so easy and frequent—he could not recall her without thinking of her laugh.

So instead, once he began making decent money, he'd flown Gram and Aunt Snag to Austin for visits, which provided plenty of distractions for all of them. As he drove them around, Grandma Lettie kept her eyes shut on the freeway, saying, "Holy crap!" The woman who'd helped homestead hundreds of acres in the wilderness beyond Caboose, who'd birthed twins—his dad and Aunt Snag—in a hand-hewn cabin with no running water, who'd faced down bears and moose as if they were the size of squirrels and rabbits, couldn't stand a semi passing them on the road. She loved the wildflowers though. At a rest stop, she walked out into the middle of a field of bluebonnets, undid her braid, and fluffed her white hair, which floated like a lone cloud in all that blue, and lay down and sang her old, big, persistent heart out. "Come on, Kache!" she called. "Sing with me, like in the old days."

He kept his arms crossed, shook his head. "Do you know that crazy lady?" he asked Snag.

Gram was of sound mind and body at the time, just being herself, the Lettie he had always adored. Every few minutes, Aunt Snag and Kache saw her arm pop out of the sapphire drift, waving a bee away.

But in the past four years, Gram's health had declined, and Aunt Snag didn't want to travel without her. When he'd talked to Snag early that morning, she'd said Lettie was deteriorating fast. "And I'm not getting any younger. You better hurry and get yourself home, or the only people you'll have left will be in an urn, waiting for you to spread us with the others on the bluff."

He'd let too much time slip by. Twenty years. He was thirty-eight, with little to show for it except a pissed off and, as of last night, officially ex-girlfriend, along with a sweet enough severance package for working his loyal ass off for sixteen years and a hell of a savings account—none of which would impress Aunt Snag or Grandma Lettie in the slightest or do them any good.

⚓

After a stop in Seattle, another three and a half hours and countless thickly frosted mountain ranges later, the plane landed in Anchorage, which Snag and Lettie grumpily called North Los Angeles. Nevertheless, it was their destination for frequent shopping trips, and they didn't hesitate to get their Costco membership when the store first opened there. The in-flight magazine said that just over six hundred thousand people lived in the state, and two-fifths of them resided in Anchorage. So even though it was Alaska's biggest city, it had over three million to go before catching up with LA.

He caught the puddle jumper to Caboose. During the short flight, he spotted a total of eight moose down through the bare birch and cottonwood trees on the Kenai Peninsula, along with gray-green spruce forests, snow-splotched brown meadows, and turquoise lakes. The plane banked where the Cook Inlet met Kachemak Bay, whose name he bore. Across it, the Kenai mountain range, home to nesting glaciers, rose mightily and stretched beyond sight.

From the other side of the inlet, Mount Iliamna, Mount Redoubt, and Mount Augustine loomed solid and strong and steady. But looks deceive—Redoubt and Augustine frequently let off steam and took turns blowing their tops every decade or so, spreading thick volcanic ash as far as Anchorage and beyond, darkening the sky with soot. Kache's mom used to say Alaska didn't forgive mistakes. As a boy, he wondered if those volcanic eruptions were symptoms of its pent-up rage.

There was the Caboose Spit, lined with fishing boats, a finger of land jutting out into the bay where the old railroad tracks ended, the rusty red caboose still there.

"See that?" his mom had shouted over the Cessna's engine that first day they'd all flown together, his dad finally realizing his dream of owning a bush plane. "The long finger with the red fingernail pointing to the mountains? I bet the earth is so proud of those mountains. Wants to make sure we don't miss seeing them." She tucked one of Kache's curls under his cap, her smile so big. "As if we could! Aren't they amazing?"

It had always been a breathtaking view, the kind that made him inhale and forget to exhale, especially when the clouds took off, as they just had, and left the sea every shade of sparkling blue and green against the purest white of the mountains. He had to admit he'd never seen anything anywhere—even now during the spring breakup, Alaska's ugliest time of year—that came close to this height or depth of wild beauty.

But the view was doing more than taking his breath away. Maybe his mom had been wrong. Maybe that strip of land was the world's middle finger, telling him to fuck off, saying, *Who you calling flat?* Today that red spot of caboose looked more like a smear of blood on the tip of a knife than a fingernail. Either way, the view stabbed its way into his chest, as if it were trying to finish him off before he even landed.

chapter
three

SNAG HADN'T STOPPED MANEUVERING through her small house since Kache's call. Kache. Finally agreeing to come *home*. In the wee hours of that morning, she'd mistaken the ringing phone for the alarm and kept hitting the snooze button until she sat up in a panic. *It's about Mom.* But no, it was Kache, calling back from Austin. Ever since they'd hung up, she'd been bathing every surface with buckets of Zoom cleaner, suctioning up the cat hair and the spilled-over cat food with the vacuum, stuffing the fridge with a ready-to-bake casserole, moose pot roast, and rhubarb crunch, wrapping the bed in clean sheets.

Snag thought she resembled a well-made bed. Polishing every last streak off the mirror, she saw her chenille robe creased under her breasts as if it were a bedspread tucked around two down pillows. They rose and fell with her deep breaths. She moved fast despite her size, wiping the counter, putting away a pepper grinder and a bottle of salad dressing with Paul Newman's mug on it. She closed the refrigerator door.

There was the memory of Kache, sitting on the kitchen stool, dark, curly head bent over his guitar, opening that same door and standing in front of the assortment of cold food like the refrigerator was some god requiring homage. How many times had she swatted him, told him to close the damn door? "A million? A billion?"

Since the day she had to put her mom into the home, Snag had been talking to herself. Before that, sometimes all Lettie had added to the conversation was, "Is that right, Eleanor?" But it was something.

No one but her mom still called her Eleanor. Around age nine, she came home from fishing the river alone for the first time, holding up a decent-size salmon. "Look, Daddy. I caught a fish all by myself."

Her daddy laughed and pulled the hook out of the side of the poor fish. "Eleanor," he said, "what you did was *snagged* yourself a fish." Glenn, jealous that he was the same age and had yet to catch or even snag anything, started calling her Snag. The name took hold and never let go. Most of the town's newcomers thought the name came from the fact that she had a gift for selling. It was true. Whether someone needed Mary Kay or Jafra cosmetics, Amway detergent, or a new house, Snag was the person to call.

Real estate had been particularly good to her. She preferred to live in her simple home, but she waxed poetic about the benefits of a sunken tub or a granite countertop. Lately, she'd stepped back from showing houses. She'd made enough money, and she wanted to give the newbies a shot. The one element in life that had come easily to Snag was money, and she didn't need to be piggy about it. She still sold products for the pyramid businesses but more as a service to the citizens of Caboose than out of her own need. The only thing she couldn't sell anyone on was the idea of getting the town mascot, the old caboose parked at the end of the spit, moving again. But she didn't have time to dwell on that.

She climbed into the car and took a deep breath. Kache. "He's going to want to kill me, and I can't blame him one bit." She wiped her eyes with the sleeve of her rain jacket, surprised to see a black smear across it. She wore the mascara for the first time in years in honor of Kache's homecoming. It was the brand she'd demonstrated at kitchen tables, rubbing it on a page of paper, dropping water on it, holding the paper up so the drop ran down clear as gin. Now she smoothed her fingers under her eyes: more black. She licked her fingers, ran them over and over her face, took the balled-up tissue from under her sleeve, and wiped more. She adjusted the rearview mirror to check herself. "Way to go, woman." It looked like someone had struck oil on her face. With all her finesse for cleaning, Snag sometimes felt that her biggest contribution to humankind was making a mess of things.

chapter

four

AT THE SMALL CABOOSE airport, Kache recognized Snag before she turned around to face him. You couldn't miss her height, a half inch shy of six feet. Long-limbed like he was, hair cropped short, with much more salt than pepper now. She was his father's twin, and they bore a strong resemblance—the deep dimples, the large gray eyes. Maybe that's why Kache had always thought of her as a handsome woman. Her back expanded. Her shoulders hung limp in her hooded jacket. She fidgeted with her sleeves, touched her face. Many times that sad spring before he'd left, Kache had seen her cry with her back to him, as if she might protect him from all the grief.

He sighed and kept standing there, observing her broad back. How was it that you could leave a place for twenty years, stay away for *twenty years*, and walk right smack into the very center of what you left behind, like it was some bull's-eye for which you were trained to aim?

"Aunt Snag?" He touched her arm and she jumped.

"Kache! Of course it's you." As tall as she was, she still had to stand on her tiptoes to swing her chubby arms around him. "Oh, hon, look at you. Your mom and dad would be so proud."

He held her soft face, wrinkled a bit more, though not as much as he'd expected, but a little…dirty? Streaked with something. With Snag, it was more likely mud than makeup. He smiled. Their eyes stayed on each other for a long minute. There was a lot to say, but all he got out was, "Let's go see Gram."

Snag blew her nose, blew some more. "She's not herself. And I tried and tried, but I couldn't keep up. It's a decent place though. It is. We can stop on the way home." She pulled his head down, ruffled his hair, like he was eight years old instead of thirty-eight. "You look so handsome. Kache Winkel, you're home. Is that your only bag?"

He nodded. He'd packed the few warm clothes he still owned, along with the old, holey green T-shirt he would never throw out, the one that said, *No, I don't play basketball.* Denny had it printed up for him, because at six-foot-six, Kache had gotten tired of being asked. And he'd packed the only item of his mom's he'd taken—her favorite silk scarf, which had smelled of her perfume for years after she died. Snag asked him where his guitar was, but he shrugged, as he had whenever she'd asked him in Austin. She raised her eyebrows and opened her mouth but let the question go, just as she had before.

Even in the middle of winter, Austin didn't get this cold. In the car, he rubbed his hands together and felt the pull and release of resistance and surrender. The place lured him back in. Then it yanked him hard with long lines of memories: Denny buying him beer at that very liquor store, which still sported the same flashing orange sign; his mom rushing him into that very emergency room when he was nine and had split his knee open; that same hardware and tackle shop his dad got lost in for hours while Kache waited in the truck, writing lyrics on the backs of old envelopes his mom kept in the glove compartment for blotting her lipstick. Kache had written around the red blooms of her lip prints.

Some things had changed, sure, and yet not enough to keep away a hollow, emanating ache.

But it was breakup. Here, early spring was the depressing time of year, when the snow and ice gave way—cracking, breaking, oozing—as if the earth bawled, spewing mud everywhere, running into the darkest lumpy blue of Cook Inlet and Kachemak Bay.

"Thought we might get to see Janie. Couldn't get away from work?" Snag asked, glancing at Kache. He shrugged. "You're awfully quiet. For you." She fiddled with the radio while she drove and then turned it off. It was true that Kache's dad had dubbed him Chatty Kachey, but that was a long, long time ago. "Ah, a break from the rain."

"We don't get enough in Austin. I'd like a good watering."

"In a few weeks, you'll be soaked through to the bone, I'm betting. Fingers crossed we'll have a decent summer. Since you don't…you know…have to get back to work. Or, apparently, Janie? You're staying a while, aren't you, hon?"

"I'm thinking a few weeks." That was the goal anyway, if he could stick it out. It would get easier in a day or two. He wanted to hang out with Snag and Lettie. Face the things he needed to face, get out to the homestead. Snag had said a nice family was renting it. He'd try to fix whatever out there needed fixing, do whatever needed to be done for Lettie and Snag, hold it together, be strong enough to look it all in the face so he could get on with his life. Janie was right. It was way past time.

Snag pulled the car into the parking lot of the low brick-and-concrete building. "Gram's a lot weaker, Kache. She asks about you still though. It depends. Some days she's clearer than most of us, and some days she's cloudy, and some days she's plain snowed in."

He got out and held open the glass door. The walls of the lobby were covered in flowery pink-and-green wallpaper and paintings of otters, puffins, and bears. He nodded approval. "Not bad, considering."

"Believe me, it's much better than the third-world prison camp they call a nursing home down in Spruce." She smiled wide. "Hello there, Gilly."

"So this is Kache." A woman, probably a little younger than Snag, reached out and shook his hand. "Not a mere figment of Snag's and Lettie's imaginations after all." She wore a name tag printed in oversize letters pinned on a cheery smock and had blue eyes with nicely placed crow's feet, the kind that told you she'd spent a lot of time laughing. "If I'd known last month you were coming up, I might have been able to talk my daughter into staying. I told her we have a boatload of single men up here, but she only lasted a couple of weeks. She said, 'Mom, I'm going back to Colorado where at least the men shave.' Plus, she heard that folks regularly get their eyebrows and noses pierced by hooks while combat-fishing the Kenai. It all fairly crushed her fantasy version of Alaska."

Snag touched Kache's face. "Five o'clock shadow."

Kache said, "Can't help that. But it'll be gone by morning."

"See, Gilly? Your daughter missed out."

Kache rubbed his chin. "It won't be long before I start forgetting how to shave, I suppose."

Even though the place was not-bad-considering, as he followed Snag down the hall, so did the faint scent of urine, medicine, and decay, with a hint of boiled root vegetables.

The TV shouted an old black-and-white film he didn't recognize, wheelchairs facing it like church pews. Grandma Lettie sat off to the side with her head in a book. Almost literally. The book lay open on her lap, her head drooping to practically touch it. She wore her hair in the same braid she always had, but it was as thin and wispy as a goose feather. In the photos of her as a young woman, it had been a thick, dark rope coiling down to her waist.

Kache knelt in front of her. A thin line of drool hung from the center of her top lip down to the page. He wiped it with his sleeve while Snag handed him one of her crumpled tissues. "Gram?"

She looked up, peering, and then her mouth opened in a smile.

"Kachemak Winkel!" The smile slipped down. "Where have you been?"

"I've been in Texas, Gram."

She shook her head. "Where've you *been*?"

"Working, Gram." His answers sounded feeble.

"No." She started to whimper and turned to Snag, whispering loudly. "Does he know about the crash?"

"Yes, Mom, he was here. Remember?"

"But he didn't die."

"That's right."

She whispered again, enunciating slowly, her eyes wide. "He was supposed to go on that plane."

Kache swallowed hard. Snag held his elbow and moved a lock of white hair from Gram's vein-mapped forehead. "Mom, Kache has been away. Just away. From here."

Gram raised her eyebrows, nodding, and rubbed Kache's long hand between her two bony, speckled ones. "Of course you have, dear. Oh, but…" She looked over her shoulder and then back at him. Her voice raised higher, almost a child's. "It was like all four of you were dead. Now at least we have you back." She picked up his hand in hers, moving it up and down to the beat of each word: "And *that* is a very good thing."

"Thanks, Gram." How had he stayed away so long? How had he come back? He was tempted to grab himself a wheelchair and steal the remote from the guy in the Hawaiian shirt and cardigan, flip the channel to the DIY Network, and let a few more decades go flickering past.

Instead, he drove with Snag over to her place. He braced himself

for the onslaught of mementos, but surprisingly, Snag didn't have one
piece of furniture or even a knickknack or painting of his mother's.
Sentimental Aunt Snag, who loved her brother and adored her sister-
in-law. Where was all their stuff? It didn't make sense to sell or give
away every single thing. And when Kache asked about heading out
to the homestead, she changed the subject. Earlier she'd said she'd
rented it. She wouldn't have sold it, would she? He knew she'd sold his
dad's fishing boat to Don Haley, but all four hundred acres, without
saying a word to Kache? It was true that Kache had given her power
of attorney, back when he was eighteen and didn't want to deal. But
she wouldn't have sold it without telling him. No way.

Later that afternoon, he went to the Safeway for her and bumped
into an old friend of his father's, Duncan Clemsky. Duncan clapped
him on the back, kept shaking his hand while he talked. "Look at you,
Mr. City Slicker. I still think of you when I have to drive by the road
to your daddy's land. Only time I get out that far is when I make a
delivery to the Russian village."

"The Old Believers are accepting deliveries these days? Progressive
of them."

"Some of them at Ural even have satellite dishes. Going soft.
Won't be long until they're wearing useless, pretty boots like those."
He nodded toward Kache's feet. "Change eventually gets ahold of
everyone, I suppose."

"Suppose so," Kache said, his face heating up. Nothing like a
lifelong Alaskan to put you in your place. He wanted to ask Duncan
if Snag had sold the land, but he wasn't about to let on that he didn't
know, if it was even true. No need to get a rumor heading through
town that would end up like one of the salmon on the conveyor belt
down at the cannery, the head and tail of the story cut off and the
middle butchered up until it became something unrecognizable.

"You're gonna need to get some real boots before folks start mistaking you for a tourist from California. Thought you were at least in Texas, my man." Duncan shook his head and winked. "You tell your aunt and grandma I said hello, will you?"

"Will do, Duncan. Same goes for Nancy and the kids."

That opened up another conversation, with ten minutes of Duncan Clemsky filling Kache in on every one of his five kids and sixteen grandchildren and seven seconds of Kache filling Duncan in on the little that he had been up to for the last twenty years. "Yeah, you know…working a lot."

On the way back to Snag's, Kache decided that if she didn't bring up the homestead that evening, he would just come out and ask her if she'd sold it. Part of him hoped she had; the other part hoped to God she hadn't.

chapter
five

SNAG FILLED THE SINK with the hottest water she could stand while Kache cleared the dinner dishes. She'd decided on Shaklee dishwashing liquid, since she'd used Amway for lunch and breakfast, and now she was trying to decide how on earth to tell Kache about the homestead.

Staring at her reflection in the kitchen window, she saw a chicken-shit and a jealous sister, and there was no hiding it. Looking at it, organizing the story in her mind, lining it up behind her lips: *This is how I let it happen. It started this way, with my good intentions but my weaknesses too, and then a day became a week became a year became a decade became another. I hadn't meant for it to happen like this. I hadn't meant to.*

She squeezed out more of the detergent, let the hot water cascade over her puffy hands. She laid her hands flat along the sink's chipped enamel bottom where she couldn't see them beneath the suds. If only she were small enough to climb into the sink and hide her whole self, just lie quietly with the forks and knives and spoons until this moment passed and she no longer had to see herself for what she really was. Sometimes drowning didn't seem so horrible when she thought of it in those terms. Better than dying the way Glenn and Bets and Denny had. She shivered even though her hands and arms were immersed in the liquid heat.

It would have brought them honor in some small way, if she'd done the simple thing everyone expected of her. Simply take care of the house and Kache. But she'd failed at both.

"Aunt Snag?" Next to her, he held the old Dutch oven with the moose pot roast drippings stuck on the bottom. There were never any leftovers with Kache, even now that he was a grown man. "Are you okay? Want me to finish up so you can catch the end of the news?"

"No... Well, okay." She dried her hands on the towel and started to walk out, but she turned back. "I've got to tell you something, hon, and it's not going to be pretty. You're going to be real upset with me, and I won't blame you one bit."

"You sold the homestead." It was a statement, not a question.

"What?" she asked, though she'd heard him perfectly.

"You sold it. You sold the homestead."

"No, hon, I didn't. I didn't sell it."

He smiled, sort of, a sad, tight turning up of his mouth while his shoulders relaxed. "I guess I'll need to go out. Check up on things. I've been meaning to ask. But it's hard, thinking about driving out, seeing it for the first time, you know? Do you go out there a lot?"

Still such youthfulness to his face. He didn't seem like a grown man who'd seen a lot of life. Snag couldn't tell what it was exactly. Trust? Vulnerability?

She said, "Not a lot, no."

"Just enough to take care of things." His voice didn't rise in a question.

"No, not that much even." She breathed in deep, searched in her pockets and up her sleeve for a tissue. "I haven't been out there at all."

"This spring?"

"No. I mean not once. Not at all."

"All *year?*"

"No, Kache. Not all year. Not ever. Not once. I never went out like I told you I did. I planned to a million times, but I never closed it up, never got all your stuff, never put things in storage. I never…"

He stood with his mouth agape for what seemed to Snag like a good five minutes. "Wait a second. You said you'd been renting it out. No one has been out there since I left? Not even the Fosters? Or the Clemskys? Jack? Any of those people? They would have been glad to help. They would have insisted on it."

Snag leaned against the counter for support, inhaled and exhaled. "Don't you see? *I* insisted it was taken care of. I told them I'd hired someone, to scrape the snow off, patch the roof, run water in the pipes."

"I don't understand. Why?"

"Embarrassed by then. I hadn't even been out since you left, to water the houseplants or—I'd never planned to be so negligent—clean out the pantry." She fell silent. The water dripped on and on into the sink. "I left it all. I tried. I drove part way dozens of times, but then I'd chicken out and turn the car around."

Kache didn't scream and holler at her like she'd expected. He hugged her, a big old bear of a hug. In his arms, she had the sense that she might not be worn down to a nub by shame after all. But grace dragged another weight of its own. He said her name tenderly and sighed. "You know it's the anniversary today, almost to the hour?"

She nodded, because she did know without thinking about it, the way she knew she was breathing. He told her it was okay, that he did understand, more than he wanted to admit, that he'd fought the same problem in trying to come back.

She was glad she didn't use the line she'd been holding on to in case she needed it, that at first, way back when, she'd waited for him to return so they might go *together*. And that's what she'd pictured happening now, the two of them braving the drive out *together*. But forgiving or not, he'd already let go of her, grabbed the car keys, and called out, "I'll be back in a while. Don't wait up."

He was starting the truck when she whispered, "Wait." But she knew. Even though he'd reacted with kindness, she had seen the shock pumping through him and that he'd needed to put some distance between them. It scared her to have him go off upset. The tires screeched like they did when Kache was still a teenager, as if they'd woken up the morning after the crash and no time had passed at all.

chapter

six

KACHE COULDN'T GET TO the house fast enough. Now that too much time had passed, and the place would most likely have rotted to ruins. The cabin Grandma Lettie and Grandpa A. R. built with their own hands in the early forties, added on to in the fifties. The place his mom and dad added on to again before transforming it into a real house in the seventies. The house Kache grew up in and loved, the only place he ever called home—reduced to a pile of moldy logs.

He guessed that it would be dark when he got out to the homestead. The days were already starting to get longer and in less than a month would go on until midnight, though that didn't help him now. He had no idea if the moon would show up full or a sliver, waxing or waning. Yes, he knew the DIY Network lineup by heart, but he'd lost track of the night sky long ago. He reached under the seat for the flashlight he figured Snag would have stowed there and set it next to him. Plenty of gas—he'd filled it that afternoon—so he'd make it out and back with some to spare.

Keeping an eye out for moose, he drove the first part of the road, the paved part, fast. Here the houses stood close enough to see one another, all facing south to take advantage of the view—the jagged horizon of mountains marooned across twenty-four miles of Kachemak Bay.

Kachemak. A difficult name to have in this town, the kids teasing him in his first years at school by adding Bay when the teacher let his full name slip out during roll call instead of the shortened version he'd insisted on—pronounced simply *catch*. Then in high school, the girls blushing and calling him *What a Kache*, asking him if he would write a song for them. Or the boys throwing balls of any type his way and saying *Here, Kache!* followed by *You can't, Kache!*, which was absolutely correct.

At first, his mom told him they named him for the bay because it was the most beautiful bay she'd ever seen and he was the most beautiful baby she'd ever laid eyes on. Whenever Denny protested, she'd laugh and say, "Den, I won't lie to you. You had the *sweetest* little squished-up turnip face. Fortunately, you *grew* into your dashingly handsome self."

Later, when Kache was sixteen and his father decided he was old enough to be let in on a secret, he told Kache that was all true, but there was more. Kache was conceived, his father said, grinning, in the fishing boat on the bay. The sun had been warm and the fishing slow—both rarities for Alaska. "Proved to be a fruitful combination, heh?" He had slapped Kache on the back so hard it had about knocked him over. "Denny, of course, was conceived on a camping trip to Denali." Kache had told his dad that he didn't need quite that much information, thank you very much.

He hit a pothole, and mud splattered on the hood and windshield. Kache knew the house was probably too far out of the way and too well hidden for anyone to stumble upon. Old Believers wouldn't want anything to do with a house outside their village, and the deepest cut of canyon on the whole peninsula added an uncrossable deterrent. Nobody with a brain would descend that canyon. The one other access besides their five-mile private road was by the beach, and only during the lowest tides.

Most likely, the house stood its ground against the snow and rain and wind until the chinking filled like sponges, the roof turned to cheesecloth, the furniture rotted with moss, all his mother's books… All those books. His mom's paintings and her quilts and the photographs. The photographs that he'd never wanted, now he wanted them—even the blurry black-and-white ones he'd taken when he was five, when he'd snapped a whole roll of film with Denny's new camera and Denny had threatened to strangle him.

Damn it, Aunt Snag.

Where you been? Where you been?

Damn it yourself, Winkel. He hit the steering wheel, pulled on the lights, and leaned forward as if that would make him get there faster.

The road turned to dirt—mud this time of year. A plastic bottle of Advil lodged between the seats rattled on and on. This was the part of the road he knew best, the part his old blue Schwinn had known so well that at one time, the bike might have found its way back home without anyone riding it.

No turning around now; the pull grew stronger, magnetic.

He wasn't the first one to leave and get pulled back. In the midsixties, even his dad couldn't wait to get away, had gone off to Vietnam in a huff of rebellion mixed with a desperation to see someone other than the all-too-familiar faces in Caboose, Alaska. But he returned with a deep disdain for the World Out There. In a few short, horrific years, he said, he'd learned a lifetime of lessons about human nature and wasn't interested in learning more.

"I'll take plain old nature with a minimum of the human element, thank you," he was fond of saying.

But then he'd met Bets, and she restored his faith in humankind, or at least in womankind, and instead of the life he'd planned as a hermit bachelor, he became a family man. Still, he answered to no one (except, it was a known fact, Bets) and lived off the sea and the land for the most part, earning a decent living as a fisherman. They'd been able to transform the cabin into a real house, with huge windows facing the bay and the Kenai Mountains. Bets had eased him into one compromise after the other over the years, first with a generator and then, once Caboose Electric Association extended their service, real electricity, although they never did have central heating. She'd confided to Kache that it was next on her list, right before the Cessna crashed.

It made sense for homesteaders, like all farmers, to have large families to help with the work. But Lettie and A. R., and later Bets and Glenn, had only had two children. Fortunately, Denny, like his father Glenn before him, had been able to do the work of three or four strapping boys. Kache, however, had been a disappointment, and his father had had a hard time hiding just how much Kache had let him down on a daily basis.

A bull moose plunged through the spruce trees, and Kache slowed to a stop and let it cross in front of him. Its long legs navigated the mud with each step before it disappeared into the alder bushes. Kache drove on and turned down their private road to the homestead, but he quickly pulled over. *Road* was an optimistic term. A churned-up pathway of sludge obstructed by downed spruce and birch trunks and overgrown alders was more like it. He grabbed the flashlight, which was also optimistic—the light dim, the battery exhausted. Aunt Snag knew to keep the battery fresh, but Kache should have checked it before he left. He didn't want to walk in the dark through moose and bear country at the onset of spring when the animals experienced the boldest of hunger pangs.

His cell phone was useless: no service. He should turn back. Get in the car and head into town and return tomorrow. But his dad, his mom, Denny—they seemed so close. A slap on his back, an arm around his shoulders, as certain as the cold on his feet, and he shivered from both. He smelled the fire from their woodstove, as if they had kept it burning all these years. All around him, they said his name in all its variations and tones, so achingly clear: "Kache, honey?" "Oh, Ka-achemak, there's my widdle brodder…" "Did you hear me, Son? Pay attention." He heard their snow machines, though there wasn't any snow, though there wasn't any *them*. He didn't believe in heaven exactly, but this place was thick with recollections and maybe something more. If their spirits watched him, somehow, from somewhere, didn't he want to prove he had become capable of more than any of them thought possible? But had he? No. A city boy number-cruncher-turned-couch-potato who wore pretty boots and forgot a decent flashlight would hardly invoke awe. Still. If they were waiting, they'd been waiting twenty years, and he didn't want to make them wait another day.

He made his way through the mud, tripping, sinking, until the full moon rose from behind the mountains. Like a helpful neighbor in the nick of time, it shone its generous golden light through the cobalt sky. A wolf howled, holding a single lonely note in the distance. The scent of spruce and mud and sea kept dredging up the imagined hint of smoke. All those scents had always come together here. Even in the summers, a fire burned in the woodstove.

Kache spotted the downed trees clearly without the flashlight, and he walked as quickly as his mud-soaked, city-boy boots would allow—until the last bend, where he stopped and readied himself for what lay ahead.

It was then, standing on the road that was no longer a road, breathing deep, his heart hammering, that the realization jarred him. The familiar scent. The spruce, the soaked loamy earth, the sea—yes, yes, yes. But wood smoke? Too strong, too distinct, not merely his imagination. It was definitely the smell of wood burning, and coal too.

He edged around the last corner and saw the house through the boughs of spruce and naked birch and cottonwoods. It stood, not a dejected pile of logs, but tall and proud, glowing with warm light.

What?

Who?

Smoke rose straight from the chimney, as if the house raised its hand. As if the house knew the answer.

chapter

seven

KACHE STOOD STARING, THE cold mud oozing into his boots and through his socks. The house stared back as it always had in his mind, glowing with light and life in the middle of the cleared ten acres.

Who in the hell?

Sweating, watching, allowing for the strangest glimmer of hope. Maybe he really *had* been dreaming, really *had* been sleeping, and now that he'd finally awoken, life might resume as it had before. Maybe all and everyone had not been lost. Maybe only he had been lost.

In these last two minutes, he felt more alive than he had in two decades. Maybe he'd been under some sort of spell, broken at last on this anniversary. His mom would love the mysticism and synchronicity of that.

He shook his head, boxed his own ears. What he needed was common sense. His dad would have reamed him for not grabbing Aunt Snag's .22 that hung on the enclosed back porch. As much as Kache hated guns, never got himself to actually shoot one, he knew it was crazy to approach the house without carrying one, especially given the lights and smoke. His dad used to say it didn't matter if you were far to the left of liberal: if you walked by yourself in the boondocks of Alaska, you should carry a gun.

His feet started moving forward anyway. Forward to his old house, his old room. *Who in the hell?*

Inside, a dog barked. A shadow passed by one of the windows. The shade went down, snapped up quick as a wink, and shut again.

He pressed his back against the old storage barn, took deep breaths, and tried to line up his thoughts, which kept ricocheting off one another. He should go back, return in daylight with the gun. Call Clemsky, Jack O'Connell, a few of the others. He licked his palm and made a small circle on the mud-covered window beside him. He peered in. It was dark, and he barely made out the outline of his dad's Ford pickup. Aunt Snag had even left that, probably driven it home that day from where his dad had parked it by the runway. She should have used it. That would have meant something.

The dog was going nuts, continuously barking. Kache pushed on the storage barn side door; it wasn't locked and opened easily. Along the wall, he felt for the shovel, the hoe, the rake. He decided on the sharp, stiff-bladed rake. Better than nothing.

Hovering behind a warped barrel and then a salmonberry bush, he tried the back door of the house, knowing it would be locked. He crept along to the first kitchen window, remembering. That window never did lock. He slid it open, pulled himself up on one knee, lowered the rake in first, jumped down inside with a thud.

The barking stopped, became a whine and growl. He pictured a hand muzzled around the dog's nose. Kache tried to make himself smaller by crouching and then slipping along the wall. The thought came to him: *I am not the intruder here. This is my house.* He'd forgotten, taken on the attitude of a thief instead of a protector, and he stood straight with his rake, as if that would shift the perspective of whoever was upstairs, as if the moment were a black-ink silhouette that changed depending on how you looked at it.

The whining, the growling. Kache could smell his own nerves, so of course the dog could. He ran his hand along the blue-tiled kitchen counter, up to the light switch, and flicked on the lights. Nothing had changed. As always, the woodstove warmed the large living room, which had once held four rooms before his mom and dad remodeled. The same furniture stood in its assigned places. His mother's paintings still hung heavily on the thick, chinked walls. Photos of the four of them—baby, wedding, Christmas pictures—all lined the top of the piano. He ran his finger along the top. Free of dust. Games and books crammed the shelves. Kache fingered the masking tape his mother had sealed along the broken seam of the Scrabble box. He fought urges to throw the rake, to vomit, to leave.

Upstairs, another growl. Kache choked out, "Hello?" He listened. Nothing. "Hello?"

Then rage. He pounded up the stairs. "Answer me. Answer me!" He flung open doors and flipped on lights to bedrooms that stood like shrines to the dead. All as they'd left it. In his room, a yellowed poster of Double Trouble was still stapled to the wall, Stevie Ray Vaughan still alive and well. As if neither his helicopter nor Kache's family's plane had ever gone down. As if Kache still slept in the bottom bunk and dreamed of playing the guitar on stage.

Under the bed, the dog let out barks like automatic ammunition, scrambling his claws on the wooden floor. Kache held out the rake. "Who's there?" An arm shot out, fist clenched around the handle of Denny's hunting knife. But even more startling than the knife was the arm, clad in the sleeve of his mother's suede paisley shirt. The shirt Kache and Denny bought in Anchorage for her birthday and that she referred to as the most stylish, most perfect-fitting shirt on the planet, a fashion statement that had forged its way to the backwoods of Alaska. "Mom?" Kache whispered under the barking dog. "Mom?" he said louder, his eyes filling.

The dog poked his nose out before being yanked back by the

collar. A husky mix. Kache bent down, trying to see through the thick darkness. "Mom? That's not you?"

The knife retreated, and the hand reappeared, unfolded. Not his mother's hand. It spread, splayed, and pressed its fingers on the floor, until a blond head emerged, and then a face looked up. Not his mother's face. That was all he saw. It was not his mother's face, and a new grief slammed him to his knees.

Mom.

The dog was still barking and this other face that was not his mother's looked up at him for some kind of mercy, and though he hated the face for not belonging to his dead mother, he saw that it was a woman's face, that it was round, that blue eyes begged him, that lips moved, saying words.

"Kachemak? It is you? You are not dead?"

chapter

eight

THERE HAD BEEN ONLY one visitor, years before.

Kachemak caught her so completely unprepared that her heart-beat seemed to be running away, down to the beach, while the rest of her waited.

He looked older, his face more angled than in the photographs. But he still had the same curly hair, though shorter now, and the same heavy brows. His height—taller than the rest of the family in every photo—also gave him away. He asked her to call the dog off, and so she did and pulled herself out from under the bed, though her arms wobbled like a moon jellyfish. She shoved her trembling hands in her pockets and tried to appear brave and confident.

And yet she felt grateful it was him. She knew that Kache, as the family called him, was a gentle soul. But she also knew it was possible for a man to appear kind and yet be brutal. She fluctuated between this wariness and wanting to reach out and hold him as a mother would a child, even though he was older by ten years.

All this time, she'd pictured him a boy like Niko, not a man like Vladimir. And all this time, she'd thought him dead. She'd figured it out on her own, but then Lettie had confirmed. "You may as well be here. They're all gone," she'd said and snapped her fingers. "And Lord knows they're never coming back."

When Nadia asked, "Was it the hunting trip?" because she'd seen a reference to it on the calendar and elsewhere, Lettie nodded and held a finger to her lips while a single tear ran down her worn cheek, and Nadia never asked her about it again. They'd had an unspoken mutual agreement not to pry, to leave certain subjects alone.

But now Kache stood before her, older, a grown man who had called her "Mom." Was Elizabeth alive too?

"Who are you?" he asked.

She shook her head. She should not have spoken earlier, should have pretended she did not understand English. But she'd already given herself away.

"Look, do you know me?" he asked. "You called me by name. You thought I was dead? Do I know you?"

She shook her head again, walked back and forth across the small room, touching the chair, lamp, bed as she went. Moving like this, she could turn her head and glimpse him sideways without feeling so exposed face-to-face. The years had marked him, but he still had a youthful expression, those big dark eyes. Though Lettie had stayed clear of certain topics, Nadia knew so much about the boy: a gifted musician, an awkward teenager who felt out of place on the homestead, who fought bitterly with his father and had been a constant disappointment to him, but whose mother understood him and felt sure he would find his way. Nadia knew when he lost his first tooth (six and a half years old), when he said his first word (*moo-moo* for *moose*, ten months old). How he cried when his mother read him *Charlotte's Web*.

"Can you stop pacing?"

She stopped. They stood in the lamplight, he staring at her, she staring at her slippers. His mother's slippers. He didn't know anything—not one thing—about her, not even her name. All those years and years nameless, unknown. Only Lettie knew her, and Lettie must be dead. Nadia was afraid to ask.

"What's your name?" Kache asked. "Let's start with that."

Leo let out a long sigh and rested his head on his paws, sensing no more danger. How could a dog get used to having another human around so quickly?

Squaring her shoulders, taking a deep breath, she said, "Nadia." She wanted to shake him and call out, *I AM NADIA!* But she kept quiet, still, erect.

He held out a large hand. "I'm Kache."

She kept her hands in her pockets and her eyes to the ground, even though part of her still wanted to hug him, to comfort him. She practiced the words in her head, moved her lips, put her voice to it without looking up. "Your mother is alive?"

"No. She died a long time ago."

At once, the new hope vanished. "Then why do you ask this, if I was your mother?"

"My brother and I gave her that shirt." She felt her face flush. "I lost my head for a minute. You scared the hell out of me. And I still have no idea who you are."

When she looked up, he crossed his arms and took an authoritative stance. She turned her eyes back to the floor. It was her turn to speak. This, a conversation. She was conversing with the boy she thought had died, whose bed she slept in, whose jeans she wore, always belted and rolled up at the cuffs. She had talked to herself, to Leo, to the chickens and the goats and the gulls and the sandhill cranes, to the feral cats, to any living being, driven by the fear that she might forget how to talk. She hadn't spoken to another human except for Lettie, four years ago. But here she was, speaking with someone, in English no less, which is what felt natural to her now after reading nothing but English all this time.

"But I tell you who I am," she said. "Nadia."

"Nadia." He nodded as he said it, as if he liked the name.

Her name. It twisted through her, and she hung her head as tears leaked down her cheeks. Soon, a sob escaped, and then another. She did not cry often. What was the point? But here she was, crying for every day she hadn't.

"What's wrong? I won't hurt you. Don't cry…"

But she could not stop. She had been so alone, so utterly alone for too many years than was possible. Here was someone she knew, someone who knew her name, knew she was alive, someone who might help her or might turn on her.

Kache touched her arm, and she jumped. He stepped back and said again, "It's okay. I won't hurt you."

Through the stuttering gasps, more words erupted, but they came in Russian, too loud, almost screams: "Я Надя! Я Надя! Я умер, когда мне было восемнадцать." *I am Nadia! I am Nadia! I died when I was eighteen.*

chapter

nine

SNAG LAY IN BED, waiting to hear the gravel popping under her truck's tires, trying not to worry but worrying anyway. Maybe Kache wouldn't come back. Maybe he'd just drive straight to the airport and take the next flight out. She hoped not. It was so good to have him home, even though he'd brought all their ghosts with him, and now those ghosts plunked down in her room, shaking their heads at her, whispering about how disappointed they were that she hadn't once gone back to the homestead, not even for the photo albums.

She did have the one photo. Opening the drawer to her rickety nightstand, she pushed aside the Jafra peppermint foot balm. She told her customers how she kept it in that drawer. "Just rub some on every night, and those calluses will feel smooth as a baby's butt." She never actually said *she* rubbed the stuff on *herself*. No one had ever felt the bottoms of her feet, and she reckoned no one ever would. Under the still-sealed Jafra foot balm was an old schedule of the tides, and under that lay a photograph wrapped in tissue with faded pink roses. This was what she was after. She carefully unwrapped it and switched on the lamp, though she almost saw the image well enough in the moonlight.

Bets at the river: tall and slender, wearing those slim, cropped pants Audrey Hepburn wore, a sleeveless, white cotton blouse, and white Keds. Her hair was swept back from her face in a black crown of soft curls. She had red lips and pierced ears, which until then Snag had thought of as slightly scandalous but on Bets looked pretty; she wore the silver drop earrings her Mexican grandmother had given her that matched the silver bangles on her delicate wrist.

Snag remembered handing her the Avon Skin So Soft spray everyone used because mosquitoes hated it. Snag had broken some company record selling bottles of the stuff to tourists. Bets had sprayed it on her arms and rubbed it in. Her skin had glistened and looked oh so soft.

Bets hadn't looked like anyone Snag had ever come across in Caboose or even Anchorage. Half Swedish and half Mexican. From Snag's perspective, the best halves of both nations had collided in Bets Jorgenson. She had grown tired of her job as an editor in New York City, jumped on a train and then a ferry, and come to visit her aunt Pat and her uncle Karl, who at the time lived in Caboose. Pat and Karl had asked Snag to take their niece fishing along the river.

That day, Bets, clearly mesmerized, had seemed content to watch Snag, so Snag had shown off something fierce. Everyone agreed: Snag was one of the best fly fishermen on the peninsula.

Bets had sighed, dropped her chin onto her fists, and said, "It's like watching the ballet. Only better." She had drawn a long cigarette out of a red leather case, lit it with a matching red lighter, and said she'd never seen a girl—or a boy, for that matter—make a fly dance like that. "It seems the fish have forgotten their hunger and are rising just to join in on the dancing." She had studied Snag late into the day, kept studying her even after Snag fastened her favorite fly back onto her vest, flipped the last Dolly Varden into the pail, pulled the camera from her backpack, and took the very picture of Bets she now held in her hand. Bets sat on a big rock, legs crossed at the ankles, pushing her dark sunglasses back on her head. The biggest, clearest smile Snag had ever seen. That picture had been taken a week and two days before Glenn returned home from Fairbanks and fell elbows over asshole in love with Bets too.

chapter

ten

THE WOMAN THREW BACK her head and screamed in a foreign language and, dragging the dog, ran into the bathroom. She locked the door. Kache pressed his ear against it and asked her to come out, but she didn't answer.

Downstairs on the hall tree hung his old green down parka with the Mount Alyeska ski badge his mother had sewn on the collar. He yanked it on over his lighter jacket.

Outside. Fresh air. Breathe. The moonlight reflected in a wide lane across the glassy bay, like some yellow brick road beckoning him to follow it. Instead, he headed through the stale snow and fresh mud of the meadow toward the trail. He walked fast, puffs of steam marking his breaths like the puffs that sometimes rose from the volcanoes across Cook Inlet.

He could erupt any moment.

He could do his own screaming.

Who the hell do you think you are? This is MY house. MY clothes. MY mother's shirt.

How long had she been here, eating, bathing, sleeping, breathing in his memories? And who else? How many others had made his home their own?

At the biggest bend, the trail opened to the left, and there, five paces away, the plunge of the canyon. He didn't go another step. He shivered, partly from the cold, partly from childhood fears.

In the quiet, a hawk owl called its *ki ki ki*, and the canyon answered Kache's ranting with questions of its own.

YOUR home?

Have you given a rat's ass about one inch of this land or one log of that house?

Has it occurred to you? The strange woman may be the only reason YOUR home is still standing?

Kache shook his head hard enough to shake his thoughts loose. The canyon obviously didn't speak to him like that. To prove it, he did what they'd all done a thousand times, whenever they'd arrived at that spot on the trail.

Across the dark, vast crevice, he yelled, "HELLO?"

And the canyon answered as it always had: "Hello?... Hello?... Hello?..."

chapter

eleven

THE FRONT DOOR CLOSING, his footsteps clunk-clunking down the porch stairs. Nadia peeled back the curtain to see him cross the meadow. Where was he going? She turned on the bathroom light and stared at her reflection in the medicine cabinet. Her hair was disheveled from climbing under the bed, so she pulled out the elastic band and brushed. Leo lay down at her feet.

Nadia touched her fingertips to her lips. "Hello," she said to the mirror. Her voice shook. All of her shook. Her throat seared from the screaming. But she did not scream now. She imagined her reflection was Kachemak, and she kept her eyes from looking away. It was one thing to talk to plants and animals and quite another to have a conversation with a human—with a man.

"I am frightened." No. "I am fine. Fine. I go now."

She raised her chin, put her hand to her hair.

"Thank you for letting me stay."

Her eyes narrowed. "Stay away from me or I kill you." She placed her fists on her hips. "Son of bitch. Damn you to hell, son of bitch."

But Kachemak's mother was Elizabeth. Kind, smart Elizabeth. And this was her Kache. "I apologize. Your mother is not bitch. Your mother is very good. Your grandmother is very good." She touched her throat. "Kache? Please? You are still good person also?"

chapter

twelve

THE SUN PULLED ITSELF up over the mountains to the east, casting salmon-tinged light on the range and all across the bay, even reaching through the large living room windows. Kache sat sipping dandelion root tea with the woman Nadia, she in his mother's red-and-white-checked chair, he on the old futon. Neither had slept. Only the fire crackling in the woodstove broke the silence between them. She burned coal and wood, which filled the tarnished and dented copper bins next to the stove. She must have collected the coal on the beach the way his family had done. It smelled like home.

The fire popped, and they both jumped. "*Bozhe moi!*" Her hand went to her mouth, her eyes still downward. "Sorry."

Wait—that language, her accent…Russian?

An Old Believer?

❧

In junior high, Kache wrote a social studies report on the Old Believer villages. The religious sect had descended from a band of immigrants who'd broken off from the Russian Orthodox Church during the schism of the seventeenth century and later, during the Revolution, fled Russian persecution, immigrated to China, then Brazil, then Oregon, before this particular group feared society encroaching, influencing their children. They moved to the Kenai Peninsula in the early 1960s, beyond the end of the railroad line, past Caboose, which was then still called Herring Town, and staked their claim to hundreds of acres beyond the Winkels' own vast acreage.

At first, everyone pitied the Old Believers. A woman was badly scarred trying to save her daughter, who died in a fire. "They'll never make it through another winter," locals predicted about the small group of long-bearded men and head-scarf-wearing women. But then a baby girl was born, and the Believers saw the tiny new life as an encouragement from God. In the spring, they began to fish and cut timber. They built wooden houses and painted them bright colors—blue and green and orange—and more Believers came from Oregon. They built a domed church. Eventually, they too divided over religious differences, and the strictest of the group ventured deeper into the woods. But both groups lived separated from the rest of the world, exempt from laws other than their own rituals, unchanged since the seventeenth century, which they believed were from God. Back in the seventies, Kache's dad said they were ignoring a lot of the fishing laws, and when the fishermen had a slow year, they often blamed the Old Believers.

"They're lowly." Kache recalled Freida, his mom's bridge partner, spitting the words across the kitchen table one night.

His parents adamantly objected, but his mom had her own concerns. "I just worry that they're so steeped in religious tradition that they have no awareness of equal rights. I've heard they marry those poor little girls off when they're thirteen."

Then Freida's husband, Roy, said, "I'll tell you where I want equal rights. Out on that water, that's where."

Kache's mom said, "I wonder if those young girls even have a prayer."

"Bets," Roy answered, "they pray all damn day."

❧

No way would an Old Believer woman step outside her village except to run an errand in town. Look at Gram's afghan, those photographs, the magazines, back from 1985 and before. Even the Rainier Beer coasters. Nothing has changed. It's like sitting in 1985 with a woman from 1685— if she even is an Old Believer. What if there's poison in the tea? Kache set down his cup. *If the tea doesn't kill me, her husband is going to come in and shoot me.*

Kache wanted to ask her many questions, but the despair rose from his spinning mind and settled in his throat, and he was afraid that if he spoke too soon, he too might succumb to tears. He'd fallen smack-dab into that day when he'd sat in this living room, a little high, playing his guitar, tired from having done his chores and Denny's as a way of apologizing, waiting for the three of them to drive up and pile in the door with stories of their weekend. His dad would be gruff at first. But once he'd seen that Kache had not only finished the chores, but also had the awful mess from the fight, repaired his bedroom door, even gone down to the beach and emptied the fishing net, all would be forgiven.

Jesus.

The dog stayed at Nadia's feet, watching Kache. A husky and something else, maybe a malamute…with big brown, loyal eyes.

"What's your dog's name?"

A long silence before she whispered, "Leo." Leo's ear went up and rotated toward her.

"Are you into astrology or literature?" he asked, mostly as a joke to himself.

But she surprised him and said, "Tolstoy. Almost I name him Anton."

His mom would be proud. "You have good taste. So…" He smiled. "I guess we've established the fact that we're not going to kill each other." He picked up the tea and sniffed. "Although I'm not sure I trust your tea."

She lowered her chin. "I would not poison."

He tried a smile again that still went unmet. "Fair enough. I do have some questions."

"Yes." She placed her hands on the knees of her jeans—his old jeans, actually. He recognized the patch his mother had sewn on the right knee. He and Denny used to tease her because sometimes she sewed patches on their patches.

"How long have you been here?"

She studied her hands as though she'd just discovered them, let a moment pass before she held them out, fingers splayed.

"Ten days?"

She shook her head.

"Ten months?"

Again, no.

"Ten *years*?"

A nod.

"How old are you?"

"I am twenty-eight years old." With this, her eyes filled again, and she quickly wiped her face.

"Do you know my aunt Snag?"

She shook her head.

"You came with your folks? Where's your family?"

"I have none."

"Who lives with you here?"

She shook her head, kept shaking it.

"But you haven't been here by yourself. Tell me who else has been living in my house."

Her hands went over her ears.

Kache took a deep breath and lowered his voice. "I'm not angry. I'm *confused*." She finally looked up, but not directly at him. "I don't know who you are and who else might come barging through the door with a gun."

"I am alone."

"I'm wondering if you're an Old Believer?"

She nodded again, one slow dip of her head.

"With an entire village? Big family? Ton of kids? But you're not wearing a long dress."

With that, she stood, and the dog rose and followed her to the stairs.

"Wait. Nadia, please. I need some answers here."

She turned and whispered, "I cannot." She was tall, sturdy. She'd rolled up his jeans and cinched them with a belt. Her back faced him again, and her gold drape of hair, which had been tied up the night before, reached past her waist. The Old Believer women he'd seen shopping in town always covered their hair with scarves.

He let her and the dog go upstairs. The door to his old room clicked shut.

No signs of anyone else, other than his own family—and those signs flashed loudly everywhere he turned. He went through the house, amazed again and again by how much remained exactly the same. Most of his mother's books filled the walls, as neat and full as rows of corn, although some books were upside down and others stood in small stacks here and there throughout the rooms. In the bathroom, there were even Amway and Shaklee products. His mom had been such a supporter of Snag, his dad would complain that the products were taking over the household. Stacked five rows deep in the barn, the pantry, the cupboards; enough, apparently, to last at least twenty years.

He turned on the faucet. The pipes seemed to be in working order. In the pantry, home-canned goods lined the shelves—garden vegetables, rhubarb and berry jams, salmon and meats, mushrooms, tomato sauces, soups, sauerkraut, relishes. Potted herbs sat along the windowsill next to the old kitchen table. He went down into the root cellar, stocked with boxes of potatoes and onions, hanging red cabbages, and some dried fish and meat. Tally marks had been carved into the wall, almost covering it. He didn't count them, but it looked like there could be enough to account for ten years. Or a lot of dead buried bodies. The family's old refrigerator held frozen fish and meats. Dried herbs hung from the ceiling.

Someone undoubtedly helped her with all of this. And who paid the electricity bill?

He climbed back up to the main floor, hesitated before heading up to the second floor. This was his house. He had every right to look around. But he paused again before he entered his parents' room. The pauses came with a sense of reverence, as if he were entering a church or a museum. Everything—every single thing—in the entire house had been so well tended, so obviously respected by this Nadia.

The quilt his mother made still covered the bed. As a small boy, he would race his matchbox cars along the quilt's patterns—roadways, as he saw them. Until a wheel caught on a stitch, pulling a piece of fabric loose, and his mother put an end to that game. He sat on the bed, running his hand along it until he found the spot where the missing piece exposed strands of batting. Even this room was not cloaked in dust as he'd expected. He opened the closet and saw their clothes, his father's heavy jackets and creased boots, his mother's red down jacket. Everyone commented on how his mother managed to look fashionable in whatever she wore, no matter how functional. He never knew much about fashion, but he knew his mom always stood out in a crowd.

"Mom," he whispered. "Mom, Mom, Mom." He stuck his nose in her sweater and inhaled, but it no longer smelled of her. On the dresser though was a bottle of her perfume: White Linen. He opened it and there it was. Once when he was Christmas shopping with Janie, he saw the perfume on display and picked up the tester, smelled it, and wished he hadn't. The saleswoman took the bottle from him, sprayed it on a piece of white textured card stock, like a bookmark to hold his place, and handed it to him. He had set the paper reminder of his mom back on the glass counter and walked away. But now he pressed the gold cylinder top on the dispenser and shot the scent of his mother across the room.

Goddamn it. There is no getting around grief.

Even if you turned your back on it, diligently refused to answer its call, it would badger you, forever demanding payment. And oh, could it wait; it would not move on. Grief was a fucking collections company, and it was never fully satisfied. It would always keep showing up out of the blue, tacking on more interest.

His mom's books lined the walls in the bedroom too. He'd known she loved to read, but he hadn't realized that they'd lived in what other people might classify as a library. She'd worked in the book business in New York before she'd met his father. She moved here willingly, even enthusiastically, carrying her designer clothes and hundreds of books to this far edge of the world.

And there was the big, old steamer trunk at the end of the bed. The one she'd kept locked, with her journals inside; the one no longer locked, the brass tongues sticking out at him. He lifted the creaky top. Empty, as he expected. He remembered Snag emptying it a few days after they'd gotten the news. Kache had sat swollen-eyed in his room and watched her blurred image go back and forth from his parents' room to a cardboard box in the hallway. She'd carried the notebooks in armfuls from the trunk to the box, and her knitted cardigan got caught on one of the wire rings so that after she released them, a single notebook hung from her sweater. It had an orangey-red cover, and it made Kache think of a king crab clinging to her. She didn't even notice until he pointed it out. Snag's own eyes were so teary that when she tried to remove it, she kept tangling the sweater and wire even more, until Kache helped release her. He handed her the journal and gently closed his door, leaving Snag to carry out his mom's one commandment that if anything ever happened to her, the journals would be burned. At least Snag had done that much.

In the bathroom, Kache blew his nose and splashed cold water on his eyes, pressed a towel against his face, holding it there for a good long minute. His great-grandfather's white enamel shaving mug, soap brush, and straight-edge razor still sat on the shelf. His mom always did love family heirlooms. Little did she know the whole house would one day be a museum full of them.

He knocked on his bedroom door. "I'm going to take off. Not sure when I'll be back, but maybe you'll be ready to talk by then?"

The dog let out a whine, but Nadia said nothing.

chapter

thirteen

THE FRONT DOOR CLOSED again, and Nadia released a sigh so long and shaky she wondered how long she'd been holding her breath. From the bedroom window, she watched him taking long strides up the road. He looked more teenager than man, still gangly and long-limbed, still moving with the slightest uncertainty.

She collapsed into the desk chair, more tired than if she'd chopped and hauled wood all day, a fatigue that started in her chest and wrapped itself around her head. She tried to think logically. Although she felt as if she knew him through the stories, he was not the same person who'd been brought up in that house. Unlike Nadia, he had lived a life. He had gone somewhere, done some things. He most likely had a wife, children, an occupation. He was a musician, or perhaps a teacher of music.

He seemed upset but mostly gentle. She wanted to trust her instinct; she was older now, knew more. It was clear he had not decided what to do about her, and she imagined him changing his mind again and again with each turn of the road. Would he bring back the police, have her arrested? Would he head out to the village to ask questions? Would he return with supplies? Or with Lettie, if she was still alive? But he hadn't mentioned her, and Nadia had long feared Lettie dead, had mourned her ever since her last visit, when she brought not one but two truckloads of supplies and Leo, who was just a puppy then.

Perhaps Kache would bring his wife to talk with her. If he did go to the village…what if Vladimir charmed Kache into coming back with him, the way he had so easily charmed her father and the others?

She should leave. She forced herself to stand, and Leo stood next to her, wagging his tail, waiting for her next move.

She'd tried to leave several times in the past years after Lettie stopped coming. Nadia had hiked down to the beach and loaded the Winkels' faded orange canoe. Leo climbed in and sat perfectly still, although his anticipation was palpable as she climbed in, paddled. Always at some point, her nerve turned to nervousness. Where was she paddling to? And then what? And so she had turned around and paddled back, Leo's ears down as if he'd been reprimanded. "For this, I am very sorry. I am such the coward, Leo."

Other times, she had hiked up to the road with a plan to walk into town and ask to trade animals for a new car battery and starter. She would offer chickens, a goat, whatever they wanted. But the downshift of a distant truck would send her into the bushes for cover. In her mind, Vladimir sat behind the wheel, and that was enough to put another end to her plans. By the time she retraced her steps, his face had faded, and she saw instead her father's kind face, heading to buy parts for his truck, and then her mother's, her sisters', her brothers' faces—all so much younger than they were now. But she had no way of knowing what the years had done to their faces. The guilt pushed her back into the Winkel house, back into bed until hunger would force her out of her self-pity, out to work the garden or to set the fishing nets and traps.

She walked down the stairs into the empty living room. Even with Leo at her heels, the emptiness had spread since Kache left. She took the dog's face in her hands. "I should not have shut him out like that, you say?" She tugged his ear. "But wasn't it so difficult? His asking these questions we do not know how to answer?"

Leo harrumphed and lay down next to the woodstove.

"You want him to come back? Like Lettie?"

Like Lettie.

❧

All those years ago, Nadia had stayed in the house through the first spring without a sign of anyone. She'd lived off fish and clams and mussels and the plants she'd foraged—sea lettuce and nori from the bay, lovage, goose tongue, and yellow monkey flower greens from the land. She snared plenty of rabbits.

One day, she hunted for morels after a week of rain, her mouth watering as she thought of sautéing them in some of the wine she'd found in the cellar, along with wild garlic and a bit of fat from the spruce hen she'd shot the day before. But she sensed, as she walked toward the house with her basket of mushrooms, that someone was there, and she slipped behind the old outhouse to hide. Her heart seemed to beat through her back, thumping the wooden siding she leaned against.

A woman's voice called out from the front porch. "Well, whoever you are, you're trespassing on my property, but I'm not gonna shoot you. You might as well show your face."

Nadia pressed harder against the building. It must be the owner. Nadia had thought it possible they would never come back. When she'd first found the house, she saw that no one had been there for months. Strangest were the signs that no one had lived there for more than a decade. The calendars, the newspapers, the magazines— everything stopped after May 1985.

"Come on now. Contrary to what you might think, I'm glad you're here," the voice called. "You seem to be taking good care of the place. I'm going to fix us something to eat. I hope you'll join me in the kitchen."

Eventually, Nadia did get hungry and cold. She smelled something meaty and sweet and delicious, along with smoke from the woodstove. Because she could not afford to pause to consider the consequences, she traversed the yard and climbed the steps to the front door without hesitation. She knocked on the door, which felt odd, and when an old woman with a white braid answered, Nadia held out the basket of morels like the neighbors attending a holy day feast back in the village. The woman smiled, her wrinkles a map of her long life. Repositioning her braid so it lay behind her shoulder, she thanked Nadia and took the basket.

She said, "You poor, sweet girl. I hope you like homemade beef vegetable soup and bread and chocolate chip cookies."

Nadia had nodded, pushing the heels of her palms against her eyes.

"Don't you worry now, you hear me? I'll tell you what. No one's going to badger you or make you go anywhere."

And Lettie had stuck to her word.

❧

If only Kachemak took after his grandmother. It seemed evident that "my nonmeddling gene," as Lettie had called it, had not traveled down through the generations.

Already Kachemak had asked more questions than Lettie. And already Nadia had decided she needed to find some way to leave, and somewhere to leave to. Somehow.

chapter

fourteen

SNAG NEEDED TO CALL Nicole Hughes to get a ride to the Caboose chamber of commerce meeting. Kache hadn't returned the previous night, which meant Snag hadn't slept even one quarter of a wink. But he called from his cell phone that morning and told her he was fine, not to worry. When she tried to ask him about the homestead, he'd only said they'd talk later and hung up.

Snag cleaned all morning, cleaned over what she'd already cleaned in preparation for his arrival, because cleaning calmed her nerves. Not this time. Everything veered off course, as if the Earth had freed itself from its steadfast journey around the sun and decided to skedaddle over to Jupiter with a side trip around Mars on the way.

She should go out to the homestead. Obviously. But she didn't have her truck, which meant she'd need a ride out there, which meant whoever drove her might detect her own unbelievable capacity for negligence, which meant, in Caboose, perhaps forty-five minutes, tops, would pass before the town and its outlying communities would hear the whole humiliating story.

Besides, she really did have to get herself to the chamber meeting. She'd been heading up a project, trying to get the train running all the way to Caboose again. A long haul, so to speak, but they'd finally gotten approval from the railroad company and the Department of Transportation, which had already begun renovation on the tracks. Now the town squabbled about one major detail.

Way back, when Caboose used to be called Herring Town with the perfectly clever slogan *The End of the Line*, the herring boom brought the train, the train brought the people, the herring were loaded onto the train by the people—everyone was happy, and everyone got down on their knees at night and thanked the good Lord for the train and the herring in all its abundance. But then, as too much of a good thing is bound to do, the herring industry dried up from overfishing as fast as it came, and the town all but dried up, and the railroad company crowned Wilbur, Alaska, as its new end of the line, about seventy-five miles up the tracks. For some reason no one quite knew, a caboose was left abandoned at the end of the Herring Town Spit, that jut of land four and a half miles long, that long finger pointing to the mountains across the bay.

About fifty years after the herring left, someone came up with the idea of changing the town name, because calling it Herring Town was a bit like calling the Mojave Desert "Seaside." A vote officially made it Caboose. They needed to change the slogan too, because it was no longer the end of the line, so some idiot, as far as Snag was concerned, came up with a zinger: *See the Moose in Caboose.* Wow. *That* was interesting. Moose appeared around every other bend in the state of Alaska and most of Canada. Not exactly bragging material.

So Snag had devised a plan to get the railroad to consider bringing the train back for the tourists and thus reestablishing the old slogan, which would once again make sense. Caboose was one of the prettiest towns in Alaska. Although, she had to admit, Alaskans used the term *pretty* rather loosely when describing towns. Caboose was a typical frontier town, where mostly ugly buildings had cropped up as needed without much of a plan, but everyone said the setting on the mountain-bordered bay wasn't just one of the prettiest in Alaska—it was one of the prettiest in the world. The tourists flocked like locusts every summer; the road backed up with motor homes all the way to Anchorage. A major cluster. Bad for the environment, and hard on everyone's nerves, locals and tourists alike. So she got the railroad to agree to bring the train back. Hallelujah, right?

Wrong. Now that they'd started refurbishing the track, everyone was pissed over the fate of the caboose, the town mascot that sat at the end of the spit and currently housed a mini museum with photos and artifacts of the early Alaskan pioneers.

Snag wanted to have the original caboose refurbished and let it run as intended, at the back end of the train, with the pioneer memorabilia on display along with souvenirs for sale. A great story, extra publicity—just like the town that had once been abandoned, the old caboose had been reborn and had a new lease on life. Stuck for all these years, and then, finally, on the *move*. She could practically write the publicity materials in her sleep.

But a big chunk of the town had their Carhartts in a bunch over the idea.

"We can't move the caboose! It's what our town was named after."

"The caboose," Snag had reminded them, "will still be here twice a day. But it will have a purpose, just like its namesake. It will be alive again, just like our town. Come on, people. Let's just get a new caboose to stick out there and use the original as it was intended."

She was beginning to realize she made up the entire minority on this issue. Snag, who'd been told by Marv Rosetter she could sell ice to an Inupiaq, had not been successful in convincing the people of Caboose of this one obvious solution. Another reason she should get herself to the meeting.

But Nicole Hughes didn't pick up the phone. Neither did Suz

Clayton. Melanie Magee's line was already busy—with one of the others calling her, Snag suspected. They, of course, played on the side of the caboose keepers. And they had caller ID. So Snag could almost see them standing in their kitchens, listening to her ask if they might be able to give her a ride. They may as well have shouted into the receiver, "No, and *hell* no!"

She pulled on her coat, stepped into her boots on the porch, and started marching toward the chamber meeting. But as she walked, she thought of Kache. Again. Where was he? Had he gone to see Lettie? She didn't know that the homestead had been abandoned. Every time she said she wanted to go out there, Snag lied. She told her there were renters who didn't want to be disturbed. She told her the road was too bad and she'd get stuck. She told her maybe next week, maybe next month, maybe in the summer.

One day, after Lettie could no longer drive, she'd set out walking toward the homestead, but luckily, Snag had come across her on the way home from the Christmas festival meeting. Winter, dusk at two in the afternoon, cold. "Mom! What were you thinking?"

But Lettie hadn't answered. She just shook her head and turned toward the window.

Now, instead of going left toward the chamber, Snag turned right onto Willow and hiked up the street to the Old Folks'. She had to get to Lettie before Kache did.

chapter

fifteen

LETTIE CLOSED HER EYES again. If only the nurses and Snag would let her be for more than ten minutes so she could enjoy this remembering, which had become so clear, as if the past were happening to her once again.

This morning, she ventured all the way back to that time she first got tangled up with the idea of Alaska. She'd thought of herself as an adulteress, but not in the common sense of the word, of course. It was the land. Damn the land. It called to her, first in a whisper, its name, *Alaska*, soft down the nape of her neck while she hung out the clothes. Then it was everywhere. It took her over. *Alaska, Alaska*, the broom said. *Alaska?* the chickens asked. She carried a picture in her pocket—of some mountain range across an inlet of water—and she took it out so often it began to peel back from the corner. At night, while A. R. slept loud and hard, she lay awake and then dreamed wet, green, mossy dreams spilling one into the other. Thick, abundant dreams that tumbled her back into morning breathless and with a feeling she guessed was yearning.

A. R. told her to forget it. "One winter," he'd said, "will send you back to Kansas, kissing the dry, cracked dirt, calling it the floor of heaven. Even *with* this great depression and all."

No, Alaska was strictly Lettie's idea.

The man who'd bought the farm from them for practically nothing was the one who told them about homesteading up north. Lettie thought it his way of trying to redeem himself for taking their land and knowing there wasn't a mud puddle in the United States they could buy with what he'd given them for it. He'd said, "In Herring Town, you can get land for free. Just like in the West way back when, but there ain't no Indians in Alaska—well, not the fighting kind." He'd handed her the photograph. "You just stake out the prettiest piece of property you ever seen in your lifetime," he'd said. "Trees and meadows, lakes and mountains and the sea too. And the moose and the berry plants, the fish and clams, the coal just waiting for you to pick it off the beach. None of them's gotten word there's a great depression going on."

A. R. kept moping around after they'd sold the farm and most of their things and moved to town, into the apartment with her uncle Fred. A. R. moped like a man whose dream had fallen down and died. But the farm wasn't *his* dream, after all, she told him carefully one morning while he still lay in bed, smoking one cigarette after the other. "It was your daddy's dream." In a rare moment of intensity between them, she grabbed his arm, tight; her fingernails made grooves in his flesh.

"I think," she said, her eyes filling with tears, "I think you gotta have your *own* dreams." He looked at her blankly, apparently as puzzled by her tears as she was. She stood. Staring into the corner of the tiny, crowded bedroom, she tried to explain, if only to herself. "It must be like what they say about religion. You can't inherit your religion. I imagine the same's true for your dreams."

❧

A. R. was a man resigned. Had he known, Lettie thought, he'd have been a man torn by jealousy. Because that place—that place she'd only heard about, only seen in a single photograph—had taken her over so completely, she thought of little else. One night, she woke from a dream that should have been a nightmare. But strangely, it wasn't. Instead of feeling frightened, she felt a freedom that *did* frighten her more than a nightmare ever had. In the dream, A. R. passed on. Lettie cried. But she left the funeral before it was over, threw her bags in a car of a northbound train, and jumped aboard with ease. Free.

The next morning she ripped up the photograph. The pieces scattered from her hand like snow. "Enough," she said aloud. She hummed familiar tunes and tried to enjoy the sun on her arms while she hung laundry on the line, as she had before this whole nonsense got started.

But the nonsense refused to let go of her. In pitiful desperation, she pleaded with A. R., afraid of that dream of his death and afraid of her own…was it *passion*?

When he finally said yes, he didn't let go gradually—he just let go. "Well, okay. We'll go to Alaska." And she did what anyone who'd grown accustomed to pulling with all her might would have done. She fell flat on her keister.

"Well, what on—?" he said, reaching a hand over to help her up.

She couldn't answer. Laughing, crying, laughing.

"Where did you come from, woman?" he asked, dusting her off. "And what on earth did you do with my Lettie?"

When she found her voice, she said, "Thank you, thank you, thank you!" while she kissed him all over his face, feeling a tenderness toward him she hadn't felt for a long time.

So many times over the next year, anyone else might have shaken a fist at her, damned her for getting them there in the first place. But A. R. never did. Not even one *I told you so.*

There was the treacherous boat trip once they ventured outside the Inside Passage, where she clung to both the fear that they might die and the fear that they might *not* die, that death might *not* come and save them from the slamming, slamming, slamming of the sea.

But they survived somehow, and they arrived somewhere. It was called Herring Town. They trudged through icy water, carrying their bags over their heads while waves leaped at them like children begging for a present. There were people on the shore too. A man, a woman, and—she counted them—ten children. Ten! The Newberrys. All of them round-faced and round-eyed, but their bodies were lean and muscled. All except for the baby, who was delightfully fat, and the toddler, who, later when the sun broke through and slapped color all over the place, ran along the beach wearing nothing but a dirty orange life preserver and a cowbell, his legs chubby and creased, his feet padding on the wet sand.

Frank Newberry had gotten word from the Rosses in Wilbur, who'd gotten word from Uncle Fred's next-door neighbor's cousin, Beck Patten, that Lettie and A. R. were due to come in to Herring Town on the *Salty Sally.* For three days, the Newberrys watched down the inlet for the promise of Lettie and A. R.

Margaret Newberry clung to Lettie as if she were a long-lost sister. She stroked Lettie's hair, most of it fallen loose from the bun she'd pinned it up in days before. A lifetime before. Lettie held her breath while Margaret stared into her face, inches away. Lettie knew she reeked of vomit and worse, but Margaret didn't seem to mind.

Margaret reassured her, reassured her again. There would someday be a train connecting them to Anchorage, and a school. More talk of a store. A post office. And soon, a church.

What Margaret didn't seem to know was that Lettie didn't need reassuring. A church? A mere glimpse of the water, which went from blue to green to red to pink, depending on what the sun and moon were up to—not as it had been earlier with the torment of waves, but now white with the sun's reflections, a thousand spots of light leaping and dancing—seemed a declaration to her, *Let there be light!* Why would anyone want to worship God in a dark log hovel?

If she could, Lettie would have stripped off her vomit-crusted clothes, pitched them into the fire, and worn nothing but a cowbell while she splashed in the icy waves.

Later, while the young women of Herring Town plotted their civilities, crowded around the Sears catalog, and tended to their children, the men helped Lettie and A. R. stake out their land. She giggled at the kissing puffins with their strange, hooked orange beaks and matching feet, cried when she first heard the lonely cry of a loon. Her heart jumped with the salmon in the river; when she saw their silver streaks through the clear water, she saw for the first time the invisible currents of her own life.

One night, she pulled A. R. close to her, unlatched his trousers, snugged them down before he'd even stopped snoring. She was not that type of woman, really. She had always been a lady, though a rather plain one. But Alaska was no place for a lady; the men in Kansas said that to A. R. Even the men on the boat said it. She kissed A. R. on the mouth, and he stopped snoring with a snort. And then he said her name, as he'd been saying it for the past few months—with a question mark. "Lettie? Lettie?" but then "*Lettie…*"

She wanted to give him some of this… What was it? Abundance. It spilled up and out and over her. Let him see it, experience it.

"Now…now…now," she said, arching her back, thinking that if A. R. went deep enough, he might touch this something inside her, take part of it for himself.

❧

The scent of the land got inside her too. A damp, sprucy, smoky, salty scent that she fancied. She smelled it in her own hair, in her clothes, and on the tips of her fingers.

She worked harder than she'd ever worked on the farm, right alongside A. R. and the other men. There was a difference between Lettie and the other women—they all soon recognized this. Instead of dissention and jealousy, the difference bore a mutual respect. Lettie had no children. And Lettie did not come to Alaska as a generous submission to her husband's quest. Alaska was Lettie's quest.

Quest. Was that the right word? Yes, she decided. *Quest* and *question* too. Alaska was her question. The one she'd had to ask. She'd been a woman who had asked few questions. Her life had been a series of neatly laid out stepping-stones, provided for her convenience. She had taken them one at a time, never skipping one or turning over another, never prying one loose to see what might lie underneath. She'd never gotten her feet muddy, so to speak. And then the next expected step was gone, simply not there. She and A. R. had not conceived. There were no children. She hadn't questioned that either. Not really. Tried not to think about it, mostly. Just stayed perched on and busy with the farm and A. R.

Until the photograph.

❧

"Mom? Are you awake?" Snag again. Snag, always trying to reel her back in to the hospital when Lettie just wanted to stay on the land.

Oh, the land. The dream she and A. R. once had to hand it down to their children and grandchildren. She must talk to Kache, tell him what she'd done, get him to go out and see if Nadia was still there.

For all she knew, the poor girl was gone now, or worse, dead. As dead and gone as A. R. himself.

Except there he'd been, as close as her own hand, there in her remembering.

chapter

sixteen

AS HE DROVE, KACHE tried to get a grip. He hadn't slept at all. Forget dandelion root tea; he needed an Americano with an extra shot. He needed answers. He needed some kind of plan. A plan would be good.

The weather could go one of many ways—big gray clouds hung around the mountain peaks, trying to decide if they wanted to get ugly, but the sun was up and shining as if to say, *Hey, calm down. I've got this one.*

Kache didn't want to turn Nadia in. So she'd been squatting on their property for the last ten years. She'd also saved it from going to ruin. But that meant it had stood empty for the decade prior to her arrival. Ten winters with no one running water in the pipes or knocking the snow off the roof or keeping the shrews and voles and mice from taking over. No way. So she was lying or Snag was lying or another strange person had holed up in the house too and might still be around, which circled back to Nadia lying.

Still, he wouldn't turn her in. He'd just ask her to find a different place. He'd help her find something suitable. If she really didn't want to go back to her village, there were people in town who'd probably trade child care or property maintenance for a room. Then, before he went back to Austin, he'd work on the homestead—she had kept up on it the best she could, but he knew it must still need some maintenance—and get it ready to rent out to a cattle rancher or someone who needed a large chunk of the land. He and Snag could deal with it together. It would feel right for them to finally step up, keep a few meaningful things, sell the rest. It would be good. Like the therapist Janie had dragged him to that one time had said: "There's healing in turning homeward, a wholeness that results from facing your history, an ability to move forward." Kache hadn't wanted to hear it and called it a bunch of poetic psychobabble. But, hell, maybe there was something to it.

He pulled up to a drive-through, an orange-and-blue coffee truck called the Caboose Cuppabrews. The brittle air blasted through his open window while a dark-haired boy of about eleven took his order.

"Aren't you a little young to be a coffee barista?"

The boy shrugged. "A bar what?"

A woman laughed from somewhere behind the boy. "We start them working young here, sir. He's my son, so we skirt around those pesky labor laws."

"Marion?"

"Yes?" She bent down, and he took in her face. She had the same dark eyes and high cheekbones and still wore her hair parted in the middle and straight. She had hardly changed. "Kache? No way!" She leaned out farther, spilling the coffee on her wrist. "Ouch! Shit. Sorry. Wait, don't move." And she disappeared back through the window, leaving the boy to sponge up the coffee, shaking his head with a small, somewhat parental smile.

Marion had pulled on a parka, sprinted out from the backside of the truck, reached in through the window, and wrapped her arms around Kache's neck before he could open his door. "I thought they were holding you hostage until we agreed to say Texas was the bigger state after all. Lettie didn't take another turn?"

He teeter-tottered his hand. "My aunt thinks she's at death's door. Gram's confused, but for someone who's ninety-eight years old…"

"You'll have to say hi to my grandpa. Remember Leroy? He's happy as long as they let him fish the hallways. My ex says Leroy's got the best fishing spot on the peninsula, right there in his head. Lettie's been so sharp until recently. How long are you here?"

He shrugged. "Not sure."

"You got someone special?" She smiled that old Marion smile.

"Not as of two days ago. You?"

Now she teeter-tottered her hand. "Still singing?"

He shook his head. "You?"

"Of course. Playing?"

He shook his head again.

"You're shittin' me. You need to come down to the Spit Tune. We still play a few nights a week. Mike, Chris, Dan—all of us. Bring your guitar and that voice of yours. Rex will do cartwheels down the bar when he sees you." She turned toward her son. "Ian, this is Kache. He's a helluva guitar player, and he's got a voice some hotshot reporter called 'both wound and wonder.'"

Kache laughed. "Is there such a thing as a hotshot reporter in Alaska?"

Several cars had pulled up behind him. "Ha-ha. Gotta get back to work, but do not leave town without us catching up. I'm here every morning except Christmas, New Year's, and Easter. Seriously. No excuses, okay?"

He smiled. "Scout's honor."

"You dropped out of the Scouts!" she shouted as he pulled away.

Wow. Marion had a kid. Marion was still singing. The band was still together.

His old house, a museum of his eighteen-year-old life. And his old girlfriend, still playing with their band. He might as well make this trip back in time complete. He turned toward the spit and headed out to see Rex. Since Kache had arrived, he'd already done more social-izing than he had in years. Janie would be shocked.

❦

Only two days before, he'd lain wedged in the permanent indent he'd caused in his and Janie's sofa, the TV cradling him in its famil-iar steel-colored light. On his chest, the cat Charlotte had purred and slept. He'd turned down the volume for the commercial, the warm Austin air carrying aching guitar riffs in D minor along with aromas of barbecue from the restaurant across the street. Another do-it-yourself show was about to start. He should get up—*Arise! Go forth!*—and turn off the TV, but he didn't. He let Charlotte sleep.

Each step of each project was vivid in his mind's eye: a version of his own hands performing every task, but calloused, surer, moving with the certainty of the experienced. Not the boy's hands his father had made fun of. "Explain to me, Son," he'd said, "how the same fingers that spin gold on that silly guitar of yours turn into flippers when you pick up a hammer?"

But some of what his father tried to teach him was at long last finding its way in, if only from a type of televised osmosis.

Janie was upstairs in the loft of their apartment, spreading on lotion, dusting on makeup, curling her hair. He must have once felt something more for her than he did now, which if he had to classify it, fell in the vicinity of a fond affection. They had traveled some, had good sex. He'd moved into her place. They'd cooked, laughed, watched movies, shared a few secrets. And yet he experienced those times as if they'd occurred in a hazy, disjointed dream.

Her footsteps clicked down the stairs and stopped in the kitchen behind him.

"Sure you don't want to join us?" she asked again.

He gently lifted Charlotte off his chest and propped himself up on his elbow so he could see Janie in the shadows, the jutted hip and crossed arms stance of late. Charlotte leaped down and began winding herself through and around Janie's ankles. "No thanks."

He sat all the way up and twisted around to face her in the kitchen, his back sore with stiffness, his arm slung along the top of the sofa in order to show her he was making an effort, paying attention. She flicked on the light. She had her hair up loose the way he liked it best, and she wore a dress he hadn't seen before. "You look nice," he said. "Really pretty."

Without a smile, she shifted her weight, unfolded her arms so they hung by her sides, her pale palms facing him. "You might surprise yourself and have fun."

How to explain the impossibility? "Not really up to it tonight."

She kept her eyes on him. She was gracious enough not to ask: *Did you apply for any jobs today? Did you make any follow-up calls? Did you even return your aunt's call? It's ironic, you know. Watching the Do-It-Yourself Network all day long and never doing a damn thing.*

She spun away, the air barely lifting the edge of her dress, and said, "I'll be home late," closing the door with force, but not quite a slam. They didn't slam doors. They didn't shout. They'd been together for more than three years and never had more than a low-heated discussion, where nothing ever boiled over, just simmered on and on until they had reached this state of bone-dry evaporation.

Kache got up to find something to eat. He stretched, muscles tight from lying down so long, his vertebrae a series of hooks and sinkers.

Janie blamed this funk he'd been in for the last six months on the fact that he'd been let go from his job. A buyout. He'd received a generous enough severance package. They called it the golden parachute, but he was too young for that. Maybe the silver? Not even. Brass. The brass-can't-save-your-ass parachute.

It wasn't that he needed the money. He'd invested well, lived far below his means. There was just nothing he could bring himself to *do*. In the quiet of their kitchen, he spread peanut butter on wheat bread. He could do that much.

The job had provided a masquerade that kept Janie from seeing the obvious: he'd been asleep for the last two decades. A relentless fog descended upon him that god-awful day, and it remained, through his college education (with the help of a fair amount of weed) and then through his job in accounting at a small high-tech company. He'd quit the weed by then but hid in the numbers for years without anyone realizing that he wasn't quite...*there*. They shrugged it off, thinking, he supposed, that he was merely distant, quiet. They, including Janie, chalked it up to personality traits of a numbers geek.

But no one in Austin had known him before the plane crash. Way back when he wrote songs and played the guitar, when he talked too much and argued with passion and was "too touchy-feely for his own good." While at work, he'd lost himself in the black and white of the numbers; their rigid columns and graphs had held him in a tight cocoon of space. Math became his new music, but without the emotions, which was a welcome relief. He had not turned out to be a "lazy, no-good rock and roller" after all.

Unlike Kache's father, Rex would find that disappointing.

chapter

seventeen

THE SPIT TUNE WAS one of the oldest buildings on the spit. It had survived the fire in 1918 and the Good Friday earthquake of 1964. Peanut shells and sawdust covered the floor. Signed dollar bills from every corner of the world hung from the ceiling and walls, and when Kache was a high school kid, he figured there was enough money there to fund their first album. Now he knew just how naive that had been. First of all, there wasn't nearly that much money, even twenty years later. And secondly, Rex, who'd owned the place forever, was fond of saying he'd shoot anyone who even tried to take one dollar down. "I won't hurt you real bad," he'd say. "Maybe just take off a finger or two to remind you to follow the rules."

Rex himself wasn't one to follow many rules. Kache, Marion, Chris, Dan, and Mike were all well underage when they started playing at the bar. Sometimes Rex even let them drink a few beers if they promised not to tell.

But Rex wasn't around. Kache didn't recognize the bartender, a young bearded guy who told him Rex was vacationing in Phoenix. Kache sat down anyway and nursed his coffee.

"Can I get you something stronger?"

"Not yet. Mind if I change the channel?"

The bartender handed him the remote. "A friend of Rex's can do anything he wants." Kache found the DIY Network. His favorite show was about to start: the father-and-son show called *The House That Jack and Jack Jr. Built*. The hosts wore their tool belts low on their hips just like Kache's father and Denny once had, sharing a similar comradeship, and when the hosts patiently began showing Kache how to build a fire pit, he felt the smallest hint of a burning in the pit between his heart and his stomach.

The hosts acted like they believed in Kache, even the father, Jack Sr. From the screen, they spoke with reassuring confidence, as if Kachemak Winkel could, in fact, do it himself; he could do any goddamn thing, if he ever decided he wanted to. He could prove his father wrong again and again. He wanted his father to be wrong. That his father had been dead since 1985 didn't matter. Kache had never wanted him to be dead, just dead *wrong*.

It was crazy, he knew, to desperately need approval and understanding from a dead man. But he did.

"Pussy Hollywood boys think they can tell us Alaskans how to build shit ourselves? I'd like to see them build a fox trap or skin a bear. Am I right, my friend?"

A large, strong-looking man sat a few stools down. Kache hadn't even heard the guy come in. "You sound like my father," Kache said. "And my brother, for that matter."

"Is that right? There's a couple of fine men I'd like to meet." He smiled warmly, eyes teasing.

"Can't. They're dead."

"Sorry to hear that. My papa too. And my mama."

Kache nodded. "Yep. Same."

"How?" The man motioned for the bartender to get Kache a beer.

"Plane crash."

"That's harsh."

"And yours?"

"Bear."

"As in a bear attack? *That's* harsh." Kache took a swig of the beer. "Were you there?"

The man said he was but that he hadn't been hurt. "No scars. At least none you can see. You know what I mean, my friend."

Kache did know what he meant, even if he didn't quite think of him as his friend just yet—he did already feel an odd kinship with him, knowing what they shared. The man had a Russian accent but was clean-shaven and sitting at a bar drinking a beer. Clearly not an Old Believer. Kache had grown up with a lot of Russians, and he wondered if they knew any of the same people. But when Kache asked him, he replied that he'd just moved here from the north slope after another failed marriage and that he lived in an old hunter's cabin. "Only place in town I go to is here for booze and music. The rest I do myself. Not pretend, like bozos." He motioned his beer toward the TV. "Don't need anybody. Tired of thinking marriage might change me. It won't. Can't. What about you? You with beautiful woman?"

That required a complicated explanation, so Kache just shook his head and turned his attention to the television, but soon, his mind looped back on Janie.

❦

The other night after she'd left to hang out with friends, Kache had noticed a light glowing from the guest room and had gone to investigate. Janie had left her computer on. Janie never left her computer on. She worked for the electric company and always not only turned off, but also unplugged every appliance, light, and electronic gadget they owned. She'd been spending a lot of time on the computer, and

Kache sometimes wondered if she'd found someone to love on the Internet. He understood why she might. He should just turn the thing off.

But the fact that he was even curious at all gave him a rare surge of energy, so he clicked the mouse, and the screen filled with tan and cream and that teal color Janie always liked.

A banner across the top read: Happenings from Our Happy Home— Welcome to My Blog.

His mom had kept journals with the commitment of keeping a religious commandment, but why anyone wanted to display a personal diary on the Internet confounded him. Below the banner, a living room basked in natural light flowing through huge windows flanked with curtains, which resembled the ones his mother had made of burlap. Now they were in style? She would have gotten a kick out of that.

Hello, Bloggers!

This weekend, Mr. Happenings has big plans to build a used-brick patio for the luau we're having in a few weeks. (Can you say pig roast? Leis? Even poi?) I have no idea where he gets his energy. It's not like his job isn't grueling enough!

Mr. *Happenings*?

But he insists he can do-it-himself, so who am I to argue?

Anyhoo, we're off to a dinner party tonight with our dear friends.

Was this just a random blog, or was this someone she envied? Did she have a crush on Mr. Happenings? Why else would she read this? This was exactly the kind of perkiness she made fun of.

Hope y'all have happy happenings this weekend. Be sure to check in on Monday for photos of our new patio project. Knowing Mr. Happenings, it will be completely finished. (And I'll be giving him one of my Swedish massages!)

Toodle-oo,
Janie

Janie? Janie *who?* He had never heard Janie once say *toodle-oo*, or *anyhoo* for that matter, not to mention the fact that none of this had anything to do with their life.

Along the right side of the screen, a cartoon caricature with Janie's long, dark hair and brown eyes grinned at him.

Click here to read About Me:

Hi, I'm Janie. I'm an Alternative Energy Specialist.

Well, he supposed that was *one* way to say she worked in collections for the electric company. She had studied modern dance and wanted to be a dancer just as he had wanted to be a musician; they shared a haunting sense of failure. Though they each bore it quietly, it was always there, as constant as the indented couch.

I'm married to Mr. Happenings, an accomplished musician and CFO who is my Renaissance man. Seriously. What can't he do? We have two darling kids, who I call the Pumpkin and the Petunia, and honestly? Most of the happenings at our home really are happy! We work hard and play hard. Check back regularly to see our do-it-yourself projects, recipes, parenting tips, decorating, crafts, and hints on how to keep your marriage and family positively happy!

He needed to stop reading, to turn it off if he could find—

"Kache. What the—?" Janie stood in the doorway, clasping her high heels in each hand.

"I'm sorry. I didn't mean to," he told her, swiping the cursor toward the X, still trying to shut it down.

"Oh, it's some work thing. I came back to turn it... Here, let me..."

"Janie." He stood and reached out, taking a shoe so he could hold her hand, so tiny inside his mammoth one. "I'm sorry, but what is this? Some kind of alternate personality?"

Her face flushed, and the pink splotch made its appearance, spreading down her neck. He felt bad, wished he had turned off the computer before she discovered what he'd discovered. "No, it's not what you think. I'm not... I was just playing around."

"Who's Mr. Happenings? Is he supposed to be me? Or I guess the anti-me? My evil twin. Or I'd be the evil twin in this scenario, I guess."

"No, no. It's silly. I'm so embarrassed. It started out... I was... bored, you know?"

"Jesus. You had to make up an entire life? It's that bad?"

She looked toward her toes as if they might have an answer. "We could change that, Kache, if you'd *try.*" Her shoulders slumped, and a few tears hit her pearly polished toenails.

He pulled her to him in a hug, Janie so short without her heels and him so tall he had to practically fold himself in half to hold her. "I will. I'll try harder."

Her muffled voice, breathy against his arm, said, "You always say that, but nothing changes. It's such a lazy-ass cliché."

He pulled back and looked at her. "Wait. You really give Swedish massages?"

She didn't smile. She didn't even respond.

He sighed. "I *am* a lazy ass."

"You didn't get all those promotions by being a lazy ass."

"I got fired."

"Laid off. Bought out. Restructuring. It's different. You ran that place."

"Hardly. I got lucky is all, but the gig's up. No, Janie. When it comes to getting things done, I'm as competent as a clam. Hence Mr. Happenings. My dad would love the guy."

She stepped back. With her small, tight fist, she punched him once firmly, squarely in his chest. "Your father has been dead twenty years. They all have been. Anniversaries are hard, I get that. But this has been going on forever. Kache, *you* didn't die."

She grabbed her shoe from him, pulled her heels back on. Balancing on one dancer's leg then the other, she kept her eyes locked on his while he stood, hands in his pockets, the slight sensation of her punch already fading. Her bottom lip trembled.

Her words had come loud and fast. "No. You know what? Forget it. We're done. I *hate* that I wrote that creepy blog. Jesus, I need an actual *life*. Get the hell out and don't come back." She'd turned and slammed the door so loud the floor quaked. Her final shout had come from the other side: "And WAKE THE FUCK UP!"

❧

"You hear anything I say, my friend? Taking nap after one beer? You need me to drive you home?" Kache wasn't sure what he'd told the man. Had he been speaking out loud? He hoped not. But the man was smiling at him again. Something about him reminded Kache of Denny. That warm familiarity. The ability to chat with anyone. Kache was so tired after staying up all night with the squatter woman, he wouldn't mind having someone drive him home. But he needed to get over to the Old Folks' and fill in Snag, visit Lettie. He thanked the man for the beer and said he hoped to see him around.

The man called after him, "Next time I see you, your life will be better. You find beautiful woman! Not like me, you live happily ever after!"

chapter
eighteen

INSTEAD OF PACKING UP a few things to leave as she'd planned, Nadia followed her morning routine. The chickens and goats shared in her jittery nervousness, calling their questions while she fed them. Feeding and tending to them usually cleared her head, but not this morning. She stopped before she began the milking and carried the eggs up to the house.

In the empty living room, the imprint of Kache remained. She could still see him running his index finger over the bump on his nose, staring at objects around the room, lost somewhere deep in his mind. She picked up one of the photos of him on the piano, and no, just as she thought, there was no bump.

She boiled thistle and drank it to soothe herself. She ran a hot bath and retrieved one of the wooden chairs from the kitchen, locked the bathroom door, and jammed the doorknob with the chair. Her shirt came off first, then her jeans, until she stood in the steam-filled room naked and gently swatted herself with the birch broom—the same calming remedy her mother had used when Nadia was young and awoke from a nightmare. Lying in the bathtub with her ears under the water, she bathed in the echoes of her mother's soothing voice, the laughter of her sisters and brothers, her father's chanting of the old scriptures, voice rich and dark as *braga*.

❧

Her family had once belonged to the small village of Ural, about a thirty-minute drive from the road that turned off toward the Winkel homestead. She grew up with a loving if strictly religious family, a close, secluded community of equally religious friends, and a boy named Nikolaus, whom she had loved since she was eight. Everyone knew she and Niko would marry as soon as she turned thirteen.

But right before her birthday, an unforeseen rift tore the village in two. Some of the Old Believers wanted to appoint a bishop to act as a leader in the church. Not allowed, not in a church committed to no hierarchy. Instead, a *nastoyatel* had always been enough, just a man in the village who volunteered to help out with church duties. Nadia's parents were strongly against a bishop. For them and nineteen other couples, this deviated from the truest interpretation of Christianity. Many before them had died in Russia trying to protect the purity of their religion. Compromise meant contamination. So thought her parents and some of the others, though they were in the minority. They devised a plan to break off from the group and settle even deeper into the wilderness in a new village they called Altai.

Niko's family stayed, and so did Niko. Nadia didn't blame them. If only the division had taken place two months later, she and Niko would have been married, and she too could have stayed. But she still fell under her father's rule, and he insisted she go with them. He had once loved Niko as a son but now treated him with disdain.

"I want my daughter and my future grandchildren to be of the purest faith. Otherwise your mama and I, we would have stayed in

Oregon, where the world weaves in and out of one's soul. You under-stand this, Nadi?"

No, she did not.

Whether they appointed a bishop did not concern her in the least. The truth—the truth that she'd shared with no one, not even with Niko—was that she didn't know if she believed any of it. She did not even know if she believed in heaven or hell. She certainly did not believe that it mattered whether you crossed yourself with three fingers or two or crossed yourself at all. She did not believe women needed to wear long skirts or scarves or men long beards. In town, she'd seen the other women in their pants with their uncovered hair and the men with their shaven faces. Lightning did not break out from the sky and strike any of them dead. It was obvious to Nadia that the world was an interesting place, but the adults spoke of it with acid on their tongues.

She believed in the mountains and the water and the trees and the animals. She believed in Niko.

When all this was happening, Niko pulled her aside from picking blueberries with her sister. They ducked into the woods. He said, "We will find a way to be together." He kissed her urgently, and his green eyes held tears. "We will. I promise you, Nadi."

The day came when the group departed, peacefully, lovingly, saying good-bye despite their differences. Except for Nadia, the once-complacent child, who had to be physically dragged away by her father and brothers. She did not scream or cry or even speak as she scratched and kicked against them, her father breaking the silence, saying, "Nadi, Nadi. *Nado privyknut*." Their lifelong dictum: *one must get used to it*.

❧

Now she stepped out of the tub to dry herself and pulled on clean clothes with a renewed awareness that they were not her clothes. Outside the bathroom door, Leo greeted her as if she'd just returned from a long journey.

chapter

nineteen

WHEN KACHE WALKED INTO the Old Folks', the nurse Gilly introduced him to a few staff and pointed him toward Lettie's room. "She's doing great today."

Where the hallway turned left, a Native man slumped in a wheelchair in the corner. He kept moving his right arm in big up and down sweeps, grabbing and pulling at the air with his left.

Gilly said, "That's Leroy's fishing hole, and you better not go putting a laundry bin or food cart anywhere near it. He makes me wheel him over to that exact spot every morning."

Leroy. Marion's grandfather. Kache bent down and said, "Hello, Mr. Tilloko. Nice to see you. It's Kache Winkel. Used to date your granddaughter years ago."

Leroy nodded and cast his line and his eyes somewhere over Kache's head. Leroy used to be strong, stoic, and intimidating as hell. But that was in 1985, when Leroy was the mayor and Kache was devising plans on how he might get into Leroy's granddaughter's pants.

In her room, Lettie sat propped up in bed, reading, open curtains revealing a killer view of the mountains of rock and snow beyond the choppy bay, which sparkled as the sun burned pale yellow through a lone cluster of pewter clouds. A skyline of family photographs topped the dresser. "Hi, Grandma Lettie," he said. "It's Kache."

She closed the book. "You're my grandson, Kache. There's no need for introduction. No matter how long it took you to get yourself home. Come here, honey. Give me a hug."

"Am I glad to see *you*." He held her close to him, her head almost covered by the expanse of his hand. Lettie must have come back and kicked out the impostor who had been hanging out in her wheelchair.

"There, there now," Lettie said into his chest, before she leaned back to look at him. "You look good. A little tired around the eyes, but not bad for an old guy."

"Thanks. I think. Where's Aunt Snag?"

"Hovering somewhere close, no doubt."

At that moment, Snag appeared in the doorway, pushing a cart with a loaded tray. "Mom. I am *not* hovering. Some might call it *helping*. Why, hello, Kache," she said rather formally. Her eyes darted between Lettie and Kache.

"I just got here," Kache said to put her mind at ease.

Snag got busy preparing Lettie's tea and toast, and Kache accepted the piece she offered. "So, Mom," Snag said. "I have something I need to talk to you about."

Lettie folded her hands and rested them on her stomach. "Shoot."

Snag kept her back toward them, occupying herself with the items on the tray. "It's about the homestead."

"Aunt Snag, we don't have to go into the details right now." Kache went over to where she stood and gently elbowed her in the side, shook his head, and took the tea to Lettie.

"Subtle, Kache. You two think you're so smart," Lettie said. "Eleanor, finish what you started. Sit down and tell me what's on your mind."

Snag glanced at Kache and obediently sat in the chair next to Lettie's bed, reaching for her hand.

"Good Lord," Lettie said. "Who died now?"

"No one died, Mom. It's just about the homestead."

"Wait, Aunt Snag. Things aren't as bad as you think. Not nearly."

"Kachemak. Let Eleanor finish. Something tells me she's had this on her chest for a while now."

"Mom?" Snag took a deep breath. "I've been lying to you for a long time."

"Aunt Snag." Kache shook his head. "Don't. It's okay."

"No, it's not okay, Kache. I did something horribly wrong, and I need to tell my mother, if you'd hold your tongue and give me a chance."

"The house is fine," he told her. "Everything looks great."

"Of course it's fine," Lettie said. "Your grandfather and I built that place with our own hands. We built it to last, to hand down through the generations. You two do remember that, don't you?"

They both nodded emphatically.

"But, Mom, I—what do you mean, it's fine, Kache?"

"I mean, it's in perfect condition."

"Impossible."

"Eleanor. Kachemak. You don't think I'd let nature have its way with that place after everything A. R. and I did to build it and Bets and Glenn did to expand and maintain it. Just because the two of you let your own demons keep you away for twenty godforsaken years, you don't really think I'd just sit here and let my legacy rot into the ground, do you?"

Snag stared at Lettie for what seemed like an eternity. "You *knew*?"

"Of course I knew. Well, at first I only suspected. Then I went out there myself and saw that my hunch was right. Renters, schmenters. We have a lot to catch up on, Eleanor. But what I need to know, Kache, is how is my sweet Nadia?"

Snag's mouth dropped open as she pressed her hand to her forehead. "Your sweet Nadia? Who the hell is Nadia?"

Kache said, "The Old Believer who's been squatting there."

Lettie pointed her chin at him. "You mean, dear boy, the conscientious caretaker who saved our asses."

"Well, yeah. I guess that is what I meant."

"Someone's *living* there?"

"Ah…that would be yes," Kache said. "Definitely yes."

chapter

twenty

AND SO IT WENT, with Kache filling in Snag and Lettie, Lettie filling in Kache and Snag, and Snag wiping her eyes with her tissues and blowing her nose in relief and regret. Apparently, Lettie had been sneaking out to the place since that first winter, running water in the pipes when the temperature took a dive, even climbing the ladder to knock snow off the roof. When Snag pictured her elderly mother finagling the broom up each rung, she started tearing up again. But the truth was that until a few years ago, Lettie was stronger than any of them, at least in spirit, which evidently compensated for a lot. As Lettie explained, she'd only had to tend to the maintenance the first ten years or so, because then this Nadia person moved in and stayed, taking care of things, hiding out from her Old Believer clan, a vague explanation that Lettie didn't delve into except to say that Nadia had never stepped foot off the property in the time that Lettie had known her.

"Are you sure, Mom? That sounds awfully strange."

"She's not strange. She's smart and responsible, and I trust her to no end." Lettie crossed her thin arms.

A wave of jealousy crashed into Snag's solar plexus. Had the Old

Believer become a surrogate daughter to Lettie? Someone who obviously did what Snag did not—take care of the property Lettie had so loved? Even Kache seemed more concerned for this woman than he did about the fact that she'd been living there scot-free for ten years. Not that Snag was complaining. She wasn't stupid. This stranger, this Old Believer woman, had saved the house from extreme disrepair. And there was the fact that Snag herself had once met an Old Believer on their beach. She was pretty sure it was an Old Believer. But that had been fifty-some years ago.

"Well, I guess I should head out there and meet this woman," Snag offered.

But Kache said, "She's going to need some time. Gram, she never left the property?"

"Nope. Not as far as I know. I took her supplies before I got sick. Last trip out there, I must have brought enough toilet paper and toothpaste and whatnot to last a decade. Now don't go plowing over her, Snag. She's not used to people."

"And neither of you find this odd?"

Neither of them said whether they did or didn't.

"Mom? Why didn't you tell me?"

"Because, Eleanor. She asked me not to, and I respected her request. It seemed important to her that I did. Besides, she's quite self-sufficient."

Snag pressed Lettie for more details, but she started getting loopy, rattling on about who knows what. One minute, she could have run the country. The next minute, she thought Eisenhower was still running it.

"Kache, can you make sure she takes those pills in the little paper cup? I'll be right back."

Snag went to get more hot water for tea and ran into Gilly. "Honey, what's wrong? Is your mom okay?" Gilly, with her limitless generosity and compassion, might have been the kindest person in Caboose.

Snag shook her head. Then she realized the question and switched to big, fast nods. "Mom's fine. A little loopy, like she gets when she's tired." But her voice cracked and gave her away even more. She felt like her head might spin clear off and veer down the hallway. "I'm a mess, but Mom's fine."

"Do you want to talk about it?" Gilly's voice alone had a calming effect. Snag suspected that when Gilly talked to her patients, their blood pressure immediately improved.

"Oh, you're so sweet, Gilly. But I know how busy they keep you. It's a story twice as long as the Caboose Spit, and I'm afraid if you knew it, you wouldn't want to be my friend any longer. And I wouldn't be able to stand that."

"Nonsense. Nothing is that bad." She held on to both sides of the stethoscope that hung around her neck. "Tell you what. Thursday's my day off. How about we go get a coffee or a drink or whatever and you can tell me about it then. Or we'll walk the spit—twice—while you tell your long story, and then we'll go for the drink. Either way."

The last thing Snag wanted to do was tell Gilly Sawyer what a neglectful aunt and daughter she was, but she nodded anyway.

chapter

twenty-one

AS SOON AS SNAG left, Lettie opened her eyes and grabbed Kache's hand. "Look," she whispered. "I'm not taking that pink pill. Makes me forget my own name. But I can't get any of them to listen to me. If my heart gives out, it gives out. I'm ninety-eight years old. I'd rather be able to feed myself a few more times than live ten more years drooling and thinking I'm Katharine Hepburn. As beautiful as she was."

"But, Gram, have you talked to the doctors?"

"I've tried. Everyone's convinced I need that damn pill. Sometimes I can be sneaky, but other times I have to swallow it because they won't leave and the stupid thing starts to dissolve on my tongue. But those pills do me in. Please, Kache. Help me out with this."

Kache didn't want to do something dangerous, but the difference in her since last night was startling. Of course she wouldn't want to take that pill. She'd obviously skipped some before and hadn't dropped dead. "Okay. But let me talk to Gilly and your doctors too, okay?"

Lettie gripped him tighter. "They think their job is to keep me alive until I break some Guinness world record. I don't want to live beyond what I'm supposed to. All these drugs! Look. Eight pills. Eight! It's ridiculous. If it's a choice between my head and my heart, or my kidneys, or my lungs—they seem to take turns these days—I'll pick my head, every time." She handed him the pink one and swallowed the rest. "See? I'm almost behaving. Now, about Nadia. Is she okay?"

"Yes, she seems to be. But she won't talk to me."

"She might, in her own time. I never did get her whole story, but she's a dear and hardworking too. I tried to talk her into coming into town and living with me, but she wouldn't have it. Never set a foot off that property. Kache, she's no 'fraidy cat. Someone must have hurt her and hurt her bad. Promise me you'll let her stay."

"Gram, don't you think we've done our part? And don't you think she'd be better off in town than alone?"

"No. Believe me, I wish I still lived out there myself."

"But you have family and friends. She needs people."

"Apparently, she doesn't. How the hell do you know what she needs, Kachemak Winkel?"

"I thought we'd rent it to someone who could use the land. Could help with the taxes."

"Pish. You and Snag hardly need help in the money department. No. Promise me, Kache. Do not kick her out. I've got an automatic payment set up with the Caboose electric. Used to bring her supplies—" Suddenly, she let go of his hand, closed her eyes, and started snoring.

Just then, Snag came in and pulled a quilt up to Lettie's chin. "Poor thing. She needed her morning nap."

Kache slipped the pink pill into his pocket.

While Kache drove Snag home, he asked if he could borrow her truck for a few more days, and she said that would be fine. Then she asked, "Do you think that woman out there is okay? Can we trust her?"

He shrugged. "She's been living there forever, presumably on her own. The place looks exactly like we left it. Exactly. It looks like Mom and Dad and Denny just walked out."

Snag's eyes got wide. "Really?"

"Really."

"I can't imagine it."

"It's—I don't know—weird…and kind of comforting…haunting… really sad."

She nodded, kept nodding. "Is that your way of saying you're leaving soon?"

He pulled into her driveway and put the gear in park. "No. Not for a couple of weeks. I was going to ask you to help me get it ready to rent, but Gram says no. She's adamant. Wants Nadia to stay."

"After everything, I guess we shouldn't fight her on this, at least not right now."

Kache saw her point, but he still didn't know if it was the best plan.

"I just hope Lettie's right about her, Kache. Hey, you look beat."

He admitted that he hadn't slept. And when Snag suggested he come in and take a nap, he agreed—and didn't wake up until late the next morning.

❦

That afternoon, Kache stopped at Safeway to pick up a battery for the flashlight and, hit with an unexpected burst of generosity, began pulling items from the shelves as if a natural disaster was predicted to hit in the next twenty-four hours. He tried to think of what might appeal to someone living alone and mostly cut off from society for the last ten years. Twenty-eight years, if he counted the time before she came to the house, when she must have lived with the Old Believers. But he saw Old Believer women in the store, shopping in pairs, their long, bright scarves and dresses tied with belts, children sitting in the carts. In some ways, the Old Believers seemed practically worldly compared to Nadia, though she'd made no attempt to cover her head and certainly seemed comfortable wearing his old jeans. He wanted to ask if they knew her, but of course he didn't.

Instead, he bought peanut butter, strawberry sorbet, and ice cream. He bought bags of chips and a couple of pounds of deli meat and Swiss cheese and Brie and bacon. He bought oranges, apples, bananas, grapes, almonds, raisins, and batteries and a pile of magazines and a newspaper. He bought boxes of cereal and salty snacks and girly stuff like lavender bubble bath and lotions and toilet paper and toothpaste—just in case Lettie's supply was getting low. He even thought about buying Tampax—God knew he'd had to run to the store for Janie—but he figured that crossed a line. He bought toothbrushes and four different high-end chocolate bars. Wait, he needed something for dinner. He bought decent wine and beer. She probably didn't drink, but he did, and he definitely wanted a drink. He bought salad fixings and crusty bread and a couple of steaks, wrapped with cellophane in their Styrofoam trays. Although she might not want any meat that came with a price sticker.

She might very well have the same philosophy as his dad.

❧

"Autumn. Tin-colored sky and bay. Already more than a foot of snow on the ground. Kache was thirteen, maybe fourteen. They'd come across a bull moose, who'd somehow snapped his leg, and his father had decided it was the perfect time for Kache to shoot his first moose. "This isn't murder, Son. It's mercy."

Kache held the gun up to his shoulder and closed one eye. He trained the bead on the head of the moose, who stopped struggling and set his eyes on Kache. Or more like *in* Kache, because that moose's eyes seemed to penetrate Kache's soul. He tried. He even closed his own eyes. But he could not bring himself to pull the trigger. The woods around them quieted and stilled, waiting.

Finally, his father swore, grabbed the gun from where Kache had lowered it, and went ahead and shot the bull right between those big pleading eyes. Kache willed back the tears, wished again he was more like Denny.

"We call it game, but this is *not* a game, Son," his dad hollered above the churning tractor as they dragged the shot moose toward home. "It's not a little ditty you can fiddle around with on that guitar of yours. You can't take it or leave it. It's life or death."

"That's because *you* choose to live this way. News flash: there's a Safeway an hour away. That sells steak."

His dad stopped the tractor, pulled Kache off the side of it, pushed him back to the moose, long-lashed eyes staring blank.

"Look at him. Know where your food came from." His father's dark eyes flashed with such intensity, it was as if they'd taken on the life force of the moose along with his own. "You can't appreciate the life of something that comes without a face, wrapped in plastic and Styrofoam. Swollen up with all kinds of chemicals. Use your brain, Kache."

Kache thought that was an ironic phrase to use just then, after his father had shot through the head of the moose that could no longer use *his* brain. "There's more than one way to live your life, Dad," he said as they climbed back on the tractor.

His dad pushed the hair back from his forehead with his gloved hand. "All I'm asking is that you make knowledgeable decisions."

"All you're asking is for me to do everything *your* way. The Holy Ordained Glenn Winkel Way."

The tractor lurched and then jerked toward home, where he helped his father rig up the pulleys and the moose spreader bar, so the six-hundred-pound moose hung upside down by his hind legs along with all the silence hanging between them. They began skinning the legs first, the fur giving way to the white fat below. They hoisted the carcass up higher so they could continue skinning down the flanks. They did this all without speaking. Kache knelt in the pink-stained snow and tried to mimic the movements of his father, concentrating so he didn't make a mistake that might set him off. When the moose was skinned, Kache closed his eyes while his father cut the head off right at the last joint at the base of the skull. Taking the saw up to just below the V of the animal's spread legs, his dad worked his way down, sawing the front of it into two perfect halves that parted like doors until he stood inside the animal. From there, he finally spoke, his voice slightly muffled but the words clear.

"This guy has a big heart. Never been one for religion, but this is the closest thing to stepping inside a confessional. This is where you understand sacrifice. Right here, Son, is where I check my own heart for unworthiness. Where I ask for forgiveness, not from God, mind you, but from God's creature." When Kache hadn't answered him, his father had resumed sawing.

❧

Well, Nadia could trap herself a squirrel or eat rabbit from the freezer if she didn't like store-bought meat. In the truck, he hummed a song he used to sing with Marion and the band—the words weren't quite coming to him—when halfway out to the homestead, he remembered the road, or lack thereof. He had been so caught up in buying out Safeway that he'd forgotten. He had a truckload of groceries and a two-mile walk ahead of him. Damn. Did the old ATV still run? Worth a try. He turned back around, filled the truck at the gas station, and filled the gas can Snag kept in the truck bed. He needed to hurry before all the ice cream melted—although that wasn't exactly an imminent threat like it would have been in Austin.

chapter

twenty-two

NADIA DRAGGED THE FADED orange canoe from the ledge of land above the beach while Leo waited below with the three boxes of provisions and clothing. It occurred to her that the clothes belonged to Kache and taking them could be considered stealing, but she was not about to paddle away with nothing but her old cotton *sarafan*.

Leo whined, sitting still in the bow and staring at her as she pushed off. There was the uncertainty of a destination. The wind would likely be picking up as the day went on, and the bay would get choppy—lumpy is what Lettie called it. Nadia knew lumpy could quickly change to deadly. She felt superstitious about canoeing on the bay. She had falsely accused the water of killing her, and she always wondered if it might act out in revenge. When she lifted the paddle, it left a trail of drops on the gray-green surface that sounded to Nadia like a line of words: *Then why not…make it so?*

To go along the shore to the northeast meant going toward her old villages; to go southwest meant to go toward Caboose. Neither was acceptable. She could set out straight across the bay, but that was twenty-four miles, and she lacked the nerve. She sat, bobbing with the waves, the paddle now resting on her lap and the edges of the canoe while she stared back at Leo, who was quite familiar with this scenario.

All morning, she'd thought of her father's words: *Nado privyknut.*
One must get used to it. How many times had she heard him say that
while growing up, and how many times had she resisted it? But the
truth was that most of her adult life had been about getting used to
one thing and one thing only: living without human contact. For the
majority of people, each day brought the noise and conversations, the
push, pull, spin of others. The coughing, the chewing, the passing
of gas. The singing, shouting, laughing, whispering. Every day, their
decisions and desires and willfulness, their opinions, sufferings, needs,
celebrations, illnesses, all butted up against one another, some wrestling
for the win, some finding joy in the yielding, contentment in the taking
or the giving. It was the human dance, and Nadia only knew how to
dance alone. To ask of no one, to answer to no one, to touch no one.

Nado privyknut.

And she had. She had gotten used to it. She had adapted to her
solitary environment, but at what cost? Acceptance, she learned,
killed the dream of something more. But to not accept? Where does
that lead? To leaving.

Always to leaving?

She picked up the paddle and turned the canoe toward the shore,
guiding it past a mass of tangled bull kelp.

"I am Nadia. I live here alone ten years." Leo tilted his head. "Please
don't ask of me so many questions. It is difficult for me to talk of this.
Thank you. Good to meet you. I am sorry your mama and papa and
brother died. This must make you very sad."

She would wait.

She would wait to see if Kachemak Winkel came back, to see what
he had to say, to see if she would be asked to leave, or what she might
be asked to accept.

And then she would decide what she could or could not get
used to.

chapter

twenty-three

KACHE CALLED OUT, BUT neither the woman nor the dog made a sound. Would he have to talk her out from under the bed every time he walked in the door? He put the ice cream and pizza in the freezer, a gallon of milk and other perishables in the fridge, and then went out to the storage barn to see if they still had the ATV so he wouldn't have to walk the other groceries in.

There she was. Nadia, out in the meadow, with two sandhill cranes. They were long-legged, large, prehistoric-looking birds with red face masks. Kache had always thought of them as mysterious. He stayed perfectly still as he watched, afraid to even breathe too loudly. The birds called out, squawking and squeaking, flapping their wings, twirling, hopping, and Nadia, unbelievably, did the same. She jutted her long neck, twisted, jumped, even squawked. The birds weren't just dancing with one another; they were dancing with her.

Who was this woman?

They went on dancing as if to music—that Stravinsky piece his mother used to play on the piano—dipping and flapping and weaving in and around one another. It was far too intimate and strange and beautiful to watch, but Kache could not turn away.

Lettie thought someone had hurt Nadia. Who had hurt her? Who *could*? And even though Kache didn't move, a shift occurred within him. Of course she could stay. And of course he would stay longer than two weeks: as long as it took to help her in whatever way she needed help.

Eventually, the cranes flew off, and Nadia watched them, waving. Kache ducked out of the old storage barn and took careful, quiet steps around the bend. He waited another minute before he started whistling loudly, kicking rocks, trying to look like he'd just arrived. But she was no longer in the yard.

He found the ATV where it always had been, parked between the tractor and Denny's Land Cruiser in the newer storage barn. The place certainly wasn't lacking in vehicles.

Once he filled the small tank with gas, it started up after several tries. He tied an old canvas bag to the handlebar. As he backed up out of the barn, the dog ran up to him. Nadia walked toward them, carrying a pail. Afraid to cut the motor in case it refused to start again, he yelled over the engine, "Groceries are in the fridge, and I'm going back to the truck to get more. The truck wouldn't make it up the road. What's in the pail? Clams?"

She shook her head and held out the pail for him to see.

"Milk?"

She nodded, eyes down.

"You have a cow?"

"Goats." She pointed toward the big barn in the distance, and when he squinted, he saw what looked like a few goats beyond it. He hadn't seen or heard them the night before. No mystery where they came from—Lettie loved goats.

"Oh. I bought cow's milk. But you probably won't like it."

She had looked so perfectly at ease dancing with the birds, but Kache wondered if she knew how to smile at a human. Or make eye contact. He gave a quick nod, revved the ATV once, and took off toward the road.

As quiet as Nadia was, he still felt excited about showing her the stash of stuff he'd bought. He wondered what might elicit a real smile from her. The ice cream? The chocolate? Or maybe she didn't want any of it. Maybe she preferred goat's milk and game and wild berries, like his dad.

It turned out to be the magazines and the newspaper that she snatched up. She didn't smile exactly, but she was clearly enthralled.

Her earlier reference to Tolstoy and Chekhov meant she at least read Russian. He almost asked her if she knew how to read English, but she said, "George Bush was elected to our president again? Bill Clinton beat him, yes? So did he run again?"

He stared at her. She waited until he finally said, "This is the younger George Bush. His son. Who is now serving his second term. You've missed out on a few things. Did Lettie ever bring you a newspaper?"

That made her smile finally and even look him in the eyes, her own eyes filled with question. "Lettie is still alive then?"

He nodded.

"I have been worried. This frightened me to ask this. In several years, she has not been here. And no, she never brought any of this news of outside world. She thought it might make things harder for me, I believe. And I never ask." She brought her hand to her throat and stood, leaving the paper and magazines on the table.

"Where did you learn to speak and read English?"

"In school, they teach us. One of few concessions to outside world."

"Are you hungry?"

"I have seen never so many types of food in one place. For only two people?"

"I didn't know if there were more to feed." He paused, but she didn't offer any information. "I don't know how you got here and where your family is. Lettie said you've never left our property? Is that true? In ten years?"

"It is difficult, this thing, to talk about."

"Okay. But I'm not sure what to do. Lettie trusts you and wants you to be here, so that's a start." She tilted her head, waited. "We can figure it out later. Right now, I'm starving. I bought a chicken and some steaks. Interested in either of those?"

"After I put milk away, I make soup. You have some of this, if you like."

"Let me make you something. Without you having to wrangle it up from the earth. How about a steak and some salad? Baked potatoes?"

She didn't say yes, but she didn't say no. Kache started preparing the meal.

chapter

twenty-four

"I HAVE NEVER SEEN men cook meals. In my village, this never happens."

Kache liked that Nadia was telling him something about herself, and he refrained from pressing her for more. "Well, 'cook meals' might be optimistic, but I can get food on the table."

"It is too much, what you buy."

He saw the piles of food and supplies through her eyes. He'd felt like a springtime Santa Claus at the store, but now he just felt like a superconsumer on steroids.

"But Lettie brought you supplies."

"Not all these many kinds of foods, because I have garden and hunt and fish. Does this mean you will go away and not return, like Lettie?"

He didn't answer. While he made dinner, she tried to make room in the fridge and the pantry.

"Who will eat all of this?" she asked as he came in carrying plates of steak from the grill.

"We will. No problem."

She shook her head vigorously, muttering in Russian.

After he set the steaks on the table, along with the potatoes, salad, and bread, he invited her to sit. "Wine?" he asked and was surprised that she nodded. They stared at the food without looking at each other. "So," Kache said. "You probably have a prayer or something. I don't want you to break any of your rules."

"I have my gratitude." She picked up her fork and her knife and began cutting her steak. "I am breaking Old Believer rules every day. I am eating off same dishes as you. This is not allowed. You are not Old Believer. Separate dishes. And no prayer with you. This is not allowed. Wine? We are allowed only to drink *braga*, wine made at home with berries. Today? Wednesday? Fasting. No dairy or meat allowed. Please, I would like for you to pass me sour cream. And this bacon." She smiled again. She had nice teeth. How did she have such good teeth without going to the dentist?

He laughed and passed her the sour cream, the bacon, the chives, the salad. "I get the feeling this is not your first introduction to worldly ways."

"When I came here, I made these decisions. I read. Watched the movies on VCR like Lettie showed me. Made my own faith." She had been holding the piece of steak on her fork as she talked. "Now I eat, yes?" She took the awaiting bite and then ate the meal with gusto, without speaking, taking second helpings and a smidgen of a third. It was good to see her eat with that kind of abandon. Janie had been a picky eater and always left food on her plate.

Nadia obviously hadn't been starving to death. She had chickens and goats; she planted a garden in the summer—a big one by the looks of all the canned goods lining the pantry. And judging by the contents of the freezer, she knew her way around a fishing pole and a rifle.

Still, she seemed to enjoy the rib eye and the salad, and she devoured the fully loaded baked potato. Kache leaned back in his chair and watched her fork moving from plate to mouth to plate to mouth, pleased at the transforming effect the meal seemed to bring to their conversation. At one point, she let out a huge belch without even a look of apology and continued right on eating, which he found much more refreshing than revolting. When she finished, she sipped the wine and said, "Thank you for this food. It is very good," which sounded to him like a prayer of sorts, especially because of the way she pronounced *good* to rhyme with *food*. She looked directly at him for an instant and smiled. The third smile she'd bestowed upon him.

He insisted on doing the dishes, and she headed down to the beach to dig up razor clams.

Kache filled the sink and began washing the same white dishes with blue flowers he had helped his mom wash countless times. Behind the faucet rested the pig-shaped cutting board he'd once made for Mother's Day. He'd painted it dark green; the pig had an orange snout, a big blue eye with coordinating blue eyelashes, and his third-grade attempt at a black-capped chickadee painted on its back, inspired by the one Kache had observed picking flies off their cow.

Above the cutting board, on a shelf, sat the Mason jar of shells and sea glass his mom had collected, a Japanese fisherman's blown glass ball, a piece of driftwood in the shape of a *W*, which Denny had found. Each one of these simple objects—everyday knickknacks he'd grown up with—now seemed to be made of gold.

A trilogy of small silver vases held dried wildflowers—forget-me-nots and beach peas, Nadia's own unassuming relics left from last summer, he guessed. Behind all the mementos, the clean, clear windowpanes looked out on the porch and beyond, to the yellow and brown clearing they'd called the meadow, occasional patches of dirty snow still hanging on. A pregnant cow moose stood out there, peeling strips of bark off a birch tree. The land tilted down toward the woods, where Kache watched Nadia head for the trail that led to the canyon and then the beach. She was wearing rubber boots, carrying a pail and a large rifle as comfortably as a woman in the city might carry a purse and umbrella. Leo pranced beside her. Ahead of them lay the ever-changing view, now a dark sage bay below the peach mountains, still soaking in the last lengthening hours of violet-washed sky. Kache had wanted to tag along—he hadn't even been down to the beach yet—but he also wanted to give her space. It must be weird for her to have him around, to have anyone around. Almost as weird as it was for him to be here, in this same kitchen, this same house. Everything the same, except, of course, nothing was the same.

But here he was, not alone exactly. He suspected Nadia knew an aloneness that even he couldn't begin to fathom. There were things he wanted to ask her, but he was learning to wait. He wouldn't bombard her. He didn't want to keep driving her to hide in his room. He rinsed the silverware and came back to her smile.

His mother had been a big smiler; it was part of her bright and undeniable beauty. She smiled easily, always. A flash of her perfect white crescent made it hard not to smile back. Maybe because of that, Kache had always been drawn to women who showed their teeth. First, there'd been Denny's poster he never took down—in fact, it still hung in his room—of Farrah Fawcett in that red bathing suit (admittedly, it was more than her big white teeth that had fueled Kache's adolescent fantasies). Marion was a smiler, Janie too, and most of the women in between.

But there was another type of smile that Kache was learning to appreciate: the shy, rare smile that presented itself as a gift. It wasn't given freely; it had to be earned. Nadia's face had been fearful, watchful. But now and then, her smile came through like determined sunlight working its way down through spruce and aspen branches, and he wanted to close his eyes and tilt back, expose his face to the unexpected warmth of it.

He shook his head, trying to shake loose this stupid fantasy edging on romance. She had lived alone for ten years. Ten *years*. She was strange…and probably married and who knew what else. Besides, she traipsed around in his mother's old clothes. Talk about Freudian.

He had just broken up with Janie, hadn't been laid in an entire month even prior to the breakup, and was letting a slight wisp of a smile stir up some ridiculous, flowery observations. Jesus. He really did need to park himself in front of the television to stop all these emerging *emotions*. It was like he was his teenaged self all over again, *feeling* every single thing that flickered across his mind.

He set the last pan in the drainer and considered whether to dry the dishes or let them drip, just as a gunshot cracked the air and rattled the glasses. And then another. Was she *hunting*? He looked out, but the cow moose was gone. No. Nadia wouldn't kill a pregnant moose. Would she? She wouldn't kill a person? Or herself? Would she?

Heart going like crazy, he pulled on his boots. He still hadn't come across a gun, had kept forgetting to even look for one. He ran out to the barn and stood, scanning the walls, seconds ticking by.

chapter

twenty-five

NADIA MADE HER WAY down to the beach, pail and clam shovel clanging, Leo following her, past the empty orange canoe that just yesterday she'd loaded with supplies. So many changing emotions in two days. And now this type of kindness from a man? No wonder she had not felt this tired in a very long time. And yet, Kache's mention of clams had reminded her the tide would be low and she wanted to fill her pail, to give something back. The dinner had been generous and satisfying. Though the meat tasted strange at first, she kept cutting off another piece and then another. It was odd to have lettuce and fresh tomatoes this time of year, and they too tasted different from those she grew every summer. Kache had even fried strips of bacon to crumble on the baked potatoes. She'd had bacon a few times when Lettie brought it, and she'd let it sit on her tongue, taking in its smoky salt.

He had insisted on washing the dishes—strange to see a man cook meals and wash dishes—so she took the opportunity to slip away, telling him she would be back in a few hours. How awkward she felt around him, and utterly exhausted. Yes, she had been so lonely at times, yearning for someone to talk to. But solitude gave her the undisturbed train of her thoughts winding toward their destinations. Her long winter nights of reading their books and listening to their records or watching their movies. Soon after she'd arrived, she'd begun thinking of all these as her own, set here only to satiate her thirst for knowledge and companionship. As soon as Kache stepped in, her perspective changed. This was his family's legacy she had been taking in, as if it were her family.

She set the shotgun on a dry piece of driftwood and began searching the sand for a small, telling indent. Then she pushed the cylinder-shaped shovel down as far and as quickly as possible, pulling it up and dumping out sand, which Leo nosed through, and there it was, a clam. She kept working like this, digging quickly and deeply, the way she'd been taught by her parents when she was a small girl, when they had worked the beach together as a family.

❧

Her family had followed the others, hiking along the recently cleared path toward the land where they would establish their new village. Nadia held on to the stone Niko had slipped into the pocket of her *sarafan*. She felt its smooth, cold surface warm up in her grasp, and then, when no one was watching, she pulled it out to look at it. It was in the shape of a heart, with a white unbroken circle around its center.

She decided then. She would leave. She would sneak back to him and marry him before her mother or father could protest. Maybe the new bishop would perform the marriage ceremony.

About a month after they'd settled at the site of the new village, nothing but a few crudely built temporary cabins and a dozen tents, she packed her clothes and hid her bag under her cot and waited for her mother and father, her brothers and sisters, to make another arduous trip into town for supplies. The timing had to coincide with when the tide reached its lowest so she would have adequate time to walk along the beach far enough behind them. She waited three more weeks. She missed Niko so much and wondered if the tears in his eyes when he'd said good-bye to her returned when he thought of her now.

She feigned a stomachache, which her mother treated with lemon juice and salt. Nadia stayed in bed until they left and then waited a bit longer because her mother always forgot one thing or another. When enough time had passed, Nadia set out to walk the seven miles back to Ural, back to Niko. The summer days spread themselves out like long, soft rugs of light, plenty of light to make the trip in one day. She'd packed only a few of her favorite dresses, hoping that her parents would forgive her. Surely, they would participate in the *devichnik* with all her female friends and come the week before the wedding, the *svadba*, to prepare the handiwork and linens, the woven belts and dresses. They would kiss and hug her and invite her and Niko back for visits, soon welcoming their new grandchildren into the family. How hopeful she was on that long hike! She clanged the bell she brought to ward off the bears, and the clanging might have been a thousand church bells declaring their newlywed love.

Even though she'd worn good hiking boots, her feet ached by the time she got to the trailhead that led up to the old village. She wished she could bathe before seeing him. But with the heart-shaped stone damp in her palm, she pressed on, imagining his expression when he opened his front door. His eyes, such a soft river green, framed in blond lashes; the dimples everyone teased him about because his beard was growing in and they wouldn't be as visible. How would he continue to be such a charmer without those dimples? the men asked. He was seventeen, almost eighteen. In the last year, he'd become more and more of a man. But a good-hearted man, and smart.

And more. Once, when he and Nadia had lagged behind on a

school outing, they had managed a few moments alone on the trail. Alone! And Niko had broken the rules. He'd turned to her and held her face in his hands, and with the confidence of a grown man, he had kissed her and kissed her until she felt her legs giving way under her long skirt. "That," he had whispered to her, "is just the beginning of what we have to look forward to." He took her hand and pulled her along the trail; if he hadn't, she suspected she'd still be standing there, trying to will her legs to move in a forward motion to keep from dissolving into the earth.

Now the anticipation of seeing him ached more than her feet, but it was a giddy ache. Almost to the village. Almost skipping. Dusk hadn't set in yet, but the sun hung low, and she guessed it was around eleven. Most of the village would still be up. It was not a day of fasting and prayer. They had to get as much work done as the summer daylight would allow.

But they were not working. The sounds of laughter and music drifted across the village—a celebration. She smiled. She would see all her friends in one place; they would welcome her, and there would be tears of joy. Look how far she'd come to return to them. *Sit, Nadia. Eat! Drink!* And they would bring her plates of *pelmeni* and *kulebiaka* and a cool pitcher of water. Pride would take over Niko's face. He would hold her hands in his.

She blotted her forehead and chin with her scarf, held her shoulders back, and smiled wide. Niko always said she had the prettiest smile in the village.

But when she had opened the door to the community center, no one noticed her. All eyes had stayed on Niko and Katarina, perched at a long table, fingers entwined, dressed in the traditional wedding clothes. Katarina, smiling her own stunning smile, already wearing the *shashmura* on her head, hair held in the two braids of a married woman instead of the single braid Nadia still wore.

❧

So many years ago, and yet her chest was squeezing as if it had just happened, as if she were thirteen years old and Niko and Katarina sat before her, holding hands, so happy. So very happy. Nadia saw their smiling faces as she dug for the razor clams, working quickly to catch them before they burrowed deeper, the wind whipping off the hood of her jacket and then working at her hair. So she had left the original village, Ural, and then she had tried to leave Altai. Those were her first two departures. Neither of her leavings led to happiness. It might even be said that her last leaving led to her death.

Leo leaped up from where he'd been crouching at the hole, stood at attention, and barked. A huge snapping of branches through the bushes. Was it a moose? A crashing, a muffled grunt. It was hard to hear over Leo's incessant barking and the wind. It sounded like a bear. Yes, a bear. She grabbed the shotgun, pointed it to the sky, and pulled the trigger. The butt kicked back, biting into her shoulder as the shot rang out. She pressed her shoulder tighter against it and pulled the trigger again. She still couldn't see the bear, but the loud lumbering faded, retreating toward the canyon.

No more sounds, except for the wind and the waves and the gathering gulls.

❧

As she headed up the trail back to the Winkel homestead, her stomach clenched. The ground seemed to ripple ahead, and a stifling warmth wrapped around her. Doubling over, she vomited onto a salmonberry bush. She was unaccustomed to food from the grocery store. This had happened before, with Lettie, after the first few visits. Nadia gagged again, and up came more of the dinner

Kache had so generously prepared. She retched and retched until there was nothing left, her throat and nose burning, eyes running. Leo paced and whined. She grabbed some snow from a clinging patch, scraped away the top dirt-crusted layer, and ate some before rubbing her face and hands with it to clean herself and put color back in her cheeks. She didn't want to reveal any sign of weakness or vulnerability to Kache. But she also didn't want to hurt his feelings after he had made her such a bountiful meal.

"Nadia?" His voice made her jump. "Are you okay?"

She turned to see him standing there, breathing hard, holding one of the Winkel rifles awkwardly away from his body. Leo hadn't warned her; instead, wagging his tail, he sniffed Kache's leg, as if to say, *He is our friend. This is the man who made us steak.*

"Yes, I am fine." She stood, trying to block the vomit-covered bushes.

"I heard gunshots."

"I thought I heard bear."

"You shot a bear?"

"No, I shoot into air only. To scare away this bear I did not actually set my eyes on."

"You scared the hell out of me."

"Your family, they never shoot guns?"

"Yes. Of course they did. I just… Okay. Right. But what about now? You're sick."

She shook her head.

"I saw you puking. Hey. You're not… Are you? Are you *pregnant*?"

Her mouth dropped open.

"None of my business. I know. Of course. Forgive me."

"If I am pregnant, it is the second coming of Messiah. Or how do they say? A freezing day in hell."

"Oh. Okay. Got it. Are you sick? Should I take you to the doctor?"

"No. I do not need doctor. Only once in many years, Lettie brings me medicine. Mostly, I make it myself. Devil's club is good for headache. Ginger root is good for this stomach. Or pickles."

"Do you throw up a lot?"

"No."

"It was my cooking."

She shook her head again. So many questions. "No, not your cooking. I am sorry." She hesitated. "It is the food I am not used to. Your cooking it is very good."

"Oh man. I'm sorry. Didn't even think of that."

"It is fine. I am fine now." And to prove herself, she grabbed the bucket and the rifle and started back up the trail, with Leo following, along with Kache, who continued on with his talking and his questions until they reached the house and she excused herself and went upstairs to wash up.

In the kitchen, she poured the clams in the colander, rinsed and gently shook them.

"Your coloring looks better now. You feel all right?"

"Yes, I told you. I am fine. I will prepare dinner tomorrow."

"I'm invited back for dinner?"

She glanced at him, turned back to the clams. "Of course. Yet I am not in this position to do this invite. I am the guest."

A pause lingered before he said, "That's not how I see it."

She shifted her weight from one foot to the other and kept shaking the clams. "How do you see it?"

"I'm not sure." He said he'd be back the next day to work on the truck and start clearing the road.

She rinsed a towel in the sink and covered the clams with it. "For this truck, you need a new battery and a starter."

"You don't say."

She looked over her shoulder at him, opened the refrigerator, and set the clams on a shelf. "You confuse me. I *do* say this."

"Just an expression. You know your way under a car hood too?"

She shrugged and let out a long sigh. She was tired. She could not answer one more question, and certainly not one about getting lost under a car. Fortunately, he said only good night and that he would see her the next day, closed the door, and was gone.

She leaned against the door, listening to the new sounds of the ATV revving up the road until the silence returned—her old, familiar silence, made of certain creaks and scratches and howls and the clickety-clack of Leo's claws across the floor.

chapter

twenty-six

GILLY WAVED FROM BEHIND the reception area and told Snag that Lettie was reading in her room, but by the time Snag got there, Lettie was asleep, the book lying open. Snag wanted desperately to talk to her, but ever since Lettie had revealed that she'd been going out to the homestead all these years, Snag couldn't catch her awake. She worried that her mom was slipping away, but everyone else, including Gilly and Kache, insisted that she was sharper than ever, that the dementia seemed to be fading rather than getting worse. Snag had bad timing, it seemed.

She plopped down in the chair. "I suppose I'll just sit here and wait." She listened to her mom's breathing; she'd been breathing ninety-eight years. Snag knew she was lucky to have her mom that long, but still, she couldn't imagine life once she was gone. "What will I do without you?"

Lettie opened one eye. "Perhaps," she said, "you will start living your *own* life."

"What's that supposed to mean?"

"Eleanor, why in the world would you sit here on this gorgeous day and watch an old woman sleep?"

"Because I want to talk to you. About the homestead and the

Russian woman and Kache and all of it. I want to apologize for not going out there. For lying to you all these years."

"I don't look at it like that. I'm your mother. And I'm the one who owes you an apology."

"What on earth for?"

Lettie started to prop herself up on her thin arms, wickered with veins, and Snag fluffed the pillow and helped her get readjusted. "Well, as far as the lying goes, you might say I've been doing the same thing. I didn't put it on the table, you see. I was waiting for you to come to me and talk. It's like when you were a baby. Glenn took off walking on his own, but you just sat on your rump, happy to play with your sweet little hands or anything I would give you. You didn't have to chase after a thing. And if I'd let you sit there, you'd probably be sitting there still. But I started collecting pretty objects and holding them in front of you until they caught the light just so and then caught your eye. When I saw that you were taken by something, I set it just beyond your reach. And I kept moving it until you finally crawled on your hands and knees and, eventually, pulled yourself up on your feet."

"So I was slow to walk. What does that have to do with anything?"

"I should have pushed you more, Eleanor."

"What, did you want me to run for the Senate?"

"Of course not. The Senate. Pish. No, I should have pushed you toward the truth. Toward not giving a care what people think of you. You, dear, beautiful Eleanor." Lettie reached out and ran her hand along Snag's hairline, the way she did when she was little.

Snag lied once again and said, "Mom, I don't know what you're talking about."

"But you do. Because *I've* suspected since you were about fourteen years old and known without a doubt since you were twenty-one. I still don't understand exactly why you couldn't go out to the homestead, but I have my theories. I just want you to be happy, Eleanor."

Snag's heart started thrumming loudly in her ears, so loudly that she had to strain to hear.

"We can't help who we love," her mom went on, "but we can help how we live. And you've been living like you made that plane go down. And as someone who's had more time on this earth than she deserves, who's staring down the barrel, I'm here to tell you life is way, way too short for this nonsense."

So there it was. Lettie was holding Snag's heart in her hand, tilting it this way and that until it caught the light and was reflecting a prism into Snag's eye. There it was, in all its pulsing glory—Snag's own old heart. Squeezed now, in the palm of her mother, just out of her reach. She felt as vulnerable as the fat baby she'd once been. She still didn't know how to speak the words. But she could walk, so Snag got up and, on her own two feet, walked out the door.

She bumped smack into Gilly, who was heading in with a small paper cup of Lettie's pills. The pills spilled all over the speckled linoleum. The two women crouched down on their hands and knees to pick them up, crawling here and there until they found every last one.

part two

land of the midnight sun

2005

chapter

twenty-seven

AND SO THEY CONTINUED, as the couple of weeks Kache had planned to stay turned into a month, and then into late June. They had agreed that he would return in the mornings after a stop by Lettie's and help Nadia around the property before leaving sometime after dinner to stay with Snag. Sometimes Nadia was warm and talkative, and other times she would grow quiet or disappear for hours at a time. If he pressed her with too many questions, she'd stop the conversation either by leaving or using her standard line: "It is difficult to talk of this." But all in all, Kache felt that she was becoming more comfortable with having him around, and surprisingly, he liked being there.

Whenever Kache went down to the root cellar, he ran his fingers along the wall, checking for Nadia's newest carved tally. He'd bought her a 2005 calendar, *Twelve Artists Paint Alaska*. He'd hung it on the kitchen wall, but that hadn't stopped her from her markings. Each day, there was another thick line made in the wood. Ten years or so of lines: that meant around 3,650 carved lines. So much time and mystery carved in those crevices. Would she stay another ten years, and then another? And what would she do once she ran out of wall? Would she engrave her lines in the kitchen, the living room, up the stairs to the bedrooms?

And how long would he stay, now that his two weeks had long passed? *As long as she needed help*, he'd told himself early on. But it quickly became apparent Nadia was helping him and not the other way around, because she knew how to do everything herself, and he knew how to do practically nothing. It was similar to the old days working with his dad, only Nadia was much more gracious and patient about teaching him, and—Kache had to admit—he tried much harder than his teenage self ever had. He was glad to note that all those hours of watching the Do-It-Yourself Network had not been a complete waste. When he held a hammer or screwdriver, his hands no longer turned into flippers. At least, not all the time. Yes, he did have a purple thumbnail and had taken a scary-ass misstep on the roof but caught himself before he fell off. Greg Barrow had ordered parts for Kache's dad's truck, and after several tries, Kache had managed to get it and the tractor running, clear the road, and, with Nadia working alongside him, finish a half dozen other projects he'd never thought he could tackle—or, at least, had never wanted to.

The warmer weather had eradicated every last patch of old snow and dried up the mud. The days lengthened so rapidly that it was as if someone tugged on each end, stretching them like taffy. He'd forgotten the way you could step outside to wash the truck and not realize until you stepped back in and looked at the clock that it was nearing midnight. Alaska created a seasonal bipolarism he couldn't deny. Summer meant fifteen-hour workdays. Energy bounced from the sun to this part of the earth and back continuously, coursing through him as it traveled in both directions. He saw himself transforming from an Alaskan Clark Kent, wearing flannel and wool socks, wrapped in a quilt by the fire, to the other dude in tights. Kache almost felt the cape fluttering behind him as he turned the wheelbarrow up toward the garden plot. He'd forgotten the miracle of this season's transformation. Not a blessed thing went untouched. The world went into fast-motion photography mode. One day, the trees' branches shivered bare, and the next, they were blanketed with buds. If he stood still long enough, he could witness those buds growing, bursting forth, unfolding to warm their faces in the sun.

All along the bench of land above the bay, fireweed spread like its namesake, setting the slope ablaze in the most vibrant fuchsia. In this land known for everything large and majestic—mountains, eagles, glaciers, bears, even its mosquitoes, which Alaskans called the state bird—the tiny, pale state flower popped up everywhere, those delicate sky-colored forget-me-nots with their pinpointed yellow centers, as if the sun had sacrificed a part of itself in order to anoint each one with a sacred droplet of light.

The place was getting to Kache. No, the place *in the summer* was getting to him, he reminded himself, barely able to recall the gray storms that had stuck around for most of breakup and kept them shivering, ducked under rain gear for days on end.

But a good summer had set in, and now it was mostly sun splashing down. It seemed that the birds never stopped singing—at the moment, a hermit thrush and kinglet were competing for the lead solo. And Nadia never stopped moving, never stopped foraging. Bending, picking, reaching, digging, pinching, plucking. Baskets, nets, pouches, slings, bags, backpacks—all filled and emptied and filled again. She knew the names, the functions, the recipes. She was wisdom and knowledge without a hint of the bored or accustomed. Always, her sense of discovery. Finding a mushroom, she'd act as excited as if it were her first one, but then she'd rattle off enough information to fill a guidebook.

She had collections of seeds: cabbage, kale, oak leaf lettuce, onions, potatoes, broccoli, carrots, and rhubarb. Plus flowers: pansies and marigolds, goldenrod and nasturtiums. She refused to go into town, but when Kache came back one warm early afternoon with pumpkin, acorn squash, and zucchini seeds, she smiled, the biggest smile yet.

She set down the hoe and took the packets in her hands. "To grow a giant pumpkin, I have always wanted this," she said.

"So it could magically turn into a horse and carriage and whisk you away from here?" He began reattaching the chicken wire that had been pulled down—probably by a moose—along the top of the fence.

"No. So I could carve the scary face and light it with candles and set on the porch."

He grinned. "For those hundreds of trick-or-treaters we get—*you* get—out in the middle of nowhere."

She shook her head, handed the seed packets back to him. "I saw photos in your mother's magazine. *Sunrise?* No, *Sunset* magazine. Jack lanterns and trickers. They made this impression on me. I'd never before seen."

"You know, a lot of people think Halloween is the devil's holiday. With your upbringing, do you pay attention to any of that?"

She gave him a long look. She said, "Kache, I have known the devil. Pumpkin? It does not scare me." She turned away and resumed attacking the soil.

Despite the midday sun, a chill skittered down his back. "Okay then. We will grow an Alaskan-size jack-o'-lantern."

"Will you still be here to help me carve it, when it grows?"

This was the first time Nadia had asked him of his plans. The truth was that he had none, other than doing more of what he was doing. He probably needed to take a trip to Austin, if just to tie up some loose ends—sell his car, pick up the rest of his stuff from Janie's. But he didn't need to stay there for a job. He had enough money to keep the homestead going and pay the taxes and, eventually, maybe build some wilderness cabins he could rent out to tourists, somewhere far enough away on the four hundred acres that the house wouldn't lose its privacy. Vague ideas, but far from a plan.

So he said, "As far as I know, yes, I'll be here. What about you?"

"I am here to stay as long as you allow me."

He knew she probably meant the word *stay* quite literally, as in not crossing her foot over the property line. He'd kept gently offering to take her into Caboose, but she adamantly refused. "Nadia, what if you had to leave? Where would you go?"

She set her shoulders back and held the hoe straight alongside her. "To San Francisco."

That was fast. "Wouldn't you like to give it some thought first?" *And wait. How will you get to San Francisco when you won't even talk about venturing the five miles to the main road, let alone into Caboose?* "I mean, you don't even want to go into our little town." He knew he shouldn't have brought this up again, but he couldn't stop himself. He went on. "Don't get me wrong. You can stay here as long as you like. My family appreciates all you've done. But don't you want to peel yourself off of this particular rock?" He took a deep breath and asked, "Does this devil you refer to live in town?"

She pulled her bandana from her jeans pocket—*his* jeans pocket, actually—and wiped her forehead. "I am going to prepare for us some lunch," she said and left.

He'd pushed too hard again. Someone had obviously scared her into staying put, like Lettie thought. Nadia showed a keen interest in the world, delighted with most of what he brought her each day: always a newspaper and a magazine, along with supplies—gasoline for his dad's old power tools, seeds, different foods to try, even a dairy cow they named Mooze, though she insisted she loved the goats' milk and had served him the delicious cheese she made from it. She'd gotten used to most of the food he bought from the store and even wrote up a list of requests. But other than the mention of San Francisco—*San Francisco? Really?*—she seemed bent on spending her entire life in isolation. All he could do was help her continue to be as self-sufficient as possible. Helping someone be *self*-sufficient. Someone who had already mastered it. Not exactly a calling.

If he couldn't take her out into the world, how much of the world to bring in? There was the question of a computer and the Internet, now available on most of the peninsula. Cable television. (His own addiction gave him pause on that one. Perhaps just upgrade the old VCR to a DVD player for movies?) It was possible now to wire in the world. She was knowledgeable, not only about how to survive by yourself on a homestead, but also much more. She'd read their books, watched their movies, listened to their albums. She'd had plenty of time, and she'd used it well.

He took off his work gloves and headed toward the house. He'd help with lunch and wouldn't say anything more about Caboose.

The windows were open, and Neil Young's voice greeted him as he stepped onto the porch. She would often put an album on the stereo when they'd come in from work. Listening to the old albums intensified the feeling of time travel he kept dipping in and out of; the scratchy sound of the vinyl made it seem as though life spun around and around, and you could almost drop in on a specific groove and replay your favorite days.

Inside, he saw that Nadia already sat at the table, eating. He untied his boots and lined them next to hers.

As he washed his hands, hunger and fatigue simultaneously hit him. He fell into the other chair and thanked her for the lunch—a salmon sandwich bordered by a pile of homemade potato chips. Though Nadia admitted she liked the Lay's he'd brought home, she still insisted on making her own, and soon, he too was eating the homemade chips instead.

Neil Young crooning "Old Man." His dad in one of his lighthearted moments doing his best Neil impression, which was amazingly good. Denny sat at this same worn spruce table with his head in

The Old Farmer's Almanac, their mom curled in her red-checked chair with her feet tucked under her, writing in her journal. The fire popped and sputtered. Everyone was tired; everyone was full. It was late autumn, and they'd been working hard to get the last of the harvesting done before the freeze set in, the last of the hay bales into the barn. Even Kache had worked hard that day. Whether his dad had noticed, Kache wasn't sure. But his dad seemed to be in good spirits. He poured himself and Bets a scotch on the rocks, toasted her, and sat down in his chair in his stocking feet. Glenn Winkel was a good-looking man. Shorter and thicker than Kache, close to Denny in size and stature, with dark, mostly straight hair that fell in one wave onto his forehead. He was clean-shaven with sideburns.

"I'm a lot like you…" his dad sang along with Neil. "Hey, Kachemak. I hardly recognized you, sitting there empty-handed. Where's your guitar, Son?"

Kache shrugged. He didn't trust this unprecedented interest in his music. But his father's eyes shone, and he smiled. Then he stood in front of Kache, holding his guitar out to him. He hadn't remembered his dad ever touching it before. "Can you play me this song? Would you?"

Kache nodded, took his guitar into his hands. It was the first and last time his dad ever asked him to play, and Kache played and played for him—with all the soul and love and attention he could muster.

Kache was so entrenched in this memory that when he came back to the present, he saw, for the first time in twenty years, his old guitar, floating ghostlike in front of him. He recoiled. It was Nadia's hand on its neck, holding his guitar out to him. The guitar he'd been sure *not* to look for since he'd returned. "Will you play it? Can you play me this song?"

He grabbed the guitar and pulled it away from her. *Can you play me this song? What?*

He wanted to say, *Quit fucking with me.* Instead, he said, "Is this some kind of joke?"

Her eyebrows darted up, and her hand went flat against her collarbone. "No, there is no laughing."

"Where did you find this? Why did you ask me to play that song?" It took all his restraint to ask this without yelling.

"Kache, wait. I am apologizing."

"Isn't it enough that you live in my house? Do you have to live in my messed-up head too?"

"I do not mean to hurt you. I—"

He didn't hear the rest, because he wedged the guitar under his arm, grabbed his boots, slammed the front door, stepped into the boots without tying them, and drove away too fast. He knew he was overreacting. Still, on the way to Snag's, he kept shaking like a birch leaf in a wind storm.

But Nadia hadn't known what those words would bring up. He already felt like an idiot for leaving her like that. There was also the ugly fear that he might be losing his mind. His guitar leaned against the passenger seat, turned slightly as if observing him, as if it might break out into its own rendition of "Hello Old Friend."

"Stop this," Kache whispered to no one. "Please. Just stop."

chapter

twenty-eight

AFTER ANOTHER FRUSTRATING CHAMBER meeting, Snag stopped by the Spit Tune to meet Gilly. Snag ordered a beer, and Gilly ordered a pink drink called a cosmo, which Snag had never heard of. "You know," Gilly explained, "like on *Sex and the City*."

"Both of those words are so far removed from my lifestyle, I'd feel like a complete fraud ordering one."

Gilly laughed, pushed her drink over for Snag to try. It was sweet and tasty, and when Snag said so, Gilly went to the bar. Snag watched as she ordered a drink from the owner, Rex. A broad-shouldered man who had been sitting a few stools down rose and leaned over to say something in Gilly's ear, and though Snag couldn't hear the conversation, she saw Gilly shake her head and smile. The man was good-looking, at least in the dim light of the bar. Snag felt a small, hot kernel of jealousy sprouting in her chest, and she knew she had to put it out immediately. Gilly? No way. She hadn't let herself feel anything for anyone for twenty years because she'd felt nothing *but* jealousy for the twenty years prior. Twenty years of consuming jealousy, followed by twenty years of remorse. Not much of a life. And she knew that little burning coal—it had already blossomed from a kernel into a coal in minutes—could ruin all the years remaining. At sixty-five, she was lucky if she had twenty years or so left. She did not want them filled with envy and unrequited, impossible love. Gilly was a decade younger than Snag and straight as an ice pick. Enough said.

Gilly returned with a pink drink for Snag, and Snag closed her eyes and downed enough of it to put out that hot coal for good.

When she opened her eyes, she saw the beer sitting to the side, sweating, and beyond it, good ol' kindhearted Gilly, her new friend and nothing more, so help her God. Snag let out a sigh of relief.

Gilly must have thought it was a sigh of appreciation for the drink, because she said, "So I see you like it."

Snag nodded and tilted her head toward the man at the bar. "An admirer?"

Gilly shrugged. "Not my type."

Snag raised her eyebrows, but Gilly didn't elaborate, so Snag started filling her in on the chamber meeting, how everyone else seemed desperate to keep the old Herring Town caboose stuck at the end of the track. "That poor old caboose has been sitting there for decades, a pitiful museum to its former life. Why wouldn't they want to see it useful and moving again?"

"Excuse me for asking this, Snag, but why not just let the old caboose stay put and let there be a new version—a reproduction of the old one? Then everyone will be happy."

"I won't be. It's the principle of the matter. That caboose makes me sad."

"Sad?"

"Yep. Sad. Doesn't it make you sad? A bygone era, a town built on an industry, and then the whole thing up and dies because of greed, and the town almost died too."

"But it didn't. It kept going. It reinvented itself."

"Exactly! Which is why I'd like to see that caboose moving again."

"I guess I'm not quite following you. Some might say the caboose has reinvented itself—as a museum."

"Museums are about the past, not the future."

"Ah." Snag took a sip of the City Sexy drink without looking at Gilly, who continued, "Okay, I'll give you that much. But I don't think that's what's been eating you up lately."

Rex came by and set a bowl of peanuts on their table. "Your boyfriend wanted to buy you another round, but I told him you were married so he'd lay off. Strange dude, even by Alaska standards."

"Oh yeah?" Snag asked. "How's that?"

"He's a drifter. Says he has a cabin off the grid by the lake. Russian."

"Old Believer?"

"Heh. Not even close. He had a job up at Prudhoe Bay, married a Native woman a while back, didn't work out, so now he's here again. Says he's a hermit except when he comes in to watch TV or listen to the band. Just want you to know I'm watching out for you two fair maidens."

"Thanks, Rex," Gilly said. "Does that mean *you're* buying the next round?"

"Hell no. Man's gotta make a living." He grinned, flipped his towel over his shoulder, and headed back to the bar.

"Rex," Snag said. "Always the gossip. I'm guessing he's scaring the guy off because Rex fancies you too."

Gilly shook her head. "Naw, not Rex. He's been in love with Tilde Miller since the mastodons walked these parts. So. Here we are, despite the fact that you've managed to cancel on me three Thursdays in a row."

"I can't even remember what I was so upset about that day you offered to talk."

Gilly popped a peanut in her mouth and smiled. "I imagine you do remember." Gilly was nice even when she was pinning you into a corner. She *gently* refused any bullshit.

Snag felt her face redden and was glad for the dim light of the bar. "I guess you're right. But it doesn't feel so urgent anymore."

"Snag, you surely don't have to tell me one iota of anything, but I do find it helps me to talk this stuff out. Life can tie a person up in knots. Talking can loosen those knots, sometimes even set us free."

"That's a nice idea, but it's not really true when you're talking about the past. Talking can't undo past mistakes. Nothing can. Especially when those mistakes set the people you love on a course bound for tragedy."

The bar was practically empty now, Gilly's admirer gone and just old Johnny Mathis-Yes-That's-My-Real-Name and his son, Bobby, sitting down at the end of the bar, eyes locked on the TV. It was early yet, and the band wasn't due to start for another forty minutes.

Snag needed to move. Now. She started to get up, but Gilly reached for her arm, pulling her back down, and Snag landed with a plop. She stared at her hands. She liked her hands, with their nicely shaped nail beds, with her father's gold wedding band settled on her middle finger. They were capable hands. Gilly rested her hand on Snag's and waited.

Ever since Kache had come back, Snag had felt ready to burst at the seams with her secrets. And here was Gilly, all concerned eyes and ears—her earrings even dangled like carrots, beckoning Snag to finally speak. And so she did. "Are you ready for this one, Gilly? You've been a friend to me, and it's been nice knowing you, but all that's about to end. And that's okay. I'll understand. Because here it is: I was in love with my own sister-in-law. For twenty-two years, I was like a puppy following her around. Pathetic. I even fantasized about my brother kicking the bucket and her declaring her love for me. And then he went and did exactly that. And so did beautiful Bets and my sweet teddy bear of a nephew, Denny. And I'm to blame."

It took all Snag had not to bolt out of there. Moments came and went. Empty glasses clinked behind the bar, and a commercial came on for a cruise line, causing Snag to wish she were in the tropics, alone on a ship of strangers rather than in the town bar confessing her sins to Gilly, who still hadn't pulled her hand away. She squeezed Snag's and said, "That is a tragic story. And I'm so sorry. But the biggest tragedy is that you've been blaming yourself for bad weather one day twenty years ago. You are a sensitive, caring, strong woman, Snag. But I'm sorry—your thoughts don't have that kind of power."

"You don't understand."

"I do understand. More than you think. And I understand that loving your sister-in-law did not make that plane crash into that mountain. I guarantee it."

"But you weren't even there. There's even more to it. I—"

"I don't need to know specifics. I don't care. I know that you weren't in that plane when it crashed. Planes crash everywhere, but they especially like to crash in Alaska. You need to knock off this excuse for not living your life. Right this second."

Snag exhaled. The breath kept coming. She had never told a soul, and now she'd just spilled her secret to a woman she didn't know all that well. True, she hadn't spilled *everything*, but she'd let go of enough to unplug the dam. Snag was making a scene, but nobody except Johnny and Bobby and Rex were there to witness it, and they were enthralled with golf up on the television. Gilly went to the bar for more drinks and brought back a stack of napkins, which Snag used to mop the tears on her face.

A crowd started gathering as the band set up. Snag waved at Marion Tilloko, Kache's old girlfriend and singing partner, whose grandfather's room was three doors down from Lettie's. Gilly waved too.

Snag leaned across her fresh drink and said, "I still have never, not once, gone out to the homestead since right after the crash. I lied to my mom and Kache about that too."

"Are they mad about it?"

Snag shook her head. "Miraculously, no."

"So there's only one thing left to do then."

"What's that?"

"Let yourself off that hook you set back in the dark ages of 1985."

chapter

twenty-nine

SNAG HAD LEFT A note for Kache—*Down at the Spit Tune listening to the band. Come join us!*—which only further intensified his anguish. Not *a* band. *The* band, still playing at the same old bar, where in the early years, Rex had ignored the fact that the band was comprised of teenagers under the legal drinking age. They were going to be *huge*. That's what they said, and that's what everyone in town said, and that's what the newspaper reporter from Anchorage said. But this was all before Kache bailed.

How was it that he'd neglected his passion? How was it that he'd left behind the most important thing in the world to him, besides his family? It had been a strange relief to head down to Austin without his guitar. Head down to the exact place he'd planned to dive into nothing but music, music, music—accepted to UT on a music scholarship. The University of Texas wasn't so quick to offer the scholarship in accounting, but when Kache pointed out his perfect grades, not just in music, but in math, science, and English, as well as his volunteer work at the native village and his SAT scores, they pulled something they referred to as a hush-hush redistribution of funds and got him into the business department on a full ride. So there had been that hurdle. And then the daily hurdles of being in a town known for its abundance of music in most every bar, on most every street corner, not to mention all the festivals the whole city embraced—South by Southwest and Austin City Limits, to name a couple—and the way he'd practically bump into people like Shawn Colvin and Steve Earle and John Prine, his heroes sitting in a restaurant having lunch with a friend or hunched down in an aisle in a used bookstore or walking out of the pharmacy as he was walking in.

But he preferred dealing with all that to dealing with what hit him when he played. He'd tried at first, still at home, in the weeks after they died. But the music always took him back to that last awful night.

❧

That last awful night, Kache had retreated to his bedroom, locked the door, and strummed as loud as possible over his dad's yelling and banging, his threatening to kick down the door, until he finally did. He pushed his face into Kache's, but Kache kept on playing as loud as possible. He smelled scotch and the onions from the casserole Aunt Snag had brought. He'd seen his dad drunk before, but not often and not like this. All three of the adults were cutting loose that night, and his dad was getting ugly. After the complaints about Kache's inability, his laziness around the homestead, it always came down to his music, as if it were a personal affront and the cause of all the evil in the world. It didn't matter that Kache worked so hard at school and his music; it only mattered that he didn't work hard enough at home.

"You goddamn lazy ass! You pompous little shit. Don't you ever lock your goddamn door on me again, you understand?" Kache didn't answer. "You understand me?"

Kache had been silently shaking, but he tried for boldness. "No. I don't understand you. I never will."

His dad pulled him up by his hair and then did what he'd never done. He punched him, hard, and blood spurted like a surprise from Kache's nose. Despite himself, tears filled his eyes while the blood filled his hand.

Kache said what he'd never said before. "I hate you. Why don't you just go fucking kill something? Go shoot your animals and leave me alone."

Snag stepped over the door, calling, "Bets, bring ice!" and chewed out Glenn, who stumbled away. "What are you, some kind of monster?" she yelled after him. But even Aunt Snag, who Kache had never seen drunk, slurred her words. She grabbed a T-shirt off the floor, not knowing it was his favorite, a Blaze Foley T-shirt that Marion had bought him at a concert in the Lower 48 and brought back last summer. Snag held Blaze Foley up to Kache's nose and let the blood soak in. Kache closed his eyes and wished for Denny, but he was out on a date. None of this would have happened if Denny had been home. His dad wouldn't dare touch Kache in Denny's presence. Kache couldn't believe he'd done it at all.

Then it was his mom crouching over him, smoothing back his hair, saying, "I'm sorry, honey, I'm so sorry. That's not your dad. It's the drink," but he smelled the scotch on her too. What the hell was everyone getting so drunk for? What had started as a nice enough meal with Aunt Snag and a game of Scrabble (planned for later but never played) had turned into a drunken brawl of an evening. Even later, as he lay on his bunk bed, pumped up with some painkillers leftover from his mom's knee surgery, he heard more yelling and crying. He rehung the door as best he could, given his drugged state and lack of carpentry skills. Then he nailed it shut and refused to come out. Maybe if Denny had come home, he might have worked himself into Kache's room and talked him into joining them. But Denny had spent the night at his girlfriend's.

The next morning, Kache wouldn't acknowledge his father's pleas for forgiveness. Instead, he played his guitar over his dad's words. "I'm sorry as a man can be, Son. It was wrong of me. Kachemak? Please forgive me."

The front door slammed. He stopped playing. His parents' footsteps on the front porch, the gravel. He quietly opened his window, straining to hear. The hunting and fishing gear thrown in the truck bed. Doors creaking open.

His dad said, "He'll be all right."

"Maybe I should stay with him." These were the last words he'd ever hear her speak.

"Sometimes, Bets, a man needs his space. Let's give him that. Come on, hon. I told Den we'd pick him up by now."

One door slammed, the engine growled into a roar, and then Kache peeked out and saw his mother look up to his window. He wanted to step forward, wave, tell her to wait, but he stayed to the side and watched her climb in and pull her door shut. It would have been so easy to stop them. The time it would have taken him to pack up his stuff would have delayed them, might have changed everything. But he didn't stop them. He watched the truck churn gravel as it turned and made its way up the road until they were gone.

This is what Kache had heard whenever he'd tried to play the guitar again all those years before: *His dad screaming, his dad threatening, Kache saying those words I hate you I hate you, go fucking kill something, his mom consoling, his dad apologizing, and then the doors shutting, the truck starting and leaving without Kache on their way to pick up Denny. Denny. The big brother who always stuck up for him.*

❧

He ran his fingers down along his nose and back up. He needed to pick up new strings. The thought taunted him as he sat on the bed in Snag's guest room, holding his old guitar. He didn't know if the background noise of that night would still be there when he played.

If he hurried, he could get to Jeff's Music to buy those strings before it closed.

Or he could turn on Snag's TV, lie back on the couch, catch *The House That Jack and Jack Jr. Built,* and call it a day. It wasn't like he hadn't been working his ass off.

chapter

thirty

IN THE LAST MONTH, Nadia had gone from plotting her escape to looking forward to Kache's arrival every morning. Now she might have ruined their friendship.

Since Kache had first shown up, she'd given up one of her favorite pastimes. What had once seemed to be intimately hers alone and a means of survival felt like rampant stealing in his presence. Even after he left in the evenings, though she was tempted, she resisted.

But she kept slipping up. Conversation was still challenging to her, and though she craved it, it drained and confounded her. How many of the thoughts in her head should she transpose into words and let out of her mouth to travel the air to Kache's ears? What was good for him to know? What would cause him unnecessary pain? What was she meant to keep for only herself?

Elizabeth had meant to keep the diaries to herself; Nadia knew this from their content. Nonetheless, she had read them so often and so thoroughly that she often had difficulty drawing the line between her thoughts and Elizabeth's. Handing Kache the guitar and asking him to play that song had been stupid, and he might be gone for good. Just like Lettie.

And so, out of loneliness for Kache and in order to stop unknow-
ingly quoting Kache's own mother, Nadia convinced herself she
should take a quick peek and refresh her memory. She took her three
favorite notebooks out of the cardboard box where she'd first found
them, packed away in Elizabeth and Glenn's closet. She positioned
herself between old boots and slippers and the hems of heavy coats,
and counting on Leo to bark if the truck turned down the road, she
opened a diary and read:

> Blessed, blessed summer is upon us, and I have the energy
> of eight of my winter selves. So much to be done, but let
> me at it and let me feel the sun on my arms and hair and
> back for eighteen hours straight. The garden is boiling over,
> the cabbage ballooning into the ridiculous. Sunflowers
> bigger than my face. Gladiolas! Pansies! Roses! The beans
> are reaching for the sky and will soon be vining themselves
> around a star. The same goes for Denny and especially
> Kache; the notches in the doorjamb need to be updated
> almost weekly.

"Oh, Elizabeth," Nadia whispered. "I have missed you."
And then this:

> We are a family of extremes, relying on one another in a land
> of extremes. We go forth in a constant state of alertness: for
> shifts in the sea and sky, for crashing of enormous antlers
> or huge claws through alders, for yet another clashing of
> personalities. We are a bear, a moose, a wolf, and an eagle,
> all living under this small roof, the illusion of shelter amid
> the magnificence.

Now she wondered who Kache was supposed to be in that scenario. She could imagine him as a moose or an eagle or even a wolf. How did his mother see him? Leo barked, and Nadia dropped the notebooks into the box, scrambled out from her hiding place, and ran down the stairs, only to see the same cow moose and her calf that showed up every day, lumbering across the yard, Kache still nowhere, and it was late morning. What if he did not forgive her?

She had pictured the two of them setting off for the beach to clear the fishing nets—much easier with two. But she shouldn't wait any longer. She certainly shouldn't be hiding in the closet when the sun gave itself so freely and completely, a thick slab of warm butter spreading out from the low sky to every corner. Brightness abounded. If only she had a big box in which she could store some of this light for the winter; when it stayed dark for most of the day, she could lift the lid and let the light reach out to warm her. But that's what the box of Elizabeth's words had done.

❧

Two salmon and four cod, along with three starfish, four sea anemones, and half a dozen Dungeness crabs, all a fraction under legal size, not that anyone was checking. Nadia let the crabs go anyway—the bigger ones had more flavorful meat—and turned her attention to the salmon and cod. They eyed her warily, flipping and then resting, stillness except for gills gasping. She did not like this particular requirement. A part of her wanted to free them, but she clubbed each once, swiftly, with enough muscle to get the job done.

She identified with each fish tangled in the net, with each rabbit she trapped, each chicken whose neck she wrung, each spruce hen she shot. She was the Vladimir in their story.

❧

He had shown up at the new village, Altai, explaining that he'd come from the community in Oregon, that he'd felt the world encroaching and wanted freedom to worship in the purest of the old ways. But it was all just a story. Vladimir did not worship anyone but himself.

He arrived two years after the villages split over their differences. Two years after Niko had married Katarina without a second thought. Nadia's parents hadn't pressured her into marriage. There were no available suitors anyway; she was the oldest of the children in their small group. She had felt such betrayal and despair over Niko that she'd put the thought of ever marrying out of her head and instead focused on her studies. But all that changed when Vladimir arrived.

At first, she'd been frightened only by his alarming beauty. He had everyone in the village swooning, even the men, who were small in number and could use his strong arms and legs to speed up the building, which had already taken too long. It didn't matter that he was already well into his thirties and unmarried—although now Nadia questioned the validity of that story too. His eyes were the color of irises; his teeth sparkled and shone white even against a backdrop of clean snow. There was his nose, strong but not too large, and the planes of his face depicted strength and wisdom. His beard looked like an inviting place to rest one's head.

Excitement rumbled through the whole village. Finally! Nadia would have a husband. If you listened hard enough, even the wind through the trees seemed to be saying the same thing. *At last! At long last!* Because Nadia, at almost sixteen, was considered an old maid. A spinster.

If they could see me now, she thought. *If they could only see me now.*

In those days, Nadia had spent much of her free time embroidering. Now she read books, but back at the village, the women were expected to become experts in handiwork. In the weeks leading up to the wedding, she and her mothers and sisters prepared her trunk with the intricately woven belts all Old Believers were required to wear, along with beautiful sheets and pillowcases, dresses, blankets, and needlepoint to hang on the walls of her new home. Vladimir, accompanied by the men, came to "buy" the trunk, another old ritual that was bathed in *braga* and full of laughter.

At their wedding party, Nadia was so nervous and excited, she didn't touch the food. *Braga* flowed freely. Plated towers of *pelmeni* and *gruzdi v pyerog* and *katleti* were passed around, aromas of meat and mushroom fillings and potatoes and dough filled the hall, but all she did was nibble on a sweet *pryanik*.

Vladimir whispered, his lips touching the lobe of her ear, "You must eat, yes? We will both need our strength." He winked and rested his hand on her thigh, over her skirt, beneath the table. The warmth of his hand spread everywhere, as if he touched much more than her skirted thigh.

But that night, he drank too much and fell into bed, snoring. She slept in the chair in her wedding dress, afraid to change if he should wake. She fingered her braids, trying to get used to wearing two instead of one.

The next morning, he didn't speak, and she wondered what she'd done wrong. She fixed him *kartoshka s echkam*—potatoes with eggs—and he shoveled them into his mouth without looking at her before leaving for the day.

Nadia stood in front of the mirror throughout the afternoon. Did she have some deformity to which she was blind, something Niko and now Vladimir had seen and been repulsed by? Certain that must be the problem, she ran to her grandmother's house. But her baba took her in, heard her fears, and reassured her she was indeed a beautiful, smart woman any man would be honored to marry. "So he had a little too much of the *braga*. The man is embarrassed, that is all. Tonight, you act like nothing happened. You make him my *galushki* for dinner, you brush your lovely hair and turn your flawless face to Vladimir— and he will be the happiest man in the village and beyond."

At dinner, he spoke kindly; the charming Vladimir was back. After she washed the dishes, she changed into the wedding night-gown she'd planned to wear the night before. Vladimir approached her gently at first, kissing her for a long time. Then he turned over abruptly, punched the pillow, swore, and went to sleep. This contin-ued for many nights. Long sessions of kissing—sometimes he would touch her breasts—but then he would stop suddenly and fall asleep or get up and clomp outside. Had she been misinformed about sex? She had definitely expected more than this. She definitely wanted more than this.

But the fifth night, after he kissed her for a while, when he pulled away, he reached under the bed and brought out a hunting knife.

"Let us try this," he said. "It will help me." He held the knife by the opening to Nadia's nightclothes and sliced apart the blue ribbons she and her mother had sewn on. Terror pulsed through her. She opened her mouth to scream, but the scream came out soundless.

"Why would you try to scream, my princess? I am your husband. I mean no harm." His eyes teased; he seemed amused as he unbuttoned his pants. "Ah, this is what I was looking for. Look at that piece of steel, would you? They call me the Stallion. I knew I still had this. Just needed a little prop is all."

He grinned almost sheepishly and held the knife to her neck. "I am sorry you have been full of desire for so many days. You are going to forget that you ever had to wait for me."

chapter

thirty-one

LEO BARKED, AND NADIA, who was hunched over the fishing net, jumped and then slowly straightened, thinking about her shotgun five paces away, expecting to see a bear thrashing through the bushes to the beach. Sometimes the bears stole from her net and tore huge holes in it that required mending. But she saw nothing. When Leo stopped barking briefly to listen, she heard music. Guitar music, but from over by the trailhead.

Kache emerged from the woods, walking and playing like one of the minstrels in a king's court she'd read about. Nadia couldn't keep from smiling and then laughing—not at him but out of relief that he was no longer angry and from the joy spread across his face as he sang out. His voice was as Elizabeth had quoted a reporter, "both wound and wonder."

He threw back his head and sang:

*"**Nadia**, you unknotted me.*
Nadia, you undeniably
Nadia, you unarguably...
Nadia ah ah... Nadia ah ah... Nadiaaah..."

He splayed his arms, held out his guitar by its neck, and shook it. "Twenty years! Twenty years, and no one could get me to get my nose out of my navel long enough to play. And all you did was hand me my guitar when a certain heartbreaker of a song was playing. I swear, you're psychic." He waited for her to respond. She'd never heard so many words come out of his mouth at once. He went on. "Thank you. I'm sorry for being such an asshole. I freaked out, but I can't believe how quickly it's coming back. My fingers keep tripping over one another, but they know where to go. They're just out of shape. Wow. Looks like you've been busy." He bent down to examine the pail of fish. "I figured I'd find you down here, but I thought we might have to collect mussels. Let's eat right here. We can make a fire and cook that salmon." He pulled his backpack off. "Look, I brought a couple of beers and some green beans and bread."

How quickly his moods shifted. She finally saw the joy Elizabeth had written about surging out of him. He chattered as fast as a squirrel, and she half expected him to race up a tree trunk next, jump across from branch to branch before inviting her for a dinner of gathered pine nuts.

Instead, he handed her a beer and got busy collecting driftwood and coal for the fire, humming his new song with all the inflections of her name. She hadn't heard her name spoken in all those years alone, had never heard it sung. The acknowledgment of her existence bloomed a bit in her chest. Why was pride so highly ranked by those who ranked sins, always followed by an inevitable fall? Why was pride even a sin? A little pride seemed like a good thing, something that sent the shoulders back, the chin up, made you feel like you wanted to give even more of yourself to the betterment of the world…or at the very least to the betterment of a man named Kachemak Winkel.

From the backpack, he pulled out a lighter, the rack from the roasting pan, a knife—even though she'd brought hers to clean the fish. Seeing the knife held in his hand made her wince, but it was a physical reaction, not from her head; she understood now that she didn't need to fear Kache. He opened his own beer and then clinked his bottle to hers. "To...what?"

"What?" She tilted her head and waited.

"I don't know what to call this."

"Call what?"

"This...this!" He grabbed her arm, but not the way Vladimir grabbed it. Instead, it was with a childlike excitement. "It's strange. Sad. But I feel we could help each other. If you're willing?"

"I do not understand."

"I've been thinking. You keep teaching me about running this place, and I'll bring a computer out, hook us up to the Internet. You can go anywhere, see anything. Without leaving. Not that you don't already know a lot; you've read more books than I'll ever read. But there's so much out there that will blow your mind."

What he couldn't know from her staring wordlessly back at him was that this was exactly what she wanted. She was afraid to go to town, to even go up to the main road. But if she could see the world? If she might somehow be lifted from this piece of land and bypass the road and town and be dropped at the Golden Gate Bridge, would she do it? Without hesitation. She wasn't afraid of the world out there. She was afraid of Vladimir. She was afraid of the pain it would cause her family if they discovered she'd been lying to them all this time. She was as alive as she'd ever been, right that minute, standing on a beach next to a fire, toasting to...what?...with Kache.

"Yes," she finally said.

"Yes to...?"

"The computer. The interconnect. All of it, I would like. Oh, and of course I am more than willing to teach you what I know about this land. For this, I would be privileged."

"Okay. Then it's not just a toast. It's a deal. We need to shake on it."

"Shake on it? Ah, a handshake, yes?"

He held out his hand, and then she held out hers, both of their hands suspended until he reached forward and took hers—so odd to be touching, skin to skin—and pumped her hand up and down until she couldn't help smiling again.

After they ate, they followed Leo up the trail, but then he veered right instead of left, and so they took the longer way home, along the canyon. She loved the canyon. It was an extremely deep and sudden jagged cut into the land, and sometimes she stood and stared down into it, trying to imagine what had caused it. A glacier? An earthquake? A meteorite? Elizabeth had written about this canyon many times, describing it as the largest and deepest on the peninsula. It was mysteriously stunning but dangerous, and it had haunted Elizabeth.

Kache said, "Come here, Leo. Don't let him get too close to the edge."

Nadia knew why, but she wasn't worried. All she ever needed to do was share a look with Leo—which she now did—and he walked alongside her as they passed the canyon.

"When I was a kid," Kache began, "I had a dog named Walter. He was a great dog, except he had this thing about chasing birds and butterflies. He would jump and run as if his hundred pounds of dog had a chance in hell of taking flight. It was the funniest thing to watch. Pure joy, determination, and frustration all at once. We all loved that dog." Kache stopped walking, took a deep breath. "One day, when I was ten, he and I were heading down this same path. He started chasing some butterfly, and I thought nothing of it. He chased it—he chased it right off the edge of the canyon. I watched him leap, and when I raced to the edge, he was still falling, you know? Falling into that great abyss, a tiny drop of black. I ran to get my dad. He followed me to the edge and put his arm around me. But he refused to go get him. It was too dangerous. He and my mom told me that Walter was probably fine and would have a good life down in the canyon, as if I were young enough to believe *that*." He smoothed his hand from his forehead back over his curls. "The next night, I snuck out and tried to hike down, but I knew I'd never make it out alive either. I never forgave myself—or my dad—for not going down there. I'm sure Walter was dead on impact. Still, the possibility of him all broken up and suffering haunts me."

Nadia knew she should not say anything, but she could not keep entirely quiet. She said, "Have you considered ever that perhaps your father, he did go down this hill to get your dog?"

Kache shook his head. "He was adamant. Besides, if he had, they would have told me so I'd quit harping on them about it."

"You were a boy, yes? And if Walter the dog was dead, which we both know that he most likely was, or close to death, your parents, they might have thought they were protecting you from the truth. You can see this?"

Kache kept shaking his head. "No, look at that incline. My dad was a tough man, but he wasn't an expert climber. It might have taken ropes to get all the way down there. Hell, they'd need some kind of search and rescue team. I understand that now. I've been mad at him my whole life for so many things. Some of them are justified. But maybe this wasn't."

"So about Walter, you are no longer angry?"

Kache started toward the homestead while Nadia and Leo followed. "There was this song that came out several years later. It was a big hit, and they played it on the radio all the time. 'Dog and Butterfly.' Whenever it came on, my mom would change the station. There weren't many stations, and sometimes it was playing on the other station, so my mom would flip off the radio. Not a memory any of us wanted to dwell on." Kache leaned down, rubbed Leo between the ears, looked up at Nadia, and smiled. "But you know?" His voice caught, and he shook his head. "That dog finally *did* fly."

chapter
thirty-two

SNAG STOOD ON HER front step, gripping the banister. Faint guitar music trickled from inside. These had been the strangest couple of weeks she'd ever experienced, and things were only getting stranger. She was lodged in a slingshot, pulled back, back, back. All this tension, pulling, resistance. Pretty soon, she'd have to change her name to Snap.

But there it was, and you had to love it: Kache picking up the guitar again. Playing. She pressed her ear to the door and listened. The music worked like a massage on her temples, her shoulders, her arms. Even her grip on the doorknob relaxed. What a gift that boy had. That *man*, she reminded herself once again, not *boy*. He was a grown man now. And she was an old, tired, stressed-out woman, suddenly feeling not so tired, not so stressed-out.

"If you feel the need to hide
I'll cover you and go bare.
If you can't walk another mile
On my back I'll take you there.

"If you can't cross the water
I'll lie down and be your bridge.
And if you lose all hope and vision
I'll paint the sky from edge to edge."

When the music stopped, Snag wiped her eyes and then her feet and opened the door. Kache sat on the edge of the sofa, the guitar still on his knee. He jumped up, a little embarrassed, a little pleased too, she decided.

She untied her laces and set her shoes next to Kache's boots. "Oh, good," she said. "I was afraid your gorgeous playing was just a forlorn memory acting up. But it was real, Kache. Real." She hugged him and his guitar with one wrap of her arms. "It sounds like you never stopped."

"Thanks, but no. I'm beyond rusty. Still, I've got to admit, it feels good."

She sat in the rocking chair by the woodstove. The cat jumped onto her lap. She liked coming home to a warm house. "I don't remember that song, and it's beautiful."

"Thanks. Something I'm working on. Where were you?"

"Oh, I left the same note sitting there from last night because I was at the same place."

"The Spit Tune again?"

"Gilly's been playing therapist for me. She gives good advice, and all it costs me is to buy her a Sexy City or whatever-you-call-it drink. Then we listen to the band play."

"How are they?"

"All right. They'd be a helluva lot better if you were playing with them."

He shook his head. "I'm already spending my days in the same house I did as a teenager. If I start playing with them again, I'm liable to start breaking out in acne and having to take ridiculously long showers."

Snag snorted. "Oh, stop it, Kache." It was better than wonderful to have him playing again, and he seemed lighter every day. "Speaking of the house, should I plan on a trip out soon?"

He was back to picking out a tune on his guitar, just playing background to his thinking. "I guess it's about time. It's just... Nadia. I know it sounds strange, but I have to prepare her. She knows a lot, but she's experienced so little. I'm going to get us hooked up to the Internet."

"Ugh. Does it have to take over every single corner of the world?"

"Yeah, I know. But it might help Nadia. And I just bought us both cell phones that get good reception."

"Kache? Are you going back to Austin?"

He told her how he'd received a couple of friendly emails from Janie asking about what to do with his car and his stuff in her garage. She'd been patient, and so he needed to book a flight down there and sell his car, take care of the loose ends.

"Will Nadia be okay? Want me to check on her?"

Kache smiled. "Knowing her, she'll welcome the peace and quiet. I'll give her your phone number and ask her, but I'm guessing she'll want to be left alone. We should plan something after I get back—if she's ready. Gram asks about her and wants to go out there."

"She doesn't ask me." Snag set down the cat. "I guess she gave up on me taking her. Besides, I'm not sure she's really strong enough."

"Did you ever hear back from the doctor about her pink pill? Or Gilly? Because I think she flushes the pink ones."

"She better not. Not if she wants to live. It's the new one for her blood pressure."

"Like I said before, she doesn't want to live if she's not right in her head, and she's convinced that those pills make her delirious. And I think she's probably right. Isn't there an alternative?"

"I asked. I haven't heard back from her doc, but I'll ask again."

"Aunt Snag?" Kache laid the guitar next to him on the sofa. "Why didn't you ever go out to the homestead anyway?"

She chose her words carefully. "Lots of reasons, I guess. What about you? Just wanted to forget?"

"If it hadn't been for that fight my dad and I had the night before... and then the next day, he kept apologizing, and I wouldn't talk to him. If I hadn't been such a prick, I think Dad would have been able to fly the plane better, even in that cloud cover."

Snag stared at Kache. Wait. *He'd* been feeling guilty all this time? "Oh, hon." Her throat barely let the words out. "Hon, it's not your fault. You have to believe that."

But he didn't say any more, just kept playing.

Snag went to change into her pajamas and robe and slippers. Alone in her room, the gravity of what she now knew pressed down on her, demanding she take a seat on the edge of the bed. Kache had felt responsible, and she had let him. Unforgivable. While he tried out different melodies, she planned how she'd tell him the story. So she was a lesbian. So what? Kache was a thoughtful, evolved person. She doubted that would shake up his world too much. It was the being in love with his mother part she'd rather continue to keep to herself. Because that led to an even bigger screwup, the stupidest thing she'd ever done, the one deed she would do anything, everything, to take back. It was the thing she hadn't told anyone—not Gilly, not Lettie— and it was what ended up ruining Kache's life. Ruined it in even more ways than she'd imagined.

chapter

thirty-three

IN THE TWO WEEKS Kache was gone to Texas, Nadia was surprised first by the return of the quiet and then how, after several days, it began to unsettle her. On the fourth day, he called. When they hung up, he reminded her to keep her cell phone charged, and so she plugged it in and found herself waiting beside it in the evening for his call, which came every night thereafter. She would tell him about her day—what vegetables she'd harvested and what fish she'd caught and the silly things the goats had done and how the weather had been. One day, she paced in front of the phone, hardly able to wait to tell him she'd seen two orcas leaping out of the bay. "At first, I thought they were strange birds with giant wingspan, but then I see that is only their tails," she told him. "Then they burst forth like huge, hidden joy. 'What a lark! What a plunge!' as Clarissa would say." She'd been rereading *Mrs. Dalloway* once again to fill the lonely evenings.

Kache would tell her about the people he dined with and all the different kinds of food he'd had, and he complained about the thick heat and loud city noises and traffic, but she asked him to hold the phone so she could hear the honking and sirens and talking and laughter, imagining what it would be like to sit with him on a patio outside a restaurant on a warm evening.

And then, finally, he came back.

She heard the truck door slam and raced down the stairs and flung open the door. He was crouched over, taking off his boots. When he stood, she felt her smile drop.

"You came back."

"I told you I would."

"But…"

She saw his smile drop too. "Aren't you glad to see me?" he asked.

"Yes, but…"

"I can leave if you—"

"No, but…"

"What is it, Nadia? What's wrong?" Her hand went to her chin, and he laughed. "The beard? You don't like me embracing my inner mountain man?"

She kept her eyes locked on his feet. It was more than that. She could not bear to look at him.

"I forgot my razor at Snag's and thought I'd just go for it. Everyone in Austin liked it. They say I'm not a computer geek anymore. And speaking of computers…"

She turned and went to the kitchen, picked up a pan to scrub, and scrubbed furiously. What she thought was that her revulsion was ridiculous; they looked nothing alike. But what she knew was that she could not stand the beard another minute.

"I'll shave it tomorrow. My razor's at Snag's."

"Come with me," she said and led the way upstairs.

She motioned for him to sit on the closed lid of the toilet. His eyebrows arched up, but he sat. From the shelf above, she took down the old razor and mug and soap brush.

Kache grimaced. "That old thing is my great-grandfather's. At least let me look for my dad's or Denny's." But he sat back, and his changing expression told her that although Denny and Glenn were rugged Alaskan men, both of them shaved every day, even when they went on hunting trips. Their razors were buried in plane rubble on a mountain.

"This will work," Nadia told him. She rinsed the dust out of the mug and stuck in a small bar of soap that smelled of lemons, ran the wet brush over the soap until there was enough to lather Kache's face. She took the razor in her hand and flipped it open.

"Have you ever done this before?" he asked.

"No."

"Let me."

"No." She turned the water on and, when it was warm to her touch, plugged the sink.

"Nadia?"

She looked straight into his eyes with a willfulness she hadn't before experienced. She had to do this, and he had to let her. That was all there was to it.

He must have understood, because after that, he kept his eyes straight ahead while his knee bumped up and down. She turned off the water. He held his breath while Nadia touched her hand to his forehead, tilted his head back, and assessed the planes of his face.

"Are you sure you've never—?"

"Old Believer men do not shave, and Old Believer women are not allowed even to witness haircuts of men. So yes, I am sure. But I skin animals. You know I am good with knife."

"I would rather not be skinned."

"Now you are quiet."

Water dripped rhythmically into the half-full sink. The overhead light reflected in the razor as she angled it and pressed it against Kache's face, in front of his ear.

She had missed him.

She scraped overlapping trails, concentrating on the smaller space between his nose and lips and in the crevice of his chin. She dipped the razor in the sink.

There was so much she wanted to tell him, but she didn't know how.

She lifted his chin, brought the blade to his throat. Kache swallowed, and their eyes met for an instant before his retreated to the cabinet ahead and hers to the curve of his Adam's apple.

So instead, she would do this: a tenderness attempting to replace the wreckage. Was she too ruined? If only she could still the trembling of her hand.

He swallowed again, and she scraped upward until the white suds were nothing but slivered remnants.

"Kache? Thank you." A single teardrop escaped, and she caught it with the back of her wrist.

His eyebrows drew together. He started to reach out, but she stepped back, so he dropped his hand to his knee. "You're welcome."

She dabbed his face with a towel. She handed him the mirror. She smiled.

She said, "There you are."

chapter

thirty-four

"SO IT IS LIKE television? I know about television," Nadia said.

Kache saw her stocking-clad feet pacing back and forth from where he lay under his mom's old desk, hooking up the modem for the laptop. Maybe he should just start with the computer itself and leave the Internet out completely. After all, that's how he—and the rest of society, now that he thought about it—had gotten accustomed to the whole thing.

Nadia continued. "It was not allowed, the television. As you understand, not much was."

"But I've heard of some Old Believers having television. Things change. Even in this house, which seems to have a supernatural resistance to change, change is upon us as we speak. Maybe your little religious village transformed into some cool bohemian colony of forward thinkers."

"What have you been smoking?"

Kache laughed. "Where did you get *that* line?"

She lifted her shoulders. "I do not remember. Somewhere I read it."

"What books have you read?"

"You mean of the ones in this house only, of course? I think you ask me which have I not read. And the answer would be—zero."

"You've read them all? Even my mom didn't claim that."

"Because she had all of you to talk with, yes? These books, they are my friends, my teachers, my family, my everyone. They keep me alive. Every one I have read at least once. Even *How to Care for Your Pet Turtle*. If I like a book, I read it at least twice. I started out, I turn each one upside down on shelf after I finish. Then right side up when I read again. But now I lose track. Some up, some down, some I read over once, some five times, I do not know."

Kache wondered but didn't ask how many times she'd read *The Joy of Sex*. Probably not nearly as many times as he and Denny snuck it into Denny's closet, making fun of all the cooking metaphors and trying not to show how completely enthralled they both were by the drawings, let alone all the helpful information. What a goddamn gold mine that book had been to them. Then there was the other one. What was it? The yellow paperback. *Everything You Always Wanted to Know about Sex (but Were Afraid to Ask)*. No pictures in that one that he remembered though, and he would have remembered.

She was saying something about getting more books. He said, "Maybe bringing the Internet in here isn't such a good idea."

"Why?"

"Because most people today read *fewer* books because there's so much information streaming in. You won't believe how much you can access."

"I cannot wait. I cannot." Her face appeared underneath the desk, sideways. "How much longer?"

Her eyelashes had become his latest fascination. She had blond hair, but her lashes were dark and long and curled at the tips. Sometimes they made shadows on her cheeks. He'd been thinking of her differently since the night she shaved his face, but it was one-sided, apparently, because she acted as if they'd never shared those intimate, almost scary moments. *It was just a shave, and she's a committed hermit*, he once again reminded himself. *Get over it and get the computer hooked up.*

He said, "Give me a few more minutes."

She sat back at the kitchen table and resumed shelling the peas. Kache couldn't remember all they'd scheduled for this week, but canning was a priority item according to Nadia. Which meant she was planning on staying for the winter. Which meant that at some point, they needed to talk, because he'd decided he wasn't going back to Austin. Even Janie had said it looked like Alaska had been good to him.

It would be much easier if he stayed at the homestead instead of driving back to Snag's every night. There were three bedrooms, and they worked until midnight anyway, and they started early in the morning. And although Snag always made him feel at home, her place was small, and he was living out of his suitcase. However, asking Nadia if he could stay crossed a very thick, high border.

He should figure out this whole soft spot for the Old Believer squatting on the family property dilemma, but still he kept showing up every morning, helping and learning and enjoying the hell out of being on his family's memory-laden land. He had one foot so rooted in 1985, Denny might drive up any moment and give Kache one of his bear hugs. He'd say something like, "Hey, Moose Legs, the kings are running. Hurry up and bring your guitar. I'll lure in the fish, and you lure in the beautiful women."

Kache now at least played the guitar without hearing the background of his father's yelling, and that was a start. Nadia had helped him overcome his fear of playing, and he wanted to help her overcome her own fears. She wouldn't speak of her past when he'd asked, so he'd tried to stop asking. But maybe he could convince her to take a step off the property. She was an Old Believer living in his old house, among all of his family's old possessions, but maybe, if he didn't screw up, maybe he could help her get a *new* lease on life. He'd like to at least try to pay her back for helping him find music again.

"I'll tell you what," he said as he crawled out from under the desk. "I will let you explore the whole world on this computer, but I want you to do one thing first."

"Teach you how to make goat cheese?"

"Come into town with me."

She dropped the pea pod and stood.

He grabbed both hands before she ran upstairs. There had been the awkward handshake at the beach, and she'd touched his face, albeit mostly with a razor, but he had never touched her like this—hands to hands, skin to skin—and he felt her flinch. He tried to make eye contact, but she kept her eyes downward, and he suddenly wanted to feel those lashes against his rib cage. "Listen," he said, trying to keep his mind on topic. "Caboose is a good stepping-stone. Don't you want to experience things firsthand before you see them on a screen? You've been to Caboose before, right? When you were a kid?"

She pulled her hands back, shoved them in her pockets, and nodded.

"Good. It's no metropolis, and we're slow to change, so things are pretty much the same. I'll be with you. You can wear a hat and sunglasses, and you don't have to talk to anyone if you don't want to. I'll just tell them you're my cousin. What do you say?"

She stared at him, shifting her weight back and forth, left to right.

"I will go if you promise to take me one place only."

"Where?"

"I want to go to Lettie."

What a moron I am, he thought. "Of course," he said. Of course that's where she'd want to go.

chapter

thirty-five

SHE ASKED HIM TO pull over so she could vomit. Her nerves, the passing trees with their long shadows, the bumpy road. Afterward, while she leaned against the truck, trying to breathe in enough fresh air to make the ground stop feeling like the bottom of a boat, he handed her a bottle of water and some gray, fabric-covered elastics. "Wristbands," he said, "for car sickness. Hold out your hands." He started to put one band on but stopped. "Okay if I help you?" She nodded, and he showed her where to place them so the white plastic button hit between the two corded veins in her wrist. She concentrated so she wouldn't react by pulling away again when his skin touched hers. The new calluses on his fingertips felt like a cat's tongue, but his pressure was light and sure. "I bought them for you a few weeks ago and stuck them in the glove compartment and, like an idiot, forgot about them until now. I'm sorry. Did you always get sick?"

"I should have brought pickle. That's what my grandmother always gave us for car rides."

"It's probably just because it's been so long since you've been in a moving vehicle."

"I am better somewhat now." She really didn't want to be standing on the side of the road, exposed to anyone from the village who might drive by, although they probably wouldn't recognize her; she wore jeans and a jacket, a baseball hat of Denny's, and Bets's old sunglasses. Her hair was tucked up into the hat. Still, she wanted the coverage of the truck's cab.

Kache was nervous too, she could tell, even though he was trying to hide it. He didn't know what to expect of her as much as she didn't know what to expect of the town. She had been here as a child, but then when her family moved deeper into the woods, their trips became more infrequent, and then Vladimir had forbidden her to go at all. But she wasn't supposed to tell her family that, so she feigned a headache or a chore she must get done whenever someone invited her along, making it even longer than ten years, more like twelve years, since she had been.

From what she could see, the town was basically the same. There were more stores and a big new building with a sign that said *The Slim Gym*. More motor homes, more people, but Caboose had not changed nearly as much as she had.

The nausea had subsided, and her head filled with the shifting colors and the laughter and the smells of food cooking and fish and cinnamon and exhaust and even perfume. Music playing from a street band and, at the same time, coming from a motor home's radio created a strange harmony. A dog barked, and another one answered, and she worried again about Leo, if he would be okay left alone in the house. He had never been without her before.

Kache turned up the hill and into an almost vacant lot and parked. "Ready?"

"No," she said, but she opened her car door anyway.

They approached a building with big glass doors, which slid open for them. The warm air hit her, along with the aromas of bacon and coffee mixed with cleaning products and the urine smell of a bathroom that needed to be cleaned. She felt a little queasy again. Kache led the way, stopping to talk to old people sitting in wheelchairs or making their way down the hall, taking slow half steps with canes or leaning on metal contraptions.

So much to see. She tried taking off her sunglasses, but even then, she could not focus on any one thing; it seemed like an abstract painting in one of Elizabeth's art books. Kache was introducing her, which made her uncomfortable, so she replaced her glasses and nodded and stayed behind him. She did hear one man ask, "Where's your guitar, boy?" and Kache replied that he would bring it tomorrow. He'd never mentioned playing for them.

He took her to a small room, where Lettie sat in a wheelchair, looking out at the view of the bay. Kache knelt beside her and said, "Hey, Gram. I brought someone."

Lettie turned and smiled, but then her eyes grew wide behind her glasses. "Nadia!"

Nadia's shyness disappeared, and she bent to hug her. Lettie was the only person who had held Nadia in the past decade, and their embrace felt so familiar, even now, that Nadia sighed and tried unsuccessfully to will the tears away.

"How good of you to come. How brave. You leave the homestead now?"

Nadia and Kache exchanged a look. "This is my first time."

"Your first time ever? And you came to this old, smelly place?"

"I missed you."

Lettie gripped her hand. "I missed *you*. Look at you. Young and beautiful and strong and full of life. Tell me what you've been up to."

So Nadia told her about the garden expansion and how the goats and chickens were doing and about the addition of the cow, Mooze. "And Leo has grown up to be a wonderful friend to me."

Kache said, "Hey, me too."

Lettie said, "Hey, you too have become a wonderful friend to her?"

Kache turned a shade of red. "Well, yeah, I guess so. I was talking about Leo. He's my buddy too. But Nadia and I are buddies, right, Nadia?"

She smiled, but she couldn't quite meet his eyes. Watching him interact with all the older people, and seeing his bond with Lettie… She'd never seen him with others like this, his goodness and kindness; he was the same with them as he had been with her.

"I miss those days working in the garden, going into town and chatting with the locals, even the tourists and all their wide-eyed wonder. Energy. I miss all that shared energy. Now you two get out of here and go enjoy some of it for me, will you? It goes by lickety-split."

But they lingered and talked a bit more, until Lettie insisted she needed her nap. After they hugged good-bye, Lettie said, "Will you please help me convince my overprotective daughter and grandson that I can handle a road trip out to the homestead?" Nadia assured her she would try.

In the truck on the way back, Nadia fell quiet, thinking how all of those people who couldn't walk or see or remember their own names were stuck in one place and that, eventually, she would be too.

"Turn around this truck, please?"

Kache glanced in the rearview mirror and slowed down. "Did you forget something?"

"Yes." She lifted her shoulders the way he always did. "I forgot to see the rest of Caboose."

❧

As they came back into town, Kache pointed to the glove compartment. "I bought earplugs too if you need them. I imagine Caboose might seem loud to you."

"Haven't you heard the gulls and crows and blue jays when they're all bickering? But thank you for thinking of these things."

"Even blue jays seem peaceful when you start hearing motorcycles and horns and fishermen shouting, so keep them in your pocket just in case."

"I promise I will not start this tearing out of my hair and banging of my head against a post if it is loud."

He smiled. "I'm so relieved." He drove up and down, looking for a parking spot so they could walk along the spit. Colorful tents still lined the beach on the north side, where the Spit Rats, out of college for the summer, camped and worked at the fish processing plant. When Nadia was a little girl, she asked her mother if she could join them.

Kache said, "Maybe we should have come a different day of the week, or better, waited until fall. It's so crazy with all the tourists."

"I like it," she said. "Please, no worrying. I am fine."

And she was more than fine while they browsed in shops overflowing with a kaleidoscope of bright things, things, things, and ate fish and chips and drank a beer and picked out gladiolas. ("My mother loved those," Kache said, staring at her again, and Nadia had to stop herself from saying *I know*.) Tourists lined up for photographs alongside their enormous bear-size hanging halibuts.

A wonderland. Rows upon rows of docked boats, tourist shops, a handful of restaurants, a bar, and the still caboose, sitting at the end of the spit. And this was not San Francisco, not even close. She shut her eyes and tried to picture the Golden Gate Bridge, the Coit Tower, the pyramid—imagine a tall skinny mountain in the middle of a city!—the rivers of people, and the clanging cable cars.

"Let's go in," Kache said, holding open the door of the caboose and motioning her inside.

It took a few minutes for her eyes to adjust to the dim light. Old photographs and tools that the homesteaders used lined the shelves. It smelled like the inside of some of Elizabeth's oldest books. A slide show flashed onto one wall. An older woman sat behind the counter, talking on the phone. As Nadia looked around, she heard her hang up and say, "Look at you! How many years has it been?" and Nadia's heart started pumping double time. But the woman was looking at Kache, not Nadia.

"Hi there, Miss Rose."

"I just saw your aunt a few weeks ago, and she mentioned you were in town. And who's your lovely friend?"

"This is my cousin," Kache said without hesitation. "Gretchen. From Colorado."

"Well, hello, Gretchen from Colorado. I taught this boy everything he knows about math and science, didn't I, Kache?"

"Yes, you did."

Nadia managed to smile, but she didn't know what to say, so she said nothing. Kache and Miss Rose continued to talk while Nadia looked at the various exhibits until she came across an enlarged photograph with a caption that read *The Winkel family on their homestead.* A couple and a young boy and girl. She didn't recognize any of them, until she noticed the way the thick braid ran down the right shoulder of the young woman. Lettie! So the man was A. R. and the boy was Glenn and the girl was Snag. All bundled up and stiff-armed in their layers of clothes, propped up on the front porch of the home where Nadia had lived for the last ten years. The home had expanded since the photo was taken and now had another floor.

She searched for more photographs of the family and then noticed a sign at another display:

> "Only one thing was certain. We weren't in Kansas anymore." —A. R. Winkel, Caboose homesteader

*"It was hard work, but it was worth every sore muscle. No
regrets. I never wanted to live anywhere else."—Lettie Winkel,
Caboose homesteader*

Nadia tried to imagine what it would be like to never want to live
anywhere else, when she constantly obsessed about living somewhere
else. She remembered Lettie telling her that she'd moved here from
Kansas. Maybe if Lettie had lived in San Francisco, she would have
never moved here; she would have been so happy to be in the hilly
city with all its beautiful architecture and views of the bay and the
bridges and museums twenty or more times the size of this one.

"Ready?" Kache stood next to her. She pointed to the sign with
his grandparents' words, and he nodded. "Yep. That land was always
imprinted on her heart."

"Was this true for him?"

Kache shrugged. "He died when I was pretty young."

❧

Back in the truck, sitting at a stop sign, Nadia asked Kache to pull the
truck over again.

"You sick?"

She shook her head and pointed to Salon & Saloon.

"That's the women's version. The guy's is called Beer & Barber.
A wife and husband own them. You can drink while you get your
hair done."

"I want to."

"We can get a drink down at the Spit Tune. Want to go there?
Here, it's more about the haircut."

"I want to get that, my hair cut."

"I thought you Old Believer women don't cut your hair."

"They do not. That is why I want to cut mine. Plus, it will be less recognizable."

"Don't you want to think about it for a few days first?"

"I have been thinking for many years about it. Once, myself, I cut it, but I did not do this good, so I only now trim the ends. I want it short and how did the magazine say it? Sassy? Like boy."

"You can try all you want, but you will never look like a boy."

"No, I want only this short hair like boy. Not to look like boy. Like girls in magazines. Your mother, she had this shorter hair, yes?"

"Yes, she did. Short with curls."

"I like this short hair. I want to have it now."

By then, Kache had found a parking place and turned off the truck. "Okay then. A haircut it is."

But as they approached the shop, Nadia remembered that it would cost money to have her hair cut, and she slowed down.

"Maybe not. Never mind." She turned away.

"You don't want to cut it?"

"No, I do it myself. This way is too much money."

"Nadia, I have money. I owe you for taking such good care of the place. Come on." He stepped toward the door and opened it, waiting for her. She paused, people veering around her, the wind blowing the bells on the door. "Hurry," he said. "My treat."

Kache sat and read a newspaper while a woman about Nadia's age, with pink-and-orange hair shaved on one side and longer on the other, looked at the photographs Nadia pointed out in the magazines. She said Nadia would look awesome with her hair short. "You definitely have the cheekbones for it." She led Nadia to the back of the salon where there were large brown sinks. Nadia sat in a black chair that leaned back so that her neck rested on the cool rim. The woman ran warm water over her head and commented on how long Nadia's hair was. She washed her hair with something that smelled like honey and flowers Nadia couldn't name, rubbing her scalp and her temples, the back of her neck. Her fingers were strong and careful, and Nadia felt herself relaxing her head into the woman's hands. She remembered her mother washing her hair when she was a child, but her mother never rubbed her head and neck like this. No one ever had, and the gentleness made Nadia's throat ache a little.

The woman walked Nadia back to her chair in front of the mirror and began snipping off long sheaths to Nadia's shoulders. "You've got so much hair I'm going to dry it before I cut anymore." The hair dryer thrummed warm and loud, and the woman, whose name was Katy, continued to rub Nadia's head and run her fingers up through the hair closest to her scalp. She shouted over the hair dryer that she just wanted to get some of the moisture out before she started cutting. While she picked out scissors from her drawer, she talked loudly of her boyfriend, how they were renting an apartment in Caboose, that she was from Seattle.

"I love it here, but there are some things you'd never guess from the postcard version. Like, for instance, the best place for spotting bald eagles? The town dump. Who would have thunk it? Kind of depressing, if you ask me."

Nadia didn't know what to say when she asked her questions like, "You live here or just up visiting?" So Nadia would nod or just answer yes or no. She didn't want to give away too much information, and then she wondered if Katy knew Miss Rose, and should Nadia be going with the Gretchen-from-Colorado story Kache had concocted? Probably. But it was too late.

Nadia soon forgot all that, and Katy grew quiet as she snipped and combed, snipped and combed. She took out a razor not unlike the one Nadia had shaved Kache's face with and started working on her bangs; the pull of it felt good, the sound of it sawing and chewing through her hair. The hair fell off, first in longer strands, then in chunks, then in smaller and smaller flakes, like the softest snowfall. Except, instead of covering everything up, it was revealing. Revealing Nadia. There were her eyes, huge and blue, staring back at her. Her ears, small. Her bare neck, long. She smiled, and Katy smiled back. "Look at you, girl. You're gorgeous. I wish I had your collarbones. And those cheekbones."

Nadia wondered why someone would want her bones, but she just smiled back. She looked completely different, like another person altogether. Like a young woman who lived in San Francisco and drove a little convertible, and when the wind blew, it didn't even bother her; her hair never got in her eyes. She could always see where she was going, and she was always going somewhere.

Nadia pointed to Katy's ears, the line of earrings going up them. "I want those too," she said. Many of the girls in the village had pierced ears, but Nadia's father had prohibited it.

Katy smiled. She had a dimple in one cheek. "You want me to pierce your ears? I can't today, because I have another client coming in. And we're not really set up for it, so my boss would get pissed. But I totally know how to pierce ears. Here's my number"—she started writing on a pink card—"and if you call me, you can come over, or I can come to your house, and I'll pierce your ears. Ten bucks a hole is all I'd charge, but you'll have to buy the earrings."

Nadia took the card and held it under the smock that was covered with her blond hair. Once they stepped foot off the homestead, everything cost money. Could she trade eggs for earrings? Katy removed the smock and brushed Nadia's neck with a soft brush. She handed her a mirror and turned Nadia's chair so she could see the back. She was facing Kache, who shook his head and smiled, smiled so big, back at her.

"Wow, you two," Katy said. "You better get out of here and go get a room."

Kache said, "It's not like that." *Like what?* But Nadia didn't bother to ask because their talking faded as she focused on the person in the mirror. *Yes, yes, this is me.*

She stared at her reflection, tilted her head. Like a woman in a magazine. Like a woman finally stepping off the page.

chapter

thirty-six

THE MORE THEY WORKED in the garden, the more the garden—and workload—grew. Kache stood, straightened his back, and pulled the spade behind his shoulders to stretch. He'd spent the early morning getting the smoker ready for the salmon, and the wondrous scent of fish and wood smoke permeated the air. The sun, unleashing itself on the bay, flashed a multitude of lights at him like he was some kind of celebrity. A thin silver band of clouds rested between water and peaks, and on days like this, it seemed he could reach across the water and leave his handprint on one of the pale blue glaciers wedged between those mountains.

Why had he hated this place so much growing up? Why couldn't he wait to leave, even before the accident? But he knew why: it was his father's extremism, the homestead zealot, that turned Kache off. It didn't have to be that way. There could be some kind of compromise, where you gave of yourself and took from the land and sometimes gave your cash and took from the Safeway. You could hook up a computer and even the Internet and live in paradise at the edge of the earth and still have a front-row seat to whatever was going down in New York City.

In order to survive, you didn't have to shoot big, brown-eyed creatures if you didn't want to, and you didn't have to leave the world behind. It was 2005. A good time to be alive.

Maybe that was the bridge for those lyrics he was working on.

He hauled the basket of potatoes and carrots and onions along with the smoked salmon into the kitchen and set it on the counter next to the sink, still full of lettuce and a cabbage the size of a basketball. He tore off a couple of pieces of the salmon and offered one to Nadia. Man, it was almost as good as his dad's.

"Delicious." Nadia sat on the couch with her legs crossed under her, the Mac on her lap, her short blond hair sticking up in the back like a beautiful Russian version of Dennis the Menace. Her lips were oily from the salmon, and a tiny track of four gold dots ran up her right ear, with just one gold dot in her left. He'd insisted on paying for the earrings as a gift, but he also wanted to pay her a salary and back pay for all her years of caretaking. She'd said no, but she might feel differently if she ever spent more time out in the world.

It was getting more and more difficult for him not to reach out and touch her hair. Could it possibly be as soft as it looked?

But he couldn't. He wouldn't. She was still skittish sometimes and reluctant to talk about her fears. She'd lived alone all of her adult life. He'd hardly lived at all most of his. They would mess each other up worse than they already were.

Still, he wondered if the span of his large hands would reach all the way around her waist. He wondered how it was that he felt so completely known when he was with her. Maybe all the solitude made her especially intuitive and sensitive to other people. Or maybe it was just that he knew so little about her in comparison.

Leo leaped from his nap to snap at a fly but missed. Kache picked up his guitar and started playing with a ditty going through his head that he was calling "Young at Heart."

"I read about a fellah who's a hundred and two.
Makes pottery for something to do.
Has a girlfriend who's fifty with eyes of blue.
Five wives behind him,
What's he gonna do?

"Sells his pottery, they say, for a thousand and two.
I'm only thirty-eight, so whoop-de-do.
Man, I think I'm coming down with the flu.
Yeah, I'm pretty sure
I'm coming down with the flu."

He kept playing while he watched Nadia at the computer, her earrings catching the light. He sang, "If you look closer, it's easy to trace, the track on Nadia's ears, whoa, oh." She kept typing. "Nadia?"

She looked up but kept her fingers on the keys. She had taught herself to type on his mother's old typewriter. Of course she had. "Yes?"

"You know that story I told you about our dog Walter and the cliff?" She nodded.

"You insisted my father might have gone down there after him. Why do you think that?"

She tilted her head. "Why do you ask?"

"I keep thinking about it...and some other things. You're either psychic or... Did you know my mom somehow? Or did Lettie tell you? And, if so, what can you tell me about Walter?"

She studied the keys in front of her, dropped her hands to her sides, scrunched her fingers under her thighs.

She took a deep breath and said, "Your mother's diaries."

He watched her watching him. Outside, a few of the goats berated one another. "But Aunt Snag told me years ago, right after the accident, that she burned them. And I saw her take them out of the trunk."

"No, you must come with me." She set the computer down on the couch next to her, and Kache followed her upstairs, up to his parents' room, to her hiding place in the closet, to the cardboard box. It was true that Snag had packed them in a box, but it was also true that she had not followed through and burned them.

"So you've read some of these? She said they weren't that kind of journal—she never wanted anyone to read them. Snag had explicit instructions to burn them."

"I think we know by now that your aunt Snag, she does not keep promises about these things."

"Did you read some of them?"

"Kache, I am sorry. I was alone, and the loneliness tightens my bones. Like a friend, your mother felt to me."

"So how many have you read?"

She bowed her head, her hair still sticking up in the back. "I have read them all. Many, many times."

He sucked in air. "Were you planning on telling me? Or just letting me think you had all this intuition and wise insight? That you just instinctively knew when to hand me my guitar? Or how to make my favorite casserole? Or weird shit, like the way you organize the pantry by colors? None of that's you, right? It's just you mimicking my mother, because you've had no life of your own." He stood and walked the length of the bedroom, still gripping the neck of his guitar. "Why don't you just change your name to Bets? Or better yet, why don't you tell me why you didn't learn things from your own mother? Since you know every goddamn thing about me since I was born—from when I said my first word and when I took my first shit to the night I screamed at my father to go fucking kill something—why don't you tell me *one goddamn thing* about you?"

He waited for her to bolt, to take Leo and run into her

room—his old room—and lock the door, but she didn't. She stood there, taking it.

"It was wrong of me. I knew when I was reading that her writing, this was not intended for anyone but herself. Yet I could not stop. It was so much a comfort. I believe her words; they keep me *alive*. The books, yes. And your mother's words also. Do you understand what I say? Alone, it would be okay to slip out of this life. But I was having a mom and a best friend and a sister all at once that kept me here. And you and Denny, you were brothers to me."

"Great." Kache stopped himself from saying she probably liked Denny better anyway. Jesus. Was he still a teenager? "This is way too weird. You're a Russian spy, a blond voyeur who's been sitting here absorbing everything I've been avoiding for the last twenty years."

"Perhaps this is time for you to read some of your mother's words."

"And go against her wishes? No. See, I *respect* her."

She picked one up. It had a blue tattered cover. "Start with this one."

"I guess I should pay heed to your recommendation, since you're the head librarian of my mother's soul."

"This is dramatic thing you say. To read them all is not necessary. But read this one at the least. And this one." She handed him another notebook with a red cover.

He took them only so she wouldn't have them, threw them in the box, took that too, and headed downstairs. He wanted to get into the truck and drive away, but he stood in the living room instead, holding his mother in his arms. Her journals had not been burned. She was there, in the box, and Nadia knew her better than he did.

Dust motes danced in the sunlight, the only things in the house that weren't stagnant. The same photos, the same afghan draped over the back of the couch. The same doodads and trinkets, the same three throw pillows, the same yellowed magazines, the same carpets, the same mismatched lamps. *Same as it ever was, same as it ever was.* He would chop some wood. That would be better than a drive, better than standing here, and it might help clear his head. Nadia had taught him a trick or two about chopping wood, and he had become much better at it than he had been as a teenager. *That* was something new.

He carried the box outside and set it down next to him. He almost saw his dad, walking in front of him, that apelike gait, hunched over, determined, not just walking the land but taking it on. Swinging the ax with equal parts ease and force. The crack through the logs might have been his voice. Then a flash of movement in the peripheral. He turned his head but saw nothing. This was different from the clear memories of his dad—and it had happened a few times. He was sure it was a wild animal minding its own business, but sometimes he felt like maybe his dad or Denny really were watching him, assessing his new skills. Crazy.

As Kache split and stacked the wood, he wished he could split his thoughts that cleanly and pull them apart. Throw his love for this place in this pile, the haunting sadness of it and the strange tricks his mind insisted on playing in that one. His desire to hold Nadia's jewel of a face up to his? In the first pile. The weird fact that she knew more about his early life than he did would go in the other pile. And so on, sorting it out, splitting the darkness and the light until he had enough to build a bonfire of the darkness and build a life with all the rest.

Enough to build a bonfire. Would he burn the journals?

He had said mean things to Nadia, things he already regretted. But…like a *brother*? Add the fact that she kept doing things that reminded him of his mother. There was Freud again, fingers on chin, nodding. But if you took all that away, which would happen in time, once they knew each other, the real person would emerge and not just these glimpses through the ghosts. He needed to know more about her—*her, Nadia*. He didn't even know her last name. Why exactly was she here? A fair question. A start. She had listened to his rage and hadn't run for cover. She was getting stronger day by day, just as he was. She could handle some gentle interrogation now without running to hide under the bed. But then her answers would move into the house too, along with all the ghosts and all the relics.

Shit, the place was already way past crowded.

Even so, he wouldn't burn those journals. He couldn't. Nadia still needed them. Maybe he did too.

He stuck the ax into the stump and started stacking the wood.

chapter

thirty-seven

LETTIE AND A. R. hurried to get the cabin done before winter busted in. While she split wood, aiming for the tree stump beneath the log, instead of for the log—Frank Newberry had taught her that after she'd hounded him—she lost herself in the rhythm of it. Up, back, over, crack, pull, her feet planted out to the sides. Up, back, over, crack, pull. Muddy? Hell yes. Her feet, her trousers, her hair even. Up, back, over, crack, pull.

The rhythm of it reminded her of the rhythm of the wooden swing her father had hung for her when she was small, intending it to amuse her for a year or two until she outgrew it. But she never outgrew the swing, not really. From the first time she got it going by herself, pumping her thick legs hard enough, she thought, *Leave the adults indoors to do their washing and futzing; this is what they mean when they sing those songs, with their hopeful words and their tears, despite themselves, slipping down their cheeks: "Nearer, My God, to Thee."* If she kept trying, maybe she might touch heaven with her toes; it certainly seemed possible from her perspective in the swing. "Nearer, My God, to Thee." It never happened like that exactly. But sometimes, with the sun just so on her face, sometimes she had a feeling. The breeze picked up her hair and smoothed it back from her face as if something—or someone maybe—was telling her she was indeed *beautiful*. She knew she was not, was quite plain, in fact—big-rumped, wide-faced, and bespectacled as she was—though everyone agreed she had a fine nose. But that *feeling*. She thought it might be the presence of God everyone talked about. She didn't feel compelled to define it. The presence of love? She didn't know the answer. She didn't have to. But it was because of that silly swing that, in her own small way, she did believe in miracles, in mystery.

So it wasn't beyond her scope of belief when, after three months in Alaska, she, Lettie Winkel, missed her first period. And then her second. At age thirty-four, she was going to be a mother. A *mother*. She watched the other women with interest. How those with babies let them suckle at their full breasts. How a woman might take her toddler's face in her hands, kiss his forehead, and pat him on his bottom as he turned to seek out more mischief. How they were always, always tending to meals, whether it be preparing, dishing up, washing up, or putting away. And in the middle of this, Lettie stood, her hand on her belly, amazed. The wonder!

There was the nausea, exhaustion too. She fought the intense desire to lie down and sleep the next seven months away, to become a bear, perhaps. But her desire to finish the cabin won out. Now it *had* to be done. And A. R., so tickled about the baby he seemed more energetic, even sang while he fit logs, started the chinking.

They finished just before the first snow. Huddled inside, with two small windows and a door, Lettie and A. R. were as proud and giggly as two kids who'd just finished their very own blanket fort on a clothesline pole.

"I love you, Lettie," he said to her that night. Ran his hand over and over her stomach. "You were right, you know. About coming here. It was the right thing for us."

"Because of the baby?"

"Well, the baby, yeah. But not just the baby. It's you. And me too."

The snow gave the land a singularity of purpose. During the summer, there was so much to do, so much to see, taste, touch, smell, hear. But in the winter, it was the silence she heard. Whiteness was what she smelled, touched, tasted, saw. A big, thick blanket tucked around her, summoning her to do nothing but rest in the womb of the cabin. And wait.

Inside her too, the baby rested. Waited. Moved about. The baby was all she thought about, it seemed. She touched her belly and closed her eyes. Tried to imagine the unseen face, the unheard cry. Tried to feel the knob of the baby's head inside her, imagine it curled into the nape of her neck, where she stroked its tiny hairs with her own strong and able fingers.

One of the younger women commented on Lettie's age. She hadn't meant to be unkind, but it stung. Certainly, Lettie wasn't young, but women older than her became mothers. She looked out and felt as cragged and ancient as the mountains. But the jolt inside her, a romp like a bear cub, and then another, said something else. There was one window of opportunity for Lettie to be a mother (perhaps it was more like the tiny porthole on that slamming ship), and this was it.

She was embarking on change as deep and quick as the Alaskan tides. She knew then she wasn't having a baby. She was having *two* babies. She knew it in the marrow of those tired bones, where earned wisdom flowed. And if she could survive the birth—*Oh please, let me survive it*—she would be the best damn mother any of those younger women had ever laid their clear, wide eyes on.

chapter

thirty-eight

SNAG SAT, WATCHING HER mother breathe. The in, the out, the up, the down of Lettie's breath filled Snag's own chest with a sweet sadness—gratitude for what had been, dread of what was to come.

She started singing her mom's favorite song. "The water is wide. I can't cross over. And neither have I wings to fly…"

Gilly stuck her head through the doorway. "I just love that song. You are one sweet daughter, Snag Winkel. Sweet voice too." And then she was gone down the hall in a flurry of nurse busyness.

Snag felt her cheeks go red and turned back to her mom. "Build me a boat, that can carry two…" Theirs had been an easy mother-daughter relationship, as far as mother-daughter relationships went. Snag grew up worshipping the ground Lettie walked on, which also happened to be the ground Lettie worshipped. Because Lettie's religion, if you chose to call it that, was steeped in those four hundred acres overlooking Kachemak Bay. Lettie told Snag she'd only been half alive before she and A. R. moved to Alaska from Kansas. She was even convinced whatever had caused her infertility had died on the boat trip up; Lettie arrived on this shore, suddenly Mrs. Fertile Myrtle. As a token of her gratitude for Snag and Glenn, she'd offered up herself—with years and years of hard work and dedication to their land.

But Alaska was the same land that had taken away not only Glenn, but Bets and dear Denny too. When Snag had brought that up once after the accident, Lettie had said she didn't see it that way. They'd loved their lives here in Alaska, doing what they enjoyed. Sure, they might not have gotten in a plane crash if they'd lived in LA or Tallahassee, but who was to say? Lettie didn't blame Alaska for the accident. But she might blame her daughter, once she heard the whole story.

When Lettie woke, Snag didn't waste any time. "Mom, I really need to talk with you."

Lettie rubbed her eyes and reached for her glasses. "Last time I tried to have a heart-to-heart with you, you ran out of the room. Or crawled was more like it."

"Well, I've been thinking of everything you said. Thinking and thinking. All this time, I didn't know you had a clue about me, and I wonder why we didn't talk about this back when it would have been helpful—back when I was a young woman instead of an old lady."

"You've still got time to get it right." Lettie sighed. "But that's no excuse for me. I thought I was being a good mom to keep quiet and let you find your way. But we didn't live in an area where you got much guidance. It wasn't like we had a gay pride parade on the spit. You could have used some straight talk about being a lesbian. There, I said it."

Snag's ears felt hot. The heat spread down her chest, and she took off her cardigan.

"But I felt ill-equipped back then," Lettie continued. "Honey, I didn't even know what a lesbian was when I was growing up."

"I didn't either. I thought I had a horrible affliction."

"That's my fault. Because, by then, I knew better and should've helped." Lettie leaned in and lowered her voice. "And then the whole thing with Bets."

Snag stared at her mom, her ears pounding. "Wait. You knew?"

"It was obvious you always had feelings for her. It wasn't a big secret."

"It wasn't?" Snag felt the blush wash over her from forehead to toes. They kept the place so warm.

"Not to me, anyway. It was all over you every day."

"Oh. That's great, Mom. Thanks."

"Honey. You can't hide what you can't hide." Lettie took Snag's hand in her own even more brown-spotted, vein-mapped one. They sat in the silence for a while, Lettie drawing her thumb back and forth over Snag's knuckles, the way she had since Snag was a little girl, as if each knuckle were a large, treasured pearl.

Snag finally spoke. "Since we're confessing all today"—though Snag was decidedly not confessing *all*—"I have a question for you."

"Go ahead."

"You're not taking your pink pill, are you?"

"Hell no."

"And you know you will probably die without it?"

"I know I'll die with it or without it, and I know I'm ninety-eight. I'm sufficiently aware of the consequences."

Snag bent over Lettie and cradled her in her arms, and her mother grabbed onto her shoulders. They held each other while the squeak of a cart went past the room. Snag was sixty-five years old, and she wanted to stay right there, forever and a day, finally fully exposed but still tight in this nook of arms where she'd always felt safe.

chapter
thirty-nine

KACHE LAY ON THE bed in Aunt Snag's guest room and turned to the place in his mother's journal that Nadia had marked with a cloudberry leaf. This is what he read:

FIGHT IN WINTER

We woke to the aluminum morning
Our fight hanging low over us
Like smoke in the cold.

Outside the smoke from our chimney fails
To rise, carves an ugly road that runs
Parallel to earth but goes nowhere.

On a warmer day, the smoke could sail.
In a warmer place, it would lift easily as a sigh
Instead of lie here a scar.

He closed the notebook. He had a decision to make. He knew Bets

Winkel one way, as a boy knows his mother. She'd made it clear these notebooks were for her eyes only, and he had always honored that. Truth be told, he hadn't had the slightest hint of interest as a kid. But those few lines revealed a side to her he'd never even glimpsed. Was he meant to? After all these years, he still missed her, at times even desperately. But he realized he missed his *idea* of her, because he never got the chance to know her fully. He only knew her in relation to him. She was the one who had fed *him*, taught *him*, stuck up for *him*, encouraged *him*. Who was Bets Winkel when she wasn't mothering him? And did he have a right to know all the things that Nadia already knew?

He buried the notebook in the bottom of the suitcase and drove to the homestead with a plan to sit Nadia down and ask her to tell him *her* life story, or at the very least her last name. Instead, when he pulled up in the truck, she jumped in and pulled the door shut.

"I'm ready for another trip to town."

"That's a change. Wristbands?"

She lifted her sleeves to show him.

"Check. Okay then," Kache said. Nadia looked like she was ready for a fight, both her arms up, fists clenched above the gray wristbands. But she was smiling. He turned the truck around. "I guess my back needs a rest from gardening and roof repair."

She made it the whole way without getting sick, nibbling on what she called her "Russian stomach medicine"—a homemade dill pickle. In town, they ordered some feed for the animals. When they approached the airport, Nadia asked him to turn in. "Does it bother you to see the planes?" she asked.

"No, not really. I've flown a lot since then, mostly for work."

"I have never flown. I would love to get on one of those and have it take me far, far away." He followed her gaze to the blue sky, where clouds lay here and there like exotic, uncharted countries.

He faced her. "That's pretty bold for someone who wouldn't get in a truck a few weeks ago."

"It's because of your help. And the Internet. There is so much to see, so much to do. But this is just talk." She held her hands out, palms up. "I will live and die here without knowing other places."

Kache fixed his eyes on the mountains. "I have an idea." He pulled the truck onto the road, onto the spit, and then into the parking lot of the Spit Tune. "First, a bathroom break," he said as he parked.

Inside the alcove, before it opened up to the main bar, he pointed out the women's room. "Go ahead. I'll meet you back here." The men's room was locked. Kache waited a minute before the door popped open.

"Hey, my friend." It was the man who'd bought Kache a beer that day, right after he'd first discovered Nadia. "I wonder if I see you here again. I forgot to get your name."

Kache told him, and when the man questioned its origin, he explained.

"I see. A man truly of this place. I am Tol. You find yourself beautiful woman now?"

"I'm working on it." Kache couldn't believe he'd admitted that and fervently hoped Nadia couldn't hear them through the women's room door.

"Excellent. Good for you! You have beer with me again?"

When Kache told him that he was just making a pit stop, Tol clapped him on the back and said he'd see him next time. Kache used the bathroom and was still done before Nadia. He waited a few more minutes before he knocked on the door. He had a plan and didn't want to miss the boat—as in literally miss the *Danny J.*

"Nadia?"

No answer.

"Nadia?" He tried the knob. Locked. He went around the corner and scanned the bar, but there was just the Tol guy watching the droning TV with the same bartender. In the old days, Rex would never have let another soul tend that bar.

He heard a door open and turned back. Nadia said, "Sorry I take long. So many things to read on wall. Why people giving their good heads away? Is this like writing or teaching?"

"Not exactly." Kache laughed as she exited in front of him. He heard a "Good day, Kachemak Winkel" from the bar, ducked, and waved good-bye to Tol.

They walked past boat after boat, some of the charters and private yachts gleaming in their showcase perfection, but most of the fishing boats—gillnetters, long-liners, combinations—rusty with history and livelihood, their decks piled with glistening, blank-eyed salmon, cod, and halibut. His dad had tried to get Kache to join him and Denny on the fishing boat, but after one vomit-filled, miserable storm of a trip, watching his dad shoot the caught but flailing giant halibuts before Denny hauled them on deck, Kache refused to go back out. He worked at the movie theater and later sang at the Spit Tune, handing over portions of his paychecks to his dad instead of helping in the family business.

Kache took Nadia's elbow for a moment to steer her, and they boarded the old fishing boat that served as a ferry, the *Danny J*, bound for Halibut Cove, the tiny artist community across the bay.

The wind pulled their hair back, teared up their eyes, and reddened their cheeks. "Have you ever been to the other side?"

She shook her head. "Never. Sometimes I dream there was bridge here, like the Golden Gate."

One of the few splurges his dad had made was taking the whole family over to the Saltry, at the time Halibut Cove's new and only restaurant, which the owner had brought in by barge during a high tide. His mom had said the food was as good as any she'd had in New York. She'd worn a black dress and a long string of pearls under her

red parka. Kache and Denny wore their best Sears catalog sweaters. While part of him wished there was somewhere to escape the
memories, a better part of him was beginning to welcome these old
slide shows in his head.

"Look," Nadia said, pointing to the wide natural arch in the rock,
which marked the beginning of the cove. "It is in the cliff, a doorway!"

It had been twenty years, but the cove looked very similar to how
it had the last time he'd visited. Many of the buildings sat perched
on stilted docks, with others dotting the hills. No cars; people got
by with a boat and a pair of hiking boots. Less than fifty people
lived there in the winter, with the population growing as fast as an
Alaskan cabbage to over a hundred in the summer. The boat held
about two dozen tourists. When he'd gone with his family, they'd
been the only passengers.

Kache leaned down so his mouth was almost touching Nadia's
gold-studded earlobe. "I'm sorry I got so mad about the journals."

"I am sorry I read them."

"Don't be. I'm glad they were here for you." And part of him was.
But it still felt odd that she knew so many details about him, knew
things his mom thought and felt that he didn't know.

"What I gave to you? Did you read?"

"No. I tried. Not ready. But I kept the two you gave me. And I put
the box back in the closet. So you'll have them."

She nodded and kept her eyes on the approaching mountains.

He said, "Let's leave all that behind for a while, okay? Today you'll
be farther away than you've ever been."

chapter

forty

THE BOAT MOTOR CHUGGED, and the bay flurried along the hull's waterline. A pink-nosed sea otter floated on its back, entertaining the tourists as if it were a paid employee. Downshifting into a purr, the captain steered the boat around a jut of land and there, as miraculous as the fact that she had finally made her way across the water—a passageway through the rock! Then the cove opened up to share its treasured secret. The water glistened and sparkled like the inside of Elizabeth's jewelry box, but nothing dazzled on the shore, which was pure and lovely in its simplicity: docked boats, small homes on pilings, tree-covered mountains plunging behind. All the years Nadia had lived on the other side of the vast bay, looking across and seeing none of this, seeing only impassable mountains.

She and Kache followed the others up the studded plank, along one dock to another dock that connected the artists' galleries. On the walls hung watercolors and oils—paintings of fishing boats and skiffs, of the otters and the puffins. One artist painted with octopus ink. Octopus ink! There was so much in this bay, not only to live on, but also to create with. And this was just one tiny piece of the whole world. What if she had stayed in the canoe and paddled across the bay and ended up here, in this cove, surrounded by artists instead of living all alone? There were no Old Believers over here. She would have been far enough away that she needn't have worried about them, except when she took the boat into Caboose. Which she eventually would have needed to do.

No. The homestead had pulled her to it; she believed that. And while she didn't believe in the way her family worshipped, she believed in something unseen, some kind of force, working, providing, demanding, providing again. Or perhaps shaping, chipping, letting her rest. Not unlike one of the beautiful bowls or vases in the galleries. How else would she end up in a home in the middle of nowhere that needed her as much as she needed it, a home stocked with everything she required—except human companionship, of course.

And then, finally, Kache.

So yes, the house had everything she'd ever need, but still. There was this cove, and beyond it there lay a world, and it was worth seeing, worth trying to capture. With nothing but octopus ink, paper, and a brush, the artist had done exactly that—captured the sweet simple buildings, docks, and boats.

"You like her work?"

"Very much."

"Octopus ink. Cool, huh? Would you like to take it home? Can you think of a place to hang it?"

Nadia had never hung anything on the walls, never moved a picture or a painting. She hadn't felt like she had a right to. But here was Kache, inviting her to change something.

She turned her head to him, raised her eyebrows in a question. He said, "Let's do it."

The galleries ran on an honor system, with a jar left out in each one in case you saw a painting you wanted to buy and the artist wasn't around. Kache put a thick wad of folded bills in the jar and lifted the small painting off the wall. "You have good taste," he said and laughed. "Or maybe it's just because we grew up looking at the same paintings and flipping through the same art books from my mom's shelves. Maybe it's not that it's good, but that it's similar to mine. Maybe we both have lousy taste."

"Never. Because your mother had excellent taste. She said so herself."

This too made him laugh. It was good to see him laughing so much. They continued along the dock and approached a young couple, kissing. They kept kissing as if they weren't blocking Kache and Nadia, like the kissing couple was alone on the dock, alone in the cove. Kache cleared his throat, and the man looked up.

"Oh, sorry, dude," the man said. The woman peeked up over his shoulder but then hid her face in his chest. "We're on our honeymoon."

"Hey, congratulations," Kache said. He let Nadia go in front of him so they passed the couple single file.

"Maybe they're Old Believers," he whispered.

"Why do you say this?"

"He has a beard. I mean, they look young, but I guess they're still much too old to be newlywed Old Believers. Don't you all get married when you hit puberty?"

Nadia lifted her shoulders. "Some do."

"Some do, including you?"

"I thought we are getting away today."

"We are. From work but not from each other. I was hoping to get to know each other away from that house and all its memories."

"Yet you are asking about my own memories. It is for me much harder work than gardening and canning to talk of these things, and much less pleasant."

"Nadia." He stopped walking and turned to her. They were at the end of a dock, where they would need to turn back or take wooden stairs down to the beach. She waited for what seemed to be working its way out of him. But he turned away from her suddenly. "Let's go this way."

On the beach, big rocks appeared almost black because of the scores of mussels that had attached themselves. A dark-headed little boy of about four, wearing a blue plaid flannel shirt, held up a mussel in victory and ran to drop it into his father's bucket.

The waves stayed small, gently licking the shore. Kache looked out across the water as he spoke. "Nadia, I want to know you. You've helped me, and I want to help you. Somehow."

"Your home, it shelters me all these years. I would say that is helping me."

"There's a lot more I can do, if you'd just talk to me."

"The computer. The Internet. These help me learn about the world. And you haven't made it that I must leave. This too helps me."

"When I went back to Austin, everything was smooth and easy. The air, the way people talk—*so good to see y'all*. The way you can walk at night without wearing a jacket and take your pick of where to eat and what live music you want to listen to. A part of me was tempted to just sink back into it."

"Why did you not?"

"Two reasons. I couldn't stop missing the homestead. I finally get it—it's where I belong."

"There is another reason? You say two."

He looked into her eyes, and she felt heat prickling up her throat. "Yeah. I couldn't stop missing you." He shoved his hands in both pockets. "And I don't even know your last name."

Now she was the one who laughed. "Is that all it will take to stop these questionings? Oleska. My name is Nadia Oleska." But what she thought was: *He missed me too.*

They stayed for dinner. The light changed and changed again to a gold-infused pink. The waitress lit small candles in old tin cans with holes punched in them so that white glowed in pointed patterns on the surfaces of the room and reflected in the windows. Kache ordered wine. They ate, they talked, they whispered, they laughed. They sipped the wine. Kache kept his gaze steady, deep into Nadia's eyes, and she let herself stay there with him. She didn't look away or restart the conversation; she looked back. The waitress approached their table but then left without saying anything or taking their empty dessert plates. The voices around them dimmed to a low melodic hum, and still they kept their eyes on each other. They had spent months together, working together, eating together, sidestepping each other, but they had never spent time like this, only looking at each other.

His hand rested on the table, and Nadia's rested not far from his. They joked about their hands—how his were blistered then calloused from hoes and pitchforks and axes and shovels, and the tips from getting reacquainted with guitar strings, and how her wrists and fingertips were sore from tapping the computer keys for such long intervals. He put his long, blistered, calloused hand over hers and slipped his thumb under her wristband for a moment. She didn't flinch or pull away.

She swallowed and said, "I do not think I'll need these anymore."

"No?"

"I am growing accustomed to motion."

Somehow he managed to pay the bill without letting go of her hand, and except for brief partings, such as while he helped her with her jacket and slipped on his own, their hands stayed together, fingers interlaced now—on the walk back to the boat, on the last late-night boat ride, rushing through the darkened sea below the purple velvet sky, to the truck, on the quiet ride home. By then, their hands pulsed with electric currents that traveled up her arm and down to her feet. When they released to get out of the truck, she slipped off the wristbands and stuck them in the glove compartment.

They kept holding hands while Leo came to greet them and Kache opened the door and she set down the painting on the kitchen table. The fire was ready to be lit, and he did so with a flick of the lighter. Moonlight and firelight filled the house as they had the first night he'd come crouching in. But that time, he and Nadia stood straight in the light, tethered together by this ongoing hand-holding, as if they might break loose from each other and this place, rambling through the stars like wayward kites if either was to let go for more than a moment. He touched her hair, her short bits of hair, touched her cheek and tilted her chin up toward him.

"Nadia Oleska," he whispered.

He kissed her. Noses, lips, tongues, lips, tongues. And she was not scared. He held her so close to him. Her solitude, her resolute oneness, slipped off her with her clothes, and she stood before him, feeling seen for the first time. His large hands held her face, ran down her arms, and pressed against her back, pressed her even closer. His jeans against the skin on her legs, his sweater soft against her breasts and stomach. He pulled her with him to the futon. "Come here."

She did not flounder. She tugged off his sweater while he kicked off his jeans, both of them laughing when one leg got stuck. Lying with him, his skin touching hers in all its hidden places, tender and wild. For the rest of that night, she was fearless, falling down and in, into this love, falling out of her mind and through her body, through every one of her pulsing veins, unfolding, unbounded, unafraid.

chapter
forty-one

EVER SINCE KACHE TOOK Snag's truck those first days and she'd had to walk, she'd discovered that she liked it and had been walking every chance she got. Who knew? Caboose was not a town designed for pedestrians. It was a quirky place with a certain charm and a boastful view—a view that melted your heart on a minus-fifteen-degree day. But like most Alaskan towns, it had been born and grown without any plan whatsoever. Buildings went up, an eyesore business next to the house of the business owner without anyone complaining. There were no zoning laws and certainly no homeowners' associations telling you what color you could or could not paint your garage door. Snag had heard about those kinds of places down in the Lower 48. Houses built so close together that whenever your neighbor farted, you felt your own walls shake. She couldn't imagine. Although one of the downsides of the do-as-you-like Alaskan mind-set was that you might have to look at your neighbors' eight nonrunning vehicles and a plethora of parts spread over the lawn for six years and counting, Snag wouldn't trade that for someone telling her she needed to trim her hedges to the standard three feet, two inches.

All this walking—past junkyards and abundant summer gardens, along busy streets packed with motor homes, and up dirt roads in desperate need of grading—created a pleasant side effect, which for the first time in her life was simply a side effect and not a long-sought-after but elusive goal: Snag was beginning to lose weight. For the first time that she could remember, her pants were baggy. Her shirts were loose. Even her bras had room to spare. And people were beginning to notice, paying her compliments, telling her how great she looked when she dropped off their latest order of laundry detergent or vitamins.

She did not look *great*, exactly. But she did look better, and she was happy about that. She felt lighter physically, and she also felt lighter in her soul since she'd talked first to Gilly and then her mom. She was explaining this to Gilly on Gilly's front porch when she dropped off her Skin So Soft and Jafra peppermint foot balm.

"Eleanor," Gilly said. She had been calling Snag Eleanor. Gilly agreed with Lettie that it suited her better. "I'm hiking the Clammit Dymit trail tomorrow. Want to join me?"

"That's a steep one. I don't know if I'm ready for that."

"We can take it slow. My friend Jackie had to cancel because she's going in for a root canal, and I don't want to go alone. Come with me."

Snag hadn't been on a hike in several decades. She used to go with Bets and Glenn and the boys, and with Lettie and A. R. and Glenn when she was a kid. She'd been walking the roads up and down with her red Radio Flyer wagon loaded with orders, and though she'd been winded and sweaty at first, lately, it had been easier and easier. Why not give an honest to goodness hike a try? When she said she would, Gilly high-fived her. "I'll pick you up at nine. Bring a sandwich, but nothing too smelly. There've been a lot of bear sightings lately."

"What would be classified as a not-too-smelly sandwich?"

"I don't know. Chicken instead of tuna, I suppose. Turkey would be okay. No fish. No liverwurst."

"You are such a cheechako, Gilly. How long've you lived here? You think a bear isn't going to smell chicken or turkey?"

"But they might be willing to overlook it, maybe wait to see what the next hiker packed."

"If a bear is hungry enough, it will smell toothpaste and break into a locked car in order to eat it. You know *that*."

"Okay, okay. Maybe just eat a big breakfast and we'll get dinner afterward?"

"Just how long is this hike?"

"Long enough."

Snag didn't sleep well that night. At about midnight, she realized she didn't have any respectable hiking boots except for Lettie's old ones, and those were at least a size too small. Snag had lost weight, but would that affect a person's shoe size? At about two in the morning, she realized Kache hadn't come home, so she worried about him. She thought about calling his cell phone, but she resisted butting in. The odds were that he was sleeping at the house and not in a ditch somewhere, and she really didn't want to wake him up, but damn it, she wished he would call.

At around four, she had visions of Gilly running up the trail with Snag hoisting herself up behind her, reaching for birch trunks and clutching at salmonberry bushes before sliding back to the bottom of the hill. Why, oh why had she said she would go on a stupid hike?

At eight, she was exhausted, hungry, wondering why Kache hadn't called and hoping he didn't do something stupid like get himself wrapped up in bed with the Old Believer hermit woman. No, Kache was too levelheaded to do something so mindless. But wait. He was a man, and the Old Believer was a woman, and a pretty and smart one, according to Lettie. Snag called and left a message and told him she was hiking the Clammit Dymit trail. She ate breakfast, stuck her feet into Lettie's ancient hiking boots, packed some water and a canister of mace the size of a large can of hair spray to ward off the bears, and tried to look cheerful when she heard Gilly's honk.

chapter

forty-two

IN THE LIVING ROOM on the opened futon, Kache lay on his side, Nadia's back to him, Leo stretched out at the foot of the bed so that Kache's feet veered off the edge. He needed to get up and get the fire going, but he didn't want to move or change anything about the moment. Other than the fact he was hard—part desire, part morning wood—everything around him was soft. The rain, the dove-gray light, the skin on Nadia's shoulder, the blanket tucked under her arm, her short wisps of hair, her sweet snore, Leo's occasional sigh. Even the stone that had settled deep in Kache's chest all those years ago might now float away, light as dandelion fluff.

Contentment. The way hard physical work let you sleep easily through the night, the way a woman who understood loneliness made you feel less alone. The way the rain might make it okay to stay tangled in bed for the day—the whole, livelong day.

He eased himself quietly, carefully, out of bed, went to the bathroom, put the coffee on, stoked the fire, and set another two logs in the woodstove. When he pulled the covers down to climb back in, he saw a large scar on Nadia's beautiful buttock. Had she had some kind of surgery? She was still sleeping. He didn't want to stare, so he covered her back up. He lay there, not exactly sure what he had seen. What he thought he saw didn't look like a surgical scar; there was something sinister to it. A strange shape to it. Like two circles.

No, more like the letter *B*.

Nadia still didn't stir, but Kache felt restless and went outside. While he collected eggs from the hens, who seemed to be having a conversation among themselves, complaining about the turn in the weather maybe, he pondered the letter *B*. He drummed up the little he knew about the Old Believers, and none of it included branding a woman on her ass with a *B*, or any letter for that matter. When he thought of Nadia's skin being burned or pierced through with a knife, he wanted to take a knife to whoever was responsible.

He knew so little about her. Nadia Oleska. He knew only that she was kind and gentle and a strong, hard worker. And smart. A Renaissance woman who could do just about anything but who also danced with birds and talked to vegetables in the garden when she thought no one was around.

And in bed, she had been surprisingly uninhibited with him. But who had she been before she came to this house?

He cooked up the eggs with some morel mushrooms they'd gathered and brought them to her so she could eat without leaving the futon, so they might spend the whole day alone on that raft, drifting and talking and touching. She smiled and sat up against the pillows after he fluffed them behind her. The rain had built itself into a frenzy of a downpour, clouds ganging up around the mountains and pinging dimples into the bay by the millions.

The shyness that disappeared the night before returned, but it was a transformed shyness. They looked at each other with raised eyebrows and closed-lip smiles, like two kids who had stumbled upon some secret, magical wonderland and now didn't speak of it or anything else, each afraid they'd imagined the whole thing, until finally, Nadia's plate cleaned, Kache blurted out, "God. That was fucking fantastic."

Nadia laughed. "It was. Fantastic fucking." She wiped her mouth with the napkin. "More please."

"Breakfast?"

She laughed again. "If this is what you wish to call it." She set the tray down on the floor and leaned back over to kiss him with a bit of rhubarb jam still on her upper lip.

The morning shed light on the things he hadn't seen the night before. On her stomach, the small birthmark like another spot of jam, the exact pink of her nipples. The tuft of hair slightly darker than her blond head, almost brown like her eyebrows and long eyelashes. He saw tiny scars scattered randomly over her torso, almost like bird footprints in the snow or the tally marks she kept carving into the wall, and there, on her left cheek, he felt the large jagged *B*. He traced it with his finger, and she flipped off him.

"What?" he asked, already wishing he hadn't touched it.

"What are you doing?"

"Nadia. What is it? Was it some kind of rite of passage?"

"You could call it this."

She lay on her back, quiet. The fire let out a loud snap, and she jumped. Kache held her tighter. He didn't know what to say, so he said he was sorry. He lay back and looked at the coal-smoked beams on the ceiling, listened to the rain and the sizzling fire, and waited.

chapter

forty-three

NADIA LISTENED TO KACHE'S heart beating until she felt brave enough to speak. She started slowly, hesitating, not sure how much to tell but then needing, finally, to tell everything. She told him about Niko and the move her family made deeper into the woods and Niko's marriage to Katarina. She told him about the years that followed and how she'd turned her focus from marriage to her studies. She started to tell him about the arrival of Vladimir, but the words caught in her throat.

"I think," she said, "we take break, yes?" They needed to go to the bathroom and refill the woodstove. Kache ran out to feed the animals, and Nadia heated up leftover potato soup for lunch. While the rain kept thrashing the roof and windows and the fire kept sputtering and breaking apart with loud cracks, they ate their soup silently.

They left their bowls in the sink for later and returned to the living room. Kache lay down on the futon and patted the space beside him, under his arm, and Nadia climbed in.

"Are you okay?" he asked her.

She nodded. "Are you?"

"Yes. I want to hear more. But only if you feel ready."

She did. In the crook of his arm, she told him how Vladimir had swooped in, a stranger who charmed everyone in their tiny village, and how once they married, he changed. He hurt her.

"Hurt you how?" Kache asked.

"It is ugly to hear this," she said. The shame felt so hot on her face. But he held her tighter, and she told him about her wedding night and the impotent nights that followed until Vladimir brought out the knife. "From then on, there was always a knife and so there was always an erection." Finally putting this into words made her scars ache, as if newly drawn blood might appear. "Soon, there was often my blood too. But never enough for anyone to see, once the bandages were in their places. He promised me he would set the village on fire. He said he is destroying everything and everyone if I tell a soul—and I believe him.

"He said, 'I will make it look like accident. A dog knocked over candle.' He snap his fingers in my face. 'Altai, the lost village. No one will suspect.'"

Wiping her eyes with the corner of the quilt, she told Kache how she kept silent. She began her tasks as if she were a happy wife washing the shirts of a kind husband. But as the evening approached, the quaking in her limbs set in and wouldn't stop, and this angered Vladimir. "He said, 'You act like one of the foxes or squirrels in my traps. Or are you shaking with desire, you slut? You are little rabbit is what you are. A horny little cottontail.'" He would threaten to cut her more severely if she did not lie still, which, of course, made her tremble more. "His anger, it grew. He liked to hold knife against my throat especially. But he would move it lower to cut me, so the wound it will not be seen. His knife began to pierce my skin; this happens deeply and more frequently, the wounds more severe. He would come back from town with gauze and medical tape and ointment. He pulls them out of bag as if these are gift, in the way some men they bring their wives flowers." In an attempt to steady her voice, she lowered it back down from where it had climbed higher. "Kache, I was very scared. But not outside our home. Outside our home, he was still good-natured Vladimir, and I do not show this fear. It was crazy time, and I myself felt crazy and ended up doing a crazy thing."

"Did you kill him? I hope you killed him."

"No." She turned her head to the side, looking directly at Kache. She said, "I should have. Instead, I kill me."

She told Kache how it went on for two years until after a night too brutal to fully recollect, Nadia hobbled, hunched in pain, along the zigzagged path alone to the beach. She climbed into a canoe, and she began to paddle.

But she realized he would come after her. Of course he would. She had to time this right. She paddled back, walked home, and made Vladimir dinner. "His frustration turned its focus on this fact that we do not conceive, and so torture, it was now long, nightly sessions. I knew I had little time before he lost control of the knife and pressed this too hard into vital organs or my veins. But I was at mercy of the tides."

She returned when the tide was low enough for her to run along the beach, but she had to hurry—the tides turned quickly and dramatically. The previous night with Vladimir had been the worst yet. The night he had carved the *B*. It was the first letter in his name when it was spelled with letters from the Russian alphabet: Владимир.

Nadia did not pay a last visit to her parents or grandmother, her brothers or sisters, because she felt she would begin to weep and never stop. She brought an extra pair of shoes and left them on the shore, full of wet sand and shells. A jacket, wrapped in kelp and thrown into the water. She left the canoe, tipped over. Her cross, wrapped and tangled around the oar. Her handwoven belt—mandatory attire, along with the cross, for all Old Believers—half buried in sand. And then she ran along in the waves, ran and ran and ran, carrying her extra shoes, wearing her extra coat. She ran until the tide came in, and then she climbed through the woods, angling west but close enough to the shore to avoid Ural.

As she neared the end of her story, the words tumbled and crashed out of her, rushing toward the finish. "I slept in the woods six nights, eating clams and berries and mushrooms. I was so very, very cold and tired, thinking I might die, when I stumble upon this homestead. I am prepared to beg for mercy of some kind. I think perhaps I can trade work for room. But what I found is this place abandoned as my own life, waiting for me to step inside." She took a deep breath, looked up at him, at the up and down of his Adam's apple, the stubbled underside of his chin, the bump on his nose, which she traced with the tip of her finger. "And so, I step inside."

chapter

forty-four

KACHE LISTENED. HOLDING NADIA, he smoothed her bangs back off her forehead. He didn't reply for some time, watching the story unfold in his mind, turning it over and over. His throat ached, and all he managed to get out at first was "I'm so sorry, Nadia."

He saw Vladimir crashing through the woods—a grizzly dressed as a jovial, strong, and devout man—who claimed he saw things their way, believed in the perfect order of their ancient faith as it was and always should be, forever and ever amen.

Fucking psycho liar.

With his fucking pervert knife.

It must have taken an unbelievable amount of courage for Nadia to leave the way she had. Kache brought her closer, trying to hold her more tightly and more gently at the same time. But she wasn't fragile. Far from it.

Later, after dinner, after Nadia carved her tally mark in the wall in the stairwell, settling back on the futon on which they'd spent most of the day, he failed to keep down one of the questions he'd been fighting.

"So your mom? Your dad? Your sisters and brothers? You have never seen them?"

She shook her head.

"They think you're dead?"

"Yes. I am certain."

"I'm pissed that they didn't see that freak for what he was." Kache tucked a piece of her short hair behind her ear, even though it did not need to be tucked. "You went through an agonizing, horrific hell, and I'm amazed at how you saved yourself." He took her hand and held it as he spoke. "But I can't help thinking, you know, from where I stand, I can't help wondering what your family would think if they knew you were alive."

She had stayed calm while she'd told the story, but her eyes filled again, and she said, "I have thought of this every day. That thought, and fear of seeing Vladimir and what he would do to me, but mostly to them, is what keeps me here."

"What if you went back to see them? It's been so long. I can find out if Vladimir is gone."

She looked up. "Gone? No. Not likely."

"People like that, their true colors start to leak through if they stay too long. I bet he's gone. If he is, I can go back to the village with you."

"No. I will never do that. It would cause them such pain. Too much time, it has gone by." She twisted the gold posts in her ear, as if adjusting the volume in her head. "Kache, you see…they have gotten used to my death. *Nado privyknut.* This is their motto: one must get used to it."

"No, Nadia. There are some things one can never get used to." Of course, she already knew this, and yes, she even had the scars. Kache held back from saying all that ran through his head: *They would be overjoyed, Nadia. They would be so happy. They would be shouting from their domed church rooftop. Trust me on this. I know they would.*

He could see them: Denny, his mom and dad, passing the big window as they walked across the front porch, carrying their gear, waving, Denny wearing their mom's old straw hat with the orange flowers and her huge sunglasses—the guy would stop at nothing to make Kache laugh. *Hey, you'll never believe this, but...* But what? What could they possibly say that Kache would understand? There was nothing. Nothing less than a story that an alien spaceship had abducted their plane in flight and cloned them so that their cloned, smashed bodies would be retrieved on the mountainside, their cloned ashes spread on this very land, and then had taken them for a twenty-year orbit. There was nothing they could say to him that would make sense or erase the pain of their absence, and probably nothing Nadia could say to her family. Still...

He held her there on the futon while she cried silently and the rain came down noisily, and they sat in a strange, time-warped capsule, the dead and the asleep, the stopped and the stalled, in this house where everything had stayed the same for too long. He pulled his arm out from where it held her and stood.

"Let's hang that picture we bought." He reached out his hand for her to take and pulled her up with him. "Come on. Let's hang it now."

forty-five

SNAG WONDERED IF LETTIE'S boots were lined with the sharp edges of knives. Somehow she had made it up to the top of the Clammit Dymit trail and was now heading down. With all the precautionary measures about not bringing smelly sandwiches, she was afraid her boots were probably filling with blood anyway, that the bears would smell the raw, ravaged meat of her heels and soles and toes. She thought of them as separate, not as one foot but as five toes, one heel, one sole—seven different points of agonizing pain on the right and seven more on the left. Fourteen different wounds that made her want to scream with each step down the mountain. She almost heard the bears smacking their lips, dripping their bear drool.

"How you doing, Eleanor?" Gilly asked, looking back over her shoulder.

"Fine! Just fine!" Snag shaded her eyes. "Wow, would you look at that view?" She used this as an excuse to stop momentarily. A middle-aged German couple nodded as they passed her. Obviously Germans because they were überprepared and had top-of-the-line shoes and hiking poles. Snag was obviously Not German.

After they were out of sight, Gilly said, "Talk about shooting a mosquito with a bazooka—although, a bazooka wouldn't really *be* overkill for one of our mosquitoes, now, would it?" Gilly had been trying to engage Snag all day in conversation, but all Snag could think about was her feet, and so she knew she was coming across as quite the dullard. That was fine. She would dazzle Gilly with her brilliance tomorrow when she was sitting comfortably in her mom's room wearing her tennies or perhaps her lamb's-wool slippers. Yes, she would wear those slippers for the rest of her life, and she silently promised her feet this, if they would just get her off the mountain and home to her recliner.

And then she was no longer thinking about her feet. It began with the sound of a twig snapping, a crash crashing, and she grabbed the mace canister hanging from her pack and held it out in front of her, her finger poised and ready to activate it while Gilly yelled, "SHOO, BEAR! GO AWAY!" clapping loudly while the crashing continued toward them, through the thicket of alder bushes on the upper side of the trail, until someone yelled, "DO NOT SHOOT!" and jumped out three feet in front of them.

By then, Gilly and Snag were clinging to each other, screaming girly screams. When they saw it was just one man, they both put their hands to their hearts and blew out sighs of relief that were so long, they seemed more likely to come from a pair of belugas than from two women with average lung capacity.

"Please forgive me," the man said. "I did not mean to scare you." The man had an accent. "Nothing like having strange-looking man jumping out of bushes," he said. But he was extremely *good*-looking, Snag thought. His eyes were the bluest—deep, deep violet—that Snag ever remembered having seen shining from the head of a human being. Maybe she'd seen a doll with eyes that shade of blue, or a pair of eyes that blue in a painting, but surely never coming from the real thing.

Gilly said, "I'll take a strange-looking man over a bear any day," and laughed. Snag heard relief in her voice. Gilly surely didn't think he was really strange-looking? Did she like him? Snag reminded herself once again that it was none of her damn concern if Gilly, her friend, liked someone.

"I did earlier this week come across bear," the man with the blue eyes said, smiling. The accent was Russian. "It wandered away into bushes, more interested in blueberries than in me."

Snag thought to warn him that the bears might accidentally pluck his blueberry eyes clean out of their sockets.

The man tipped his hat and continued down the trail. He carried sacks on his back, and Snag guessed he was out checking his traps. He was probably after fox. She wondered if he knew Nadia.

"Hey!" she called after him, but he was already around the bend.

O Handsome One stuck his head back and asked, "Yes?"

But Snag thought better of it. There were lots of Russians on the peninsula, and he was clean-shaven, not an ounce of stubble— obviously not an Old Believer. She didn't want to sound ignorant. "Oh, never mind, nothing. Just be careful."

He must have thought she was joking, because he laughed and then disappeared for good.

"Okay," Snag said. "That scared the bejesus out of me. But that was one beautiful man. If you're into men."

"You know who that was?"

"No. You know him?"

"That was the guy who tried to buy our drinks at the bar that night."

"It was? Do you think he recognized you?"

"Probably not. It's always dark in there. Which was why he probably tried to pick me up in the first place."

"I doubt that very much, Gilly. Why'd you say no?" Snag silently congratulated herself for sounding so cool and encouraging. Like a true friend.

Gilly shook her head and grinned. "Rex said he's a weirdo, remember?"

"Since when does anyone believe Rex?"

"Not to mention, the guy's too young. I'm done with youngsters. I'm looking for someone more mature."

"Well, you've got lots of *very* mature men to choose from at work." They both laughed. It was good to talk like this despite the initial twinge of jealousy. She'd been successful at squashing the feelings before they'd taken root. Gilly was a good friend, and that's exactly what Snag needed from her.

Gilly resumed walking on her own comfortable feet in their perfectly fitted hiking boots while Snag hobbled behind.

❧

Snag leaned her back against the inside of her front door. She'd begged off dinner with Gilly, saying she would just pop something in the microwave. Inside her boots, her feet lay decimated, dying. "I'm so sorry. Let's get these torture chambers off you," she said and trudged the six excruciating steps over to the couch, where she eased the boots off, peeling off her socks to assess the damage.

Forget the knives. Someone had set off an atomic bomb inside her mother's boots, and her feet were the victims of the nuclear fallout. She grimaced. "You silly woman." The cat came out to inspect her feet and even licked her little toe once before Snag shooed her away.

That's when she heard a car pull up on the gravel and then a knock on the door.

"Kache?" she called.

"No, it's Gilly."

Crap. Snag thought about trying to cover her feet, but she couldn't bear it. She sighed resignation and yelled, "There's a key under the pot of pansies."

Gilly let herself in. She took one look at Snag's feet and asked, "Why didn't you say something?"

"Pride."

Gilly silently went to get a Tupperware tub, filled it with warm water, got a towel, sat down, and pulled Snag's feet into her lap, where she took a good look at them. She bent Snag's legs and put her feet in the tub. "They're going to be okay." She went into the bathroom, came out with the Neosporin, and turned into Snag's bedroom.

"Ah?" Snag said, starting to get up but surrendering back into the comfort of the warm water and the couch.

"If I remember correctly, you keep your foot balm in your bedside table drawer so you can apply it every night, right? That's what you said when you sold me the stuff." She came back out holding the still-sealed balm. If she'd seen the photo of Bets, she said nothing.

Snag said, "My feet haven't hurt this much since the earthquake of '64."

"What happened to your feet then?"

"It was just one foot, actually. I was at the bowling alley when the quake hit. A bowling ball fell on my foot. Holy mother of mackerel, did that hurt! I limped outside, and all hell and earth were breaking loose. We lost a good portion of the spit that day. Houses floated away. Cars too."

"I remember. I lived in West Seattle, and we felt it, but not like you. The dry cleaners' windows busted out. We rushed home, and the only thing that was broken in the whole house was one saucer in the cupboard. My mother cried relief."

Snag closed her eyes and let Gilly have her way with her feet. Gilly's hands had some kind of miraculous gift. "It was crazy here. I thought the world might end. My friends helped me limp over to the drugstore, who knows why. A Band-Aid? I remember the whole town outside smelling like liquor and inside the drugstore smelling like a hundred perfumes." Snag stopped to take in the memory of that day while Gilly began applying the Neosporin. "Everything toppling onto everything else. I've never been suicidal or anything, but I remember that day, feeling like I might die and being okay with that. Knowing it might just be easier than continuing on as the confused wreck I was at twenty-four."

Gilly looked up from her work on Snag's feet. "Oh, Eleanor. I can't say I haven't felt that way myself a time or two. Now, your feet can't take this peppermint oil, but it will feel like heaven on your calves."

Snag started to protest, but she didn't have the energy. For the first time since she was a baby, she let someone baby her. After Gilly finished treating Snag's blisters and sores, she massaged her calves with the Jafra peppermint balm until Snag oohed and aahed and then, before she could stop herself, let out a moan.

"Damn you, Gilly," she finally said.

"Is it my fault that you wore boots from the last century?"

"No, but you know… You know I spent too much of my life in love with a straight woman."

Gilly stopped her massaging. "Who says I'm straight?"

Snag opened one eye. "Who says I'm in love with you?"

"Who says I didn't feel the ground below me shake and shudder the first time I heard that laugh of yours coming from Lettie's room? Or those sweet lullabies? Not to mention that first time I laid eyes on you and your dimples and every time I've seen you since?"

"But…but you're divorced. I met your daughter."

"So? You're not really that naive, are you, Eleanor?" And with that, Gilly set Snag's feet on the towel, scooted along the couch on her knees up to where Snag rested with her hands behind her head, leaned over, and kissed her so deeply, so completely, so at once urgently and gently, that Snag felt the tingle all the way down her pepperminted calves, to her tender, bleeding Neosporined toes, and lots of other places too.

chapter

forty-six

AT FIRST, TIME SEEMED to stop its forward trek. Instead, it looped around and around this beginning of Kache and Nadia. Nadia would be untangling the fishing net with her hands, but her mind stayed tangled in the sheets with Kache. She would be out in the garden alone, talking to the vegetables as she watered them—out of habit now rather than loneliness—but her mind was going over all she had told Kache. She didn't regret telling him. But the hollowness left behind felt unnerving. The hauntings giving way, making room for this…this new and vibrant good thing.

It was a good thing. But she walked around in a type of trance, forgetting the order of her chores or even if she had done some of them at all.

"Who am I?" she asked aloud one day to Kache as they sat eating breakfast.

"It depends. Is this an existential question? Or a rhetorical one?"

"Everything is changed. I am changing."

He placed his fingers over hers, which were gripping the table, gently loosened them, and took her hand. "I know. Me too."

"I am so happy. But I am sad also. Does that make sense? I think not!"

"No. But I feel that way too. We can both make nonsense together."
He took a sip of his coffee. "It does make sense though. You've been
through a lot. I don't want to rush you, Nadia, if you feel like it's moving
too fast. Or that we shouldn't be this close, you know, physically?"

She shook her head. "It's not the problem. I do want this closeness
with you. It is just, I don't know. The old sad things—it is as if they
make more noise now that they are saying good-bye? Ack! See? I
make no sense."

"We've both been *not* changing for so long. Now, it's like Mother
May I finally said, 'Nadia, Kache, you can take five giant leaps.'"

"Your mother said this?"

"Yeah. Didn't you read it in her journal?"

Nadia shook her head.

"I'm kidding. It's a kids' game, Mother May I. You didn't have it
in the village?"

"No. We had lots of games, but not this one about mothers. We have
Klushki, Lapta, Pognali, Zaets, Shalachkee, Sharovki, Knaz, Jaunza—"

Kache laughed. "Okay, okay, you had a lot of games. Any chance
I'll ever get to play *Shalachkee* with you?"

"Yes. But I warn you that I am really very good." This made Kache
laugh again. She always felt his laugh turn into a smile inside her.

❧

So time circled for days and then weeks, drawing Kache and Nadia
closer and closer, and then when they had caught up with this new
love and were again able to take care of the chores and all the rest,
time expanded. There seemed to be so much more. More time, more
life, more everything.

Nadia grew up following the Julian calendar, thirteen days and
several centuries behind most of the world. Her sense of the days

and months passing was tightly interwoven with religious observations and rituals. Fasting on Wednesdays and Fridays. More than forty holy days, when school and work were forbidden. Holy days of solemn fasting followed by holy days of feasting and celebration, full of laughter and delicious foods and *braga* to drink. Even her birthday she never celebrated on the actual date of her birth but on her designated saint's day. The days that weren't designated as holy were days of preparation leading up to the next holy day. Every hour was steeped in faith; even the clock seemed to tick off prayers.

But when she lived alone at the Winkels' house, she paid closer attention—it became an obsession, really—to the constant changes in nature that marked the hours and the days and the months and the seasons. Route of the sun, cycle of the moon, position of the stars. The life cycles of the flowers, their subtle routines from dawn until dusk, their journey to full bloom peak, their decline until they withered, hung, and spread over the land, creating a new generation. She felt joy when the cow moose and calves appeared in the spring and a sense of loss when the geese honked their good-byes, heading south in the fall. With nothing but Elizabeth's old 1985 calendar and the notches in the root cellar wall, nature provided the only milestones in Nadia's life.

Yet since Kache had arrived, every day was full of milestones, natural and otherwise. The computer with the bitten apple on its cover, the Internet, Kache's never-ending bags of products and supplies, their trips to Caboose and Halibut Cove.

And now, all the changing in the space between her and Kache, and the spaces inside them. So much had happened in such little time, Nadia simply could not keep up with it all. The plants and the animals, the weather and the soil moisture, all blended into one big blur somewhere out there; she didn't feel such an integral part of it, and that was okay. She focused on what was directly in front of her, usually Kache or the computer screen. So much to know about both of them. He would stomp on the front porch, slip his boots off, and burst in, smelling of spruce or fish, carrying eggs or a pail of milk. He had stronger muscles. He smiled more. When he wasn't working, he played his guitar and sang. His voice, his lyrics, his guitar playing— she marked the passing of time in how he got better and better each time he picked up his guitar, so good now, as if he had been playing all the years he was gone instead of only keeping track of numbers. She'd heard people in Caboose ask when he would play at the Spit Tune again. They asked him why he hadn't gone off to become a famous rock and roller. Kache would just shrug, smile, and say, "Well, you know how it is."

Nadia didn't really understand. She didn't quite know how it was, but she strove to learn. Every morning, she felt compelled to look up something new.

One morning, she drummed up the courage to look up something old.

"Did you know," she asked Kache, who had just walked in with an armful of firewood, "that there is actually information on the Old Believers? For anyone to read? Listen:

> "The schism, or *Raskol*, occurred in the mid-1600s when Patriarch Nikon of the Russian Orthodox Church decided to implement relatively minor reforms in rituals of worship, such as using three fingers instead of two to make the sign of the cross. Many were deeply offended, but the reforms were adopted, and those who refused to adapt broke off from the church and were persecuted, with persecution intensifying during the Bolshevik Revolution. These Old Believers fled to China,

then Brazil, and eventually different parts of the
United States, including Alaska. While beliefs and
practices do vary between villages, each Old Believer
village considers themselves the keepers of the true
faith, requiring followers to keep rigorous religious
practices and rituals. There is a general tendency to
live separately from 'outsiders' and eschew modern
culture. This is becoming more difficult as the
Internet and satellite television encroach on even the
most remote locations."

Nadia stared at Kache with her mouth hanging open.

He said, "Things are changing fast. I wouldn't be shocked if they
themselves posted that information for all to see. If you look long
enough, you'll probably find an Old Believer's blog."

"Never."

"The irony in all this? You have been living isolated from the
media, and some of them have satellite dishes on their homes."

"Never," she said. "Not in Altai." Kache didn't seem to understand
that if the Old Believers had not changed during the revolution or
the *Raskol*, or anytime in the four hundred years since, they certainly
weren't going to change during some little technology revolution. No
matter how many people used the Internet, her village would stay
outside of it; they would not be like salmon swooped up in the net.
They would not.

But she would. Oh yes, she would.

For so long, she had no options. But now! She could do anything
if she was brave enough. She could apply to college far away and learn
how to make films. She could live in an apartment in a big city and
find a job working in a tall glass building. She could become a teacher
or a golf pro or a biologist or a doctor. Or she could stay exactly where

she was and love Kache, as she had for the last decade, but differently, of course, because the boy in her head had materialized, grown into a man who was sitting on that chair, singing his sweet heart out to her, and that was the best change of all.

So many ways to live one life!

Her favorite poem of Elizabeth's went like this:

DEVOURED

Oh, to be young and beautiful.
I was young once
But never quite beautiful enough.
Though I felt it on a few occasions.
Usually the color black was involved.
The night of the black opera gloves
And the strapless black evening gown, the black diamond earrings.
The night a black man whispered "beautiful" in my unadorned ear.
The night you and I swam beneath a black sky in icy black water,
hot on my skin.
The night I met a black bear on the path to the cabin.
How it lumbered away, but then turned and stood to watch me
With hunger in its eyes.

If Nadia were to write a similar poem, it might be in reverse, beginning with the woods and the bear. And perhaps, maybe, the last lines would include an evening gown?

Not that Nadia hadn't explored the back of Elizabeth's closet and tried on the same black strapless gown and long black gloves she'd written about. Ten years came with a lot of evenings to fill. It turned out that Nadia filled the dress perfectly. But no one had ever seen her wearing an evening gown, besides Leo. She had never had an occasion to wear one. A long dress, yes—she'd grown up wearing a *sarafan* every day. It was interesting how the same length of fabric might be used to thwart as easily as it might be used to seduce.

Apparently, she didn't need an evening gown to seduce Kache. Because it was then, while she wore his rolled-up jeans and old T-shirt, that he closed the top of the computer so that the upside down apple with the bite out of it stared up at her. He took the computer from her lap and rested his dark, curly head there so it was Kache staring up at her. She leaned down and kissed him and kept kissing him until they squirmed out of their jeans, shirts, socks, and underwear, and her naked lap was on top of his naked lap—a whole different version of a laptop, she told him, and he laughed. He touched her with a knowing ease and intensity, as if she were the guitar in his hands. His fingers kept making new songs inside her. He pulled on the condom and slid into her, and she was amazed once again how good this sex felt, that what she and Vladimir did was also called sex, but that it felt nothing like this; it felt the opposite of this. Sex, long dresses. A *sarafan* was nothing like an evening gown. She needed to learn more words, or create them, as Shakespeare had. Kache ran his tongue around her nipple. There weren't enough words.

part three

the fall

2005

chapter

forty-seven

THE FALL CAME ON quickly. Suddenly, the pink fireweed was gone, its leaves turned dark red. Kache remembered how summer never lingered; it just up and left. But even the crisping air felt hopeful to him. Nothing but bright gold leaves hung in the birch groves, glowing with exaggerated promise, as if the hillside had flipped open to reveal layers and layers of shimmering treasure.

Why not be hopeful?

Today, his hope lay in a couple of specific things: he'd planned a weekend in Anchorage and wanted to talk Nadia into going with him. He needed to be careful; it would be overwhelming for her to be in a city. Anchorage wasn't a big city, but it was the biggest they had, and if you were used to talking to only one person and a few vegetables, magpies, and moose, it was big enough.

Because she had gone to Caboose several times, this trip would be the logical next step. It might be easier, in fact, because in Anchorage, she wouldn't have to look over her shoulder for Old Believers. As soon as Nadia told him about Vladimir, Kache had started asking around to see if anyone knew him. His mechanic, Greg Barrow, a guy he'd gone to school with, had a lot of Old Believer customers and said he'd never heard of him but he'd look into it. But Old Believers didn't hang out in the city, stay at the Hilton, shop at Nordstrom, or eat at high-end restaurants, which were all part of Kache's plan.

He had bought Nadia a gift, and so he was also hopeful that she would like it and that it might help persuade her to go to Anchorage with him—a small video camera. She'd expressed an interest in learning how to film, and he thought it might help provide a filter so she wouldn't be bombarded with everything at once. Through the camera, she could pick and choose what to see.

She sat at the table, watching video clips on YouTube. He held the camera behind his back.

"How would you like to be able to film things like that?"

"Like this?" She shut the computer. "Ach. That was only people playing mean jokes on one another. I would like to do something much better."

"If only you had a camera?"

"Well, yes, but these cost great deal of money, I believe."

"Not that much," he said and set the camera down on the table.

"This is a video camera?" Her hands fluttered around it. "It is so small!"

"It's really easy to use."

"I can use this?"

"Of course. It's yours. And please, no more talk about money. It's a gift. I want you to have it."

A smile spread across her face, and she jumped up and swung her arms around his neck, kissing him.

"Come to Anchorage with me," he said.

She let go of him. "When?"

"Today is good."

"Is this bribery that you are doing?"

"Maybe a little." He grinned. "You don't have to go. But it would be good for us to get away for a couple of days. One night."

"What about Leo?"

"He'll be fine. That's why I've been having him sleep in the barn the last few nights, so he could get used to it. And he was fine both times when we went to Caboose. It's just one night. We'll feed him before we go and bring him home a treat."

"I do not know. The city?"

"Far, far away from Altai or Ural."

"And Leo will be fine, you think?"

"I do."

"Yes."

"Are you agreeing with me or agreeing to go?"

"Both. I will pack."

Kache stood there, hands on hips, while she ran upstairs, taking them two at a time. *Well*, he thought. *That was easy.*

☙

As they stood on a street corner, waiting for the light to change, Nadia tilted her head back, staring through the camera at one of Anchorage's few tall buildings, her mouth gaping. She had recently gotten her hair cut again and another piercing. She wore a tiny diamond on the side of her perfect nose. (After many discussions, Kache had insisted he pay for these things, finally promising he would deduct the amount from the caretaking back pay he felt the family owed her.) She wore the earplugs to guard her sensitive hearing against the traffic, so she talked a little louder than usual. "Were the Twin Towers that high?"

Kache shook his head. "They were much, much higher. These wouldn't even be considered skyscrapers."

"Like mountains."

"Man-made mountains." They fell into a trance, staring at the building. Mountains and skyscrapers. Kache thought of the planes flying into the Twin Towers and of his parents' plane flying into the mountain. The light changed, and he pulled gently on Nadia's hand. "It's okay. We can go now."

There were no tall buildings or traffic lights in Caboose. So the woman who understood the chemical properties of soil now needed to be reminded that red meant stop and green meant go.

In the department store, she touched everything. "We sew all our *sarafans*, everything." She walked around all the shoes, picking them up, smelling the leather, putting them back down. She ran her hands along the racks of clothes. "I do not need these. It is too much. You spend too much of the money."

"No, I want to."

She shook her head. "I cannot. The camera? Now this? No."

"Look, you saved our entire house. Believe me, I owe you a lot more money than this. Please. It makes me happy."

"It does?"

"It does. You need clothes." He elbowed her. "Besides, I want my old jeans and T-shirts back."

Her eyes veered up, and she pursed her lips. Finally, she nodded. "Okay. But only if you promise to deduct."

Nadia circled around the floor and came back empty-handed. "How do you choose something from all of this? Where do you begin?"

"Well, let's see" is what he said, but what he thought was that he had absolutely no idea and that he didn't want to let on that he didn't know his way around the women's department of Nordstrom. He could do this. Sure, Nadia could do just about anything, but he had the upper hand on this one.

She pulled out one of her earplugs, tilted her head, and then said, "Come with me," offering her hand. She followed the music pumping from the lower level, where the younger styles were. The escalator held her in a daze until Kache demonstrated how to step onto it, insisting that she not try to film and step on at the same time. Once downstairs, she went straight to a pair of jeans and pulled the hanger off the rack. "I like these," she said. Silver studs curving along the front pockets, not unlike the gold studs that curved along her ear. Nadia had a sense of style. She picked out long sweaters with big, loose necks and tall boots that wouldn't last a day on the homestead. "That's okay," she explained. "I can wear them tonight." She picked out a few short skirts and some tights. (*For gathering coal on the beach?* he thought but didn't say.) A black leather jacket and a more practical brown wool one that fit her perfectly. Almost everything she tried on looked damn good on her. He sat outside the dressing room and kept his mind busy thinking about sneaking in and helping her shed that last pair of snug-fitting corduroys.

They carried big bags to the truck. Then he took her to the museum, but she kept her movie camera in her backpack and told him she'd been living in the past her entire life—she already knew the way people used to live. "Who cares about these things? I still use that tool right there for berry picking. And they keep it in glass case? I want to see something new. I want to see how city behaves."

So Kache took her downtown during the lunch hour. It wasn't Manhattan, but people were out walking quickly, crowding up the street corners, filling up the restaurants. Huge baskets overflowing with flowers hung from the lampposts. Down on Spenard Road, the homeless men slouched with outstretched cups and the drug dealers asked them if they wanted to get high and the alcoholics zigzagged out of the bars. Nadia filmed everything, but when she finally pulled the camera away from her face, Kache saw that she was crying.

"I understand this homelessness. If it had not been for your house, I would have died alone, outside, cold, hungry."

"I doubt that," Kache said, tucking her under his arm. "Knowing you, you would have gnawed enough branches to build yourself a shelter and a hunting spear in no time."

"You are a funny one, Kachemak Winkel." She used his full name sometimes, the way his mother had. He dug into his wallet to hand her a small wedge of bills to pass out, and she thanked him earnestly, again promising to pay him back.

When the sun began to set, she stood in front of another glass building and watched the reflected yellows and pinks and reds splash across the facade, pointing her camera at the actual mountain scene, back to the reflection, and to the mountains again.

They drove to the airport so she could see the jets and down to the harbor so she could see the last of the season's cruise ships. They walked around the university because she said she wanted to pretend she was a college student.

As bicycles and pedestrians passed them, rushing to classes, Nadia smiled, tilted her head, and said, "Did you study for that test?"

"Which one? Human biology? I pulled an all-nighter. I'm gonna ace it."

Nadia grinned. "You are very serious student of this subject."

"You're the *valedictorian*."

Kache had wanted to take her to a nice restaurant for dinner, but she opted for a movie at a theater because she'd never seen a movie on the big screen. They watched *Batman Begins*. Actually, Kache watched Nadia watching *Batman Begins*. And he took the popcorn from her to hold because she kept spilling it when she jumped.

She had never been in a hotel. When the elevator lurched, she laughed and grabbed him. Then she said, "Why is there no thirteen?"

"Because people think it's bad luck. Thirteen is supposed to be an unlucky number, so no one wants to stay on the thirteenth floor."

"So there it is empty with no rooms on this floor?"

"No, there really is no floor."

"There is only big gap of air? Layers of clouds?" She scoffed, shaking her head.

"No. They name one floor twelve, and the next one right after that is fourteen. They just skip thirteen."

"And people do not know that fourteen is really thirteen? That people on the floor fourteen are—how do you say that?—really *screwed*?"

A man who'd just entered the elevator chuckled. Kache smiled. "It's more of a gesture, I think. Everyone overlooks it."

"I have a secret for you," Nadia whispered. "People are strange. And not very smart."

The man laughed again as he stepped out—onto the fourteenth floor. "Wish me luck, sweetheart," he said.

The man was old enough to be her father. Kache wondered what her father and mother were like. Which of her brothers and sisters looked like her? Were they smart like she was?

What a loss for the family. The grief they must have felt, must still feel. He wished he could somehow talk her into visiting them. Highly unlikely, he knew. As unlikely as his mom, dad, and Denny running to catch the elevator, saying they were so sorry they'd been gone so long; they had been stuck on the thirteenth floor.

When the elevator door closed and the elevator resumed its trip upward, Nadia said, "Why did he call me 'sweetheart'? I am not his sweetheart. This man, I do not know. See what I say? Strange cookies, these people."

In their room, she stood and filmed the view through the window, the cars and the people down below. She had never been more than two stories up. She was starting to commentate what she filmed. "Here we are, on the eighteenth floor, which is really the seventeenth floor. Apparently, this is secret phenomenon. You heard it here first, folks."

"Where did you hear that?"

She sighed. "From you. About ten minutes ago. Do you not remember having this discussion in elevator?"

"No, I mean the 'you heard it here first, folks.'"

"I do not know. The movie, perhaps? Something I read?"

"You're all eyes and ears."

"And camera." She patted the side of it. "I want to make beautiful movies."

"And so you will, I suspect."

"I need to learn how."

"You mean my mom didn't have a book on filmmaking?"

She shook her head.

"Well, let's go to the bookstore and buy one, and you'll be making Academy Award–winning films by the time you flip through it."

She touched his shoulder. "You are angry?"

"No, of course not. Why?"

"You are talking funny. You are angry I read your mother's books?"

"No, no, not at all. I'm just…kind of in awe. It seems like there's nothing you can't do."

"You are wrong. There is much I have not done and cannot do. I cannot even leave the homestead until you came there. And I cannot sing like you or understand talking in groups of people, and many other things. I need college."

"Nadia, you could *teach* at a college."

She shook her head and dropped her chin.

"What's wrong?"

"I hide away in stillness, and the world spins on. I have wasted much."

He put his arms around her. "Nothing has been wasted on you."

"A mind is a terrible thing to waste."

"See? Now, where did you hear *that*?"

"Many times, in the old magazines. Advertisements for United Negro College Fund. But I am not Negro."

"No. And you might want to say 'African American' instead of 'Negro.'"

"Okay. But I still have a mind I do not want to waste. Is there United Ex-Old Believer College Fund?"

"No. But it's not a bad idea." Kache leaned his butt against the ledge that stuck out from the window. He tried imagining Nadia going to college. She looked like a college student. But he couldn't see her there, because then he would have to see his home without her in it.

He gently pulled her to him, and they stood at the window, looking out at the wide vista of city lights between them and the Chugach Mountains.

"I like being here," she said. "Way up in the sky."

🍂

The next morning, after they ordered room service and had breakfast in bed, Nadia talked Kache into singing and playing his guitar in a park so she could film him. At first, he resisted. But she had agreed to come to Anchorage, so he agreed to play a song for a couple of squirrels.

Before long, there was a crowd not just of squirrels, but clapping, foot-stomping people. Bills and coins dropped into his guitar case by the handfuls and soon covered the felt lining in the bottom of it. Kache hadn't played in public since he was eighteen. People kept approaching him, asking where he played. Did he have a CD or a website? Was he on iTunes? Kache kept shaking his head, saying, "No, man, sorry. This is all I have, right here."

A short, sinewy man handed Nadia his card and told her to have Kache call him. Nadia laughed when she showed it to Kache. "As if I am in charge of you. Your boss."

"He owns a bar. He probably thought you were my manager. Like a guy playing for pennies at the park has a manager."

"Pennies? You make three hundred fifty-seven dollars."

"*You* made it. It was your idea. You were the event coordinator. And you inspired their favorite song. Did you see how much they liked the 'Nadia, You Unknotted Me' song?"

"Everyone was clapping to it, and some even danced."

Kache lifted his shoulders. "I just showed up and played, so give me ten bucks and we'll call it good."

"Really? I have never had money."

"That three hundred forty-seven bucks will last you a long time back at home."

Her eyes flashed, and she started to respond but stopped.

"What?" he asked.

"Nothing. It is very much money. I know it will not pay for all, but I want to pay for some of my clothes, not only this deduct you pretend to do."

"Wait. I have an idea. Put this in your college fund."

She smiled at that and agreed that she would.

❧

Nadia slept the entire four-hour drive to Caboose. She had been a trooper, but although she seemed to want to take the whole city in her arms and bring it back with them—a huge bouquet of street-lights and cars and people and buildings—she was also exhausted by it.

His cell phone rang. It was Greg Barrow, reporting that Vladimir

Tolov had left the Old Believer village about ten years ago. None of them had heard from him since. He'd asked around town too, and no one he'd talked to knew him.

Kache thanked Greg and pulled into the Caboose Safeway parking lot to pick up a few things they needed. The news about Vladimir wasn't a surprise. Still, he couldn't wait to tell Nadia. But she was sound asleep. He would just be a minute. He covered her with his jacket so she wouldn't get cold and locked up the truck, cupped his hand against the window, and looked in. She was so tired and so pretty. He'd surprise her with a bag of peanut M&M's. She couldn't get enough of the things.

Inspired by the Halloween display, he grabbed a fancy, five-piece carving set. The photos on the back looked like the pumpkins had been carved up by Renoir. Those definitely hadn't been around when he was a kid—at least, not in Caboose.

In the dairy aisle, while he checked dates on yogurt, he heard a familiar voice sing, "My boyfriend's back and he's looking at the yogurt. Hey la, hey la, my boyfriend's back."

He turned to see Marion pushing a cart up the aisle. "Hey, Mare," he said and gave her a hug.

"I keep telling the guys you'll be down to the Spit Tune. I say, 'Don't worry. He *promised.*'"

"I did?"

"Practically. Almost, anyway. How's it going?" Her dark eyes went from teasing to genuine. "Snag said you're working hard at the homestead. God, I'd love to see that place again. Lots of memories. Is it tough to be out there?"

"Thanks for asking. Actually, I'm enjoying it. Surprised?"

"Yes. But I'm glad to hear it. Glad you're back too. I've missed you, Kache."

Marion would make a good friend for Nadia. The thought of

Nadia made him drop his yogurt in the basket, grab a gallon of milk, and say, "I've gotta run."

"Kache, I—"

"I really am going to try to come play with you guys soon."

They kissed cheeks, and he rushed to the candy aisle to grab the peanut M&M's.

chapter

forty-eight

IN NADIA'S DREAM, KACHE was singing, interrupted by Russian voices calling back and forth as if she'd last heard them only hours ago instead of a decade. Some were complaining about the cost of toilet paper, and she wondered how this fit into her dream about flying from building top to building top with Kache. Then there they were, a few Old Believers soaring alongside them, asking one another if they remembered to pick up the oranges that were on sale. It would be good to have the oranges. And then they were throwing the oranges at her, and she woke up, sitting up in the truck. Where was Kache? Where was she?

The Safeway parking lot. And in front of her, two Old Believer women in their bright, printed *sarafans*, loading groceries into their truck. Did she know them? Had they seen her? She lay back down, straining to hear, but they said nothing more. The doors slammed, the engine started, and the headlights glared through the windshield while Nadia kept her face pressed to the vinyl seat. Those women could have been her little sisters, and she would not know them by their voices, and perhaps not even by their faces. They were ten and eleven when she last saw them. Now they were older than she had been then, wearing two braids instead of one. Married. Grown women with families who went shopping for oranges and paper towels. It could have been her sisters or someone else from the village. It even could have been Katarina.

When Kache finally unlocked the door, she bolted up. She shook all over. "Why did you leave me?"

He apologized before she told him what happened and then apologized again after. He was sincere, but she still could not believe he left her like that, asleep and unaware. Anyone might have wandered up to the truck and seen her.

"Will these help my standing?" He held out a bag of the chocolate-and-peanut candies she loved.

She grabbed them. "No. But I will eat them anyway."

"I won't ever do that again. No matter how peaceful and beautiful you look sleeping, I will wake up your sorry ass. Deal?"

"My sorry ass? What are you saying? Because of the scar you say this?"

"Nadia. Oh God, no. I am so sorry. It's just an expression. I wasn't thinking." They were quiet until they pulled onto the road that led out of town. "I'm an idiot."

"What if Vladimir had seen me?"

"Vladimir is long gone."

"How are you this certain?"

He tried to take her hand, but she slipped out of his grasp and folded her arms. He let out a long sigh and rubbed his eyebrows with his thumb and forefinger. "I've asked around." He told her that his friend the mechanic knew many of the Old Believers and had found out about Vladimir from numerous sources.

"So he has been gone all this time?"

"He has." Kache stayed silent for several miles until he said, "I bet he went back to Oregon. You said he wandered into your village one day, telling a tale, right? There were no other women of marrying age."

Nadia's face fell into her hands. "I worry about my sweet sisters, if he somehow got to them. I only fled. I didn't protect them."

"You protected them and yourself by leaving. He told you he would kill them all if you said anything. My guess is he moved on a long time ago. Your sisters weren't of age yet, right? There was nothing for him there. Nadia, I can go and scope things out, pretend I just took a wrong turn."

"That is old trick. It is not possible to just wander in without trying with all your might to find this place. You can so-call 'wander' into the bigger village, Ural—even though everyone knows you are snooping, they will probably be friendly. But you have to hike into Altai or take ATV. They are not believing it was accidental, and it may make them suspicious, especially if you ask any questions related to me."

A truck approached from the other direction, and she dove down to the floorboard until they passed.

"We've got to think of some solution so you don't have to hide. Look, you've been hinting around about going to college. You went to school when you lived at home, right?"

"Of course. I learn English, math, many things."

"Then you're going to need your school transcripts, the record of your education, and your birth certificate too."

She stared at him. "Shit damn."

He smiled. He always smiled when she swore, which seemed to make it less effective, less satisfying, but she still liked to swear whenever the occasion called for it. "Shit," she said again.

"They say it happens," he said and reached across the back of the seat to place his large hand on that soft space he liked between her shoulder and her neck.

chapter

forty-nine

AS SLEEP DEPRIVED AS she felt with all the late-night goings-on with Gilly, Snag set her mind to scheduling a dinner with Kache out at the homestead. She hadn't seen him in weeks. She dialed his number as she walked, pulling the wagon with her deliveries, waving to the passersby who called out to her. Kache didn't answer, which wasn't a big surprise. He was busting out ten different projects. But Snag swore she'd keep calling until they set a date.

Nadia had been allowed more than enough time to acclimate to people. She'd been in town—Snag had heard it from about five different people. Something about Kache's cousin.

Ha! More like kissing cousin. If she could sleep with Kache, she could certainly say howdy and shake hands with Snag. She'd been out to see Lettie and even to Anchorage, for Pete's sake.

Not that Snag had minded delaying the visit for her own reasons. But now she was determined to face down her failure and her breach and stand herself in that house, come what may.

Snag had procrastinated on scheduling the dinner for another reason besides her own issues and trying to accommodate the Old Believer: it was worry over Lettie. Lettie wasn't very strong, and it was a long trip, a long way from the hospital if anything should go wrong. Since they'd stopped giving Lettie the blood pressure meds, she was doing much better mentally. Snag knew that wasn't so physically. But Gilly had said she'd go, and since Gilly was a nurse, that made Snag feel better.

Kache and Snag kept missing each other at the Old Folks', playing a lot of phone tag, leaving rambling messages to keep each other caught up. The fact that he was not only sleeping with, but also *living* with this woman gave Snag some concerns. But it wasn't her business. She was finally in her own business, and what a joyous relief. She was sixty-five and in love, and for the first time, someone loved her right back.

But she had to at least get out and meet Nadia. It was odd, first of all, that Kache was involved with a woman from the Old Believer village—it wasn't like they mingled with the heathen much. But even odder, Snag herself had once, long ago, had an encounter with an Old Believer. At least, she was pretty sure she was an Old Believer. It was so long ago but still vivid in her mind. The Winkels' was the very last homestead before you reached the remote Russian villages, so Snag supposed that if any family were to have multiple rendezvous with Old Believers, it could very well be the Winkels of Caboose, Alaska.

❧

Snag was thirteen years old, down at the beach, loading the wheelbarrow with coal and a metal pail with mussels. It was one of those summer days that stretches on and on. She was content, alone, with the sunshine warm on the back of her neck and arms as she foraged among the rocks. The tide was out, and it was so bright that the dimpled wet sand mirrored the mountains. She heard something and looked up, half expecting the bear and cubs they'd been spotting all summer, but instead, she saw a girl about her age, strolling down the beach. She wore a long, brightly flowered dress and carried a kerchief, her blond hair blowing behind her. She walked directly up to Snag and said hello. Snag heard an accent but didn't know where the girl was from. She could have come walking across the water from the USSR for all Snag knew.

The girl asked if she had water, and Snag let her drink from the thermos. The girl said, "I walk much farther than I plan. Are you boy?"

"No."

"But your hair is short and you wear trousers and you are tall like boy."

"Yep. That's right. But I'm a girl."

The girl flung her hair so that the wind caught it again, a silk flag threaded with gold. "I am girl also."

"Obviously."

"I am married. I am going to have baby."

"No way. You're too young for all that."

"It is because of my culture." Her lip trembled, and her chin crinkled up.

Snag nodded as if she understood.

The girl said, "You have this pretty face. Like pretty boy."

Surprisingly, this didn't sting. It sounded like a compliment. Snag grinned despite herself.

"Will you do me favor?" the girl asked. "This secret favor?"

Snag nodded, knowing she would do whatever the girl asked.

"Will you kiss me?"

Kiss her? That was the last thing Snag had imagined, but it began to seem like the most natural thing in the world, kissing this girl, on this beach, on this day.

So Snag said, "Yes." She set down her pail of mussels next to the wheelbarrow half-filled with coal, and she placed her arms around the girl's waist, the way she had seen men do in the movies. The girl knew what she was doing far more than Snag did, which, of course, wasn't saying much, but they managed to kiss and kiss some more. It still remained one of Snag's sweetest, loveliest memories. They took a break from the kissing and watched the sky settle into layers of reds, yellows, and lavenders, which reflected in foam cresting the quieted waves. Eventually, the girl rose from where they'd been sitting on a large piece of sun-bleached driftwood. She said, "Tide returning. I must to go back."

Snag asked, "Can you meet me here tomorrow?"

"No. I cannot come back again. Not ever."

Snag hung her head.

"We feel sadness together." The girl reached out and hugged Snag, and Snag held her tightly against her chest, where deep inside, she felt something shift, a permanent settling in. "Good-bye."

"So long," Snag said.

The girl let go and began to work her way back along the beach in the direction from which she'd come. Then she turned. "My name," she called out over the cries of the gulls, "is Agafia!"

❧

As vivid a memory as it was, Snag wondered many times if she'd merely imagined her. Snag was young, confused. She knew enough not to try to kiss any of her friends at school. There really weren't any she *wanted* to kiss. And then this girl with lips the color of fireweed came out of nowhere and disappeared just as quickly? Maybe it was nothing more than a desperately needed daydream of a perplexed adolescent. Still, she found herself on that particularly ordinary day pulling her red wagon with vigor, the wheels turning as her mind turned up that name: Agafia. Strange, the things we remember.

❧

As Snag rounded the bend above the McNicols's Jellies and Jams shop, she spotted a row of cormorants resting on a driftwood log, holding their wings open to dry like flashers exposing themselves. "Why, aren't you proud of yourselves?" she said.

Her phone rang, but the birds just stared at her like they were beyond annoyed with cell phones. It was Kache, inviting her and Lettie to Thanksgiving. After she asked what to bring, she asked if there was anything she needed to be careful about, that might offend Nadia.

"What do you mean?"

"You know, the religious thing. There must be a lot she doesn't approve of."

"Aunt Snag, I told you. She isn't an Old Believer. I mean, she came from them, but she doesn't subscribe to their belief system."

"I see." Snag felt as if she had one leg over the edge of a bridge. She didn't know if the water below was freezing or warm, too shallow or deep enough, but it called to her just the same. "So, Gilly's going to come with us. Is that okay? I thought it would be good for Mom to have a nurse out there."

"Of course. That would be good. I like Gilly."

"Me too. A lot."

"She's great."

"She's incredible," Snag added. "Did I tell you?"

"Tell me what?"

"Oh, just that Gilly is my girlfriend."

"Yeah, I know you're friends. You've been hanging out at the Spit Tune, right?"

"And we go other places." Snag stopped walking to catch her breath and steady herself. "Like bed. We go to bed."

"Oh?" And then, "Ohh. Oh, I get it." And then, "That's cool."

"Is it? Cool with you?"

"You know what I really want to say, Aunt Snag? Good for you. It's about fucking time. I'm happy for you. In fact, that just made my day."

A lump in her throat. Some days, it just felt like the whole world was on your side. "That's sweet of you, Kache. Thank you. And I'm looking forward to meeting your Nadia."

"Better not call her mine. It might get me in trouble. She might start quoting Mom's Betty Friedan books."

"Well, good. I like her already." Snag realized she liked everybody at that moment. Kache was cool with her and Gilly. Of course, she'd left out the other part he wouldn't be so cool with. *One step at a time,* she told herself as she took the last hill toward home.

chapter

fifty

How to explain to my passionate ten-year-old son that his beloved dog Walter was a broken and battered pile of agony at the bottom of a cliff? I can't. I won't. Glenn made his way down the treacherous drop—God only knows how he didn't kill himself in the process—to see if he could save our dear, sweet Walter, each step full of such consternation, knowing our dog would be dead or worse.

It was worse. Glenn said that when he found him, Walter was beyond any hope and suffering so that he looked to Glenn with those big dark eyes and begged for him to end the pain. I'm crying still as I write this. Glenn, of course, had brought a gun and didn't cry in front of Walter, but after he pulled the trigger, he confessed to me that he dropped to his knees, holding Walter to him and howling like they were of the same species. We all loved that dog. Glenn loved that dog. But he said he knew how much Kache *needed* that dog. And so we must lie to our own son. And this command from Glenn, who is so matter-of-fact about life and death. "It is too much for the boy," he told me, crying again. "We need to tell him the Disneyland version." And so I did, but I'm afraid it was a mistake, because Kache looks at us with an underlying suspicion, though he doesn't say anything.

KACHE CLOSED THE JOURNAL and stuck it under his arm, heavy-hearted and mystified, thinking about Walter. And his dad. It was a different version from what he'd been rehashing in his mind all these years. His father said that? *To protect Kache from the truth?* He had seen his father only as a bully. But now Kache wondered if there was another side to the man. Why else would his mother have stayed with him? She was a kind woman, a smart woman, a strong woman. She must have seen *something* in him.

Kache walked out to the canyon, and though he saw it from a new angle, it remained impossibly deep. It still scared him.

❧

They had dropped the subject of visiting Nadia's family, but that didn't mean Kache wasn't thinking about it. Now that they knew Vladimir wasn't in the picture, Kache wanted Nadia to let her family know she was alive. Reconnect with them, free herself from the grip of her painful past—who wouldn't want that? To live fully here at the homestead, she needed to be able to go into town without ducking for cover.

The college application seemed to be the strongest motivator, but she hadn't mentioned it again, and Kache suspected that Nadia liked the idea of being accepted and going to college, but just the idea, not the reality of actually leaving and traveling somewhere else to live. It would be years before she'd be ready to move away, if ever. Most likely never. That was what he kept telling himself.

He kept quiet about her family. It was her decision.

The last of the garden had been harvested. The last of the canning was done. He walked back home and set the journal inside. Then he headed back out to finish stacking the bales in the barn. Nadia was milking Mooze. When she finished, she pulled her video camera out of her pocket, filming Kache as he stacked the hay.

"Another exciting day at the homestead," he said, hamming it up.

"No. Natural," she said. So he finished his work, wondering what winter would be like, Nadia and him burrowed in the house under the new down comforter while the snow piled up and up around them for days on end. Board games, cards, movies, books. Few responsibilities except to make sure the animals weren't freezing to death, keep the fire stoked, dig out between storms, maybe knock down the icicles when they got so big that they threatened to pierce them.

The temperature had plummeted, but they hadn't seen a hint of snow yet. He knew that once winter set in, it would be harder to get back to Nadia's family's village. Nadia must have been thinking the same thing, because later, when he came back from checking the nets at the beach, she met him at the door, wearing her new brown coat and new jeans, along with her hiking boots they'd bought from the catalog—not the stylish ones from Nordstrom.

"I'm ready. Let's go," she said before he had a chance to pull his own boots off.

"Go where?" he asked, but he knew. Her eyes seemed bigger, like they had that night when he first saw her face peeking from under the bed.

She crammed her hands into her coat pockets as if she were plugging them into a source of courage. "The village. Come, let's go."

"Why this sudden change?"

"You read your mother's story of Walter."

"I did."

"And this is something you are afraid to do, yes?"

"Yes."

"And it is good that you read it, yes?"

He nodded.

"I am ready. I want to be brave also. And I see how much you miss your family and what a gift it would be to see them. You can't. But me, I have ability to make this trip. And the tide, it is very low and will get lower. Besides, if I am going to get my transcripts and birth certification for college, I must go now." She sounded like she was presenting all the reasons to herself more than to Kache. She headed for the truck, her determined, long-legged strides reminding him of a moose starting across the road no matter what. She opened the truck door, closed herself in, and rolled down the window. "Hurry before my mind changes or this tide comes in."

chapter

fifty-one

IF THERE WAS A way to present herself in the most favorable light and still be truthful, Nadia did not know of it. That morning, she had tried on her *sarafan*, the colors still fairly bright because she never once wore it after she'd first arrived at the house. She covered her head in a scarf. She stared at her reflection, her cropped bangs peeking out, her earrings, the tiny diamond in her nose. She looked like a gypsy. She did not feel like herself at all, and the one thing she wanted was to present herself truthfully. There was no redemption in facing a lie with more lies. She changed into her new clothes and tried to imagine what her family's reaction would be. Would they recognize her? There was also the temptation to present Kache as her husband and not her live-in lover. Neither was ideal, but a marriage would certainly be preferred. Except what if Vladimir was still there? What if he still claimed she was his wife? They would think of her as an adulterer. And that would only be the beginning.

She should not think ahead this much. As they bounced and swayed along the drive up to the main road, she felt for the old handgun in her coat pocket.

She inhaled deeply and said, "I do not know what to expect. But I do know we will be miles from anyone who can help us if Vladimir is there and threatening us. Therefore, I have one of your father's pistols in my pocket."

Kache raised his eyebrows. "That's probably overkill. So to speak."

"I think you are right. I hope you are right. But in case you are not."

"Do me a favor and at least put it in the glove compartment."

She obliged, taking out the pair of sunglasses she kept there and putting them on, even though metallic-rimmed clouds shrouded the sun and seemed to have hooked themselves on the jagged tips of the mountains. When they reached the end of the five-mile private drive, Kache turned right onto the main road, toward the villages, instead of left toward Caboose.

She'd started on this trip back many times over the years, when the isolation chiseled her fear down to a sharp root. She wanted her mother and father, her sisters and brothers. She heard the folk songs they would break into around the dinner table. She would sing them in Russian, alone in the house, her lone voice eerie, not in any way comforting: *Farewell, curly locks. Farewell, auburn hair. Farewell, blue eyes. I won't be seeing you again.* She would cook some of her mother's dishes—the *leposhki* and *rebnea katlette*—and sit down at the table by herself. A bite, warm, delicious—browned bread dough pancakes, the salmon and mashed potato balls—but she could not get much of it past the lump in her throat.

She'd pack a small bag, picturing her parents' full house, the noise, the laughter, the teasing, the scolding. But also, the plenty she did not miss. Even if she had married Niko instead of Vladimir, she would no longer fit back into the village. The role of being a *khoziaki*, a house-hostess, the pressure to have children one after the other. The tight, unyielding grip on a way of life that she believed was meant to be left where it belonged, hundreds of years in the past. She did not fit in with people who separated themselves over how many fingers they used to make the sign of the cross when she did not feel compelled to make the sign of the cross at all, no matter how many fingers.

No, all of that would fade away once she hugged her mama and papa again. But then there was Vladimir. Always Vladimir.

And so she would unpack her bag and go out to the lone birch tree and rest her forehead against it. "You understand," she would say. "You are not in the grove with your brothers and sisters and mother and father. I will come and talk to you, and we can ease each other's sorrow. The sparrows in your branches sing and from my hands eat. It is good for you to be here and for me to be here." This brought comfort until another bout of loneliness would take over and she would go through it all again. Sometimes it was the birch tree that would bring her back to herself. Sometimes it was the garden, or Leo, or the noble mountains across the bay. Lately, it had been Kache and the video camera.

If she were to present her truest self to her family, it would be from behind her camera, with Kache at her side, filming her parents and brothers and sisters—how odd that was, yet also true! But her parents were leery of photography of any kind, so the camera had to stay behind.

"This is Ural, where I grew up. Where we lived before the split," she told Kache as they approached her old village on the bank near the end of the road, a spread of brightly painted structures—houses, barns, a church—and plenty of tractors, trucks, SUVs. Satellite dishes?

"I told you," Kache said, as if he could read her mind.

"I am shocked. But Altai will not have this. Ural is more conforming." What she thought but didn't say was *This is where Niko and Katarina live with their children.* She wondered how many they had, if they lived in one of the houses she could see.

Kache had originally turned on the heat in the truck, but Nadia had turned it off miles ago. Still, a trickle of sweat ran down her rib cage. She felt sick to her stomach. It wasn't car sickness. Kache spoke to her, and she watched his lips move, but she barely heard him over the thrashing of her heart.

Returning was a very stupid thing to do. "Turn around," she said. "Turn *around*."

Instead, he pulled over. "Breathe. It's going to be okay."

"You do not know this. And do not stop in Ural. That is the invitation for them to approach us."

"Do you want me to keep going?"

"No. Yes. Wait," she said. She took one deep breath. "Okay, yes, keep going."

And so they drove on, until they rounded the last bend where the empty trailhead to Altai seemed to be waiting for them. Kache parked the truck, and Nadia reached for the glove compartment.

He said, "At least let me carry it."

"Kache," she said. "I mean no disrespect. But I have shot guns many, many more times than you have."

"Everyone will be hugging you. It won't be safe." He held his hand out, and she gave him the gun while she hoped and doubted and hoped again that her family would indeed hug her. "Don't worry," he said. "I promise not to shoot my own foot. It will most likely stay in my zipped pocket, with the safety on."

They began taking the switchbacks down to the beach. Nadia had already checked the tide schedule online and knew they had plenty of time to walk along the sand to the village. There was no other way in. They could have brought the ATV in the back of the truck, and if it had already snowed, she would have insisted on it. But she was glad for the time the walk took. It helped calm her nerves. Alone on the trail, Kache stopped, hugged her, and then kissed her. She remembered the time on the same trail when Niko had kissed her. It was her first kiss, snuck in, before they raced to catch up with the others.

But now, Kache and Nadia took their time. He lifted her sunglasses. "Are you okay? Do you want to keep going?"

"Do you mean keep kissing or keep walking?"

He smiled. "Either one. Both?"

"That might be difficult."

"Yeah, I suppose." He let her sunglasses fall back in place, kissed the diamond stud on the side of her nose, and turned to lead the way.

They continued down the trail. At one point, Kache bent to inspect bear scat.

Nadia examined it. "This, it is not fresh. We can always fire gun into air to scare one."

Kache gave her a look that said firing the gun might scare him worse than it would scare the bear.

The trail dropped them onto the beach, where they jogged a bit toward the end of the bay—not because they were in a hurry (they definitely weren't) but because they needed to expend their nervous energy. A lone bald eagle watched them from its perch on the top of a dead spruce where the forest met the sand. The bay had receded. The distant waves slammed out their rhythm, marking time. Almost ten years before, Nadia ran down this beach, but in the opposite direction.

She took Kache's hand, and they slowed to pick their way along the rocks, dodging driftwood, tide pools, piles of long, tangled kelp, chunks of coal. Gulls bickered over a dead lingcod. Nadia bent over an aggregate anemone. Its green tentacles seemed to invite her in, and when she placed her finger in its center, they gently grasped onto it, holding tight until she pulled back and they let go.

The clouds had darkened and swept toward them, locking the sky in, low and gray. She wished for the sun to break through and lighten her mood, which also felt low and gray, as if the sky were a lid pressing down on them. She half worried, half hoped that she wouldn't be able to find the next trailhead to Altai, that it would have been taken over by salmonberry and alder bushes. She couldn't even be sure the village was still here. Perhaps they had given in to having a priest and returned to Ural.

But there was the second trailhead, as it had been before, cleared, dirt-packed, steep switchbacks that took you one way and then another in an indecisive reverie climbing upward. Where before she had been sweating, now she pulled her coat tighter around her. Chills. Her body balked, wondering when she would turn around. She'd never come this far, not even close.

The trail seemed shorter than she remembered, and too soon, they came upon Altai, too late to turn back, because children already peeked out from behind women's long skirts and men walked toward her and Kache. Nadia's eyes filled with tears, so she could not see who these men were, whether she knew them. They spoke in Russian, greeting Kache, but when he looked to Nadia, they switched to English.

"Brother, can we help you? Are you lost?" a tall man asked. Nadia did not recognize him or the others.

"We're hoping we can speak with you."

At the word *we*, the men looked Kache and Nadia over. "What would you like to speak about?"

Nadia took a step toward them so that she was slightly in front of Kache. She said in the old Russian, "I need to talk to Irina and Dmitri Oleska. I have important information for them."

The man who'd first spoken nodded. "We will take you to their home."

Nadia said, "I appreciate your kindness, but that won't be necessary. I know where it is located. Thank you." She motioned with her head to Kache, and they walked off toward her old home.

The group that had formed followed along behind them, with

some of the children prancing ahead, calling out to her parents, "Irina, Dmitri, the strangers have come to see you!"

Nadia shook. A young woman broke through the crowd and approached her.

"If you please? Take off your glasses so I can see your eyes," she said.

Nadia took off her glasses, but her tears were already escaping, running down her cheeks. "It is me, little sister. Anna, I am your Nadi."

Anna cried out and reached her arms around Nadia, and they fell to the ground, embracing. And then Anna was yanked away, Nadia was pulled to her feet, and her mother—a bit thinner and more lined—held Nadia's shoulders and looked deep into her eyes. Her mother cupped her chin and the side of her neck. Then she slid her grasp down both of Nadia's arms. Her lips trembled, her pale eyes wet with questions. "Nadi? Nadi?"

"Yes, Mama."

"It is miracle? God has brought you back to life?"

"No, Mama. I have been alive all this time. Always alive." Nadia lay her hand flat along the side of her mother's cheek. "I am so sorry."

"You are alive? You are *alive*." Her words croaked out in the midst of laughter and cries. And then her father was twirling her around and around, holding her waist. More crying and laughter. The entire village quaked as if the land under it shifted. No one asked, "Where have you been?" or "Who is this man?" Everyone was far too overtaken by emotion, too busy praising God for the miracle to ask the obvious.

The crowd suddenly grew quiet and parted. Nadia's grandmother approached her with her crooked smile and wet eyes.

"Hi, Baba," Nadia said.

Her grandmother threw her arms around Nadia and whispered into her ear, "It is you! My precious Nadia, you are more beautiful than ever."

It wasn't until her mother and father, along with her ten siblings—for word spreads fast in so small a village—had pulled her from the mob and taken her into their home, painted a lovely robin's-egg blue and sunny yellow, and directed her and Kache to sit that the questions began. They came one after another after another, without any pause for an answer, while her grandmother sat stoically, listening.

"What happened to you?"

"Where did you go?"

"Why did you cut your hair?"

"Who is this man? Is he your husband?"

"Where are your children?"

"Are you hurt?"

"Were you held captive?"

"Why haven't you come home to us?"

"Why are you dressed in worldly clothes? What is in your nose?"

"Why are all those earrings in your ears?"

"Did you know it has been almost ten years? *Ten years?*"

With questions zooming at her from every direction, Nadia felt like she stood at one of those intersections in Anchorage—only this was where her wish to share nothing and her wish for them to know all intersected. Where to begin, how much to divulge? In the corner, the shrine of icons and hand-rolled candles, the old gold jewelry and ancient texts. The patron saints stared, waiting for her answers. Upon entering the house, every person had turned to this shrine and bowed repeatedly and made the sign of the cross. Every person except Nadia and Kache. She looked to Kache, who stood off to the side with his hands shoved deep in his pockets. He raised his eyebrows, and she gave him a slight nod.

He said, "Nadia will answer your questions. But it's difficult for her. It's not an easy thing to tell. Let's all sit back for a minute and catch our breath and let her tell you her story. But first, will you answer an important question that we have? Where is Vladimir?"

Her father answered in English, "He is no longer of us. He left this village soon after Nadia disappeared."

So it was true. Nadia hung her head and willed the next set of tears to stay put. Here, her grandmother spoke up, also in English. "Nadia and her friend must to be hungry, eh? Let your questions wait. It is not to be holy day of fasting, so let us feast. Our celebration feast of gratitude for return of our Nadia. She will answer questions later. For now, you show to her our family, your children, your husbands, your wives. You tell to her what happened in these ten years she's been gone."

In minutes, it seemed, foods piled themselves high on the table. Nadia noticed that her mother took out the mandatory outsider dishes—separate dishes in a different pattern for those who weren't Old Believers—for Kache, but also for Nadia. Her grandmother argued with her mother in Russian, but with everyone else talking, Nadia couldn't hear what the two women said. There was no prayer before the meal. Nadia knew why: the rule that Old Believers cannot pray with outsiders. But her father raised his glass and said, "I wish you all good health and the spirit of God."

Everyone gathered to greet Nadia. Warm hugs, shy smiles. Her sister Marina said, "I have always been afraid of water. I cannot go in boats. But here you are! Maybe I'm not as afraid anymore."

Her brother Alex introduced her to his wife and children. "This is your aunt Nadia. She is the one who taught me how to play *Lopta* and *Knaz*. No one ever beat her at *Knaz*! She was always the king."

Her sister Natalia said, "How we have mourned you. The forty required days were only the beginning. I have never stopped crying and praying for your soul. But now I happily stop."

There were more stories, more tears, but joking and laughing too.

Braga flowed freely. Nadia almost forgot that she had yet to explain where she'd been. She almost felt that she had never been gone. Almost. Yet not quite. Every now and then, she looked up to see Kache, chatting with Alex, looking fairly comfortable and well-fed, as he nodded and ate from his separate dishes.

chapter

fifty-two

KACHE HAD NEVER BEEN the recipient of so many sideways glances. While Nadia's return was being celebrated, his presence was definitely of the elephant-in-the-room variety. A few people addressed him in English, but the obvious question—what the hell are you doing here with Nadia?—hung unasked.

Nadia sat behind a cluster of vibrantly clothed siblings. Two of her brothers spoke quietly and urgently in the corner. They did not look happy. At one point, one actually snarled. Kache tried to appear casual as he repositioned himself between them and Nadia and her more friendly siblings. If he were the elephant in the room, the gun felt like a rhinoceros in his coat pocket.

Another brother did approach Kache just then, smiled warmly, and shook his hand. "I am Alex," he said. "How do you know my sister?" He took a bite of food and then another.

"She has been living in my parents' home," Kache offered, aiming for the most wholesome way to put it.

"She is married, you know," Alex said, talking with his mouth full. He seemed like he hadn't eaten in weeks. "But we will never see him again."

Kache wondered if Vladimir was dead. "Really? Why's that?"

"He was not truly Old Believer. He kept...uh...magazines." He set down his fork and plate and squeezed the air as if he had big breasts. "The worst acts you can imagine. We burn them—only looked at the few." He let out a long, low whistle. "Barbaric. He stopped coming to service. He smoked and drank the hard liquor. At first, we let him mourn Nadia, but then we realize this is not mourning. This is his life, you know? We ask him to leave, and he says, 'Gladly.' He says we are backward, backwoods, backass. He stumbles out. Not in good condition. We assume he dies soon after."

"Your brothers"—Kache motioned with a tilt of his head—"are not happy to see Nadia?"

"Not happy to see her stamped with the world. Me, I don't care. The world is coming more and more every day. What next? We blast out caves in mountains and hide there? Some people leave here. They don't like it. Three people last year." He shrugged. "It happens. I have beautiful wife, four children. I like my life; it is good, yes? Live and let live. But Yuri and Josiph. They want penance."

chapter
fifty-three

NADIA WATCHED ONE OF her brothers, Yuri, who even as a boy always had a dour face, clink his fork on his glass and demand quiet. He said, "It is time we let our sister speak of her absence."

They sent the children out to play. The adults sat in silence while Nadia began from the very beginning, speaking in Russian, of the night of her wedding to Vladimir, and without going into too much detail, she was able to convey how terribly wrong things turned, the insane violence that took place within the four walls of their house and the threats to set fire to the village if she told a soul. "I believed he would. And I still believe that to this day. So I left, and I faked my own drowning. It was the only answer I could think of, but I have missed you all terribly, and I am begging you for forgiveness for this terrible lie that went on all these years. It didn't have to. Vladimir is long gone. He isn't even around here, and I've been hiding all this time." The tragedy of this scraped the back of her throat as she tried to get the words out.

Tears ran down many of the faces of her family. But Yuri and Josiph, whose lips made a thin, straight line above his beard, whispered back and forth.

Yuri stood and spoke. "You are obviously living in sin. One look at you tells us this. For what, exactly, are you looking for forgiveness? Adultery, perhaps? You certainly do not wish to come back and live as family and worship with us?"

Her father waved his hand and said, "Yuri, you do not know this. Give Nadia time to speak and time to adjust to being back again. Ours is a unique culture and her absence, very many years. Give her time, and she will remember our loving and good life. She will remember the joy in living as pure a life as humanly possible."

Nadia considered keeping quiet, but this is where she knew she might begin another lie that would tangle her up and keep her. "Father, Mother, Yuri is correct. I have changed greatly since I have been gone. As much as I love you, as much as I have missed you, I no longer believe as you believe."

Her mother gasped, reached under her scarf, and pulled on one of her braids.

Her father said, "Nadi, do you know what you are saying? You are renouncing your faith?"

She couldn't speak the words, so she merely nodded, and as Kache would later say, all hell broke loose. Some of the women cried out, and many of the men groaned and shook their heads in dismay. The mood in the room went from celebratory to funereal. This was not an exaggeration. She knew that to them, she had come back to life and then was dead once again, all in a matter of hours.

She said, "I am so hoping that we can still have a relationship. That we can still be a family, and I can visit with you, and you can come and visit me. We can eat together and sing together and play games again. *Please?*" But they stared at the ground while her father said they belonged to the family of God. Her sisters did come up and hug her good-bye. Anna and Natalia clung to her longer than the other three, who probably barely remembered her. But eventually, they all let go and left.

Her baba held her and whispered in her ear in English, "You are strong woman. You are good woman, my precious Nadia. I love you always." Her three brothers left without even looking at her, except for Alex, who squeezed her hand and wished her peace. Nadia's father and mother pleaded with her to rethink her decision, hugged her long and hard. Then they walked her and Kache to the front door.

Her father said, "Nadi, it is your choice. We believe in this, freedom of choice. Know we receive you with arms and hearts open wide if you ever change your mind." Her mother held her apron to her face.

As Kache and Nadia set off down the trail, her mother's wails followed them. "Nadia. Nadia!"

And later, on the beach, when a single cry sliced the air, Nadia looked back, hoping to see her mother running after her, but it was only a lone gull, pure white against the steel sky.

chapter

fifty-four

LETTIE SLEPT. OR AT least she felt like she slept, but she wasn't quite dreaming. It was the remembering again. Such detail, such accuracy, like watching a movie of her life, of things she hadn't thought about in years and years. When she closed her eyes and let herself drift, she always went back to the land, and her memories played out before her with exact precision, her five senses and then some, all intact. There was no flying or being chased or forgetting to wear her underwear to school like your run-of-the-mill dreams. This was closer to time traveling. It was sleeping next to A. R. again—hearing him, smelling him, touching him—and holding Eleanor and Glenn on her lap, feeling the chubby weight of them, the feather down of their sweet heads of hair resting against her neck and chin and cheeks. Living in the cabin on the land with its equal parts exhilaration and exhaustion. Lettie felt happier than she had in years. She felt like herself again. Young, strong, but with the awareness time gives you to pay attention to the moments—the slanted gold bands of light, the surprise of a huge potato pulled up from its loamy womb, the shared long gaze of a gray wolf, the way you can smell the rain when it's still held by the swollen clouds.

Even the medicinal, urine, and macaroni-and-cheese aromas drifting down the hall were replaced with the Sitka spruce, the coal and wood smoke, the simmering bear stew. And there she was in the twelve-by-twelve-foot cabin, the hewn logs with the moss chinking they would replace the next year with mortar. The place seemed to be decorated by the Chevron fuel company—their wooden Blazo boxes held everything from kindling to silverware, even babies. There were the two cradles A. R. rigged up out of Blazo boxes, and inside the cradles, both babies—both of them finally!—asleep. In town, she saw women shepherding long lines of children, and she wondered at the work involved. How did they do it? She would never know, because after the touch-and-go birth of Glenn and Eleanor, the doctor told her it was a good thing she'd had twins, because she was done having children. She could conceive no more.

Privately, she thought this a blessing of sorts. She adored the babies, adored being a mother. But the work! A. R. wished they would have more help in the future, something a slew of kids could provide. But the years between now and then with a whole litter of kids would have done Lettie in. She was a hard worker, just as tough as most men. It wasn't the work but the *type* of work that scared her off. She wanted to be felling trees alongside A. R. again as soon as the twins grew old enough. She didn't want to be pregnant six more times like most women in the area were. The laundry already took all day. Twenty-eight pails of water hauled with a yoke on her shoulders, two buckets a trip. Then the heating of the water, the washing, the two rinse cycles, the flatironing (though Lettie had to admit she skipped this step more often than not and much more than her contemporaries). With more than two children, she and A. R. would be outnumbered, and that just didn't seem like a good idea. Not at all. The doctor had called her uterus "uncooperative," but to Lettie, her uterus had generously obliged her by carrying two perfect children to full term and then kindly closing shop.

Of course, she told A. R. none of this, just reassured him that once the children were older, they would all share the workload and that he should be glad he had a wife as strong and able as two full-grown men.

This was not a land for the weak-willed. Many of the women complained. More than a few left and never set foot in Caboose again. The hill where all the homesteads were being staked out had come to be called Separation Hill. Lettie knew that if any separation between A. R. and her took place (she didn't think it would, but if it did), A. R. would be the one to leave and Lettie would be the one to stay. She could never abandon this place. It was of her, and she was of it. How to explain? She knew it when she saw that photo all those years ago; she knew it more when she stepped onto this driftwood-strewn shore. She knew it when winter raged in and knew it again when the ice and snow gave way to mud. None of it scared her away. And then summer! The glorious gift of summer, where abundance sang its arias from every nook and cranny of that amazing land and sea.

But there was guilt involved in living your dream. Few spouses met at the altar carrying the same dream. Usually, one had a passion and the other did not, so he or she simply went along for the ride. The lucky few shared the same passion. The more commonly cursed had conflicting passions that ricocheted off one another and kept them fighting the duration of their lives.

A. R. complied with grace and a steadfast diligence in the work laid out before him. But there were times when his ambivalence showed, and Lettie understood. There he was, pausing to lean on a shovel, facing the bay, not in grateful wonder as she did, but maybe a different kind of wonder—wondering what their life might have been like if they'd stayed in Kansas with the peeling white picket fence and their modern conveniences, without having to travel so far just to get to a store. Sure, Kansas had been nothing but a heap of dust during the Depression, but the Depression and the dust were long gone by then. She had asked much of him, and he had been kind and sacrificial, and she was indeed grateful.

There, the twins, older, Glenn always out in front, taking whatever he wanted. Strong, stubborn, but likable Glenn. Tall, big-boned, but pretty Eleanor who didn't know she was pretty and lacked Glenn's confidence when it came to working the land, but who had a delightful laugh and knew her way around a conversation. She could usually talk her way into being given what she wanted instead of just taking it. Except when it came to Bets. Lettie saw that one unfold, and she knew what was happening and how it would play out before Eleanor even knew what hit her.

Love was like that with its victims. How everyone saw it splayed out on a person's face before that person even knew what was in his or her heart. Lettie blamed herself. She knew Eleanor had a penchant for women, but Lettie didn't know how to broach the subject. Oh, she had tried. But there was no one to sort it out with first. As kind of a soul as A. R. was, he wouldn't understand. He was still bugging Lettie about attending church, for God's sake. For her own sake, Lettie stayed away. She sang praises every time she stepped foot on her land; she didn't need a church roof over her head to feel grateful.

But she couldn't talk to A. R. about their daughter's lesbianism. More correctly, her *suspected* lesbianism, because as far as Lettie knew, Eleanor had never had a girlfriend, not in that way. Well, maybe while she was away at college. Lettie should have talked to Eleanor, but because she didn't know how, she watched her suffer an unnamed confusion. She knew that she'd failed her daughter, that she should have helped her.

And there was Bets, as heterosexual as a person could be, loving

Eleanor almost as completely as Eleanor loved Bets, but not quite. Not in that one particular area or—here is where Lettie grinned, despite herself—*areas*. Bets couldn't have if she wanted to, and knowing what a mule Glenn often was, there were times when she probably wished she were wired to love a woman instead of a man. But alas, she was not. So she looked to Eleanor as her best friend, her sister, her closest confidante. All of those things that are delightful in a friendship, but not enough for someone in love.

Lettie traveled back to before the Bets saga, and there was Glenn, enlisting to fight in Vietnam. Enlisting! All while they lived so close to the Canadian border, Lettie could have driven him over there herself. What she thought about when her nest hollowed to empty, what she obsessed over, was not all the things she'd gotten right as a mother but the few very crucial things she'd gotten wrong. A tension lay tightly coiled between Glenn and A. R. back then, with Glenn hell-bent on getting away. He wanted to see the world, but when he came back, he was, of course, wounded through and through, without a scar to show for it. Lettie wanted to save him, but he wouldn't talk to her, wouldn't talk to anyone about any of it. Not even about what they ate for breakfast in the jungle. Bets showed up, and she saved him. Bets did what Lettie couldn't do for both of her children: she helped them see who they really were.

By then, A. R. was too sick to live out at the homestead, so they divided up the acreage evenly between both children, sold the cabin off for cheap to Glenn and Bets (Eleanor had gone off to college to try to forget Bets and wasn't interested in living in the cabin anyway), and moved into town. But a day didn't go by that she didn't miss living on that land. She never spoke of this to A. R.; he'd spent the last twenty-odd years letting her live her dream. He was weak but strong enough in spirit to find comfort in resting his head on her shoulder instead of the other way around like when they were younger. If she could have, she would have moved him back to that state he missed so he could die where he belonged.

That's what Lettie wanted for herself. She wanted to go back to the homestead at least once while she was still alive. And when her time came, she wanted to become part of the land the way the land had become part of her.

chapter
fifty-five

KACHE WANTED TO SHAKE every one of Nadia's family members—shake and shake them—until they saw that they were turning their backs on their blood, their love, their history, and all the infinite possibilities that future days with their Nadia would have brought them. He hadn't needed a translator to see their initial joy wiped out by their indisputable rejection. There was even a moment he considered taking out the gun and firing it in the air, just to wake them all up.

Didn't they realize? Very few people get offered a second chance like that.

The walk back to the truck was quiet between them, the bay lying down flat for the evening, the cold piercing their eyes, cheeks, and noses. Every so often, Nadia would stop walking. Kache would turn back to her so she could lean into him. They stood, her forehead pressed against his chest, his arms tucked around her. Out on the long beach, the piles of bleached driftwood looked like prehistoric bones, as if he and Nadia had stumbled upon an archaeological dig.

She would let out a long, stuttered sigh, wipe her eyes on the inside of his jacket, and resume walking. He thought she was the bravest person he had ever known.

❦

The truck heater blasted, and when it finally turned from icy air to warm, they held their open hands to the vents.

"Damn hell it," Nadia said, hitting the dash. "We forgot to ask for school records and birth certification. Because I have been banished now, how will we ever get them? How do we forget this?"

There, the truth that had been dripping down the back of his neck, cold and persistent: *he* hadn't forgotten. He had remembered, but he hadn't spoken up, and he wasn't sure why. But he was sure he wasn't about to admit it to Nadia, not now—if ever. What made him more uneasy? That he'd purposely not asked for what they'd come for, or that he was determined to withhold information from the woman he loved?

"The only good things that come from this trip?" she said as he replaced the gun in the glove compartment. "We didn't need the gun. And we found out we won't. Vladimir, he is gone."

The mood stayed pensive as they started the drive back. Then Nadia broke the silence. "One of my sisters said there is one television at the school in Altai. Some of the people have computers. Everything is different. This is painfully ironic, no? They have modern technology while I stayed living without it. They have all gone on with their lives."

"Of course. That's what the living have to do."

"*You* did not. *I* did not."

He steered sharply to avoid yet another huge pothole. "Point taken. But we can agree that might not have been the best tactic."

"I do not know what I think."

"Some things haven't changed for them. Not at all."

Gazing out the window, she nodded and said, "You heard them. I was only alive for few hours. Dead again to them. We accomplished nothing. We only make it worse. They did not even ask where I live. They do not even want to know this."

"They may come around."

"Did you hear them? My grandmother was the only one who wasn't wailing when I said I no longer am Old Believer. She was unlike her, quiet."

"She didn't look old enough to be your grandmother. But then again, your mom is closer to my age than my mom's age."

"You must remember, they have children when they were teenagers. My grandmother is sixty-six. My mother is…let me think…forty-three? My grandmother, she is my father's mother, and he greatly admires her. My father behaves like submissive little boy in her presence. It is quite funny to see." Her chin trembled. "I mean, it once *was*…"

"Come here."

She scooted over, rested her head against Kache's rib cage, and let the tears fall the rest of the way home. He should have gotten the papers for her. He should have at least done that.

The temperature dropped again that night, and snow covered everything. It had been many years since Kache had woken to the first snowfall. The spruce looked like giant, eager brides. The ground basked in its perfection, untouched even by tracks.

Inside, the house was taking on a different look too, which had begun with the hanging of the octopus-ink painting and proceeded with throw pillows they purchased in Anchorage, along with new sheets and a down comforter for his parents' room, which Nadia and Kache had moved into. They'd even ordered a new bed. Though the changes felt a bit ruthless, Kache swore he heard his mother saying, "Kache, honey, it's about time."

That first day of snow, unable to do much outside, they began moving furniture, as if they could rearrange the previous day's events. Later, they stepped into cross-country skis and crossed over the fresh, sugary white while lazy fat flakes floated down, sticking to their knitted hats. They didn't throw snowballs. Didn't even talk much about the day before. The world was pure and silent and easily traversable, only their two pairs of ski tracks etching the snow.

Inside the cabin that evening, the world shrank. They turned on every lamp downstairs and built a fire. Kache looked out the window. Nothing out there but darkness and hidden night creatures. Perhaps they were watching Nadia and him, exposed in the house's glaring light. He felt oddly unsettled and on display by this one-way mirror. Instead of the grand vistas of the summer and fall, all he could see was his own reflection, along with the fact that he had caused Nadia pain by encouraging her to return to her family and—as if that wasn't enough—had kept quiet about her documents.

part four

winter tracks

2005–2006

chapter

fifty-six

TOO MUCH, TOO MUCH, too much. Nadia needed to be alone. Away from the Internet, away from her family's judgments, away from Kache, sharing the same stifled air day after snowed-in day. She loved Kache, loved being with him, but she had no time to herself, no room to grieve the loss of her family. *Again.* It was as if her thoughts and emotions piled up on a chair and she had to sort through them to see what still fit and what only took up space. Instead, she just kept throwing one sad thought on top of the other.

She was tired. She wanted to climb under the down comforter and stay there, waiting it out like the garden under the snow. But she did not. Instead, she laughed and helped Kache move things around and plan for Lettie and Snag's visit. She cooked with him. She played Scrabble and cards with him.

It was easy between Kache and Nadia, most of the time. The talking, the laughing, the having sex. Making love. The closer she and Kache became, the further away she moved from Vladimir. He'd been gone ten years and had still managed to hold her prisoner—no, *she* had held herself prisoner. She was finished with that. She would not let fear hold her away from life.

On the third day of the snowstorm, she said to Kache, who sat on the futon checking his email, which he rarely did, "Would you be offended or worried if I go into the bedroom with door locked and only come out for food and water and to go to the bathroom?"

He watched her for a long minute. "Too much togetherness?"

She nodded. "I believe so."

He sighed, got up, and stretched. "I need to call Clemsky and see if I can borrow his snowplow anyway. I was using you as an excuse to be lazy. Convinced myself that you didn't want to be alone after the family stuff."

"I have never before gone so long without being alone. I love having you here. It is only that… I don't know how to say this."

"Nadia, your family. You need space, and there's plenty I can do. The snow's stopped, so I need to start digging out."

"But I should help."

"Not this time." He had already pulled on his jacket and was punching numbers into his cell phone. "I'll start with the walkway and driveway until Clemsky can get out here."

Kache was so agreeable, but Nadia still had to fight the impulse to place both of her hands on his back and push him out the front door.

❦

She kept a file on the computer. Into it, she dragged her favorite photographs of San Francisco from the Internet. When she felt confused or anxious, like she did now, she opened the file, and she soon felt full of something that might be called hopefulness. If they could build a city like that? If they could build a bridge like that?

She stared at the orangey-red bridge, the blue water, the white city, the blue sky. She looked out past the porch's log pillars, the blue water, the white mountains, the blue sky.

All the sadness of the visit with her family sat like a piece of steel lodged in her throat. There was always this—and that. The hope. The sorrow. Her baba. Her precious baba. Her mama. Her precious mama. Her mama's arms around her. Her mama's disbelief turning to delight before being taken over again by a new grief. Her papa's features dancing in recognition, shadowing over. Nadia understood why they could not accept her. She understood. Because there was a part of her that wished to forget everything she'd learned and go back to them.

But no. She had changed. There was no bridge back, only forward. And yet she hadn't asked for the papers she needed to apply to school.

There was something else though, Nadia knew, something she needed to pay attention to. What was it?

She went upstairs and lay under the new down comforter. She pulled it over her head and let the images of that day play on the white screen of the blanket. She viewed it all with new perspective. There was Kache, standing in a corner, ready to intervene if need be. There was her grandmother, sitting in her chair, watching her, listening to Nadia tell her story. It was as if Nadia were the center of the sea anemone, with all her siblings and her parents crowding around her like tentacles, coming in closer, backing off. But her grandmother's face stayed calm when Nadia said she no longer believed. Now, under the covers, Nadia watched her again closely, the slightest upturn at the corner of her mouth, the touch of light radiating from her eyes. And she had told Nadia she was strong, that she would always love her. Nadia was sure of it; she was not dead to her grandmother.

Yes, all of the tendrils of the anemone she found at the beach were green, but Nadia imagined there might be a red one, not swaying with the others, still attached but distinct.

❧

With Kache gone for the day, Nadia found herself opening one of the boxes of journals. She turned to Elizabeth's last entry.

Last night was the darkest night in the history of the Winkel family, or so it felt. We are all of us extremes, living on the extreme edge of the world, where the mountains themselves were shaped by the force of colliding tectonic plates.

And so it is for this family. What will be the shape of us after last night? An impassable range of great height between us? Time will tell. The lemony morning sky already casts new light, healing light.

I wish I could shine that light into Glenn's heart and reveal the dark corners. Lord knows we all have our blind spots, but sometimes I think Glenn's has become a full eclipse. He is a stubborn bull of a man, and I don't imagine he could have gleaned a life from this land were he not. But he rules over the boys like the military he despised—giving them little freedom to make decisions, let alone mistakes. He is stifling them. And while Denny seems to everyone else the stronger of the two, I know this is not the case. Denny is a pleaser. Plus, he loves this land as much as his grandmother and father do. It's natural for him to pick up a rifle, to use his back more than his brain. He is agile and strong, and he wears this yoke without complaint because it's been tailor-made to fit him.

But Kache. Strong-willed, independent Kache, who was given a gift none of us could ever begin to master. The gift of music. And yet you would think the guitar was a machete raised over his father's head.

Jealousy is part of it. It's painful to watch a parent jealous of his own child. But there it is. It may as well be spelled out

in the tread of the man's boot, the word with a capital J left
wherever he walks.

The other part of it is fear. Glenn ran off to Vietnam, intent
on seeing the world, and then came back to duck and cover
from it for the rest of his life. Deep down, he is afraid that the
world out there will kill his boys just like it killed his friends.
But Alaska is just as dangerous, if not more so, than any city
in the Lower 48. Alaska does not forgive mistakes. We all say
it because it's true.

Nadia always wondered what Elizabeth meant by the phrase
Alaska does not forgive mistakes. That you could not be forgiven when
you lived here? She needed to ask Kache about it. She would wait
until the time was right. She skipped to the last lines, for these had
become a totem to her.

But for now, I will gather these men together, and we will
fly away from here for a few days. We will look down on this
house, this land—free from it—and the perspective will do
us good.

Nadia had never failed to notice that Elizabeth's last written
words were *Do us good*. She often thought of them as a new type of
commandment for her to follow, and she thought of it often when
she was tending the house in the years before Kache returned. But
now that she knew him, now that Snag and Lettie were coming out
to the homestead for Thanksgiving, the commandment felt more
weighted—and broader. It wasn't just about tending the house and
land. There were many ways to do good—and not to do good—by
someone. To do good to the people you loved and still be truthful to
yourself. That was the narrowest of bridges.

chapter

fifty-seven

IT WAS LIFE'S OBSESSIONS that Snag found herself obsessing over as she sat in her robe, drinking her coffee, looking over her calendar, and realizing she'd missed the last two Caboose chamber meetings. Without her there to argue her point, the chamber most likely had voted 33–0 in favor of leaving the red caboose in its most likely final resting spot at the end of the tracks, at the end of the Caboose Spit, where it housed memorabilia of days of yore and looked complacently out over one of the prettiest views on the planet. What Snag found most bewildering was that she didn't give a hoot. Not even a snort. She simply no longer cared.

And yet, and yet. She had raised her voice at countless meetings, handed out flyers, even carried a sign in protest. And why? *Why?* It had felt necessary. And now it did not. *Hmph*, she thought. She looked at her watch and realized she had to get moving if she was going to get all her deliveries made before she went to see her mom—and Gilly, of course. Now that there was so much snow, she wasn't delivering by foot and wagon. But she did schedule in a stop at the gym. She'd even ordered herself a bathing suit from Lands' End and had taken up swimming laps.

Her body hadn't experienced stuffing itself into a bathing suit in nearly forty years. But there she was, in all her glory. She loved the lukewarm water, even the smell of the chlorine. She loved the kickboards and the linked plastic lane dividers and the old people (even older than her) swimming (even more slowly than she was) with such good intentions. It made her feel happily tolerant—no, way beyond tolerant, even proud. Here they all were, putting forth such effort for the strength of their bodies, for the strength of humankind.

Easing herself into the water, she thought of Nadia, of how they would all be celebrating Thanksgiving together. She thought of the young girl she first kissed at the beach. Agafia. How one sweet, brief encounter set her on the path to Gilly. She wondered if Nadia knew Agafia. She thought of the strange way her actions—and *non*actions—had led Kache to Nadia. And as Snag swam, she felt herself linked to each person, if only briefly, like the chain of buoys that floated beside her in the pool, creating a lane, keeping her going in a single direction so she didn't spin in circles, one linked to the other to the other, this way, this way, this way, and then back again.

chapter

fifty-eight

KACHE COULD SEE THAT Nadia had taken once again to killing things. A skinned rabbit and a plucked spruce hen hung from string in the barn. The woman could skin a rabbit without a knife. The first time, he'd watched with uneasy awe as she grabbed its legs and, holding it upside down, firmly pulled the leg fur up like socks and then the tail and all the rest of it in one continuous motion, as quickly and easily as if merely removing its sweater.

Kache jumped when he heard another shot go off from the west. He liked it much better when she was shooting movies rather than animals, but there seemed to be no stopping her.

In the bracing cold, he fed the cow, goats, and chickens, all under-standably a bit on edge. The pure white goat, gentle Buttercup, stuck by Kache's side the whole time he worked. He offered them all gentle reassurances along with the hay and grain, but who could be sure? Nadia's nerves were shot too. The idea of preparing a Thanksgiving meal for five had the most capable woman he knew wringing her hands—along with a spruce hen neck.

He wanted to head out to the woods to remind her they had an eighteen-pound turkey—bought from Safeway already plucked, gutted clean, and now brined and stuffed and roasting in the oven—but he didn't want to join the casualties, so instead, he removed his boots, entered the warm house, and basted the turkey.

He sifted through the pile of his mother's recipe cards until he came to the recipe for cranberry relish. They'd always used the lowbush cranberries they picked every August—the lingonberries. He and Nadia had picked enough to can and freeze some, and they glistened in a bowl, waiting for him to chop the walnuts and add the sugar and the whole orange. Staring at the recipe card with its hard chunk of lingonberry sauce still attached to it, he realized, *That lingonberry is over twenty years old.* The last time that card had been pulled out, it had been by the hands of his mother. She had no idea that the speckle of lingonberry she smudged on it when she picked it up—perhaps to check again on the amount of sugar, because she'd always complained that including the orange rind required that you add a ridiculous amount of sugar—would still be tenaciously clinging to the index card long after she'd let go of it and had to let go of this life.

So there Kache stood, holding the card his mother once held, his eyes misting up. When a tear splashed onto the card, he wiped it away quickly so it would not upset the persistent lingonberry remnant, so it might stay on the lined index card with the folksy mushroom artwork above the olive-green type that said *Our Family Recipe.*

All these years of not celebrating, declining most invitations to other families' celebrations. He'd accepted a few. One of the guys at work had told Kache that since he and his wife lived far away from their families, they always hosted a "Homeless Waif Thanksgiving," inviting people who had nowhere else to go. Kache went to that one, ended up driving home a tall, brunette, fellow homeless waif and sleeping with her. She talked about how she was definitely going home for Christmas, that she'd already shopped and had shipped her parents' and six siblings' presents. He left before morning.

Years later, Janie had tried, and Kache had tried along with her, helping her make family recipes that her mom had emailed her. But, of course, it was never the same. It never is.

But this? This was as close as it came without having those three walk in, and he let himself imagine it once again, and soon, he was thinking about the village and what it must have been like for Nadia's family to see her standing there in real flesh and blood and bones, talking, reminding them of the way she creased her brow and fluttered her hands sometimes when she spoke.

Nadia came in through the side kitchen door, hoisting up the skinned rabbit, Leo following close behind with a triumphant grin, head and tail held high. "Time to put stew in the oven." When Kache raised his eyebrows, she added that she would happily freeze the spruce hen, but she really wanted to serve the rabbit for Thanksgiving.

"But the turkey. There's no room in the oven."

"Shit damn."

Kache cracked up.

"What?"

"I swear, the way you swear."

"I don't understand."

"I love your original combinations."

"'It is better to fail in originality than to succeed in imitation.'"

"Huh?"

"Melville."

"Of course. Anyway, it's fine. We don't need rabbit stew. We have turkey. We have dressing. Mashed potatoes. Green bean casserole. Shall I go on?"

"But Lettie loves rabbit stew." There was such insistence in her voice, he half expected her to stamp her foot.

"She does?" He stared at her, her nose red and running a bit from the cold. "But of course *you* would know that."

Kache cleared a pan off one of the burners, which worked fine for the stew. He managed to set the table with his mom's china without blubbering, and Nadia managed to stop shooting innocent animals. "At some point," she said, fluffing the new pillows on the couch yet another time, "you are going to have to learn how to shoot gun."

"I told you. I'd rather my protein sources come in those Styrofoam trays wrapped in Saran wrap with stickers. Hypocrite that I am, I don't want to kill anything. I'm the guy who takes even poisonous spiders outside, remember?"

"There are no poisonous spiders in Alaska, remember?"

"Oh, but there are in Austin. And scorpions. And rattlesnakes. And all kinds of things that creep in the night. And I didn't even shoot *them*."

"You are—how is the word?—a pacifist."

"So you get my point."

"Still, you live in Alaska. I am going to teach you how to shoot tin cans at very least."

"Right now?"

"No, right now, we get this house looking like perfection, like it is on one of those Internet websites about beautiful homes."

"You're kidding, right?"

"Only little bit."

"Next, you're going to want me to build you a brick patio."

She scrunched her eyebrows together. "Why? Can you do that?" She ran her finger along the coffee table, inspecting it for dust, and then she looked at him. "What?"

"Just don't ever call me Mr. Happenings." He took her up in his arms and kissed the gold-studded track along her ear. "Hey, are you the same woman who was hiding under the bed screaming in Russian while your ferocious dog lurched at me?" She nodded. "Look, you've gotta stop. It's going to be fine. They're going to love you. Lettie already does."

"I am afraid I am just 'that squatter' to them. But to me, they mean something. I feel that I know them, that I even love them."

"You know Lettie doesn't think of you as a squatter. Never has. They're grateful to you. And so am I. Very grateful. And don't worry about Snag. She'll love you too once she meets you."

Nadia kissed him once on the nose, the forehead, and the neck before she went up to change into her new Nordstrom clothes. Kache stuck another log in the woodstove, waited on the couch with Leo snoring at his feet, and was dumbfounded to realize he'd been imagining two little kids—a blond girl, a dark, curly-headed boy—jumping on him, climbing on Leo, disturbing the peace and quiet with their miraculous little *Daddy! Daddy!* screeches.

chapter

fifty-nine

NADIA AND KACHE HAD been sure to shovel the walkway wide
enough to fit a wheelchair, but in the end, Kache lifted Lettie out of
the car and carried her up the porch steps she and A. R. had once built
and through the doorway into the living room, which had once served
as their whole cabin.

Nadia held the door open as they filed in. Leo barked, alarmed at
the idea of visitors, but once Nadia reassured him, he calmed down.
The woman she assumed was Snag carried the pies, and the other
woman, Gilly, heaved the folded wheelchair up the steps and opened
it in the living room.

"Well," Lettie said, settling into the wheelchair, "I don't think my
husband ever carried me over the threshold, and I certainly didn't
think my grandson would, but thank you, Kache. That made things
easier, didn't it?" She looked up at Nadia and said, "Why, there you are.
How are you, my dear?" Nadia bent to hug her. Lettie said over Nadia's
shoulder, "And that must be Leo. A fine dog he turned out to be. I
knew it. Best of the litter."

Nadia had read that a hostess should offer to take her guests' coats,
but when she did so after Snag set down the pumpkin pie and rhubarb

crunch, Snag said, "That's okay. I know where they go, believe me. I'm Snag, by the way. Nice to finally meet you." She shook Nadia's hand with vigor and introduced Gilly, who smiled warmly and gave Nadia a hug.

There was an awkward moment of silence while the women took in their surroundings. Nadia almost felt an inventory occurring. She understood how strange it must be for them to be here, with some things finally changed but so many still the same.

"It's as if time folded back on itself," Snag finally said.

"We've changed things a lot," Kache said. "You should have seen it before. It was exactly the same as we left it."

"This feels pretty exact to me." Snag walked around, staring at the walls, at the bookshelves and the paintings, at the old Japanese fisherman ball and the photographs along the top of the piano.

Nadia saw the little difference their attempts had made. Moving the furniture, adding a coffee table, pillows, some artwork... That barely dented the accumulation of memories Snag and Lettie must have been poring through.

Everyone held their breath, and then Lettie sighed. It was a long sigh, as if she'd inhaled all the air in the room and let it all back out so that everyone could resume breathing. "All I can say is it sure feels good to be home."

While Kache went to put the goats and Mooze in the barn for the expected cold snap, the women arranged themselves in the living room, Lettie accepting the afghan Nadia offered her for her lap—the afghan Lettie had once crocheted—and a small pillow to somewhat cushion the back of the wheelchair. Snag took the red-checked chair, and Nadia and Gilly sat on the futon. The fire crackled and sputtered, suddenly burning brighter.

"So, my dear," Lettie said, looking at Nadia. "Tell me how your life has changed since the last time I saw you. Kache tells me you've been filming. Still dream of San Francisco?"

Nadia had once admitted to Lettie that she stared for hours at a time at one of the Winkels' oversize photography books that said *San Francisco, City by the Bay* on the cover. Until she'd seen those pictures, she hadn't imagined that such a place existed.

"Yes," she said. "Sometimes. You remembered. Now I have a file on my computer, and it is there I keep photos of San Francisco, so I can click over and pretend I am in this great city."

"I remembered because you reminded me of me. There was one bent-up little photo that pulled me here to Alaska. I seem to recall that one photo pulled you the most. One taken from the Golden Gate Bridge, looking toward the city. I understand that kind of magnetic force. No denying it."

Snag said, "I didn't know that, Mom. A picture started it all for you and Daddy? Really?"

Lettie rested her chin on her fist while she spoke from her wheelchair, and Nadia thought how she looked like a much older version of Rodin's *The Thinker*. "Your poor father. He came along, of course. But he was doing it all for me. I was the one. Alaska this! Alaska that! If I hadn't heeded that call, I would have lived my life in regret."

"But Daddy came around. He loved it here as much as you did."

"Your father loved *me*. But if I would've just once said 'Let's move back,' he would've had the moving truck loaded before I finished my sentence. I feel bad about it now."

"But," Gilly said, "you wouldn't change anything, would you?"

"Well, I'm the one who got what she wanted. He's the one to answer *that* question, but he's not available at the moment. Sometimes I think he would have lived longer had he been happier."

Snag waved her hand. "Oh, Mom. Daddy *was* happy."

"He loved his family. But I think he would have preferred a different kind of life, in a different kind of place. I knew him like no one else did, Eleanor."

Nadia took this all in, and when Snag and Lettie fell silent, she turned their conversation over and over in her mind. She stared at the fire. Then she looked around to see the others also transfixed by the flames.

Long ago, she had begun seeing herself somehow, someway, finding her way to San Francisco. More recently, she'd added the idea of film school. It was what they called a long shot, followed with an "excuse the pun," but she dreamed about it constantly. Lately, on the movie screen in her head, images flashed of her and Kache living in one of those houses like the painted ladies, a colorful Victorian with a bay window that looked out over the street where they'd watch the passersby, the cars, and the buses taking people here and there.

But Kache increasingly mentioned how much this place, this land, meant to him. How he'd always thought Denny would take it over and keep it in the family but that now he saw himself doing just that. How he was beginning to understand what his father and grandmother had meant when they talked about the way a place called you and staked its claim on your mind and heart, might even heal you and make you whole.

Lettie finally spoke. "Nadia, what will you do next? Do you know?"

Nadia hesitated but said, "I know what I would love most to do. I would love to go to film school in San Francisco. I have filled out my application on the line, but there is problem." She told them about the missing school transcripts and birth certificate, how they were at her mother's house but she doubted her mother would turn them over to her now. Nadia should have thought to ask her before she admitted she'd "gone heathen" as Kache called it, but alas, she had been overwhelmed by the reality of her family standing before her.

Snag sat up suddenly and said, "Nadia, tell me. Do you know a woman named Agafia?"

"I know of two. One is my grandmother."

"No, this woman would be younger than your grandmother. More along the lines of my age."

Nadia smiled. "But my grandmother *is* about your age. My mother is only forty-three. Remember, we start young in the villages. Why? Do you know my grandmother?"

"I doubt it was her. I met an Agafia once, when I was just a girl."

"My baba lived in Oregon most of her childhood. The other Agafia lives in Ural."

Snag nodded but said nothing more. Through the windows, the outdoor lights illuminated plump snowflakes lolling down. Inside, the fire waltzed around in the woodstove. Nadia went to take care of the last preparations for dinner and light the candles.

The table and the faces around it were bathed in an enchanting amber. The silver and the china and the crystal all reflected the candlelight, sparkling. Steam rose from the serving dishes, piled high with three days' worth of preparations, and Nadia allowed herself a moment of pure pride while Kache poured wine. They raised their glasses, and Lettie said the only blessing the family ever said, if you could call it a blessing. Nadia knew it from Elizabeth's journal: "Good wine. Good meat. Good God, let's eat." They clinked glasses until everyone had toasted everyone and said, "*Gracias, merci, grazie*, thank you," and Lettie asked, "Wait, how do you say thank you in Russian?"

And Nadia said, "*Spasiba.*"

"*Spasiba!*" they said in unison, and then they took a sip and started passing the food around.

Soon, Nadia was lost within her own memories of family and celebration. This is what she missed most. She did not miss the outdated rules and regulations, the never-ending church services, the squabbles about how and when and where to worship, but she missed the rituals that came with all that. The rituals were needed. *Everyone has them, even us heathens,* she thought. Humankind must have come up with rituals to help counter all the chaos and despair.

"Is that right, Nadia?" Gilly was asking her a question. Had she spoken her thoughts aloud? She found it difficult to stay alert in a group when everyone was conversing and you had to be ready to add your opinion when there was a lull or especially a direct question. She felt her face redden.

"What was that? I am sorry. I was thinking."

"What were you thinking about, dear?" Lettie asked while she dug into her rabbit stew. She'd passed on the turkey, saying the Old Folks' served it every Sunday and she was tired of it.

"I was thinking of my family," Nadia admitted. As they ate and helped themselves to seconds and thirds, Kache and Nadia filled them in on their trip to the village, which required the backstory of why Nadia had fled in the first place. Nadia suggested they wait for another time for her to talk about it, but they insisted that now was as good a time as any.

When Nadia finished her story, Snag set her glass down, wiped her eyes with one of the cloth napkins she had once given to Bets and Glenn for Christmas, leaned her forearms on the table, and said, "You *faked* your own death?"

Nadia nodded, red again, she was sure.

"That takes some *cojones.*"

Nadia wondered what *cojones* were while Lettie said, "You are miles beyond smart and brave, Nadia."

"But now I have no family."

"We will be your family," Lettie said with a nod. "We're not perfect, but we'll do."

"Far from perfect," Snag said. "I'm so far from perfect, you'd be better off leaving me out of it. In fact, Kache would have had an entirely different, much better life if—"

Lettie said, "Eleanor, no one blames you."

"Blames you for what?" Kache asked.

Gilly sat back in her chair, shaking her head, but Snag kept on talking. Now she was the one confessing. She confessed a whole story about how she met Kache's mom before his dad did, how she fell in love with her and never stopped loving her, even after Glenn and Bets got married and had kids.

"But I kept my mouth shut until that night before the plane crash. You remember, Kache? How I came over and we were all celebrating some silly sales award I'd received? We got to drinking. I got hammered like I've never been before or since." She took a deep breath and placed her hand on her heart. "Not that I'm trying to make excuses. There was a weird moment with your mom in the root cellar, and I…" She looked around the room. "I kissed her."

"You what?" Lettie's wrinkled lids lifted away from her pale, magnified eyes behind her glasses.

Gilly reached out and took Snag's hand, and Snag seemed to summon the words again. "I kissed her."

"Good Lord. Did she kiss you back?"

"No, no. But Glenn walked in before Bets even realized what was going on. And you can imagine how pissed off he was."

"Yes, I can." Lettie nodded.

"He took it out on you, Kache. Your dad could be a bully, but I'd never seen him like that. I had to pull him off you. So you see, Glenn wasn't in his right mind when they took off the next morning."

Kache stared, openmouthed, silent.

A long, quiet moment ticked by before Lettie said, "Eleanor, your brother flew in the *war*. He was an exceptional pilot. I'm sure Bets explained the context. A drunken mistake. He would have never knowingly put his family in jeopardy. He had a temper, and he was bulldog stubborn, but that man loved his family. So stop this now."

Snag bit her lip and shook her head. The room fell quiet again. "You want to know the worst thing? *You* felt guilty, Kachemak Winkel. I didn't know that you carried the burden of guilt over that fight you and your dad had the night before. Not until you told me this summer. And I've been trying ever since to find a way to tell you the fight wasn't what did it. The reason your dad was drunk and angry in the first place was because of me stepping so ridiculously far out of line. I am beyond sorry." Snag cried so heavily, her napkin became soaked. Gilly handed over hers and Lettie's too.

Gilly said, "Neither one of you are taking into account that 22 percent of all U.S. plane crashes occur in Alaska. And that's not because of a family quarrel."

Lettie added, "Or that they were flying through that horrible Rainy Pass, and you all know it's one of the worst blind corridors in the state. On a day when there was a three-thousand-foot ceiling with poor visibility. And that cloud cover comes out of nowhere."

Kache kept staring at his aunt, not speaking.

Pushing her chair back from the table, Nadia said, "Elizabeth didn't blame either of you for anything."

Snag blew her nose. "With all due respect, how would you know?"

Nadia said she'd be right back and went to retrieve Elizabeth's last journal. She returned, sat down, and opened the pages. This made Snag drop her head in her hands in more shame. "I told Kache I burned them like I was supposed to. I didn't even manage to do that right."

"You will be glad you did not burn them when I read you this," Nadia said.

But Snag reached across and grabbed the notebook from Nadia's hands, cranked open the woodstove, and tossed the whole thing into the fire.

"What the hell are you doing?" Kache yelled. He lunged for the fire poker and pulled the journal out. He grabbed a boot, hit the burning edges until the flames died, and then held the smoldering cover by the corner.

"She didn't want us to read them!" Snag tried to snatch it from him, but he lifted it far above his head.

"It's a little too late for that, isn't it? Do you really think she cares now?"

Lettie turned to Nadia. "Go ahead and read what you were going to read, dear."

Without saying a word, Kache handed it over to Nadia. The pages felt warm on her fingertips. She began Elizabeth's account of their last night together as a family, reading aloud the part about Alaska not forgiving mistakes and stopped to ask what it meant.

Snag said, "It's because the weather and conditions are so extreme. If you make the smallest mistake—like not dress warm enough, or fly a plane when you're angry—you might end up dead."

"Or," Lettie added, "you could do everything right and fly a plane when the weather looks fine but a storm comes up out of nowhere. These things happen, and too many times."

Nadia nodded and continued reading out loud. She was at the part she really wanted them to hear.

We drank too much last night, and we'll be paying for it for years, if not forever. I cannot believe that Glenn went after Kache like he did—out of control. It was always words, never physical until now. The saying of it is bad enough, and all of it needs to stop. I am ashamed I haven't put an end to it by now, and I swear it will not happen again in this household.

As for dear, kind Snag, I must talk with her. She thinks that the kiss was some kind of horrible revelation to Glenn and me—as if her feelings were something we weren't aware of. I think Glenn was just shocked and angry that she acted on it. But she was drunk. We all drank too much. I must tell her that if it were anywhere in me to love a woman fully—physically as well as emotionally—she would be that woman. That she will someday make a woman astonishingly happy. And that somehow, call me psychic if you must, I know this to be true.

We are all flying to Gunnysack for the hunting trip as planned. Ha! Lord help us, if we don't all kill one another first.

But for now, I will gather these men together, and we will fly away from here for a few days. We will look down on this house, this land—free from it—and the perspective will do us good.

When Nadia got to the last line, which ended with *do us good*, she added, "I don't think all this blaming yourselves over and over is doing them or you good. Twenty years is too long. Living in the past, like we are all of us Old Believers."

Snag's arms were folded on the table and held her buried head. The candles had burned down to nothing but lighted wicks floating in their holders, the wineglasses empty except for puddled stains, the leftover food turning hard and cold.

Snag finally stood. She let out a long sigh, looked at Kache through her swollen eyes, and said, "I'm not going to ask for your forgiveness. Not yet." Her voice squeaked, but she continued. "I know you need some time."

Kache looked up at his aunt.

Snag said, "I can take it."

"Honestly? I don't know what to say."

"Just know how sorry I am about the whole awful mess."

"Awful mess?" He shook his head. "That's a euphemism if I ever heard one."

He excused himself, silently pulled on his boots, and went outside. Nadia rose and cupped her hands around her eyes, the window cool on her fingers. His silhouette stood black against the snow, as if someone had cut a Kache-size hole out of the meadow.

She felt a pat on her leg and looked down at Lettie in her chair, who whispered, "This is how our family is, you see. Awfully messy. You still want in?"

Nadia said yes, she did.

chapter

sixty

AFTER THANKSGIVING, GILLY TOLD Snag she needed to have a talk, which sent Snag into another cleaning frenzy. By the time Gilly arrived, the house sparkled, but the mood between them felt dark and heavy.

"Please don't tell me you're moving on," Snag spilled before Gilly opened her mouth.

Gilly took Snag's hand in hers and looked deep into her eyes. "You know how much I love you. But I can't stand by and keep watching you beat yourself up. There's so much more we could be doing with ourselves, with our love. Either you forgive yourself, Eleanor, in a put-it-out-to-pasture type of way, or I think—no, I know—we should go our separate ways. Which would break my heart."

"But Kache is mad at me."

Gilly let out an exasperated sigh, and Snag shut up. Gilly's voice was soft but sure. "So let him be mad. He just found out, and he'll work through it. But you've known for two decades. You need to sing a different song."

Gilly left without kissing her, without even a hug, determined, it seemed, to mean business. Snag knew Gilly was right. Hell, Snag was sick and tired of herself too, and now sufficiently scared that she might lose the best person that had ever happened to her.

So late that night, after watching too many numbers on her alarm clock slide by, Snag devised a plan of penance. If she were Catholic, she'd go to confession and say a boatload of prayers afterward. But she wasn't Catholic, and so she thought that because she had hurt someone—a lot of someones, most of them dead—she should now set out to do something difficult in order to help another someone. She didn't for a second think it was enough to make up for her transgression. But it was a symbol she might stamp in her mind, a single gold star she could turn to.

It took her about a week to prepare, to talk over the details with Nadia and pick up her letter.

Snag reached the end of the snow-plowed road, climbed down the snow-packed trail to the beach, where the low tide she'd been promised by the tide book awaited her, the sand, rocks, and long ropes of kelp glistening with hoarfrost. She trudged along the beach until she spotted the next trailhead. She would work her way to the end of this second trail and soon step foot in Nadia's village. In her pocket was Nadia's letter to her grandmother.

Eleanor Snag Winkel. Embarking on a mission. And grateful she had been getting in better shape. She almost felt like running.

No one but Nadia knew that Snag had set off for the village. Both Kache and Gilly would have insisted on joining her, and that would get complicated. Well, Kache might not, considering he hadn't talked to her since Thanksgiving. And Gilly was about to cut her loose, so she might not have been quick to come along either. A verbal protest from both of them then, at least. Snag was, after all, a sixty-five-year-old woman traipsing through some pretty rugged country in the snow, on her way to confront a band of outsiders who would likely not be thrilled to see her. But the trail was firmly packed, and she had finally purchased several good, comfortable pairs of boots—the ones she wore now made to tackle snow—so all good so far. She fantasized that there might be a shot or two of decent vodka served up for her, but she wasn't counting on it. Hot coffee, maybe. Wait. She'd heard coffee and hard liquor were off-limits for Old Believers. Water then. She could use some water. Sweat trickled under her layers of clothes, and her mouth was dry. But as far as penance went, this journey didn't land all that high on the difficulty scale.

Here is how it played out in Snag's mind: For so many years, she had seen the time she kissed Bets as the most destructive kiss in history since the kiss of Judas. So maybe the time she kissed Agafia might end up being a positive, something Snag could use for good. She liked the symmetry of that thinking.

And yes, it was true that Snag was officially done—*done!*—beating herself up about kissing Bets. Nadia had helped Snag by reading Bets's journal to her that night. The poor young woman had been living alone for ten years, squandering the best years of her life. Snag related on some level. Time now for all of them to step forward. She saw that Nadia and Kache cared a lot about each other. She also believed that Nadia needed to fulfill her dreams, to experience the world outside the homestead. Even Snag herself had gone away to college for her business degree.

The woods opened into the village with its colorful homes, and a couple of boys who looked about thirteen greeted Snag. When she asked for Agafia, she told them she was an old friend, and they took her directly to her front door, painted bright green. Agafia shooed away the boys with some Russian scolding—at least it sounded like scolding—and asked Snag, with a guarded tone, "Who are you, and what will you want with me?"

"You are Agafia?"

The woman wore a head scarf and had wrinkles and kind eyes. She didn't answer but waited.

"You… I think…" How could she know for sure? It had been over fifty years, and she'd spent only a few hours with that young girl one day when she was thirteen.

"Yes?"

"I don't think you're the Agafia I know."

"You may be looking for Agafia Ruskoff. In Ural, other village. You come much too far out of your way." Agafia began to close the door, but Snag wedged her foot in the threshold.

"Wait, I…" Snag held out the envelope, and Agafia took and read it, and then she placed her hand on her heart.

"You come to talk about my granddaughter?" she asked. She touched her aqua blue scarf where it was knotted behind her neck. She invited Snag in, offered water, and insisted she sit at her kitchen table. Snag took the glass and thanked her.

"I don't suppose you have vodka," Snag said, mostly as an attempted joke.

One of Agafia's eyebrows went up. "Yes, I have. But this information, do not share with anyone, inside village or out. Except to maybe Nadia. Nadia is okay."

"Of course."

"This excellent way to start our mysterious conversation." Agafia went to open the freezer and returned with two teacups and a frosty clear bottle, which she poured from until the cups were full. Then she hid the bottle again in the back of the freezer.

"Oh, my word," Snag said and lifted the full teacup to toast the woman sitting across from her. To sip like tea or take as a shot? She decided to sip.

"Let me tell you before you begin. No use to going to her parents. They are people of strongest conviction and are mourning again for forty days, as if she dies all over again! I woman of deep faith. These, my people. Good people. Big hearts, hardworking people. But I do not agree with everything they believe. Heritage of my blood, not my brain, eh? Still, I am old, my husband dead, my children, grandchildren, great-grandchildren, they all to live here." She sat back, folded her arms across her chest. "So you see, I here to stay. But my heart, it breaks for Nadi."

"Will you just try to talk to her parents? Her father is your son, correct? She says he listens to you."

Agafia shook her head. "No. This causes big problem."

"Agafia, do I seem familiar to you at all?"

Startled, Agafia jerked her chin upward. "Do I know you?"

She leaned in, peered into Snag's eyes, kept peering, until Snag said, "It has been a very, very long time. Fifty-two years. There was one day. On the beach."

Agafia went back to the refrigerator to retrieve the vodka. As she opened it, one eyebrow raised. "You speak of when Nadia left us?"

"Sorry," Snag said. "It must have been the other Agafia."

"You make habit out of being social with Old Believers?"

While Agafia seemed to be appraising Snag, she topped her own cup off. (Snag had placed her hand over hers; she did have to make her way back before dark.) Snag told her of Nadia's desire to go to art school and how she needed the transcripts and birth certificate.

"Yes, I read this in letter. Ah, much easier than you think. Me, I keep copies of children's and grandchildren's documents in fire-safe box. After youngest son's house burns down, we do this. So I will send them with you today, no problems. Except then we have no record of Nadia, as if she never exists here. This, not good."

"Maybe you'll visit her where she lives now."

"Perhaps, but not likely. Not so easy for me to get around these days. Not like when I am young."

Snag wanted to ask her if she went on extremely long walks when she was young. She opened her mouth but stopped herself with another sip of vodka.

Agafia tilted her head. "What?"

"Nothing."

"But you are able to walk all this way here to help my Nadia? What is your name?"

"Eleanor."

"Eleanor. This is nice, beautiful name for you."

Snag felt the heat rush from her face down her chest. Blushing at age sixty-five. The vodka was getting to her. She wanted to stay and talk with Agafia all day and into the night, but the light was already fading, and she loved Gilly. She stood.

"I'm sorry, but I have to go. If I don't, I'll be stuck in the woods when it gets dark, and I'm liable to end up fending off a pack of wolves. Not to mention the tide. Can you give me the papers?"

"But these are the only records."

"What if I promise to mail them to you?"

"Ach. Mail is no good. What if they are lost?"

"I'll take good care of them," Snag said and knew she would. "I'll make copies and send them to you," she said and knew she would do this as well. "Give me a pencil and paper and we'll both write our post office boxes so you can reach me if you don't receive them."

With this, Agafia nodded. "Okay. Wait." She returned with a manila envelope with *Nadia Oleska Tolov, May 31, 1977* printed in English and again in Russian. Her scarf was gone, and her gray hair fell down her back. Snag thought she might indeed be the girl who once asked her for a kiss and she might just as well not be. The only thing that mattered was that she was Nadia's grandmother and she was handing over the papers Nadia needed.

"Now go, before darkness comes." She took Snag's arm and led her to the door. "Please you tell Nadia her baba loves her." Her voice became high and tight. "Loves her so very, very much." She handed her the envelope with Nadia's name on it. "This, all I have of her. Hide it from others under jacket. Do not lose. Do you to need directions to other Agafia's house?"

Snag said no, it wasn't necessary. She had everything she needed.

❧

Snag turned up the radio and hummed along. Mission most definitely accomplished. She couldn't wait to get home and tell Gilly. "Woman," Snag said aloud, practicing, "I'm finally, truly free. And I'm all yours. Plan on sticking around for a long, long time, Ms. Gilly Sawyer."

At the gas station on the outskirts of town, all lit up and welcoming, Snag filled the truck. She had to pee, so she left the gas pumping and went to the women's room. When she came out, several cars and a motorcycle had pulled in. A man stood with his hand on the same nozzle Snag had used, ready to remove it from her truck.

"Excuse me? Can I help you?" she called, irritated. *Why not use another pump?*

The man lifted his head and said with an accent, "Oh, your gas. It is done pumping. I was going to remove for you." He stepped back to pull the nozzle out.

As she moved closer, she recognized him. O Handsome One. She had definitely named him correctly. "Hey, I know you," she said and smiled. "Remember me? At the Spit Tune with my friend? Actually, you didn't see me then. But on the trail? We thought you were a bear, and you thought we might shoot?"

He tilted his head, tapped his chin. "Ah, yes! Yes, I do remember now. Please forgive me. The cold is dulling my brain, I am afraid. But you recognize me. You have good memory."

"I guess it was your eyes," she said while she thought, *Obviously.* Those lupine eyes with black, curly eyelashes. But his jawline, that was striking too. "That's a weird coincidence. I was just speaking to another Russian."

"Is that so?"

"Old Believer. Out at the village. Altai."

"I am not Old Believer. Only Russian. There are big differences."

"Of course. You can shave when you want."

He chuckled. "For starters, yes. I am not one for living with big group. So what is this business you have with the people of Altai?"

"Oh, long story."

He smiled his movie star smile. He said, "I have got quite a lot of time."

"I wish *I* did, but I have to get going. But nice talking to you."

"Likewise. Perhaps our paths continue to cross."

"You take care now." *Man,* Snag thought as she climbed into the truck, watching him fill up his motorcycle. *A motorcycle on a night like this?* He must be made of rugged stock. And there he was, flirting with *her*—she thought it might be flirting—even when Gilly wasn't around. Maybe she hadn't needed to feel jealous about him. Maybe, possibly, it was Snag he was interested in. Ha! Lose a little weight, and they start coming out of the woodwork, all walks of life, all genders. She had to admit, if every man in the world looked like that, she might have been tempted to play for the other team a time or two.

As she pulled away, she realized that she'd left the manila envelope on the passenger seat while she went to the ladies' room. There it was, with Nadia's name and birth date printed in English and Russian. She'd promised Agafia she wouldn't let it out of her sight, and she'd already done exactly that. She felt inside for the papers. Still there. Of course they were. Who else would want them? Nevertheless, she pulled a U-turn. She was tired and couldn't wait to get to Gilly's to

share her news, but Snag would go back. She would take them to
Nadia right away. With Snag's luck, if she took the papers home, the
cat would shred them before morning. She noticed the single lamp
of the motorcycle in the distance behind her until she turned off to
head toward the homestead, and she wondered where in tarnation O
Handsome One lived.

chapter

sixty-one

THE NEXT MORNING, KACHE tramped through the fresh snowfall
to feed the goats and found one of them, the pure white one Nadia
had named Buttercup, dead. From a distance, he thought fireweed had
somehow bloomed in winter. As he got closer, his stomach tightened.
Not sweet Buttercup. He might have missed seeing her if her blood
hadn't seeped pink through the fresh layer of snow. The poor thing
had probably been the prey of some hungry animal—a bear or a wolf,
but since they were still in the middle of winter, the bear was unlikely.
It looked like the beach hawks and eagles had been working on her
too. Kache looked around for evidence. The wind-brushed new snow
covered any tracks left behind.

Both Nadia and Kache took it hard. Especially Nadia. She'd grown
attached to all the goats, and Buttercup had been her favorite. But
Nadia had lost her share of animals over the years, and though she
shed tears, there was a practicality in her sadness that Kache admired.

A few days later, he helped her set up the tin cans on various-size
pillars of snow. The long winter twilight cast its palest violet veil over
the trees, the land, Nadia, everything. Kache stamped his feet to try to
get the blood moving faster.

"I think Buttercup would be very proud of you," Nadia said, stepping back to appraise their work.

He shrugged, checked his voice to make sure it sounded casual and wasn't laden with this shift he'd been feeling. He'd always hated guns. But they lived out in the middle of the wilderness, and he'd begun realizing the responsibility his father bore. He'd been able to keep them all safe, no small feat in Alaska—at least until the plane crash. A gun couldn't protect you from everything, but if you ran into a sow and her cubs, a pack of wolves, or an angry mother moose, a gun might be necessary, if to do nothing else but scare them away. It would soon be spring, and the bears would be waking up, cranky and hungry. "I just got to thinking. You're probably right. If I'm going to stay here, I should know how to shoot a gun. I shouldn't leave everything up to you. We're a team now, right?"

She nodded. "But your father, he did teach you the basics, yes?"

"He tried. I wasn't a very willing or attentive student."

"But you got straight A's."

He shook his head. "Is there nothing you don't know about me? Yeah, okay. But it wasn't my dad teaching trig or world history. This was different."

"I see. I understand." She stepped back. "Now, shoot."

As Kache held the .22 up to his shoulder, closed his eye, and lined up the bead on the first can, he knew he'd need to learn how to shoot the bigger shotgun if he actually needed to kill a bear or an angry moose. But this was a start. His numb finger pulled the cold trigger, and to both his and Nadia's amazement, he hit the can.

"You are lying. You know how to shoot gun."

"Some of what he taught me must have sunk in there and stayed after all."

He took another shot, missed, and then another and hit the next can. Nadia exchanged the .22 for the handgun. "Here, try this. We'll save the shotgun for another day."

He blew on his hands, and then he missed a few times. It was harder to steady the handgun. She wrapped her arms around him from behind and helped him secure his right arm with his left. The next shot nailed it.

"Kachemak Winkel, I think you are turning me on," she said. She stepped back. He took another perfect shot. "Very—how do you say it?—macho? Yes."

"I thought you liked the sensitive songwriter types."

"I do. Especially when they can shoot like that."

❧

They celebrated the successful target practice session with a different type of session on a stack of blankets in front of the woodstove. The spruce tree they'd chopped down stood in the corner, branches heavy with lights and all of his mom's decorations. Almost all of them, anyway. They'd had to throw out one box that shrews had taken over, but the rest of the ornaments were still in the paper his mom had carefully wrapped around them her last Christmas. She had let the boys pick out their own ornament every year and marked them, so along with the pretty glass balls, the handmade cloth Santas, and the painted wooden gingerbread houses, there were Star Wars characters and baseball bats and a tiny guitar. Kache wondered what he and Nadia would do once they had kids. They'd have to get a bigger tree.

It felt good to glow and sweat together, when outside the frozen dregs of winter surrounded them. He appreciated that Nadia was so willing to let him explore her. After everything she'd been through, she'd told Kache that making love with him felt something like grace.

She slept on her side, facing away from him, her body illuminated by the fire and the twinkling white lights of the tree, and he saw plainly not only the carved *B*, but also the small dashes of scars where Vladimir had pressed his knife. Sometimes Vladimir pressed the knife into her skin, far enough to draw blood, and sometimes deeper. She'd said that he liked to see terror in her eyes, that he held the knife to her breast or her throat and watched her face twist into panic until he grew stiff. The night he carved his initial into her was the night she'd refused him, and soon after, she had fled.

The dashes looked like some strange code or tracks in a field of snow; a message, a remnant, a territorial marking. She'd said he had been a trapper—an extremely patient and efficient one.

Kache was filled with wanting to protect her. He wanted her to know she would always be safe right there with him. He would be vigilant against any threat. Bad men. Hungry bears. Crashing planes.

She stretched like a silky pale cat and said over her shoulder, "Are you staring at my ass again?"

"It is lovely."

"Kache, we both know that is not quite true. Last time I got my hair cut, I admire Katy's tattoos. I am thinking of getting one to be as camouflage."

"What would you get?"

"I was thinking of butterfly. See?" And she stretched her arm back and showed him how the *B* might form the right side of the wings, tracing, retracing with her finger, and then with his, where the other colorful wings would go.

❧

With her video camera plugged into her Mac, her stylish elfin haircut, and her new clothing, Nadia looked as if she might already be at film school. While she worked, she sang along with one of his mom's many Joni Mitchell albums—or tried to sing, anyway. "Oh, but California…" Kache would never wince openly; he would never say to Nadia, *You sound like a cat in heat, who is dying and fighting at the same time*, because even though it was the god-awful truth, he knew she felt self-conscious about her voice, and this singing in front of him was her way of trusting him. It was a little disappointing that they would never sing in harmony, but also a relief; the woman couldn't do every single thing perfectly after all. Well, that and never charging her cell phone. Which reminded him to remind her.

"Did you happen to charge your cell phone?"

She tilted her head way over to her shoulder, smacked her forehead, and grinned.

"How can you be such a technology guru and not remember to plug in your phone?"

She'd picked up on the computer so quickly that she was now telling Kache how easy it was to edit a video. He knew nothing about film editing and could offer no help. Instead, he busied himself with snow shoveling, songwriting, and target practice. And plugging in her phone.

"I'm going to need one more scene," she said, leaning back in her chair, twisting from side to side to stretch her back.

"Oh yeah?"

"Yes. You at the Spit Tune place. Singing."

"Well, I don't know. It's been a long, long time."

"Snag says to me they ask about you all the time. And your friend Marion sings there, yes? With old band? It will be reuniting. I want to film there at this place. Please?"

He could swear she was actually batting her long eyelashes at him. Was this universal? Where did women learn these things?

❧

Finally, Rex was tending bar. He'd hit his sixties and had a lot less hair on his head with a lot more on his upper lip. When Kache said, "Hey Rex," the man almost jumped over the bar to hug him.

"Winkel, my man, it's good to see you. Snag and Marion said you were back in town. But it sure as hell took you long enough to come by."

"Hey, I've been by, but you've been down in the Lower 48 working on your tan. I can see business is as good as ever."

"We're in Alaska, and this is a bar. Of course business is good. And Marion and the boys still keep everyone coming back. Rumor has it you're playing and singing with them tonight."

"I heard a rumor like that too."

"Marion and Danny Boy are already setting up. Go say hi. And don't you dare leave here without having a beer with me. Who's the pretty gal?"

"Oh, I'm sorry. Nadia, meet Rex."

They shook hands and Rex said, "You always did have a way with the ladies, Winkel." Nadia blushed.

And then, as if on cue, Marion came up from behind him and pressed her hands on his eyes. He knew it was Marion because that is how she used to greet him in high school, and he knew she was doing it for old time's sake. "Marion," he said. "The only person who would try that on me at this age."

"Finally, you bless us with your presence. I haven't even bumped into you at the Old Folks' in a while."

"Marion, this is Nadia. Nadia, Marion." Nadia reached out, and they shook hands.

"So this is who's been keeping you so busy. You're the one with the camera, right? Nice to meet you. Kache, can you come and do a sound check with me?"

He looked to Nadia, and she smiled and waved him off.

"She's precious," Marion said as they pressed their way through the packed room to the small stage in the corner. "A little young, but darling."

"She looks a lot younger than she is."

"Oh good. Then we won't have to have you arrested." Marion stepped onto the stage to test the mic.

A deep, somewhat familiar voice said, "Arrested? You breaking laws, my friend?"

Kache glanced around before the man at his side momentarily lifted his cap and pulled his sunglasses down his nose. "Oh, it's Tol, right? Are you going all movie star on me? Going to do an Alaskan version of a do-it-yourself show?"

Tol laughed. "You are wishing. You might learn something. No, too many lights and people for me here. I must get to door and get some air. I can't stay long, but I look forward to hearing you sing your music," he said and disappeared into the crowd.

Dan, Mike, and Chris all hugged Kache at once, and soon, everyone was slapping him on the back, taking out their wallets to show him photos of their kids and wives. It seemed to be as Marion had told him: all had been forgiven. He'd left without a word and never looked back, but it was as if they'd played together last week. He was hoping the music would sound that way too.

Marion said, "So shall we play some old stuff to warm up? Then you can go through your song for the video, and we'll see where we can jump in."

He felt exposed, singing such a personal love song in this crowd. He'd done it in Anchorage, but he didn't know anyone there. Still, when the time came, he went for it, put it all out there, and Nadia filmed him.

"If you feel the need to hide,
I'll cover you and go bare.

If you can't walk another mile,
On my back I'll take you there.

"If you can't cross the river,
I'll lie down and be your bridge.
And if you lose all hope and vision,
I'll paint the sky from edge to edge.

"Because **Na***dia, you unknotted me.*
Na*dia, you undeniably*
Na*dia, you unarguably*
Made me a better man.

"If your eyes let go their tears,
I'll drink them like sweet wine.
If your gentle heart goes unclaimed,
I will gladly call it mine.

"If no one smiles at your jokes,
I'll laugh until I split in two.
Then there will be one more of me,
And I'll spend both lives loving you.

"Because **Na***dia, you unknotted me.*
Na*dia, you undeniably*
Na*dia, you unarguably*
Made me a better a man."

Marion and the guys rounded it out, and it sounded good. The whole place stood and clapped when they were done, and when Nadia took the camera away from her face, Kache saw that she beamed.

Marion must have seen it too, because she started speaking into the mic just as the applause finally died down. "Now we're going to go way back to the sweet and innocent old days. I know Kache remembers this one…" and she started in on the love song the two of them had written together. It was one of their best songs from back then, and they'd sung it when they were in love, with their lips almost touching, looking into each other's eyes, and this was what Marion did now. She walked over to Kache's mic and looked into his eyes while Dan started in on the piano.

Kache didn't play the guitar for this one. There was only the piano, soft and slow, and Marion's voice and Kache's voice, always in such close harmonies, and this song always did flay him. "I don't want to try…to deny…this love anymore. I'm falling faster…and further…than I ever have before." He forgot momentarily about Nadia, about the camera, about the crowded bar, about Rex filling glasses behind the counter, and he looked into Marion's deep brown eyes and remembered how fully he loved music back when they used to sing together, how nothing had scarred him over yet. His family was back with him in those words and notes; in fact, they hadn't even left. He remembered how much his mom and dad liked Marion and how Denny said he was jealous because she was such a fox. He remembered how when she came over, they treated her like family, and sometimes if it got too late, his mom would call her mom to see if it was okay if Marion spent the night on the couch instead of having to drive her all the way into town since it was so late and the roads were so icy. And when his dad's snores filled the upstairs, Kache would open his door ever so carefully, tiptoe down each stair, avoiding the places that creaked, and Marion would be waiting, would lift the sleeping bag and let him in.

The song ended, and with it, its spell. Kache blinked and turned away from Marion and saw Nadia, no longer filming, only watching, and all Kache said was, "Damn it." Unfortunately, he said this into the mic, so the crowd heard him and stopped clapping, waiting for him to finish saying whatever it was he was going to say. "So yeah. That was an oldie. Really old. Let's liven things up a bit. The band's going to play some of their new stuff, and I'll chime in when it feels right."

So that's what they did, and at the end of the night, when they were all sitting at the bar chatting with Rex, Kache heard Nadia ask Marion, "So you have always lived here in the town Caboose?"

Marion said that she had.

"You did not ever wish to leave?"

"Why would I, when I live in the most beautiful spot on earth? Where else is there?"

It seemed like Nadia wasn't sure how to answer this question. She picked up her camera bag. "Kache?"

Kache took that as his cue. "Yeah, we've gotta get going. Thanks. And guys, I promise it won't be so long. Let's do this again soon." Everyone hugged both him and Nadia good-bye. The bitter night air startled them when they walked outside, so that they both paused, held their breath for an instant, pulled their coats tighter, and dashed to the truck.

Kache attempted to begin a few conversations, but nothing stuck, like the wispy snow flurries that had started but wouldn't amount to much, needing only the wipers' lowest setting. He knew what was bugging her. He'd be bugged too. He'd blown it, but he didn't know what to say, and starting a conversation about the song seemed like admitting guilt. He'd gotten lost in the moment. Yes, he'd loved Marion once long ago, but it was Nadia he loved now and had even daydreamed of their kids. He knew not to tell her about that particular daydream just yet, because that would freak her out even more than him getting all moony-eyed with Marion. *Marion, you made me moony-eyed.* What an asshole. It was another memory, a good memory of his family, which singing with Marion had brought on. Totally innocent except for that one flashback regarding climbing into her sleeping bag, but that was quick—both the memory and the event itself. He must have smiled at this, because Nadia finally said something.

"So you are very happy and smiling. Tonight made you very happy."

"No. I mean, yes, but not in the way you're thinking."

"How do you know what I am thinking?"

"You seem to know what I'm thinking all the time. Maybe I found a journal about *you*."

The look on his face meant to say that he was only joking, that he loved her beyond anything he'd ever felt for any woman anywhere, but it didn't seem to translate, because her eyes held tears.

"Hell shit," she said. She wiped her eyes with her mitten and cursed again because a piece of the wool from the mitten had lodged itself in her eye. Kache switched on the overhead light so she could look in the visor mirror. He waited while she ran her finger over and over the surface of her eye. "There," she said, and he turned the light off.

"Nadia. I'm so sorry. I love you."

"You love a lot of people, I believe. Your heart, it is getting crowded."

"No. I don't know how to explain it. I was caught in the memories. My family really liked Marion."

"This is not helping me. I love your family! I have love for all of you for ten years. But none of them ever know me. Only you. You, who perhaps prefer Marion." She crossed her arms. "After all, she *sings*."

"Nadia, I love *you*. And my family would have fallen madly in love with you. Like Lettie and Snag have. Come here." He reached around, pulled her from her farthest shoulder, and she scooted across the bench seat. He put his arm around her, and she leaned into him. The wipers continued their steady back and forth, and the snow kept on dancing, fluttering in the beam of the headlights.

chapter

sixty-two

NADIA COULD NOT STOP working on her video. Up late at night while Kache slept upstairs, she thought she was close to finishing. But then she'd started reading about special effects. She wanted to try different techniques, especially slow motion, in a few spots. She loved how it created a heightened view of the action. Looking at what she had now, frame by frame, intrigued her.

She'd been studying some of the videos people posted on the Internet, especially on YouTube, and when she was done, she wanted to figure out how to post hers—which was not as brilliant as some, but better than most. No one would know about it. But how satisfying it would be for her to know it was out there, that she had created it and put it into the world beyond these four walls.

She'd been so busy working, she'd forgotten to carve her mark in the wall earlier that night. She rose to do this now, quickly, in order to get back to her video, looking for a clear space to begin the next grouping of five—she might need to start on a new wall soon. She stuck the knife into the wood and bore down, careful to make the line as straight as possible.

Back in the chair, something snapped outside, and her awareness

broadened from the computer screen to the tablecloth with its colorful fruit print to her own reflection in the dark window. Another snap,
and Leo scrambled from the floor and twitched his ears up. "Probably
just a moose, Leo. Or is it a wolf?" She and Kache had secured the
barn and added more chicken wire on the fencing to keep the animals
safe. Nadia rubbed her forearms to calm down the risen hairs—she
felt them beneath her sweater—then rubbed the top of Leo's head to
calm him down too.

No more sounds from outside, but as she worked, Nadia sometimes
felt as if she were being watched. Perhaps this happened when you
spent so much time behind a video camera. You began to see your own
life as a film. The great director, or whomever, calling for another take.

And if her life were a film, where would the next scenes take place?
Was she living out a love story? A tragedy? A comedy? That indeed
was a mystery. If only life fell into such neat categorizations.

Ever since the night at the Spit Tune, Nadia had been thinking
about how her and Kache's lives might or might not fit together.
Actually, she'd started even before then, when Lettie told her and
Snag about A. R.'s desire to live elsewhere. His sacrifice. It was so
much to ask of someone. Too much. When Nadia saw the connection
between Marion and Kache, she knew that it went beyond history
and music. They were bonded too by this place.

This place! This place had saved her long ago, and she was grateful, but it also became her prison. She knew only this place and the
Winkel family. She knew only how they had chosen to live their lives.
She had not yet chosen how to live hers. She'd taken on everything they
had built and made and even thought. Until this film, she had made
nothing lasting of her own. She had filled her mind with the words of
others from the bookshelves of another woman, from her diaries too.
But Nadia felt that she had not taken in enough of the world firsthand
nor given enough, and she wanted to. Oh, how she wanted to.

❧

She must have fallen asleep with her head on the keyboard, because Kache was touching her arm, his voice pulling her awake. "Nadia. The northern lights."

Her arms and feet flopped behind him as he led her to the coatrack, buttoned up her jacket, and held her boots for her to slip into. She was fully awake by the time they got to the back of the truck, where he'd lined the bed with sleeping bags and pillows and blankets, and there they lay to watch the sky pull its miraculous long green and rose curtains to and fro. The curtains transformed into running giants, falling ribbons, winding rivers, and huge tidal waves, crashing through the heavens.

Kache said, "The Native legends say they're spirits of those who've passed on."

"Have you seen them before?" she asked.

He said that he had. "Here's a story you haven't read in my mother's journal." He told her about the night he and Denny, teenagers and left alone for the weekend, raided the liquor cabinet out of boredom, and then out of even more boredom—drunken boredom—decided it would be a good idea to take down their father's beloved bear head, Anthony, from above the piano and go scare some tourists.

"You did not do this."

"We did."

"I have never seen this bear head Anthony."

Kache told her that's where the northern lights came in. "We take the ATV up the main road. It's almost dark, and Denny decides he'll keep the ATV light on and flag down the cars and I'll stand in the bushes holding up Anthony and, of course, growling, like this," and Kache growled.

"Not very frightening, Kachemak Winkel."

"Oh, come on. You're terrified, I can tell. Anyway, the only problem is that I've gotta pee, and if I stop and put Anthony down, that will be the very moment a car finally pulls over, and all the tourists see is some stupid drunk kid peeing in the bushes, and God knows they can see that anytime in the Lower 48. So I'm holding Anthony above my head for a good hour and doing the pee-pee dance and no cars come. Not one."

Kache stood and demonstrated a little jig while he held up the imaginary bear head, and Nadia laughed. He plopped back down and said that he finally set Anthony in the bushes and relieved himself, and that's when the northern lights made their appearance. "They don't show up much on the peninsula, and we'd never seen them like that. And we were absolutely blown away." They raced home on the ATV, the green splashing out above and beyond them, and they climbed up on the roof and watched until dawn.

It was then that they realized they'd left the bear head in the bushes on the side of the road. They went back and looked and looked, but the alcohol had dulled their memories. Denny thought someone had spotted it and carted it off. They made up a story about going into town for a movie and returning to find Anthony gone. *Stolen.*

"My father was bereft. He filed a report with the police. My mom corralled us into my room the next night and said, 'Boys. Do not tell me a thing. I don't want to know. I just want to thank you from the bottom of my weary heart.'" Kache laughed—a sharp croak of a laugh.

Nadia hugged him. "You are right. I did not know this story."

"Good." He squeezed her. "That's good." They too watched and talked until dawn, gazing at the incredible mystery of the sky, and Nadia told him she'd seen the northern lights a number of times.

"Were they as beautiful as tonight?"

"No," she said, resting her head inside his jacket, against his ribs, watching the roses and greens waltz with one another, on and on and on. "Not like this." She was sure that nothing in her life, in fact, had ever been as beautiful as this.

part five

breakup

2006

chapter
sixty-three

KACHE STRADDLED TWO SHIFTING plates of dirty snow and ice in the garden while Leo dug at something of interest. Underneath and all around, water gurgled, cutting the hillside loose from its winter acquiescence. Breakup was ugly, but man, was it full of promise. In less than a month, the whole land would burst forth in a showy display of fireweed and Indian paintbrush, forget-me-nots, lupine, five different kinds of berry bushes, not to mention the alders, cottonwoods, and groves of birch trees, leaves filling in with every shade of shimmering green. And that was just the start of it. He'd ordered so many new types of seeds for the garden, he couldn't wait to see the look on Nadia's face when they started arriving. He'd already sketched out plans for a greenhouse.

Night was receding earlier, letting the sun make up for its winter laziness, working overtime now, staying lower to the horizon, casting longer shadows. There was nothing like Alaskan light and all the astonishing subtleties that lay between the midnight sun and the winter darkness. A thousand varieties of light. Every day now, the snow shrank and trickled, and the mud oozed in growing patches, exposing everything from crocus shoots to fossils of frozen dog shit to a rusty oilcan and a trash bag left in the yard last autumn.

It had been almost one year since he'd returned. He had lived more in this one year than he had in the two decades he'd been gone, and that was no exaggeration. Frozen plates had shifted within him as well. He felt closer to his mother here, and Denny. Sometimes he even felt that the memories he had of his father were incomplete, perhaps unfair. That he and his dad had lived their relationship in a sort of endless winter, cold and cut off from each other, shouting through blizzard after blizzard of misunderstanding. He wished there was a way to go back and get to know him better.

Being here was one way to try at least. And he knew that becoming a father himself was another way. Not that *that* was any reason to have kids. But now he wanted them. He wanted Nadia and a couple of kids and a life right here on this land his grandparents had homesteaded and his father had lovingly and tenaciously tended. Wasn't that strange? To want exactly what his father had once had? Sure, Kache wanted to be a different kind of father. Gentler, much less controlling and stubborn. But not entirely different, not 100 percent different. "And that," he said to Leo, who had given up on the mysterious rodent and now tilted his head, waiting for Kache at the gate, "is damn near a revelation."

As they walked toward the house, Kache removed his glove and checked inside the pocket of his down vest. Still there. The envelope he'd folded and stuck in there earlier that morning when he'd picked up the mail at the post office. She'd gotten her application in late, after Snag had somehow come up with the necessary papers, practically bursting with pride when she presented them but not offering up any details, at least not in front of him. Snag and Kache still hadn't really spoken other than quick exchanges about Lettie, and he knew it was up to him to change that.

The envelope was addressed to Nadia and had a return address with the words *Academy of Art* and *San Francisco* in it. The envelope was too thick to see through, even when he snuck in and held it up to the high-watt sunlamp Aunt Snag kept under her bathroom sink for when she was experiencing seasonal affective disorder and needed to get her serotonin level up. Kache hoped Nadia wouldn't need the lamp after she read the contents of the envelope.

He loved that she had this dream, that she had already learned so much about film and art and life and the world on her own. He loved that she was so well-read and capable, so talented at whatever she tried. Yes, he was taken aback at times, insecure, especially at first. But he had grown; he could handle it. He felt challenged by her in the best way possible. He knew that a college application was not enough. Not enough to adequately prove all of her astounding qualities to skimming eyes looking for SAT scores and athletics and volunteerism and debate club involvement. And he knew that she liked the *idea* of living in a city but would despise the reality. The crowds, the pollution, the constant noise, the push and pull and hustle. She was a woman of this land. It was woven into her very being, as it was into his. They were relaxing into a life together. He'd even gotten Denny's old Land Cruiser running again, thinking maybe—who knew?—one day Nadia would want to drive again. She'd said her dad had taught her years ago. Now that Vladimir was gone and her family knew she was alive, he could picture her eventually driving to town herself, maybe even with a couple of kids buckled in the back seat.

But he would not say any of this to Nadia right now. He would let her open the letter, and he would hold her and assure her that all would be well, because he knew it would be.

But when she opened the letter, instead of dropping her head into her hands as he had predicted, her eyes widened, and she said, "Holy damn, holy hell, holy SHIT DAMN!" and she grabbed his arms and jumped up and down and then ran to the door, flung it open, and shouted, "HOLY SHIT DAMN!" once more.

He stood in the same spot by the kitchen while she humming-birded around him until she finally flopped herself over the arm of the futon and lay there, the missing tears making their late entrance, pooling in her eyes.

Kache closed the door and sat at the end of the couch. He lifted her stockinged feet, placed them in his lap, and said, "I take it that means you got in?"

She laughed and nodded, and the nod set the tears free so they slid down the sides of her temples toward her ears.

"Nadia, I'm so proud and happy for you," he said, and he meant it.

She sat up and threw her arms around his neck. "You are? Really? Thank you."

"Of course I am. How could I not be?"

She sat back and looked at him directly, wiping her eyes and nose with her sleeve. "Wait, let me get Kleenex," she said before hopping up and then returning to rest her gaze on him. A particle of Kleenex stayed trapped in one of her eyebrows. "Kache, you know this means many changes for us."

He chuckled, though he didn't mean to. "You're thinking of accepting? Of actually going?"

"No, I am not thinking. I have already thought, for many years. I am going."

"And how are you going to manage that?"

"Read this letter. There is scholarship. And work studies. They say I can get loan for remaining. And to assist me to adjust to this city living, there are people. I am part of their 'unique circumstances' program."

A scholarship? "I'm not talking about the money. I'm talking about conducting yourself in a city of hundreds and hundreds of thousands of people. I'm talking about a million different stimuli bombarding your senses twenty-four hours a day."

"You need to stop this talk. Now."

"Nadia, do you need me to point out to you that you were afraid to step foot off this property because of one man who probably left Alaska a decade ago?" Kache could not believe what was pouring out of his mouth. He *did* need to stop. He took a deep breath and took another.

"You are mocking me?"

"No, of course not. Forget all that. Look, Nadia, I'm sorry. That's not what I meant. You'll go, and of course I'll go with you. I'm really happy for you. I'm being an asshole. As cities go, San Francisco is one of the best. It will be an adventure. We can go for what? A couple of years? How long is art school?"

Nadia stood. She crossed her arms, uncrossed them, let them down at her sides. "Kache...you know I love you, yes? You know how grateful to you I am? I hope you can understand this thing that is very hard to understand. Even for me it is hard. This is something I am afraid to ask of you. Here is where you should be. Here you are happy."

He held both her hands, even went down on one knee, and it all came out. "It's because of you I'm finally at home here. I love you, Nadia." He said it. But that wasn't all, and there was no more holding back; the words had a will all their own. "I want to marry you. I want us to have kids if you want that too. Marry me, marry me, Nadia. Please?"

"Kache." She knelt too, held his face to hers, her breath a little stale, but he wanted to gulp it in anyway. "I love you. So very much. But I—I am not right for you. There is this thing I must do. This thing I must, to go and do alone. Please try to understand."

He stood. "Oh, that's great." He laughed again. His voice trembled. He was fucking out of control. "Yeah, you haven't had enough ME time, right? Ten goddamn years was not enough. We finally found this, what we have, each other, this place, all the good goddamn stuff that *everybody* wants, and you're going to throw it away so you can learn how to make better videos to post on YouTube? That is perfect."

"Your mother was right about your sarcastic streak, I see."

"Would you please stop doing that? I hate that shit. You're such a voyeur."

Nadia winced, still kneeling on the floor where Kache had left her. "I know you hate it. That is another reason—it can never be right between us. All I know is *you* and *your* family. I have no me to know."

"That's such classic bullshit. What, did you get that from one of my mother's self-help books? And now we're talking *never*? To think I wanted us to have kids, to be a family. What an idiot I am. We went from *for always* to *never* because of one typed letter with an impressive letterhead? Wow, *you're loyal.* I get it. You're only loyal when you have to be. When there's nowhere else to go." He got off the couch and threw the pillow they'd bought together in town. It hit the lamp they'd ordered online, which crashed to the floor. "Well, *I* do have somewhere to go. See ya." He grabbed his coat and stopped to pull on his boots.

Nadia finally rose from her knees. "Is that why you push me to see my family? Knowing they will not accept me? Knowing I will only have you, *your* family, *your* house, *your* history?"

"Nadia, is that what you think?"

"I do not know what *I* think! What is me, and what is—"

"I've gotta get out of here."

She grabbed his arm. "No, *I* go. This is your home."

"*How* will you go?"

"What about the Spit Tune? You are supposed to play there again tonight, yes?"

"I'll still do it. You're worried you won't be able to film it, is that it? You can drive the Land Cruiser. Drive yourself there." He pulled away from her.

"I have enough footage."

"That's what I thought. You've gotten everything you need."

"Kache, this you do not understand. I do not mean to hurt you. I do not want you to feel like your grandfather."

"My grandfather? What, did you find a journal of his too?"

Nadia wept so hard that Leo started whining, pressing his nose against her legs and hands. The Kleenex was now useless, and Kache watched her try to stop the deluge on her face with both sleeves of her sweater. He grabbed his scarf off the coatrack and handed it to her.

He wanted to hold her, to tell her again how much he loved her and wanted her to stay, but instead, he stepped over the ice and mud to his truck, started it, and turned the radio up so loud he heard nothing else, not the engine roaring, or Nadia crying, or Leo whining, or the voice in his head telling him he was quite the asshole after all.

chapter

sixty-four

KACHE HAD NOWHERE TO go but Snag's. A Honda sat next to her truck in the carport—Gilly's, no doubt. He knocked on the door and waited. He didn't remember ever knocking on Snag's door.

She called to come in and waved through the kitchen window. They both said hi and stood in the living room while Gilly grabbed her keys and purse and said she needed to head back to work. After she left, Snag started to get her cleaning supplies out, but Kache took her arm and pulled her back into the living room. They both sat, Snag in her rocker and Kache on the sofa, and Kache dropped his head into his hands.

"Oh, hon. Does that mean you forgive me?"

He nodded. "We all wish we'd handled things differently." Was it fair to blame Snag for falling in love with his mom? It turned out he and Snag both fell for smart, brave, kind women they couldn't have. He was so tempted to turn on the television, but he let the sadness keep rolling in until it filled every corner of the room, of him.

In time, Snag cleared her throat and began to speak. "There's something I've been wanting to tell you, Kache. It's a long story, but I want you to know it."

Kache nodded, leaning back on the couch to listen.

"I was home from college, cleaning windows for the summer. One day, your mom talks me into playing hooky from work. We head toward Anchorage, up by Turnagain Arm, and the tide was out, coming in, but still way out there. This is long before they put up all those warning signs. Bets got an inkling that we should go clamming. 'Oh, Snag, let's!' she said. She had never been, and of course I wanted to be the first to take her, so I said, 'Why not?' I had pails in the back of the truck for cleaning windows, and I always kept a shovel and a couple of pairs of hip boots on hand."

She told Kache how the extra hip boots had been his dad's and four sizes too big, but Bets wore them anyway, and Snag teased her about swimming in boots before they ever got to the water. "But she traipsed along against the wind—your mom always was such a trooper—her hood tied tight around her head like a little kid." Snag gave her a couple of pointers about looking for the indent in the sand and how you had to dig fast before the clam burrowed itself deeper. "Pretty soon, I was loading my pail and Bets had gone off to load up her own. I got lost in the hunt, and next thing I know, Bets is yelling, 'Snag! Help! I'm stuck in the sand!'"

Snag said she looked up, and her heart stopped. "You know that crude saying about the Alaskan tide comes faster than a sailor just home from leave? It was never so true." Bets had gone out too far, and Snag saw where the darker glacial silt, the stuff they call Alaskan quicksand, began. There was no way Snag could reach her without getting stuck herself. The water soon swirled around Bets's ankles.

"Any other person would have been screaming their fool head off. But not your mom. She stayed calm, staring down the waves. Such dignity. She yelled over the wind, 'Snag Winkel, don't you go blaming yourself for this, okay? I should have never insisted in the first place, and then to wander out here like an idiot. I'm a few rungs short of a full ladder.' She was thinking of *me* while she faced her death head on. And then she hollered. 'Wait, the *ladder*!'"

Snag told him she'd understood immediately. She tore up to the parking lot and drove the truck right onto the beach, stopping to check the sand so she could get as close to Bets as possible. She pulled open the long steel ladder and, with every ounce of strength she had, flung it out and aimed it at Bets, who was eventually able to grab the end of it. Snag rested the other end on the tail of the truck bed, and with Snag's guidance, Bets pulled one leg out of the oversize hip boot and then the other and crawled up the ladder, onto the truck bed, and into Snag's embrace.

"She had been so brave, so composed. We clung on for dear life and kissed each other's wet freezing cold cheeks, and I remember the taste of salt—all mixed in from our tears and our sweat and the ocean—and we swore we'd never tell a soul how stupid we'd been, how close we'd come to tragedy, and I kept that promise until now."

Kache leaned forward and let his elbows rest on his knees. "Wow. She always warned us about those mudflats but never said she had personal experience with them."

"The reason I'm telling you all this now, Kache? When that plane went down, I think your mom somehow gave them courage like she'd given it to me. In those split seconds? When someone else would have been screaming obscenities, she took in all their fear and wrapped them in her love and acceptance. That's who she was."

Kache liked hearing this about his mom. But he knew Snag was wrong about one thing. He shook his head. "It's nice to tell ourselves these stories, ease our survivor's guilt. But no. You know they were scared shitless, Mom included, no matter how brave she was, no matter how amazing she was, and no matter how none of them deserved to die that way. They did. And it was fucking terrifying. Every goddamn second of it. You know it and I know it. And to make it less than that seems cowardly. There's no way we can rely on lines like, 'At least they didn't suffer,' because they *did*, and we can't say, 'At least they're in a better place,' because there was no better place to the three of them than that homestead."

Kache took a deep breath. "We'll never know if Dad was thinking of you or me or anything other than getting through the cloud-filled corridor. We'll never know, Snag. All we know is that they died and we'll miss them every single day for the rest of our lives."

He went on. He couldn't stop talking. He told her about Nadia and the fight.

Snag said, "You are so much like your dad."

"You mean my mom."

"Well, that too. But you've definitely got some Winkel in you."

"Such as?"

"Winkels never forget anything."

He laughed. "Yeah, I've definitely got that gene."

"Which is why I know you didn't just *forget* to ask for Nadia's school papers."

He stared at her. "Yes, I did."

"Hon, if you really want to call off the bullshit, let's be consistent. You didn't want her going off to art school, just like your dad didn't want you going off to music school. I'm not saying it was completely conscious. But we instinctively want to keep those we love close and safe. Problem is irony kicks in when we try to play that game. Your dad, for instance, used to say how rock and rollers always died in plane crashes."

"He did not."

"He did."

Kache ran his finger down his nose. "He just hated my music."

"Then why did I always catch him on the nights your band played, parked outside the Spit Tune with the heater blasting and his windows rolled down?"

"You did not."

"I did." She sighed. "Your daddy loved you, Kache. He just had strange ways of showing it sometimes. But you've got your mama in you too. You can do better than he did."

Kache leaned back against the sofa cushion and stared at a crack in the plaster. "I guess I won't be needing to stay here tonight after all."

"Well, there's a piece of good news." She stretched and hugged him. She said that she had to run some errands, that she'd see him later at the Spit Tune. Kache tried Nadia's cell phone, but it went straight to voice mail. He thought she might at least charge it after he'd left. An hour to kill—not enough time to drive out and apologize before the show. So he grabbed his guitar, sat back down, and started playing with a song idea that had come to him when he was driving into town. He just needed to remember to leave early enough to get some gas on his way to the Spit Tune.

chapter

sixty-five

IN KACHE'S OLD ROOM, where she'd slept for the ten years before he came back, she patted the bottom bunk to tell Leo it was okay, and he curled up at her feet and watched her, worrying.

She never imagined that a dream coming true would be so difficult. She never thought it possible to love someone this much and still feel it might be right to say good-bye. She loved him more than she'd ever imagined caring for another person. But still Nadia felt that what she had to offer him lacked a wholeness.

And now he said he wanted children. She wished she could talk to Lettie again, or Snag. But talking about this meant crying, and she did not want anyone to see her weakness.

Leo followed her outside into the lingering twilight. A lone sandhill crane took a few steps on its long delicate legs and bent its long delicate neck to stab its beak at a worm.

"Is it you?" she asked. "Where is your love?" With so many predators to worry about—even bald eagles, and certainly dogs—this crane held itself on the land in a confident familiarity. It shared a long look with her; its yellow eyes behind the red mask took inventory of Leo, who would not leave her side that evening even to scare off a bird. It went back to its worm. Nadia walked over to the single birch tree that stood alone and pressed her forehead to it, asking it to share some of its strength. She went to the barn and ran her hands over the sheep and remaining goats, patted the cow, clucked at the chickens in their coop. "I am not alone," she said aloud.

When the darkness forced the last light away, it was almost 10:00 p.m. No sign of Kache. She sat at the kitchen table, checking to see how many more views her video had received from strangers. Kache had asked to see it for weeks, but she'd told him she still wasn't finished, when, in fact, she'd posted it on YouTube and sent it to film school. She'd wanted to wait and surprise him for his birthday. Something crackled outside, but she hadn't heard Kache's truck pull up. It was the very pregnant cow moose or the sandhill crane that half considered themselves seasonal pets, showing up through summer. Or perhaps a bear or another wolf. She hoped not; she would have to shoot whatever started threatening the barn animals.

The house creaked and settled. Outside, the wind picked up, cried, and whistled, scraping tree branches against the upstairs windows. In the city, there would be many more sounds. Sirens and neighbors' laughter and yelling. People running down stairs and doorbells and music and even, sometimes, maybe someone scream-ing, like in the movies.

She wrapped Lettie's afghan around her and buried her nose in the fur of Leo's neck.

She didn't know what to do.

And then she did.

She grabbed her video camera. She pulled the Land Cruiser keys out of the drawer. Yes, it was crazy, but Kache said you never really forgot how. If she hurried, she could catch the very end of the show.

chapter

sixty-six

KACHE SANG HIS BUTCHERED heart out. He sang every song he could think of other than "The Nadia Song." He had the band, the crowd—they were all with him, upturned faces, raised hands clapping—and he never wanted to stop singing.

He took out the crumpled envelope he'd written the lyrics on, smoothed it out, stuck it on a music stand, pulled the stand in front of him, and said, "You heard it here first, folks. This song's a virgin, have never once sung it. So bear with me. Still don't have a chorus, so let me know if you think it needs one." He took a sip of water, checked the tuning on his guitar, and began.

"I believe in our old windowpanes
and how they catch light like the water.
I believe in the dimpled cheeks
of our future son and daughter.
And I believe in the first time
I held your hand on that old water bus.
But I can't believe this is happening to us.

"I believe in the forget-me-nots
we arranged in that crooked vase.
I believe in the soft, sweet smell
of your kind and pretty face.
And I believe in you and me
growing old and gray together.
But I can't believe you're changing with the weather.

"I believe in strength and frailty
of the body, mind, and spirit.
I believe love fades sometimes
to a whisper, but I still hear it.
And I believe in honesty
and wearing my heart on my sleeve.
But I can't believe you said you have to leave.

"No, I don't want to believe you said you have to leave."

Marion tucked her long hair behind both ears, placed her hands on her hips, and waited for the applause to die down. "I think we all need to take a break after that one."

Kache went to the bar, and Rex slid him a beer.

Before long, the Russian guy Tol greeted Kache and said, "You are quite a good singer and writer of songs, my friend." Kache thanked him. "My friend, Kachemak Winkel." Tol drank, looking straight ahead. He had a strong jawline.

Suddenly, Tol leaned over and placed his hand on the back of Kache's neck like they were coconspirators. "I wish for you to play that song you played the last time you were here. What is the name of it? 'Nadia'?"

Someone else elbowed their way in next to him. "Hi there,

Nephew." It was Snag, who leaned over and patted him on the back. "You made me cry. Gilly too. Hey, you *again*?" She was talking to Tol. Snag knew Tol? "Saw you at the gas station, and before that on the mountain, and what is it, three times here now? Weird that I never once ran into you and now you're everywhere."

"It must be destiny, eh?" he said, raising his hands, palms up. "Actually, I come and go. A nomad."

"Hey, do you live way out at the east end? I could have sworn I saw your motorcycle behind me that night, when I turned back to the homestead after I left the gas station?"

At that point, Marion said into the mic, "Let's get the star of the show up here, and we'll be ready to sing a few for you before you have to head out in that wind. Kache?"

Tol yanked hard on Kache's sleeve and held on. "That Nadia song, it is not finished, I think. Too much happy. It needs sadder ending. A tragedy."

His face was too close. *Asshole.* Kache jerked his arm away and took his beer and his place back on stage. They started in with that old Tom Waits song, "Grapefruit Moon," but Tol called out, "Hey, play song called 'Poor White Goat,'" and Kache stopped singing and looked for Vladimir, because at that moment, he knew—every blood cell pummeling through his body knew—that Tol was Vladimir, the man who was no longer seated at the bar.

Panic squeezed Kache while he scanned the room. *Where is he? Where is he?* "Gotta run," he said and felt in his pocket for his keys, but they must have been in his jacket. "Marion, take it from here."

Kache pushed his way through the crowd, ignoring everyone who tried talking to him, looking everywhere for his jacket. Where the hell did he leave it?

He yelled, "Where's my jacket?" and Marion, looking confused, stopped singing and asked if anyone had seen Kache's jacket.

"What color is it, Kache?" she asked into the mic.

"Dark blue!" Kache was about to ask Snag if he could borrow her truck when someone held up his jacket, and Kache grabbed it, felt for the keys, and ran outside.

In the center of the parking lot, he spun around, scanning for taillights or exhaust, but there were none. He ran to his truck, peeled out of the lot and onto the spit, and drove as fast as he could but saw no taillights in front of him either. He hit the steering wheel, kept hitting it, and tried to call Nadia on his cell, but it went straight to voice mail. He thought, *That woman could not keep her phone charged if her life depended on it*, and then regretted the thought immediately.

Leaning forward, he pressed down on the gas pedal and tried to think. Who could he call? No one. Should he call the police? And say what? *There was a guy with a Russian accent who requested a song about a goat and it spooked me?* By the time the Caboose police found their friendly way to the homestead…no. Kache reached across to the glove compartment and popped it open. Nadia had talked him into keeping the handgun in there. "Even what you call the hippies in Alaska have their rifles on a rack. You can at least hide a gun in your glove compartment, yes?" And so he had. And there it was.

He knew he was not overreacting. He knew it. Everything merged together in his mind, how Tol—Vladimir, Vladimir *Tolov*—kept running into Snag, how he probably trailed her to see her turn down the road to the homestead. Or maybe he'd been trailing Kache too. Shit. The asshole was at the Spit Tune the night Kache and Nadia were there. How long had he been following them around? Had he been lurking around the homestead, waiting for an opportunity?

Kache had given her a false sense of security, insisting he was long gone, all while drinking beer and chatting it up with the psychopath.

And then all the horrible things Kache had said to her earlier started shooting through his head, but he stopped himself. He needed to think clearly. To be smart and do everything exactly right. He needed to not fuck this up.

"Nadia, Nadia, Nadia." He wasn't singing; he was pleading. "Don't open the door. Wait for me."

Almost there. But the truck lagged as he approached the turn off the main road. Another lag, and then it died. No. He turned the ignition. *No, no, no. Shit.* His head had been so far up his ass and then so lost in that damn song, he'd forgotten to get gas. Stupid and dangerous, even on a normal day.

Wait. A full gas can in the back.

At an unbearably slow speed, the gasoline meandered its way through the long spout into the tank, Kache urging and cursing it.

ꙮ

Denny's Land Cruiser sat parked in the middle of the road where it turned into the driveway, blocking Kache's truck. A motorcycle lay on the ground next to the driver's side. Kache grabbed the gun and jumped out: Nadia's uncharged cell phone was on the seat, keys gone. He took off running toward the house. Had she tried to drive the Land Cruiser? Had it died?

He heard Leo going crazy in the house, like he had that very first night. Trying to catch his breath, Kache kept the gun down close to his side and ran up the steps. Leo was behind the front door, scratching, barking even at Kache. He turned the knob and pushed open the door, and Leo bolted out, ran down the porch steps sniffing, ran back to Kache and then out the gate toward the beach trail, nose to the ground, fur standing up in its own path on his back. Kache grabbed the flashlight that they kept on a hook in the kitchen and followed Leo. "Good boy, good boy. Where is she, Leo? Where is Nadia?"

He wanted to scream her name, but he didn't want Vladimir to know he was there. How far could he have taken her, through the patches of snow and ice and mud? The moon hung fully ripe, casting silver light on the land, and he saw clearly enough, even without the flashlight. Wind whipped and roared so loudly, it sounded like the ocean crashing through the trees. Why the beach? But Kache knew.

Nadia. *Wait.*

Leo zigzagged ahead of him, sniffing the mud and snow. He never lifted his head, just kept in a staggering, frantic line while Kache followed. "Where is she, Leo? Find Nadia."

"Kache!" Nadia screamed. "Here!" He rounded the bend to see her kicking and twisting while Vladimir dragged her by the waist off the path that crested the ridge, toward the cliff.

There they stayed, on the precipice, the moon spotlighting them. Vladimir held his knife to her throat, and Nadia had stopped fighting. She clung onto the arm that gripped the knife, but she did not flinch. Her eyes wide with terror and locked on Kache. Leo crouched, growling. Kache raised the gun.

"Hello, my friend," Vladimir shouted over the wind. "Took you a long while, eh?"

"Let her go and I won't shoot."

"You will hit her instead, pussy boy."

"Put the knife down. Put the knife down and leave and no one gets shot." His voice and hands shook, and he fought to keep them steady. He sounded like he'd watched too many cop shows as a kid. Trying to be the tough guy he so obviously wasn't. He wished he had the .22 rifle instead of the handgun.

"I must look like fool," Vladimir shouted. "I *am* fool. I thought she was dead." He spit his words in Nadia's face. "You think you can just leave again? You trick me. Why not drown yourself for real? Leave me dirty work. It's always left to Vlad."

Leo was still crouched, growling, at Kache's side.

"No. Just put the knife down." *I cannot let her die. I cannot let her die.*

"Say good-bye to Nadia. This makes good song. At least she told you she has to leave. Me she only tricks." He continued talking, most of it gibberish. Kache remembered that Nadia called Vladimir a patient trapper, and he wondered if that's what this was, him feigning insanity while waiting for his moment. While Kache waited for his.

"Let her go. She hasn't hurt you. Just let her go, and I'll let *you* go."

"You will *let* me? How kind." Vladimir laughed, his disturbingly amiable laugh, as if they were all close friends.

As if he didn't hold his hunting knife to Nadia's throat.

chapter

sixty-seven

NADIA LOCKED EYES WITH Leo, not Kache. She didn't want Kache to look at her, because it would be the death of them. *Yes,* she told Leo without speaking. *Keep your eyes on Vladimir's knife.*

The knife glinted moonlight in her eyes. She knew why he had a knife instead of the easier gun, knew that Kache had interrupted his long-thought-out plan. He had told her as much. He did not want to only kill her—the killing would be the last act of a winding story, and that is why he hadn't yet cut her throat. Now he muttered about sacrificial lambs and goats and how the bear must always be fed.

For an instant, she imagined the thin red line and how it would spread. She closed her eyes, opened them. There were special effects. The silver light on the trees could be turned up so that it too had a sinister glint.

Slow motion set in. Frame by frame. Kache holding the gun in place, Leo crouched, silent now. Close up to his eyes on her, waiting.

❧

There are different ways to tell a story. One second can be slowed down, dissected for all its worth: life, death, retribution. But whose?

What has been unclear for a decade comes into a single, focused frame.

You. Me. A knife.

Again.

But I said never again, and I meant it.

I built my life around never again.

And yet here we are.

You. Me. A knife.

But there is more now.

There is them.

Cut to them.

Look in their eyes and admit you see that I have found love despite you.

That alone is my revenge.

But what will be yours?

Killing me?

Or forcing me to kill you?

You think this choice belongs to you.

It does not.

It is mine.

❧

She silently said *Now* to Leo with a nod. He snarled and leaped onto Vladimir, going for his throat. The man reeled back, trying to regain his balance. Leo released his hold, but Vladimir stumbled back, twisted around, hung on to Nadia.

Leo attacked again, and her feet went out from under her. Was this it? Her face was covered by his open jacket, falling. But then ground, not a freefall over the edge. She lay on top of him, scrambled up. Vladimir jumped to his feet, but before he could regain his balance,

Leo pounced. Nadia thought but didn't say, *Kache, don't shoot now. Don't shoot Leo.*

With all the strength Vladimir had given her—for his wickedness had given birth to her courage as well as her fear, she knew that—Nadia reached out and placed her hands on his back, the heft of him crashing against her, but then came another pounce from Leo, a final heave from the deepest part of Nadia, and Vladimir became weightless. He plummeted off the edge, into the canyon.

His howls joined the wind. His screams—"MY GOD... My God... my god..."—faded into the infinite sea of trees.

chapter

sixty-eight

KACHE RAN TO NADIA, gathering her up in his arms, asking, "Are you okay? Are you okay?" and she insisted she was while Leo jumped on both of them.

"Good boy, Leo, good boy," Kache said, rubbing his head. They took small, careful steps nearer to the edge of the canyon, but not all the way. They held back, looking down. Nothing but the black, pointed shapes of the tops of trees. Kache took out his flashlight, but it provided a pinprick of light in the vastness.

Nadia said, "We should call the police." She heard the tremble in her own voice.

They started back, but about halfway, Kache stopped. "Nadia. I don't think we should call."

"What if he's not dead?"

"Exactly. Listen to me. If we call the police, there will be a huge media frenzy. It will become all about you—the hermit woman who fled her backwoods village. The Old Believer who faked her own death. They will put some strange spin on it, and you'll be hounded by every talk show host and news agency in the country. And I know you did the bravest possible thing—but you may still be charged with murder."

She understood. He was right about that. "What is it that we do?"

Kache began walking in fast circles around her, lost in thought. "I should go. I'll go and find him."

"And then what?"

"I just want to make sure he's dead. No one could survive that fall. But just in case…"

"And if he isn't dead?"

"I'll decide what to do then. It depends…"

"On what? What if *he* kills *you*?"

"He won't. He's going to already be dead. I just want to make sure. I want to know, to see him with my own eyes so we both know."

"How will you ever make it down there? It's way too steep."

"My dad did it. I can do it. I'll take it slow."

She didn't want him to go, but she saw a determination cross his face that she understood. He would go anyway. It would do no good to fight him. It would undermine his confidence when he needed all of it. And she too wanted to know that Vladimir was dead for certain.

"Only if you take Leo with you."

"Then I'll have to worry about *him* falling. I've already lost one dog to this canyon."

"But that was because Walter chased butterfly, dreaming and distracted. Leo is good on his feet. He will show you the way. And he will protect you if Vladimir…" But she couldn't finish. She watched Kache while he considered her proposal.

"Okay," he finally said. "There will be enough light soon. Let me get some supplies and one of the smaller packs. And rope in case I need it. Call Snag and have her come out to stay with you. Hurry."

She could not keep her hands and words from quivering. "He was taking me to the beach, Kache. He said if I want to drown so badly, I should ask him for help the first time." She left out all the other things he'd promised he would do to her.

"I'm so sorry. I should have never left you. But it's over now. It's almost over."

She knew how wretched that canyon descent was and that they were still a long way from "almost over." The adrenaline kept her legs moving forward as they raced their way up the hill toward the house.

❧

A few hours after Kache and Leo had left, Snag paced a pathway from the homestead's kitchen sink to the woodstove and back. She stared out the window. "Part of me—a big part of me—thinks we should call the police. But Kache is right about the media. It will be endless. It will be twisted. And it will be hard for you to survive it." She'd started by holding out one finger, and with each point she made, she stuck out another finger. "And there's no way a man could survive a fall like that. And this is Alaska. It's the Wild, Wild West. And you're saying he didn't have any family or friends?"

"No, none. He was always loner. He came from the village in Oregon, but he left Altai not long after I did. He never mentioned anyone this whole time I knew him."

Snag kept pacing. She called Gilly, and Nadia could hear them going over the story again until Snag said, "Yes, yes. You're right. Okay. I'll wait." Then she turned to Nadia.

"If Kache doesn't return by midmorning, I'm calling the police *and* search and rescue."

chapter

sixty-nine

IF IT WASN'T FOR Leo, Kache wouldn't have known where to break trail, but the dog seemed to have a sixth sense or at least a plan about how to go about descending the crevice—and that was more than Kache had.

So Leo led the way in the first breaking light, creating his own switchbacks when he could or stopping when he couldn't and waiting for Kache to take his scythe to the profuse underbrush, alder, and berry bushes. Much of the still-clinging snow was mud streaked and not in the least bit stable, and Kache would often call Leo to his side and test it with the ski pole before they stepped. When they weren't managing the rickety patches of snow, they were bogging through mud and newly released creeks. Every five or six steps, Kache stopped to listen for Vladimir, or for a bear and then set down the ski pole, picked up the scythe, and hacked at another gristly bush.

The sweat poured from him, even through the ridiculous cold. His clothes went from mud crusted to damp with sweat to washed clean but soaking wet from slipping in the creek water. His boots—good mountain-man boots—helped, but Kache needed much more than a good pair of boots.

How absurd. How cavalier of him, a man so ill equipped, to tell the fair maiden he would slay the dragon, the dragon she'd had the courage to kill. The dragon probably lay dead, and odds were that Kache would end up dead too before this thing played out. But he had to go. What else could he have done? He wanted only to get this one thing right.

"Keep going. Not much farther now, Kachemak." He was so far gone that he heard his dead father talking to him. But he let him. Kache needed the company. "There's a bench of land you can't quite see yet. A nice big ledge that rises out of nowhere."

"Is that where you found Walter?"

"Yes, Son, it is."

Sure enough, the bench presented itself. Kache must have heard a tidbit of his parents' discussion to have this information lodged in his subconscious and hear it resurface in his dad's voice.

But all the same, Kache said aloud, "Thanks, Dad."

"If he's alive, you know what you have to do. I'll be here for you, you understand?" Kache nodded that he did. "Now head west about fifty yards."

Kache and Leo inched on in a westerly direction and came to a cleared area where large rocks—maybe a dozen of them—lined up, and when he stepped back, he saw that they were spaced in the shape of a *W*.

Walter. Good Walter.

Throat tight, he said, "Thanks for showing me this. It means something to me. It does. But I misunderstood."

"You want to find the Russian. Keep going. About forty more yards."

Milky light filled the sky. The cold and wet had ravaged his clothing, and he wished he could discard it. Leo sniffed the air incessantly, whined, snarled, and began barking. "Shh. Quiet, boy."

Vladimir lay on the blood-soaked snow, which had turned a

disturbing pink. A branch pinned him down, both legs bent in unbendable directions. "Thank God you have come. Thank God you are here," he whispered, his face contorted, his breathing shallow. Kache checked his coat and pants for the knife or a gun and then knelt to give him water. He saw then that Vladimir wasn't under the branch but had been impaled through the gut by it. The branch was so thick, it must have been the top part of the trunk of a birch tree. Kache looked away when he thought he saw a smear of the man's intestines on the bark.

"Vodka…in my pack…there. Then you shoot… Quick, my friend."

"I'm not your friend. I should carve my initials all over you," Kache said, but he found the pack a few yards away, retrieved the canister, and held it to Vladimir's lips. "I can go and get help. We can helicopter you out." He said this knowing that Vladimir would not survive the time it would take.

"Dying. Must shoot."

"I don't want to fucking shoot you."

Vladimir grimaced. "You owe…nothing…but I beg…mercy." He was crying now, coughing up blood. "Here." He tapped his chest. "Shoot…"

Kache swigged the vodka out of the canister. Swigged again. Saw the dark eyes of the crippled moose, that day with his father. *This isn't murder, Son. It's mercy.* Kache put his hand in his pocket and set his fingers in their places. He said, "Vladimir, let's talk about—" And in one fluid motion, Kache pulled the gun out and shot Vladimir in his dark heart above his pierced stomach.

The dead man stared at him, his eyes blank in their sinister beauty. Vladimir's eyes truly were unique, almost purple, set off with black brows and thick eyelashes. His mother must have loved those eyelashes. Nadia must have too, at the very beginning.

I won't tell her how much you suffered or how you begged, Kache thought. *Even though I want to.* He hung his head and cried out with relief and gratitude and shame. Leo whined and scratched at his leg.

❧

Kache wept while he dug the shallow grave with a rock and the scythe, while he spread the mud and snow over Vladimir, the tree branch ironically serving as a headstone, the nubs of new leaf buds that would never unfurl. With a pocketknife, he carved the letter *B* into the wet ground and watched it disappear just as quickly. It most likely wasn't enough of a grave to keep away a pack of wolves, or bears coming out of hibernation.

He and Leo began their way back up the canyon. At least they had done the trailblazing on the way down. But as Leo trotted up a pile of rocks, he lost his footing and took several hard, twisted bounces.

"Leo!" Kache called out. "You okay?" The dog jumped up before Kache got to him, but it was already obvious Leo was not okay. His front leg, badly broken, hung bleeding. He whined and licked at it, and Kache tilted his head back and yelled at the sky, "GOD *DAMN* IT!"

The look on Leo's face was so full of pain and apology and worry that Kache ripped off his jacket and his shirt and got to work making a splint for Leo's leg with the shirt and a stick.

"Don't you worry, boy. It's gonna be okay," he said while he wondered how in the living hell he would ever make it back up so steep of a grade carrying a seventy-pound dog when he'd barely made it down carrying nothing.

"Dad!" His father didn't answer him. He needed the help, but at least Kache wasn't hallucinating anymore. He hunched down, positioned his head under Leo, and tried to stand up wearing Leo over his shoulders. At first, he wavered like a top-heavy tree about to go down, but he finally found his balance, using the ski pole to help him with the extra weight.

"It's just backpacking now," he said. "We can do this. Right, Dad?" All he heard was the wind and the whoo-whoo-whoo of an owl. Kache closed his eyes tight, willing forth what he needed most: the one thing he'd fought against his whole life. When he looked up to find the wisp of their trail, his father stood waiting for him, carrying a man on his shoulders. They were both dressed in army fatigues. His dad didn't say a word, just shared a long look with Kache and proceeded ahead of him. He'd turn and wait whenever Kache slipped or when he hesitated, shivering, aching, nauseous with exhaustion and the compression of his spine—there was his father, his face full of a compassion Kache had never seen, or maybe never noticed, when he was a kid.

His dad led him up and up, switching back, higher and higher, until Kache clawed his way through the final ascent and crawled over the ledge, where he collapsed. He heard voices, Leo barking, and he tried to get up, but it felt so good to close his eyes, just for a minute.

❧

When he opened his eyes, it was Nadia's face he saw, her hands on his temples.

"You are okay? You are okay?" When he nodded, she said, "Snag is taking Leo to vet. It is going to be fixed, the leg." They were still outside, his head in her lap. She tilted water through his lips.

She asked, "You found him?"

Kache nodded. She didn't ask further. She had draped a wool blanket over him. "Dad…" But his father was gone. He sat up, half wondering if he'd appear. Kache wanted to say good-bye. He wanted to thank him. But there was no sign of him anywhere. Still, Snag was right. He knew now that his father's blood coursed through him—his blind devotion to this land, his self-righteous anger, born from his stubborn strive to control, to do whatever was necessary to keep those he loved close and safe.

chapter

seventy

NADIA STOOD WITH HER hands in her coat pockets and watched Kache empty the gas tank of Vladimir's motorcycle, wheel it out to the canyon ledge, and push it over.

At first, she felt nothing but relief. Relief that Vladimir was dead. Relief that Kache was alive. In the days that followed, the relief began to give way to dread. She had to reply to the school's offer. Neither she nor Kache had said a word about it since their fight. She wanted the answer that didn't involve pain, but that answer didn't exist. Every direction required a huge sacrifice—hers or Kache's or both.

She and Kache sat on opposite sides of the couch, Nadia reading while Kache checked his emails on the laptop, their legs wrapped around each other and Leo, who snored, his casted leg sticking straight up.

Kache said, "Is there something you want to show me?"

"What is it you mean?"

"Well, there's a strange email here from my old girlfriend Janie. It's forwarded from her friend who wrote 'This looks like Kache' in the subject line. Then a note from Janie. Do you want me to read it?"

Nadia felt her neck getting hot. "If you want."

"It says, 'Wow. You've gone viral. I never imagined you were that good. So glad you're playing again. And look at you. You look like Mr. Happenings himself.' Then she goes on to say how happy she is that I found someone and that she's getting married next month."

"Who is this Mr. Happenings?"

"Long story."

"I see."

"So there's a link here I can click on, but I thought you might have something to tell me before I do."

"I was going to wait until your birthday, but now it is good time, yes?" She started to lean toward him, but her nerves forced her up, out to the kitchen, where she began washing the breakfast dishes. She washed each one carefully, taking her time, afraid to turn around.

When she turned off the water, she heard the song coming to its end, the last chorus.

"Nadia, you unknotted me.
Nadia, you undeniably
Nadia, you unarguably
Made me a better man."

There were Kache's hands on her hips, turning her away from the sink, his arms wrapping her in a hug.

"I had no idea. How did you learn to do that?"

She shrugged, trying not to smile quite so big. "You gave me the camera."

"It's as if... I don't know. As if I were seeing a sunset reflected in a building for the first time. As if I'd never seen a homeless woman until now. Like I'm seeing not just what you're seeing but *how* you see it. Even those mountains. And those shots of me working. How'd you make me look like I know what I'm doing?"

"Because." She laughed. "Now you do."

He went on. "And I love how the chopping wood works in time to the beat, the way you slow it down in spots, and how the visuals reflect the lyrics, but not too overtly."

She laughed again. She couldn't help it. "So you like it?"

"I'm blown away by it."

They both fell quiet. She stayed in his arms, his praise filling her.

Kache leaned back and tilted her face up toward his. "Nadia," he said.

She waited.

"You're right to want this." He let out a long sigh. There was so much sadness in that sigh. His dark eyes seemed as deep as the canyon. "It was wrong of me to try to keep you here. You have to go. And I have to stay."

She pressed her ear against the place where she always heard his heart beat, and she nodded.

chapter

seventy-one

THEY'D DECIDED THAT LEO would stay with Kache, so for the first time he could remember, Leo didn't follow him down to the barn when he did the milking that morning. It was as if the dog knew he had limited time with Nadia. Kache understood. He too wanted to sit at her heels while she packed.

"Settle down, Mooze, girl," he told the cow, but she might as well have said the same thing to him. It was funny how sensitive the animals were, how they picked up on human emotions so easily. Both Mooze and Kache finally did settle down, and the steady stream of milk, the *zip-zip-zip* rhythm, calmed him even more.

In the past few months, Kache had tried to imagine what his life might be like on the homestead once Nadia was gone. He couldn't picture it. But he knew there would be good moments like this one, little surprises here and there, glimpses of grace. Nothing like what they'd had here together, not entire days and even weeks that were downright wondrous. But there would be good moments—and they would not be wasted on him.

A loud squawking and squeaking erupted outside. He gave Mooze a grateful pat on her hide and went out to investigate. The sandhill cranes had returned, and they'd brought friends. There must have been thirty, maybe forty of them, and they were dancing. Flapping their wings, hopping, and twirling. Kache looked back at the house; no one was out.

He watched a while longer, but he couldn't help himself. He set down the pail of milk and, timidly at first, took a few steps toward the birds. They hardly noticed. Admittedly, with his long skinny legs and arms, he probably didn't look all that foreign. He tried flapping his arms and took a few hops. As musical as he was, he had two left feet. But he seemed made for the sandhill crane dance. He spread his arms even wider, picked up his legs, and took high prances, and those birds let him in. They let him in.

Then Nadia was beside him, dressed in her city-girl leather jacket, her slim jeans, her pretty riding boots. She flapped her arms and stretched her long neck, stepping up, twirling, hopping. They ran, skipped, jumped, flapping, fluttering, squawking. They danced and they danced. He opened his arms, and she twirled to him, and they held each other, her soft golden feathers of hair on his chin. The birds lost interest and flew away, but Kache and Nadia stayed like that while they laughed and cried and caught their breath, hearts pounding.

He wanted to remind her that sandhill cranes mated for life. But then she would have to remind him that the two of them were not sandhill cranes.

❧

At the airport, Kache took the silk scarf he'd kept with him all those years in Austin—gold, black, cobalt, sage, and rose—out of his pocket. "This was my mom's," he told Nadia. "It was the only thing I took with me when I left here. I want you to take it with you."

She hesitated but then nodded, and he wrapped it loosely around her neck. "I know you won't ever be needing it for your head, but this looks really fashionable. It's from New York. You look like a real city woman. Oh, and this." He handed her a leather-bound notebook. "Your own journal."

She tiptoed and wrapped her arms around his neck. He pulled her to him, and they stayed like this, breathing in each other, not talking until her flight was called.

"You have your earplugs and your wristbands? Someone from the school will meet you, right?" She nodded. "And your cell phone is charged?"

She nodded again, tears streaming down her beautiful, beautiful face. "I know! I remember to charge. A miracle!" She told him to take good care of Leo. She told Kache how much she loved him, and he told her how much he loved her. Still, she turned and left and flew away, and he stayed. He waved to her, watching her from the ground until the plane flew above the clouds and he could see her no more.

❧

Lettie, Snag, and Gilly had come out for a good-bye dinner and were staying for a few days. That evening, Lettie asked Kache to wheel her out on the property. He sat on a log next to her. They looked out at the sky. It was the kind of sky that might make a devout atheist reconsider the possibility of heaven. Some clouds ran themselves in silver layers upon layers, and some formed golden vertical towers. Still others billowed in a bouquet of pinks and oranges. And the light—it seemed to emanate from all different sources, bordering around and spotlighting from above and below and exploding through. It was a sky for everyone, everywhere.

They sat, taking it in. When Kache stood to begin pushing her back up the hill, Lettie reached behind her and said, "Here you are," but when he went to take whatever it was she was offering, her hand was empty. She gripped his fingers and said it again. "*Here* you *are*. This place—it means something to you, Kache."

He said, "More than I wish it did, Gram."

"You got that gene from me."

He squeezed back. "Yeah, I guess I did. Whaddya know? Here I am."

⚘

Lettie died in her sleep two days later, in the cabin that she and A. R. had built, exactly how she always said she would go. The next week, the town of Caboose came out to the homestead. It was an honest to God summer day, breezy but shirtsleeves-warm, Kache's garden overflowing, the bay sparkling. Snag and Kache spread the ashes on the land where they had once spread Denny, Bets, and Glenn, and before them, A. R.

Kache sang Lettie's favorite song.

> *"The water is wide,*
> *I can't cross over,*
> *And neither have*
> *I wings to fly.*
> *Build me a boat*
> *That can carry two,*
> *And both shall row,*
> *My love and I."*

His voice caught, and the crowd waited patiently while he took a deep breath and then another. He'd always thought of *my love* as the physical person, sitting there in the boat rowing with you, but he saw how in the end, maybe it wasn't the actual person who helped you across whatever you needed to cross over. Maybe it was simply your love for that person.

"And both shall row,
My love and I."

When Snag—Eleanor, she was officially going by Eleanor now—heard Kache's voice break out into her mom's favorite song, she started to cry, and Gilly took her hand. Eleanor squeezed Gilly's fingers, held on. Then she rested her head on Gilly's lovely shoulder and kept it there for the whole town of Caboose to see.

❦

Sixteen hundred miles away, Nadia walked across the Golden Gate Bridge for the first time. With her camera in hand, she filmed up the big reddish steel trusses and back down to the wide, cobalt water reflecting the sun, the ivory city—her city!—risen against clear blue sky. People were passing her in cars, buses, taxis, trucks, on bikes, walking hand in hand, running in packs. Noise and movement and mayhem. She let the camera come down from her face, taking it all in. The rumbling of traffic came up through her feet in what seemed like a gesture of connection.

A couple walking toward her stopped, and the smiling young woman offered to film Nadia for a moment. Nadia stood against the railing and waved at the couple. A wind gust picked up the silk scarf she'd worn around her neck, but she caught it and held on.

The woman handed the camera back to her, still smiling. She said, "For a second there, it looked like you had grown wings."

Later that evening, in her tiny rented room, Nadia ate her carton of Chinese takeout and wrote in her journal while lonely violin music arched its way up through the window. When she finished writing, she closed the notebook. She sat, listening to the aching notes, the impatient horns, and frantic sirens, the single long screech of a bus coming to its stop.

She remembered the film clip and downloaded it onto her computer. There she was on the bridge: laughing, waving, with her city in the background. And when the scarf Kache had given her—Elizabeth's scarf—rose behind her in the wind and ballooned out for an instant on each side, Nadia saw that what the woman had said was true.

reading group guide

1. Discuss the title of the novel and how you feel it connects with the story.

2. Discuss the role of the homestead and the role of the setting in Kache's and Nadia's lives, both individually and together.

3. How did you feel about Snag and her actions? How did time and place affect her, and how might her story be different today?

4. Discuss the nature of choice and loss for Kache and Nadia.

5. How do you think the seasons reflect Nadia's and Kache's emotional journeys?

6. Nadia's family chose their religion above continuing a relationship with Nadia. How do you perceive this choice? Have you ever faced such a life-altering choice in your own life, and if so, what was it?

7. Kache and his father appear to have a fractured relationship, but Kache is gradually able to see his father's actions from a grown perspective, and it changes how he sees their relationship—and ultimately saves his life. Discuss the importance of parental relationships and the differences in this perception as children and as adults.

8. Nadia falls in love with Kache as a young man through reading his mother's journals, and although this enables her to fall in love with him as an adult, it causes friction in their relationship. Do you think she should have read the journals? What could she have done differently with the knowledge?

9. At the end of the novel, Kache and Nadia are unable to find a way to continue their relationship. How did you feel about this? Do you believe they did the right thing?

10. What do you believe happens to Kache and Nadia after the end of the story?

a conversation
with the author

What was your inspiration for *All the Winters After*?

When I made my first trip to Homer, Alaska, I immediately fell under its spell. The *mountains*. The *bay*. The *wildlife*. The *people*. Circumstances prevented me from hopping on a boat and moving there like Lettie did. But because I'm a writer, my mind, at least, can move anywhere it pleases. And my mind was already packing. At the Homer Bookstore, I came upon a book of autobiographical accounts from the area's homesteaders. I saw Old Believer women shopping at the Safeway, wearing long, colorful skirts and head scarves. Intrigued by the place, the homesteaders, and the Old Believers, I had an idea for a novel. I wrote about fifty pages. But life got complicated, and my mind was needed elsewhere. So I put that novel away. For about, oh, twenty years. I wrote two other books before I finally picked those fifty pages back up.

Can you share how the actual Old Believers' villages became Ural and Altai and how Homer became Caboose?

By the time I returned to this story, there was a lot more information available on the Old Believers than there had been all those years before, both in print and on the Internet. There are several Old Believer villages on the outskirts of Homer. Altai and Ural are fictionalized versions of two of those villages; I created them from what I've read and imagined, but they are not meant to be factual representations. They were seeds of inspiration mixed with my imagination. That is also true for Homer in its transformation to Caboose. I borrowed heavily from the town, especially its location, but I also had fun making things up and altering them. I combined real history and locations with creative license.

One more inspiration: One of my favorite books as a child was *Island of the Blue Dolphins*, about a woman stranded on an island, completely independent and cut off from civilization for years. Although Nadia's situation is different, I think the seed for her isolation probably sprung from my early fascination with that kind of ongoing solitude.

All the Winters After has a stunning setting in Alaska, and as a reader, I felt your love and enthusiasm for it as a remote and exhilarating destination. What type of research did you do?

I have a lot of ties to Alaska. My first husband grew up on the Kenai Peninsula, and my oldest son went to college in Anchorage. In addition to family trips, I traveled there for my work as a creative director. For a long time, I wanted to live in Alaska, and I subscribed to *Alaska* magazine and read everything I could on the subject. A few years ago, while working on the book, I stayed in a log cabin on the Kilcher Family Homestead on the outskirts of Homer, right about where I'd envisioned the Winkel homestead to be and where they have a living museum in the old homesteaders' cabin. I also lost myself in the Pratt Museum in Homer for hours and hours, where I loaded up on more books and visited the Anchorage Museum at Rasmuson Center and the beautiful Museum of the North at the

University of Alaska–Fairbanks. I have a pile of field guides, but if I couldn't find the answer I needed, I'd call my son, Daniel. He earned a degree in biology in Anchorage and spent five summers working for the U.S. Fish and Wildlife Service in the Alaskan wilderness. He was my go-to guy.

A lot of the characters in this book have unique names. How did you come up with them, and what is their significance, if any?

With the exception of the family name of Winkel, which I changed after many drafts and which was an intentional nod to Rip Van Winkle and his long nap, most of the names just came to me early on, and I'll admit that I didn't see their significance until later. Kache was always Kache, after the Kachemak Bay—but it's pronounced *catch*, and he is clearly caught, unable to move forward, as are Snag and Nadia. Aunt Snag stepped onto the page already christened, along with the story of how Glenn gave her the nickname, long before I knew what her problems were. And Nadia? I wanted something that sounded Russian, so I grabbed that one from the air. It wasn't until years later, when I was trying to write the song lyrics, that I realized Nadia sounds a lot like *knotted*. I must have known at some subconscious level, but I'm a bit baffled that I didn't notice that their names reflected their conditions.

I really yearned for Kache and Nadia to find some way to make things work between them. Do you know what happens to them next, and if so, will you share that? Or would you rather leave it to the imagination of the reader?

I don't know what happens to them next. (However, I do know what my mother would like to see happen!) I would need to write another book about them in order to find out. I will say that Kache and Nadia freed each other, but, in choosing to be true to that hard-earned freedom, they had to lose each other too. And yet not entirely. The kind of change they brought into each other's lives leaves a significant and lasting impression, whether or not they reunite.

This is also a very sad story in a lot of ways—the death of Kache's family and the subsequent fracturing of relationships for those left behind, Nadia's self-imposed isolation, Nadia's family's rejection of her. As an author, how do you leave that emotion behind when you're not writing?

Most of my angst comes beforehand, circling around a tough scene before I delve in. I know what it's going to require, so there's this pondering and buildup, but the actual writing of it can be cathartic. I'll admit to a transitional period after, a reentry from the world in my head that I'm trying to get onto the page, back to the world on which I try to plant my feet. I can be a bit distracted and foggy-headed when I first step out of my writing room. It's good that I'm not a surgeon. I do have a very understanding spouse. That helps.

Lettie is irresistibly drawn to Alaska and changes her whole life, possibly sacrificing an element of her relationship with her husband, to achieve her goal. Have you ever felt drawn to anywhere in this way?

Oh yes. I've already hinted at this, but I guess I'll come out and call it what it was—my obsession. My first husband and I had planned to move to Alaska, where he was from, but we ended up in San Diego instead—practically the polar opposite, so to speak. I remained obsessed with Alaska for years, and Lettie's story grew from that. Unlike me, she made it happen.

These days, I no longer obsess about moving north, but I do live in a house in the woods, a remodeled and expanded cabin, not far from a bay where we kayak and my husband goes crabbing and salmon fishing. I joke that it's the closest I can get to living in Alaska and still get to live in California. My son has plans to finish his doctorate and return to Alaska, so I'll probably get to spend a lot more time there in the future.

Are your characters based on anyone in particular?

No. I wrote a lot of material in my twenties and thirties that was never published, and much to my family's relief, most likely never will be. After excavating my childhood, my writing process changed and became more imaginative. Now I excavate my obsessions, my fears, my observations, certainly my sense of place, and yes, my characters. But they're not thinly disguised people from my real life. I definitely borrow from stories friends tell me, as well as lines of dialogue, and I'm sure there are traces of me and people I've known in characters, but that's as far as it goes. I enjoy making stuff up.

The story of Kache's dog and the butterfly that led to his end was a story that really stayed with me. What inspired this incident?

Here's an example of one of the stories mentioned above that inspired a story in the book. While I was staying at the homestead, the host pointed to the cliff and told me about her childhood dog chasing a butterfly right over it. As a dog lover, that vision haunted me. As a writer, I had to include a fictionalized version of it in the book. In fact, at one time, the title was *The Dog and the Butterfly*.

The homestead is filled with books that likely save Nadia's life. What books would be on your shelves if you had to live in a homestead for a decade?

Well, first of all, every how-to book and field guide ever written! After that, I would include my favorites—the complete collections of Annie Dillard, Barbara Kingsolver, Ann Patchett, Anne Tyler, Geraldine Brooks, Jane Hamilton, Alice Munro, Elizabeth

Strout... I could go on all day. More novels I love, sitting on this shelf next to me: *Middlesex, The History of Love, The Sandalwood Tree, Never Let Me Go, Cold Mountain, Let the Great World Spin, We Are All Completely Beside Ourselves, The Handmaid's Tale, A Prayer for Owen Meany, The Snow Child, Beautiful Ruins, Room, The Signature of All Things, Life After Life, The Hours, Wuthering Heights, The Awakening.* I would need volumes and volumes of poetry—Mary Oliver, Billy Collins, Emily Dickinson, Ted Kooser, Walt Whitman, for starters. Books on travel to help any wanderlust I'd likely experience. This list is obviously off the top of my head and nowhere near complete. But I would also want all those books I've been meaning to read and haven't. And lots of big, thick classics. A decade isn't nearly long enough, but I could make a serious dent.

What would you like the reader to take away from your novel?

I'd like the reader to experience a deep sense of place and of time well spent—of escape and connection, longing and fulfillment, recognition and discovery. The feeling of having walked in these characters' boots. And maybe a cramp or two from sitting and reading too long. That's a lot to ask, but I can hope.

acknowledgments

Once, long ago, I wrote about fifty pages of a book and then put it aside, and for complicated reasons, I didn't pick it up again until twenty years later. That book eventually became this one. I guess you could say I now have about twenty years of accumulated gratitude spilling over, and much of it goes to my godsend of an agent, Elisabeth Weed, who believed in this story and who took the time to read and reread as the novel found its shape. She and her assistant, Dana Murphy, offered thoughtful feedback that made all the difference. I'm so fortunate that I get to work with Jenny Meyer, foreign agent extraordinaire, who has made it possible for me to reach readers in other countries. Special thanks to her and hard-working assistants Shane King and Zoe Weitzman.

A deep bow of appreciation goes to Dominique Raccah and the amazing team at Sourcebooks, especially to my esteemed editor, Shana Drehs, a bright star who led the way, and to Anna Michels, for her smart editorial guidance. Heather Moore, Valerie Pierce, Beth Oleniczek, Heidi Weiland, Margaret Coffee, Chris Bauerle, Stephanie Graham, Heather Hall, Sabrina Baskey, Patricia Esposito, Adrienne Krogh, and Brittany Vibbert each played an important role in the publication process. Thank you, Sourcebooks!

I'm forever indebted to my gifted critique partners, Laurie Richards and Chelo Ludden, for marking up and talking through numerous drafts, and to those generous souls who read the manuscript in one or more of its various forms and whose comments helped immensely: Nancy Campana, Daniel Prince, Molly Eckler, Colleen Morton Busch, Amy Franklin-Willis, Suzanne Haley, Nicole Haley, Jan Aston, Shannon Barrow, and Melanie Thorne. I'm also grateful to the talented group of writer friends at Book Pregnant for support and advice on the ins and outs of writing and publishing. And Diana Foster and Angelica Allen share the award for attending more of my book readings than anyone should ever have to endure.

Thanks to Mark Madgett and Spencer Nilsen, old friends who told me a funny story about a moose head that inspired Kache and Denny's escapade with Anthony. And I'm beholden to Catkin Kilcher Burton, who, in one of those wonderfully synchronistic encounters, hosted my husband, Stan, and me at her lovely cabin in Homer (which is available on VRBO, for anyone who's interested) and took us through the old family homestead, sharing tales of growing up there—decades after I'd first read about her grandparents and many other Homer homesteaders in the book that started it all: *In Those Days: Alaska Pioneers of the Lower Kenai Peninsula.*

While that book planted the first seed, I also was lucky enough to discover the following, which all helped the story take root and grow: *Lost in the Taiga: One Russian Family's Fifty-Year Struggle for Survival and Religious Freedom in the Siberian Wilderness* by Vasily Peskov; *In the Shadow of Antichrist: The Old Believers of Alberta* by David Z. Scheffel; the booklets of Old Believers' food, clothing, history, and traditions written by the schoolchildren of Nikolaevsk School, Nikolaevsk, Alaska; *Kachemak Bay Communities: Their Histories, Their Mysteries* by Janet R. Klein; and *Kachemak Bay, Alaska* by the Homer

Foundation. A long meandering afternoon at the Pratt Museum in Homer helped fill in even more details.

I've been blessed beyond measure by a circle of loving family and friends, old and new, who've turned out in droves to support my work in a myriad of ways. A big hug of appreciation for each and every one of you, and especially to all my parents: Jan Aston, Jan Beste, Jan Halverson, and Stan Halverson Sr. (And yes, I really do have three moms named Jan.) To my boys' Grandma Alaska, Carrie Prince. And to those of you I miss every single day: my dad, Don Beste; my stepdad, Bill Aston; my writing sister, Elle Newmark; and my forever and ever friend, Shannon Barrow. I love you and thank you all.

And finally, this full heart of mine has my kids to thank: Daniel Prince, Michael Prince, Karli Halverson, and Taylor Halverson, who make it all worthwhile. And my husband, Stan Halverson, who makes it all possible. I met him in eighth grade, but it took until our twenty-year high school reunion to realize we were meant to be in this together. When it comes to getting some of the big things in life right, it seems I'm on the twenty-year plan.

about the author

Seré Prince Halverson is the international bestselling author of *The Underside of Joy*, which was published in eighteen languages. She and her husband have four grown children and live in Northern California in a house in the woods.

Photo credit: Steven Rothfield